Dear Reader,

This is my sixteenth _____ _____ching
Cowboys of Cold C_____
collection of variou_____ery
time I tell myself I'_____p
with one more ide_____e
hanging. The mor_____
last year's _The Holiday Gift_, I knew I w____ ___ __
tell her story. She played an important role in that
book by helping the hero and heroine finally come
together, but in the process, Ella ended up with her
heart bruised. I couldn't let that be the end of things
for her! I'm thrilled to have the chance to give the
earnest and caring music teacher her own happy
ending with sexy rancher Beckett McKinley—and his
unruly twin boys!

Every time I return to Pine Gulch, I feel like I'm back
among friends. Thank you for coming along!

Wishing you all the most joyous of holidays!

RaeAnne

RaeAnne Thayne

THE RANCHER'S CHRISTMAS SONG

The Cowboy's Christmas Miracle

ISBN-13: 978-1-335-14374-7

The Rancher's Christmas Song and
The Cowboy's Christmas Miracle

Copyright © 2017 by Harlequin Books S.A.

Recycling programs
for this product may
not exist in your area.

The publisher acknowledges the copyright holder of the individual works as follows:

The Rancher's Christmas Song
Copyright © 2017 by RaeAnne Thayne

The Cowboy's Christmas Miracle
Copyright © 2008 by RaeAnne Thayne

This edition published by arrangement with Harlequin Books S.A.

For questions and comments about the quality of this book, please contact us at CustomerService@Harlequin.com.

Printed in U.S.A.

www.Harlequin.com

CONTENTS

To my dad, Elden Robinson,
who loved Westerns and cowboy music and
who made the best popcorn west of the Mississippi.
I miss you more than words can say.

THE RANCHER'S
CHRISTMAS SONG

Chapter One

The twin terrors were at it again.

Ella Baker watched two seven-year-old tornadoes, otherwise known as Trevor and Colter McKinley, chase each other behind the stage curtains at the Pine Gulch Community Center.

In the half hour since they arrived at the community center with their father, they had spilled a water pitcher, knocked down a life-size cardboard Santa and broken three ornaments on the big Christmas tree in the corner.

Now they were racing around on the stage where tonight's featured act was set to perform within the next half hour.

She would have to do something. As organizer and general show-runner of this fund-raising event for the school's underfinanced music program, it was her responsibility to make sure everyone had a good time.

People's wallets tended to open a little wider when they were happy, comfortable and well fed. A gang of half-pint miscreants had the potential to ruin the evening for everyone.

She had tried to talk to them. As usual, the twins had offered her their angelic, gap-toothed smiles and had promised to behave, then moments later she saw them converge with four other boys to start playing this impromptu game of tag on the stage.

In order to tame these particular wild beasts, she was going to have to talk to someone in authority. She gave a last-ditch, desperate look around. As she had suspected, neither their uncle nor their great uncle was in sight. That left only one person who might have any chance of corralling these two little dynamos.

Their father.

Ella's stomach quivered. She did *not* enjoy talking to Beck McKinley and avoided it as much as possible.

The man made her so ridiculously nervous. He always treated her with careful politeness, but she could never read the expression on his features. Every time she spoke with him—which was more often than she liked, considering his ranch was next door to her father's—she always felt like she came out of the encounter sounding like a babbling fool.

Okay, yes. She was attracted to him, and had been since she moved back to Pine Gulch. What woman wouldn't be? Big, tough, gorgeous, with a slow smile that could charm even the most hardened heart.

She didn't *want* to be so drawn to him, especially when he hadn't once shown a glimmer of interest in return. He made her feel like she was an awkward teenager back in private school in Boston, holding up the wall at her first coed dance.

She wasn't. She was a twenty-seven-year-old professional in charge of generating funds for a cause she cared about. Sexy or not, Beck had to corral his sons before they ruined the entire evening.

Time to just suck it up and take care of business. She was a grown-up and could handle talking to anyone, even big, tough, stern-faced ranchers who made her feel like she didn't belong in Pine Gulch.

It wasn't hard to find Beck McKinley. He towered about four inches taller than the crowd of ranchers he stood among.

She sucked in a steadying breath and made her way toward the group, trying to figure out a polite way to tell him his sons were causing trouble again.

She wasn't completely surprised to find her father was part of the group around Beck. They were not only copresidents of the local cattle growers association this year, but her father also idolized the man. As far as Curt Baker was concerned, Beck McKinley was all three wise men rolled into one. Her father still relied heavily on Beck for help—more so in the last few years, as his Parkinson's disease grew more pronounced and his limitations more frustrating.

At least her father was sitting down, leaning slightly forward with his trembling hands crossed in front of him atop the cane she had insisted he bring.

He barely looked at her, too engrossed in the conversation about cattle prices and feed shortages.

She waited until the conversation lagged before stepping into the group. She was unwilling to call out the rancher over his troublemaking twins in front of all the others.

"Beckett. May I have a brief word?"

His eyebrows rose and he blinked in surprise a few times. "Sure. Excuse me, gentlemen."

Aware of curious gazes following them, Ella led Beck a short distance from his peers.

"Is there a problem?" he asked.

She pointed toward the pack of wild boys on the stage, who were chasing each other between the curtains. "Your sons are at it again."

His gaze followed her gesture and he grimaced. "I see half a dozen boys up there. Last I checked, only two of those are mine."

"Colter and Trevor are the ringleaders. You know they are. They're always the ones who come up with the mischief and convince the others to go along."

"They're natural leaders. Are you suggesting I try to put the brakes on that?"

His boys were adorable, she had to admit, but they were the bane of her existence as the music teacher at Pine Gulch Elementary School. They couldn't sit still for more than a few minutes at a time and were constantly talking to each other as well as the rest of the students in their class.

"You could try to channel it into more positive ways."

This wasn't the first time she had made this suggestion to him and she was fairly certain she wasn't the only educator to have done so. Trevor and Colter had been causing problems at Pine Gulch Elementary School since kindergarten.

"They're boys. They've got energy. It comes with the package."

She completely agreed. That was one of the reasons she incorporated movement in her music lessons with all of her students this age. All children—but especially boys, she had noticed—couldn't sit still for long hours at a time and it was cruel to expect it of them.

She was a trained educator and understood that, but she also expected that excess energy to be contained when necessary and redirected into proper behavior.

"Our performers will be taking the stage soon. Please, can you do something with the boys? I can just picture them accidentally ripping down the curtains or messing with the lights before we can even begin."

Beck glanced at his boys, then back down at her. His strong jaw tightened, and in his eyes, she saw a flash of something she couldn't read.

She didn't need to interpret it. She was fairly certain she knew what he thought of her. Like her father, Beck thought she was a soft, useless city girl.

Both of them were wrong about her, but nothing she did seemed to convince them otherwise. As far as her father was concerned, she belonged in Boston or New York, where she could attend the symphony, the ballet, art gallery openings.

Since the moment she'd arrived here with her suitcases a little more than a year ago, Curt had been trying relentlessly to convince her to go back to Boston with her mother and stepfather and the cultured life they had.

Beck seemed to share her father's views. He never seemed to want to give her the time of day and always seemed in a big hurry to escape her presence.

Whatever his true opinion, he always treated her with stiff courtesy. She would give him that. Beck McKinley was never rude to anybody—probably one of the reasons all the other ranchers seemed to cluster around the man in public. Everybody seemed to respect his opinion and want to know what he had to say about things.

The only thing she wanted from him right now was to keep his boys from ruining the night.

"I'll talk to the parents of the other boys, too. I'm just asking if you'll please try to round up Colter and Trevor and have them take their seats. I'll be introducing our performers in a moment and I would like people to focus on what they came for, instead of how many straws Colter can stick up his nose."

He unbent enough to offer that rare, delicious smile. It appeared for only a moment. His cheeks creased and his eyes sparkled and his entire face looked even more gorgeous. "Good point, I suppose. The answer is five, in case you wanted to know. I'll grab them. Sorry they caused a ruckus."

"Thank you," she said, then walked away before she was tempted to make another joke, if only to see if he would offer up that smile again.

Better to quit while she was ahead, especially since her brain was now struggling to put together any words at all.

Beck watched Ella Baker walk away, her skirt swishing and her boot heels clicking on the old wooden floor of the community center.

He had the same reaction to her that he always did—sheer, wild hunger.

Something about that sleek blond hair and her almond-shaped eyes and the soft, kissable mouth did it to him. Every. Single. Time.

What was the *matter* with him? Why did he have to

be drawn to the one woman in town who was totally wrong for him?

Ella wore tailored skirts and suede boots that probably cost as much as a hand-tooled saddle. She was always perfectly put together, from the top of her sleek blond hair to the sexy but completely impractical shoes she always wore.

When he was around her, he always felt exactly like what he was—a rough-edged cowboy.

Can you at least pretend you have a little culture? Do you have any idea how hard it is to be married to someone who doesn't know Manet from Monet?

Though it had been four years since she died—and five since she had lived with him and the twins—Stephanie's words and others she had uttered like them seemed to echo through his memory. They had lost their sting over the years, but, boy, had they burned at the time.

He sighed. Though the two had similar blue-blood backgrounds and educations, Ella Baker looked nothing like his late wife. Stephanie had been tall, statuesque, with red hair she had passed on to their sons. Ella was slim, petite and looked like an exotic blonde fairy.

Neither of them fit in here, though he had to admit Ella tried a hell of a lot harder than Stephanie ever had. She had organized this event, hadn't she?

He should probably stop staring at her. He would. Any moment now.

Why did she have to be so damn beautiful, bright and cheerful and smiling? Every time he saw her, it was like looking into the sun.

He finally forced himself to look away so he could do as she asked, quite justifiably. He should have been keeping a better eye on the boys from the beginning, but he'd been sucked into a conversation about a new ranching technique his friend Justin Hartford was trying and lost track of them.

As he made his way through the crowd, smiling at neighbors and friends, he was aware of how alone he was. He had been bringing the boys to these community things by himself for nearly five years now. He could hardly believe it.

He was ready to get out there and date again. The boys had somehow turned seven, though he had no idea how that happened.

The truth was, he was lonely. He missed having someone special in his life. He was tired of only having his uncle and his brothers to talk to.

Heaven knows, he was really tired of sleeping alone.

When he did jump back into that whole dating arena, though, he was fairly sure it wouldn't be with a soft, delicate music teacher who didn't know a mecate from a bosal.

It might be easier to remember that if the woman wasn't so darned pretty.

In short order, he found the boys on the stage and convinced all of them it was time to find their parents and take their seats, then led his own twins out of trouble.

"Hey, Dad. Guess what Thomas said?" Colter asked, as they were making their way through the crowd.

"What's that, son?" He couldn't begin to guess what another seven-year-old might pass along—and was a little afraid to ask.

"His dog is gonna have puppies right before Christmas. Can we get one? Can we?"

He did his best not to roll his eyes at the idea. "Thomas and his family have a miniature Yorkie that's no bigger than my hand. I'm not sure a little dog like that would like living on a big ranch like ours with all our horses and cattle. Besides, we've already got three dogs. And one of those is going to have her own puppies any day now."

"Yeah, but they're *your* dogs. And you always tell us they're not pets, they're working dogs," Trevor said.

"And you told us we probably can't keep any of Sal's puppies," Colter added. "We want a puppy of our very own."

Like they didn't have enough going right now. He was not only running his horse and cattle ranch, the Broken Arrow, but also helping out Curt Baker at his place as much as possible. He had help from his brother and uncle, yeah—on the ranch and with the boys. He still missed his longtime housekeeper and nanny, Judy Miller, who was having double–knee replacement and would be out for six months.

Adding a little indoor puppy into the chaos of their life right now was completely unthinkable.

"I don't think that's going to happen," he said firmly but gently.

"Maybe Santa Claus will bring us one," Colter said, nudging his brother.

At seven, the boys were pretty close to understanding the truth about Santa Claus, though they had never come right out and told them. Every once in a while he thought they might know, but were just trying to hang on to the magic as long as possible. He was okay with that. Life would be full of enough disappointments.

He was saved from having to answer them by the

sight of beautiful Ella Baker approaching the microphone.

"Hey! There's Miss Baker," Trevor said, loudly enough that she heard and looked in their direction.

Though families had been encouraged to attend the event and it was far from a formal concert, Beck was still embarrassed by the outburst.

"Shh," he said to the boys. "This is a time to listen, not talk."

"Like church?" Colter asked, with some measure of distrust.

"Sort of." *But more fun*, he thought, though of course he couldn't say to impressionable boys.

Trevor and Colter settled into their seats and Beck watched as Ella took the microphone. He figured he could watch her here without guilt, since everyone else's eyes were on her, too.

"Welcome, everyone, to this fund-raiser for the music program at the elementary and middle schools. By your presence here, it's clear you feel strongly about supporting the continued success of music education in our schools. As you know, programs like ours are constantly under the budget knife. Through your generous donations, we can continue the effort to teach music to the children of Pine Gulch. At this time, it's my great pleasure to introduce our special guests, all the way from northern Montana. Please join me in welcoming J. D. Wyatt and his Warbling Wranglers."

The introduction was met with a huge round of applause for the cowboy singers. Beck settled into his chair and prepared to savor the entertainment—and prayed it could keep his wild boys' attention.

* * *

He shouldn't have worried. An hour later, the band wrapped up with a crowd-pleasing, toe-tapping version of "Jingle Bell Rock" that had people getting up to dance in the aisle and in front of the small stage.

His twins had been utterly enthralled, from the first notes to the final chord.

"That was awesome!" Colter exclaimed.

"Yeah!" His twin glowed, as well. "Hey, Dad! Can we take fiddle lessons?"

Over the summer, they had wanted to learn to play the guitar. Now they wanted to learn the violin. Tomorrow, who knows, they might be asking for accordion lessons.

"I don't know. We'll have to see," he said.

Before the twins could press him, Ella Baker returned to the mic stand.

"Thank you all again for your support. Please remember all proceeds from ticket sales for tonight's performance, as well as our silent auction, will go toward funding music in the schools. Also, please don't forget tomorrow will be the first rehearsal for the Christmas show and dinner put on by the children of our community for our beloved senior citizens at The Christmas Ranch in Cold Creek Canyon. This isn't connected to the school and is completely voluntary. Any students ages four to sixteen are encouraged to join us."

"Hey. That's us!" Trevor said.

"Can we do it, Dad?" Colter asked, with the same pleading look on his face he wore when asking for a second scoop of ice cream. "We wanted to last year, remember? Only you said we couldn't because we were going to visit our Grandma Martin."

That had been a short-lived visit with Stephanie's mother in Connecticut, who had thought she would enjoy taking the boys into the city over the holidays and showing off her grandsons to her friends. After three days, she had called him to pick up the boys ahead of schedule, sounding ages older than she had days earlier. She hadn't called again this year.

"Can we?" Trevor persisted.

Beck didn't know how to answer as items on his massive to-do list seemed to circle around him like buzzards on a carcass. He had so much to do this time of year and didn't know how he could run the boys to and from the rehearsals at The Christmas Ranch, which was a good fifteen minutes away.

On the other hand, Ella Baker lived just next door. Maybe he could work something out with her to give the boys a ride.

Of course, that meant he would have to talk to her again, though. He did his best to avoid situations that put them into closer proximity, where he might be tempted to do something stupid.

Like ask her out.

"Please," Colter begged.

This was a good cause, a chance to reinforce to them the importance of helping others. The holiday show had become a high point to many of the senior citizens in town, and they looked forward to it all year. If the twins wanted to do it, how could he possibly refuse?

"We'll see," he hedged, not quite ready to commit.

"You always say that," Trevor said. "How come we never really *see* anything after you say we will?"

"Good question. Maybe someday, I'll answer it. We'll have to see."

The boys laughed, as he hoped, and were distracted by their friend Thomas—he, of the tiny puppies—who came over to talk to them.

"Are you gonna do the Christmas show? My mom said I could, if I wanted."

"We want to," Trevor said, with another cajoling look at Beck.

"Maybe we can have a band," Thomas said. "I'll be J.D. and you can be the Warbling Wranglers."

As they squabbled good-naturedly about which of them would make the better lead singer, Beck listened to them with a sense of resignation. If they really wanted to be in the Christmas program, he would have to figure out a way to make it happen—even if it meant talking to Ella Baker again.

The thought filled him with far more anticipation than he knew was good for him.

Chapter Two

"What a fantastic event!" Faith Brannon squeezed Ella's hand. "I haven't enjoyed a concert so much in a long time."

"Maybe that's because you never go out," Faith's younger sister, Celeste, said with a laugh.

"Newlyweds. What are you going to do?" Hope, the third Nichols sister, winked at their group of friends.

Ella had to laugh, even as she was aware of a little pang. Faith had married her neighbor, Chase Brannon, about four months earlier, in a lovely wedding in the big reception hall of The Christmas Ranch.

It had been lovely and understated, since it was a second marriage for both, but there hadn't been a dry eye in the hall. They seemed so in love and so deserving of happiness.

Ella had managed to smile all evening long. She considered that quite an accomplishment, considering once upon a time, she had completely made a fool of herself over the groom. When she first moved to Pine Gulch, she'd had a gigantic crush on Chase and had all but thrown herself at him, with no clue that he had adored Faith forever and had just been biding his time until she came to terms with her husband's premature death.

Ella had almost gotten over her embarrassment about events of the previous Christmas. It might have been easier to avoid the happy couple altogether except the Nichols sisters—all married now and with different surnames but still "the Nichols sisters" to just about everyone in town—had become some of her dearest friends.

They were warm and kind and always went out of their way to include her in activities.

"You did a great job of organizing," Hope said now. "I couldn't believe all the people who showed up. I met a couple earlier who drove all the way up from Utah because they love J.D. and his Wranglers. I hope you raked in the dough."

"Everyone has been generous," she said. "We should have enough to purchase the new piano we need in the elementary school with plenty left over for sheet music at the middle school."

She still didn't think it was right that the art and music programs had to struggle so much to make ends meet in this rural school system. Judging by tonight, though, many members of the community seemed to agree with her that it should be a priority and had donated accordingly.

"It was a great community event. What a great turnout!"

"Just think." Hope grinned. "We get to turn around

and do this again in a few weeks at The Christmas Ranch."

Faith made a face. "You wouldn't believe how many people have brought up that Christmas program to me tonight, and I'm not even involved in the show!"

"You're a Nichols, though, which makes you one of the co-queens of Christmas, like it or not," Ella said.

The Nichols family had been running The Christmas Ranch—a holiday-themed attraction filled with sleigh rides, a life-size Christmas village and even their own herd of reindeer—for many years. It was enormously successful and attracted visitors from around the region.

The popularity of the venue had grown exponentially in the last few years because of the hard work of the sisters.

A few years earlier, they had come up with the idea of providing a free catered dinner and holiday-themed show presented by area children as a gift to the local senior citizens and the event had become legendary in the community.

"We are so lucky that you've agreed to help us again this year," Celeste said now to Ella.

"Are you kidding? I've been looking forward to it all year."

The event—more like an old-fashioned variety show—wasn't professionally staged, by any means. Rehearsals didn't even start until a few weeks before the performance and there were no auditions and few soloists, but the children had fun doing it and the attendees enjoyed every moment.

The previous year's performance had been a wonderful growing experience for Ella, serving as an icebreaker of sorts to help her get to know the local children better.

She hoped this year would only build on that success.

"Wait until you see some of the songs we have planned. It's going to knock your socks off," she said.

"How can you be so excited about wrestling seventy schoolchildren already on a Christmas sugar high?" Faith shook her head. "You must be crazy."

"The very best kind of crazy," Celeste said with a smile.

"You fit right in with the rest of us," Hope assured her, then changed the subject. "Hey, did you see that good-looking guy who came in with Nate and Emery Cavazos? His name is Jess Saddler and he's temporarily staying at their cabins. Em said he's single and looking to move in and open a sporting goods store in town. He's cute, isn't he?"

She followed the direction of Hope's gaze and discovered a man she didn't know speaking with Nate and Emery, as well as Caroline and Wade Dalton. Hope was right, he was great-looking, with an outdoorsy tan and well-styled, sun-streaked hair that looked as if it had never seen a Stetson.

He also had that overchiseled look of people who earned their strength at the gym instead of through hard, productive manual labor.

"I suppose."

"You should go introduce yourself," Hope suggested, ignoring the sudden frown from both of her sisters.

"Why?" Ella asked, suspicious.

Hope's innocent shrug didn't fool her. "He's single. You're single. Em said he seems like a great guy and,

I don't know, I thought maybe the two of you would hit it off."

"Are you matchmaking for me?"

"Do you want me to?" Hope asked eagerly.

Did she? She wasn't sure how to answer. Yes, she was lonely. It was tough to be a single woman in this family-oriented community, where everyone seemed paired up. There weren't very many eligible men to even date and she often felt isolated and alone.

She wasn't sure how she felt about being the latest pity project of her friends. Did she seem desperate to them?

That was an uncomfortable thought.

"I don't need a matchmaker. I'm fine," she told Hope. "Even if I met the right guy today, I'm not sure I would have time for him, between working at two schools, doing music therapy at the senior citizen center and taking my dad to doctor appointments."

"When you care about a man, you make time," Celeste said.

"I don't think the guy is going anywhere. After Christmas, you should think about it," Hope added.

"Maybe." She could only hope a bland nonanswer would be enough for them.

Hope looked disappointed but was distracted when another neighbor came up and asked her a question about a private company party scheduled the following week at The Christmas Ranch.

While she was occupied, Faith turned to Ella with a frown on her soft, pretty features.

"It sounds like you have too much on your plate," Faith said. "Now I feel guilty we roped you into doing the Christmas show again."

"You didn't rope me into anything," she assured her. "I meant what I said. I've been looking forward to it."

"When will you have time to breathe?"

She didn't mind being busy and loved teaching music. It had been her passion through her teen years and pursuing a career in music therapy was a natural fit. She had loved her job before she came here, working at a school for students with developmental disabilities, but there was nothing like that here in this small corner of southeastern Idaho. Teaching music in the schools was the next best thing. She had to do something with her time, especially considering her father continued being completely stubborn and unreasonable about letting her take over the ranch.

She was busy. She just wasn't *that* busy.

"If you want the truth," she admitted, "I may have slightly exaggerated my overloaded schedule to keep Hope from making me her next project."

Faith looked amused. "Very wise move on your part."

"Don't get me wrong. It's sweet of her and everything. It's just…"

"You don't have to explain to me. I totally get it."

"I'm just not looking for a male right now."

"Too bad. Looks like a couple of cute ones are headed this way."

She followed Faith's gaze to find the twin terrors barreling straight toward her at full speed. To her relief, they managed to stop inches from knocking her and Faith over like bowling pins.

"Hey, Miss Baker. Miss Baker! Guess what?"

The boys' faces were both covered in chocolate, a fairly solid clue that they'd been raiding the refreshments table. How many cookies had they consumed between the pair of them? Not her problem, she supposed. Their father could deal with their upset stomachs and sugar overload.

"What's that, Trevor?" She directed her question to the one who had spoken.

He hid a grin behind his hand. "I'm not Trevor. I'm Colter."

"Are you sure?" She raised an eyebrow.

He giggled. "How come we can never fool you? You're right. I'm Trevor."

The boys were the most identical twins Ella had ever seen and they delighted in playing those kind of switch-up games with the faculty and staff at the elementary school. From the first time they met, though, Ella had never struggled to tell them apart. Colter had a slightly deeper cleft in his chin and Trevor had a few more freckles.

"Guess what?" Colter finished his brother's sentence. "We're gonna be in your Christmas show."

Beside her, Faith gave a small but audible groan that completely mirrored Ella's sudden panic.

On the heels of that initial reaction, she felt suddenly protective of the boys, defensive on their behalf. It really wasn't their fault they misbehaved. None of it was malicious. They were high-spirited in the first place and had a father who seemed more interested in taking over her father's ranch than teaching his two boys to behave like little gentlemen.

But then, she might be a tad biased against the man. Every time she offered to do something to help Curtis, her father was quick to tell her Beck would take care of it.

"Is that right?" she asked. The show was open to

any children who wanted to participate, with no auditions and guaranteed parts for all. They wouldn't win any talent competitions, but she considered the flaws and scenery mishaps all part of the charm.

"Our dad said *we'll see*," Colter informed her. "Sometimes that means no, but then I heard him asking your dad if he thought you might be able to give us a ride to and from practice on the days no one from the ranch could do it."

Her jaw tightened. The nerve of the arrogant rancher, to go to her father instead of asking her directly, as if Curt had any control over the matter.

"And what did my father say?"

"We didn't hear," Trevor confessed. "But can you?"

Their ranch was right next door to the Baker's Dozen. It would be no great hardship for her to accommodate the McKinleys and transport the twins if they wanted to participate, but it would be nice if Beck could be bothered asking her himself.

"I'll have to talk to your father first," she hedged.

The boys seemed to take her equivocation as the next best thing to a done deal.

"This will be fun," Colter said, showing off his gap-toothed grin. "We're gonna be the best singers you ever saw."

To reinforce the point, Trevor launched into a loud version of "Rudolph the Red-Nosed Reindeer" and his brother joined in. They actually had surprisingly good singing voices. She'd noticed that before during music class at school—though it was hard to confirm that now when they were singing at the tops of their lungs.

They were drawing attention, she saw. The cute guy

with Em and Nate was looking this way and so was Beck McKinley.

Ella flushed, envisioning the nightmare of trying to keep the boys from trying to ride the reindeer at The Christmas Ranch, or from knocking down the gigantic sixteen-foot-tall tree inside the St. Nicholas Lodge.

"You can be in the show on one condition," she said, using her best teacher's voice.

"What's that?" Colter asked warily.

"Children of all ages will be participating, even some kindergarten students and first graders. They're going to need someone to set a good example about how to listen and pay attention. They'll be watching you. Can you show them the correct way to behave?"

"Yeah!" Trevor exclaimed. "We can be quiet as dead mice."

That was pretty darn quiet—and she would believe *that* when she saw it.

"We can be the goodest kids in the whole place," Colter said. "You'll see, Miss Baker. You won't even know we're there, except when we're singing."

"Yeah. You'll see," Trevor said. "Thanks, Miss Baker. Come on, Colt. Let's go tell Thomas." In a blink, the two of them raced off as quickly as they had appeared by her side.

"Those boys are quite a pair, aren't they?" Faith said, watching after them with a rather bemused look on her features.

Ella was again aware of that protective impulse, the urge to defend them. Yes, they could be exhausting but she secretly admired their take-no-prisoners enthusiasm for life.

"They're good boys. Just a little energetic."

"You can say that again. They're a handful. I suppose it's only to be expected, though." Faith paused, her expression pensive. "You know, I thought for sure Beck would send them off to live with family after their mother left. I mean, here was this tough, macho rancher trying to run his place while also dealing with a couple of boys still in diapers. The twins couldn't have been more than two."

"So young? How could a mother leave her babies?"

"Yeah. I wanted to chase after her and smack her hard for leaving a good man like Beck, but he would never let anybody say a bad word about her. The only thing he ever said to me was that Stephanie was struggling with some mental health issues and needed a little time to get her head on straight. I think she had some postpartum depression and it probably didn't help that she didn't have a lot of friends here. We tried, but she wasn't really very approachable."

Faith made a face. "That sounds harsh, doesn't it? That's not what I mean. She was just not from around here."

"Neither am I," Ella pointed out.

"Yes, but you don't constantly remind us of how much better things were back east."

Because they weren't. Oh, she missed plenty of things about her life there, mostly friends and neighbors and really good clam chowder, but she had always felt as if she had a foothold in two places—her mother's upper-crust Beacon Hill society and her father's rough-and-rugged Idaho ranch.

"Anyway, she left to get her head on straight when the boys were about two and I can't imagine how hard it must have been for Beck on his own. A year later, Stephanie died of a drug overdose back east."

"Oh, how sad. Those poor boys."

"I know. Heartbreaking. Her parents are high-powered doctors. They fought for custody of the boys and I think it got pretty ugly for a while, but Beck wouldn't hear of it. He's a good dad. Why would any judge take the boys away from father and the only home they've ever known and give them to a couple of strangers?"

"He strikes me as a man who holds on to what he considers his."

"That might have been part of it. But the truth is, Beckett adores his boys. You should have seen him, driving to cattle sales and the feed store with two toddlers strapped in their car seats in the crew cab of his pickup truck."

Her heart seemed to sigh at the picture. She could see it entirely too clearly, the big, tough rancher and his adorable carbon-copy twins.

"He's a good man," Faith said. "A woman could do far worse than Beckett McKinley. If you're ever crazy enough to let Hope fix you up, you shouldn't discount Beck on account of those wild boys of his."

That wouldn't be the only reason she could never look seriously at Beck, if she was in the market for a man—which she so totally wasn't. For one thing, she became nervous and tongue-tied around him and couldn't seem to string together two coherent thoughts. For another, the man clearly didn't like her. He treated her with a cool politeness made all the more striking when she saw his warm, friendly demeanor around others. And, finally, she was more than a little jealous of his close relationship with her father. Curt treated his

neighboring rancher like the son he'd never had, trusting him with far more responsibility than he would
ever consider giving his own daughter. How could she
ever get past that?

She was saved from having to answer when Faith's
husband, Chase, came over with Faith's daughter and
son in tow.

Chase smiled at Ella and she tried to ignore the awkwardness as she greeted him. This was all she wanted.
A nice man who didn't make her nervous. Was that too
much to ask?

"Mom, can we go?" Louisa said. "I still have math
homework to finish."

"We're probably the only parents here whose kids are
begging to leave so they can get back to homework,"
Chase said with a grin.

"Thanks again for the great show, Ella," Faith said.
"We'll see you tomorrow. Now that we've been warned
the McKinley twins are coming, we'll make sure you
have reinforcements at practice tomorrow."

She could handle the twins. Their father was another story.

As much as he enjoyed hanging out with other ranchers, shooting the, er, shinola, as his dad used to call it,
Beck decided it was time to head out. It was past the
boys' bedtime and their bus would be coming early.

"Gentlemen, it's been a pleasure but I need to call
it a night," he said.

There were more than a few good-hearted groans of
disappointment.

He loved the supportive ranching community here
in Pine Gulch. Friends and neighbors came through

for each other in times of need. He couldn't count the number of guys who had stepped in to help him after his father died. When Stephanie left, he had needed help again until he could find a good nanny and more than one neighbor had come over without being asked to lend a hand on the ranch.

The Broken Arrow would have gone under without their aid and he knew he could never repay them. The only thing he could do now was help out himself where he could.

As Beck waved goodbye and headed away from the group, he saw Curt Baker climb to his feet with the aid of his cane and follow after him. Beck slowed his steps so the older man could catch up.

"Thanks again for stepping in today and helping Manny unload the feed shipment."

"Glad I could help," he answered.

It was true. He admired Curt and owed the man. After Beckett's father died, Curt had been the first neighbor to step in and help him figure out what he was doing on the ranch. Now the tables were turned. Curt's Parkinson's disease limited his ability to care for his own holdings. He had reduced his herd significantly and brought in more help, but still struggled to take care of the day-to-day tasks involved in running a cattle ranch.

He had actually talked Curt into running with him to be copresidents of the local cattle growers association. It wasn't a tough job and gave Curt something else to focus on besides his health issues.

"Have you thought more on what we talked about over lunch?"

As if he could think about anything else. As much

as he enjoyed cowboy folk songs, he'd had a hard time focusing on anything but Curt's stunning proposal that afternoon.

"You love the Baker's Dozen," he said. "There's no rush to sell it now, is there?"

Curt was quiet. "I'm not getting better. We both know that. There's only one direction this damn disease will go and that's south."

Parkinson's really sucked.

"I'm not in a hurry to sell. So far Manny and the other ranch hands are keeping things going—with help from you and Jax, of course—but you and I both know it's only a matter of time before I'll have to sell. I want to make sure I have things lined up ahead of time. Just wanted to plant the seed."

That little seed had certainly taken root. Hell, it was spreading like snakeweed.

The Broken Arrow was doing better than Beck ever dreamed, especially since he and his brother, Jax, had shifted so many of their resources to breeding exceptional cattle horses. They still ran about 500 cow-calf pair, but right now half the ranch's revenue was coming from the equine side of the business.

He would love the chance to expand his operation into the Baker's Dozen acreage, which had prime water rights along with it. He wasn't trying to build an empire here, but he had two boys to consider, as well as Jax. Though his brother seemed happy to play the field, someday that might change and he might want to settle down and become a family man.

Beck needed to make sure the Broken Arrow could support him, if that time came. It made perfect sense to grow his own operation into the adjacent property.

It would be a big financial reach, but after several re-cord-breaking years, he had the reserves to handle it.

"How does Ella feel about this?" he asked.

Curt shrugged. "What's not to like? You take over the work and we have money in the bank. She'll be fine. She could go back to Boston and not have to worry about me."

He wasn't sure he agreed with Curt's assessment of the Ella factor. Yeah, she didn't know anything about ranching and had only lived here with her father for a little longer than a year, but Ella was stubborn. She adored her father and had moved here to help him, though Curt seemed reluctant to lean on her too much.

"Anyway, we can worry about that later," Curt said. "My priority is to make sure I sell the land to someone who's actually going to ranch it, not turn it into condo-miniums. I've seen what you've done with the Broken Arrow since your father died and I have no doubt you'd give the same care to the Baker's Dozen."

"I appreciate that."

"No need to decide anything right now. We have plenty of time."

"You've given me a lot to chew on."

"That was my intent," Curt said. "Still need me to talk to Ella about taking your boys to the music thingy tomorrow?"

He winced, embarrassed that he'd even brought it up earlier. He was a grown man. He could talk to her him-self, even if the woman did make him feel like he'd just been kicked by a horse, breathless and stupid and slow.

"I'll do it," he said. "I actually have a few things in town so should be able to take them tomorrow. When

I get the chance, I'll try to talk to her then about future rehearsals."

He wasn't sure why his boys were so set on being in this Christmas program, but they were funny kids, with their own independent minds. He had always had the philosophy that he would try to support them in anything they tried. Basketball, soccer, after-school science clubs. Whatever.

Even when it meant he had to talk to Ella Baker.

Chapter Three

"Trevor. Colter. That's the last time I'm going to ask you. Please stop making silly noises. If you keep interrupting, we won't make it through all the songs we need to practice."

The twins gave Ella matching guilty looks. "Sorry, Miss Baker," Colter said.

"We'll be good. We promise," his brother added.

Somehow she was having a hard time believing that, especially given their track record in general and this practice in particular. After a full day of school, they were having a tough time sitting still and staying focused for the rehearsals, as she had fully expected.

She felt totally inadequate to deal with them on a December afternoon when they wanted to be running around outside, throwing snowballs and building snow forts.

Would it distract everyone too much if she had them stand up and do jumping jacks for a minute? She decided it was worth a try. Sometimes a little burst of energy could do wonders for focus.

"Okay, speed workout. Everyone. How many elf jumping jacks can you do in one minute? Count to yourself. Go."

She timed them on her phone and by the end the children were all laughing and trying to outdo each other.

"Excellent. Okay, now close your eyes and we'll do one more moment of deep breathing. That's it. Perfect."

That seemed to refocus everyone and they made it through nearly every number without further incident, until the last one, "Away in a Manger."

The song sounded lovely, with all the children singing in tune and even enunciating the words—until the last line of the third verse, when Trevor started making noises like a certain explosive bodily function, which made the entire back row dissolve into laughter.

By the time they finished the ninety-minute rehearsal, though, she felt as wrung out as a dirty mitten left in the snow.

As soon as parents started arriving for their children, Hope popped in from the office of The Christmas Ranch with a mug of hot chocolate, which she thrust out to Ella.

"Here you go. Extra snowflake marshmallows. You deserve it. You survived the first rehearsal. It's all uphill from here."

"I hope so," she muttered. "Today was a bit of a disaster."

"I saw Beck's boys giving you a rough time," Hope said, her voice sympathetic.

"You could say that. It must be tough on them, coming straight from school to here."

Eight rehearsals. That's all they had. She could handle that, couldn't she?

"Do you need me to find more people to help you?"

She considered, then shook her head. "I think we should be okay with the two teenagers who volunteered. Everyone is so busy this time of year. I hate to add one more thing to someone else's plate."

"Because your schedule is so free and easy over the next few weeks, right?"

Hope had a point. Between the Christmas show, the care center where she volunteered and the two schools where she worked, Ella had concerts or rehearsals every single day between now and Christmas.

"At least I'm not a bestselling illustrator who also happens to be in charge of the number-one holiday attraction for hundreds of miles around."

"Lucky you," Hope said with a grin. "Want to trade?"

"Not a chance."

Hope wouldn't trade her life, either, Ella knew. She loved creating the Sparkle the Reindeer books, which had become a worldwide sensation over the last few years. She also adored running the ranch with her husband, Rafe, and raising their beautiful son.

"Let me know if you change your mind about needing more help," Hope said.

"I will."

After Hope headed away, Ella started cleaning up the mess of paper wrappers and leftover sheet music the children had left behind. She was gathering up her own things when a couple of boys trotted out of the gift shop.

Colter and Trevor. Was she supposed to be giving

them a ride? Beck hadn't called her. He hadn't said a word to her about it. Had he just assumed she would do it without being asked?

That didn't really seem like something Beck would do. More likely, there was a miscommunication.

"Do you need me to call your dad to let him know we're done with rehearsal?"

Colter gave an exasperated sigh. "We told him and told him about it last night and this morning at breakfast. We took a note to school so we could ride a different bus here, then our dad was supposed to come get us when practice was done. I don't know where he is."

"Maybe we'll have to sleep here tonight," Trevor said. "I call under the Christmas tree!"

"You're not sleeping here tonight. I can give you a ride, but I need to talk to your dad first to make sure he's not on his way and just running late. I wouldn't want us to cross paths."

At least he hadn't just assumed she could take care of it. Slightly mollified, she pulled her phone out of her pocket. "Do you know his number?"

The boys each recited a different number, argued for a few moments, then appeared to come to a consensus.

She punched in the numbers they gave her without much confidence she would actually be connected to Beck, but to her surprise he answered.

"Broken Arrow," he said, with a brusqueness she should have expected, especially considering he probably didn't recognize her phone number.

Those two simple words in his deep, sexy voice seemed to shiver down her spine as if he'd trailed a finger down it.

"Beckett, this is Ella Baker. I was wondering…that

is, your sons were wondering, uh, are you coming to pick them up?"

Darn it, she *hated* being so tongue-tied around the man. She had all the poise and grace of a lumbering steer.

There was a long, awkward pause, then he swore. He quickly amended it. "Uh, shoot. I totally forgot about that. What time is rehearsal done?"

"About twenty minutes ago," she answered, letting a bit of tartness creep into her voice.

He sighed. "I've got the vet here looking at a sick horse. We're going to be another ten minutes or so, then I'll have to clean up a bit. Can you give me a half hour?"

He still couldn't seem to bring himself to ask for her help. Stubborn man. She glanced over at the boys, who were admiring the giant Christmas tree in the lodge. She wasn't sure she had the physical or mental capacity to keep them entertained and out of trouble for another half hour.

"I can give them a ride home, if you would like. It's an easy stop on my way back to the Baker's Dozen."

"Could you? That would be a big help. Thank you." The relief in his voice was palpable.

"You're welcome. Do you want me to drop them at the barn or the house?"

"The horse barn, if you don't mind. That's where I'm working."

She was suddenly having second thoughts, not sure she was ready to see him two days in a row.

"All right. We'll see you shortly, then."

"Thank you," he said again.

She managed to round up the boys in the nick of time, seconds before they were about to test how strong the garland over the mantel was by taking turns dangling from it.

How had Beck's house not burned down to the ground by now, with these two mischievous boys around?

"Why are you driving us home?" Colter asked when they had their seat belts on in her back seat. "Where's our dad?"

"He's taking care of a sick horse, he said. The vet's there with him and they lost track of time."

"That's Frisco. He was our mom's horse, but he's probably gonna die soon."

She wasn't sure how to reply to that, especially when he spoke in a matter-of-fact way. "I'm sorry."

"He's really old and too ornery for us to ride. He bites. Dad says he better not catch us near him," Trevor said.

She shivered, then hoped they couldn't see. She had to get over her fear of horses, darn it. After more than a year in horse and cattle country, she thought she would be past it—but then, twenty years hadn't made a difference, so why should the past year enact some miraculous change?

"You better do what he says."

"We don't want to ride that grumpy thing, anyway," Trevor said. "Why would we? We both have our own horses. Mine is named Oreo and Colt's is named Blackjack."

"Do you have a horse, Miss Baker?"

She remembered a sweet little roan mare she had adored more than anything in the world.

"I used to, when I was your age. Her name was Ruby.

But I haven't been on a horse in a long, long time. We don't have any horses on the Baker's Dozen."

In one bold sweep, her dad had gotten rid of them all twenty years ago, even though he had loved to ride, too. Thinking about it always made her sad.

"You could come ride our horses. We have like a million of them."

Familiar fear sidled up to her and said hello. "That's nice of you, Colter, but I don't know how to ride anymore. It's been a very long time since I've been in a saddle."

"We could teach you again," Trevor offered, with a sweet willingness that touched something deep inside. "I bet you'd pick it up again easy."

For a moment, she was very tempted by the offer but she would have to get past her phobia first. "That's very kind of you," she said, and left it at that. The boys didn't need to know about her issues.

"Hey, you know how to sing, right?" Colter said suddenly, changing the subject.

Considering she had one degree in music therapy and another in music education, she hoped so. "Yes. That is certainly something I do know how to do."

"And you play the guitar. You do it in school sometimes."

And the piano, violin and most other stringed instruments. "That's right."

"Could you teach us how to play a song?" Colter asked.

"And how to sing it, too?" Trevor said.

She glanced in her rearview mirror at their faces, earnestly eager. "Does either of you know how to play the guitar?"

"We both do, kind of," Colter said. "Uncle Dan taught us a couple chords last summer but then he said he wouldn't teach us anymore because we played too hard and broke all the strings on his guitar."

"Oh, dear."

These boys didn't do anything half-heartedly. She secretly hoped they would continue to be all-in as they grew up—with a little self-restraint when it was necessary, anyway.

"But we would never do that to your guitar, if you let us practice on it," he assured her with a grave solemnity that almost made her smile.

"We promise," his twin said. "We would be super careful."

She couldn't believe she would even entertain the idea for a moment, but she couldn't deny she was curious about the request. "What song are you trying to learn how to play and sing?"

"It's a good one. 'Christmas for the Cowboy.' Have you heard that one?"

"I'm not sure."

"It's about this cowboy and he has to work on Christmas Eve and ride his horse in the snow and stuff," Trevor informed her.

"He's real mad about it, and thinks it's not fair and he wants to be inside where it's warm, then the animals help him remember that Christmas is about peace on earth and stuff."

"And baby Jesus and wise men and shepherds," Trevor added.

"That sounds like a good one."

She combed through her memory bank but wasn't sure if she had ever heard it.

"It's our dad's favorite Christmas song in the whole wide world. He hums it all the time and keeps the CD in his pickup truck."

"Do you know who sings it?" she asked. It would be much easier to track down the guitar chords if she could at least have that much info.

The boys named a country music group whose name she recognized. She wasn't very familiar with their body of work.

"So can you teach us?" Colter asked as they neared the turnoff for the Broken Arrow. "It has to be with the guitar, too."

"Please?" Trevor asked. "Pretty please with Skittles on top?"

Well, she did like Skittles. She hid a smile. "Why is this so important to you? Why do you want to learn the song so badly?"

As she glanced in the rearview mirror, she saw the boys exchange looks. She had noticed before they did that quite often, as if passing along some nonverbal, invisible, twin communication that only they understood.

"It's for our dad," Trevor finally said. "He works hard all the time and takes care of us and stuff and we never have a good present to give him at Christmas."

"Except things we make in school, and that's usually just dumb crap," Colter said. "Pictures and clay bowls and stuff."

Ella had a feeling the art teacher she shared a classroom with probably wouldn't appreciate that particularly blunt assessment.

"When we went to bed last night after the concert, we decided we should learn that song and play it for our dad because he loves it so much, but we don't know the right words. We always sing it wrong."

"Hey, maybe after we learn it, we could play and sing it in the Christmas program," Colter said.

"Yeah," Trevor said, "Like that guy and his wranglers last night."

She didn't know how to respond, afraid to give the boys false hope. She didn't even know what song they were talking about, let alone whether it was appropriate for a Christmas program designed for senior citizens.

"I'm afraid I'm not familiar with that song—" she began.

"You could learn it, couldn't you?" Colter said.

"It's probably not even too hard."

As she turned into the ranch, they passed a large pasture containing about a dozen horses. Two of them cantered over to the fence line, then raced along beside her SUV, their manes and tails flying out behind them.

She felt the familiar panic, but something else, a long-buried regret for what she had lost.

"If I can find the song and agree to teach you, I need something from the two of you in return."

"Let me guess. You want us to quit messing around at rehearsal." Colter said this in the same resigned tone someone might use after being told they faced an IRS audit.

"Absolutely. That's one of my conditions. You told me you could behave, but today wasn't a very good example of that. I need to be able to trust you to keep your word."

"Sorry, Miss Baker."

"We'll do better, we promise."

How many times had the boys uttered those very

same words to one voice of authority or other? No doubt they always meant it, but something told her they would follow through this time. It touched her heart that they wanted to give this gift to their father, who had sacrificed and struggled and refused to give up custody after their mother died.

She wanted to help them give something back to him—and she wanted something in return, something that made her palms suddenly feel sweaty on the steering wheel.

"That is one of my conditions. And I'm very firm about it."

She paused, sucked in a breath, then let it out in a rush and spoke quickly before she could change her mind.

"I also have one more condition."

"What?" Trevor asked.

Her heart was pounding so hard, she could barely hear herself think. This was foolish. Why did she think two seven-year-old boys could help her overcome something she had struggled with for twenty years?

"You said you could teach me how to ride horses again. I would like that, very much. I told you it's been a long time since I've been on a horse. I…miss it."

More than she had even dared acknowledge to herself.

Once, horses had been her passion. She had dreamed about them, talked about them, drew pictures of them, even during the months when she was living in Boston during the ten months out of the year her mother had custody of her. It used to drive Elizabeth crazy.

Everything had changed when she was eight.

"You really can't ride?" Trevor said. "You said that

before but I didn't think you meant it. You're a grown-up."

These boys probably spent more time in the saddle than out of it. She had seen them before as she was driving by the ranch, racing across the field and looking utterly carefree. Until now, Ella hadn't realized how very much she had envied them.

"Not everyone is as lucky as you two," she said as she pulled up to the large red indoor horse barn and arena. "I learned how to ride when I was a child, but then I had a bad fall and it's been…hard for me ever since."

Hard was an understatement. What she didn't tell the boys was that she had a completely reasonable terror of horses.

She had been only a year older than the boys, on a visit here with her father. Her sweet little Ruby had been nursing an injury so she had insisted to her father she could handle one of the other geldings on a ride with him along their favorite trail. The horse had been jittery, though, and had ended up being spooked by a snake on the trail just as they were crossing a rocky slope.

Not only had she fallen from the horse, but she had also tumbled thirty feet down the mountainside.

After being airlifted to Idaho Falls, she had ended up in a medically induced coma, with a head injury, several broken vertebrae and a crushed leg. She had spent months in the hospital and rehab clinics. Even after extensive therapy, she still limped when she was tired.

Her injuries had marked the final death knell to the marriage her parents had tried for years to patch back together. They had been separated on and off most of her childhood before then. After her riding accident, her mother completely refused to send her to the ranch.

The custody battle had been epic. In the process, a great gulf had widened between her and her father, one that she was still trying to bridge, twenty years later.

If she could only learn to ride, conquer her fear, perhaps Curt Baker wouldn't continue to see her as a fragile doll who needed to be protected at all costs.

"I know the basics," she told the boys now. "I just need some pointers. It's a fair trade, don't you think? I teach you a few chords on the guitar and you let me practice riding horses."

The boys exchanged looks, their foreheads furrowed as they considered her request. She caught some furtive whispers but couldn't hear what they said.

While she waited for them to decide, Ella wondered if she was crazy. She couldn't believe she was actually considering this. What could these boys teach her, really? She was about to tell them she had changed her mind about the riding lessons but would still teach them the song when Trevor spoke for both of them.

"Sure. We could do that. When do you want to practice? How about Saturday?"

"We can't!" Trevor said to his brother. "We have practice Saturday, remember?"

"Oh, yeah. But maybe in the afternoon, when we're done."

Why was she even considering throwing one more thing into her packed schedule? She couldn't do it. Ella wiped her sweaty palms on her skirt. "We can forget this. It was a silly idea."

"Why?" Trevor asked, his features confused. "We want you to teach us how to play and sing a song for our dad's Christmas present and you want to learn how to ride a horse better so you don't fall off. We can teach each other."

"It will be fun. You'll see. And maybe you could even buy one of our dad's horses after you learn how to ride again."

That was pushing things. Maybe she first ought to see if she could spend five minutes around horses without having a panic attack.

"So can you come Saturday afternoon?" Trevor asked.

"Our dad won't be home, so that would be good. Then he won't need to know why we're teaching you how to ride horses. Because otherwise, we'd have to tell him it's a trade. That would ruin the surprise."

"I…think I can come Saturday." Oh, she was crazy.

"Yay! This will be fun. You'll see."

She wasn't so sure. Before she could come up with an answer, the door to the barn opened and Beck came striding out with that loose-limbed, sexy walk she always tried—and failed—to ignore.

He had someone else with him. Ben Caldwell, she realized, the veterinarian in town whose wife, Caidy, had a magical singing voice. She barely noticed the other man, too busy trying not to stare at Beckett.

Her hands felt clammy again as she opened her car door, but this time she knew it wasn't horses making her nervous.

Chapter Four

"You know, it might be time to say goodbye."

Ben Caldwell spoke gently as he ran a calming hand down Frisco's neck. "He's tired, he's cranky, he can't see and he's half-lame. I can keep coming out here and you can keep on paying me, but eventually I'm going to run out of things I can do to help him feel better."

Beckett was aware of a familiar ache in his gut. He knew it would be soon but didn't like to think about it. "I know. Not yet, though."

The vet nodded his understanding but that didn't make Beck feel any less stupid. No doubt Dr. Caldwell wondered why he had such a soft spot for this horse that nobody had been able to ride for five years. Frisco had always been bad-tempered and high-spirited, but somehow Stephanie had loved him, anyway. Beck wasn't quite ready to say goodbye yet.

He shook the vet's hand. "Thanks, Ben. I appreciate you coming by."

"You got it."

Sal, one of Beck's border collies, waddled over to them, panting a welcome. The veterinarian scratched her under the chin and gently patted her side.

"She hasn't had those pups yet."

"Any day now. We're on puppy watch."

"You'll call me if she has any troubles, right?"

"You know it."

He had great respect for Ben. Though Beck hadn't been too sure about the city vet when the man moved to town a handful of years ago, Dr. Caldwell had proved himself over and over. He'd also married a friend of his, Caidy Bowman, who had gone to school with Beck.

They were finishing up with Frisco when he heard a vehicle pull up outside. Beck's heartbeat accelerated, much to his chagrin.

"You expecting somebody?" Ben asked.

"That would be Ella Baker. I, uh, forgot to pick the boys up from rehearsal at The Christmas Ranch and she was nice enough to bring them home for me."

"That Christmas program is all the buzz at my place, too," Ben said. "My kids can't wait."

Ben had been a widower with two children, a boy and a girl, when he moved to town. Beck sometimes had Ben's daughter babysit the twins in a pinch.

The two men walked outside and Beck was again aware of his pulse in his ears. This was so stupid, that he couldn't manage to stop staring at Ella as she climbed out of her SUV.

Ben sent him a sidelong look and Beck really hoped the man didn't notice his ridiculous reaction.

"I'll get out of your way," Ben said. "Think about what I said."

"I will. Thanks again."

Ella and the boys both waved at the veterinarian as they climbed out of her vehicle.

"Hey, Dad! Hey!" His boys rushed over to him, arms wide, and he hugged them, wondering if there would ever come a time in his life when they didn't feel like the best damn thing that had ever happened to him.

He doubted it. He couldn't even imagine how much poorer his life would be without Trevor and Colter. Whenever he was tempted to regret his ill-conceived marriage, he only had to hug his boys and remember that all the rest of the mess and ugliness had been worth it.

"Hey, guys. How was practice? Did you behave yourselves?"

"Um, sure," Colter said.

"Kind of," his brother hedged.

Which meant not at all. He winced.

"We're gonna do better," Colter assured him. "We promised Miss Baker. Me and Trevor thought maybe we could run around the building three times before we go inside to practice, to get our energy out."

"That sounds like a plan."

It was a strategy he sometimes employed when they struggled to focus on homework at night, taking them on a good walk around the ranch so they could focus better.

"I'm starving," Trevor said. "Can I have a cheese stick?"

"Me, too!" Colter said.

"Yeah. You know where they are."

The boys ran into the barn, heading for the fridge inside the office, where he kept a few snacks.

He turned to her. Like his father always said, better to eat crow when it was fresh. It tasted better hot and was much easier to swallow.

"How big of an apology do I owe you for the boys' behavior?"

To his surprise, she smiled, something she didn't do around him very often. For some reason, the woman didn't seem to like him very much.

"On a scale of one to ten?" she asked. "Probably a seven."

"I'm going to take that as a win."

Her smile widened. It made her whole face glow. With a few snowflakes falling in her hair and the slanted afternoon sun hitting her just right, the universe seemed to be making it impossible for him to look away.

"It's hard for two seven-year-old boys to be in school all day, then take a long bus ride, then have to sit and behave for another hour and a half," she said. "I understand that. They have energy to burn and need somewhere to put it. Today was hard because there was a lot of sitting around while we practiced songs. Things won't be as crazy for our next practice, I'm sure."

"It really does help if they can work out a little energy."

"We did elf jumping jacks. You're right, things were better after that."

She paused, her smile sliding away. He had the feeling she was uncomfortable about something. Or maybe he was the only uncomfortable one here.

"Do you need me to give the boys a ride to the rest of our practices?" she finally asked. "I can take them with me to The Christmas Ranch after school and bring them back here when practice is over."

Her generous offer startled him. The night before, he had wanted to ask her the same thing, but in the light of day, the request had seemed entirely too presumptuous.

"Are you sure that wouldn't be a problem?"

"You're right next door. It's only five minutes out of my way, to bring them up here to the house. I don't mind, really."

"That's very gracious of you. If you're sure it won't be an inconvenience, I would appreciate it."

"I don't mind. I should warn you, they might be a little later coming home than some of the other children, since I have to straighten up our rehearsal space after we're done. Perhaps they can help me put away chairs after practice."

"Absolutely. They're good boys and will work hard, as long as they have a little direction."

The wind was kicking up, blowing down out of the foothills with that peculiar smell of an approaching storm. She shivered a little and he felt bad for keeping her standing out here. He could have invited her inside the horse barn, at least.

"I really do appreciate it," he said, feeling as big and rough and awkward as he always did around her soft, graceful beauty. "To be honest, I wasn't sure how I would juggle everything this week. I'm supposed to be going out of town tomorrow until Monday to look at a couple of horses and I hate complicating the boys' schedule more than I have to for Uncle Dan and Jax."

"No problem."

"Thanks. I owe you one."

"You do," she answered firmly. "And here's how you

can pay me back. We're signing up drivers for the night of the show to pick up some of the senior citizens who don't like driving in the snow. Add your name to the list and we can be even."

That would be no hardship for him. It would take up one evening of his life and he could fit a half-dozen senior citizens in his crew cab pickup.

"Sure. I can do that."

"Okay. Deal."

To his surprise, she thrust out her hand to seal the agreement, as if they were bartering cattle or signing a treaty. After a beat, he took it. Her fingers were cool, small, smooth, and he didn't want to let go. He was stunned by his urge to tug her against him and kiss that soft, sweet mouth.

He came to his senses just an instant before he might have acted on the impulse and released her fingers. He saw confusion cloud her gaze but something else, too. A little spark of awareness he instantly recognized.

"I need to, that is, I have to…my dad will be waiting for me."

"Give my best regards to Curt," he said.

The words were a mistake. He knew it as soon as he spoke them. Her mouth tightened and that little glimmer of awareness disappeared, crowded out by something that looked like resentment.

"I'll do that, though I'm sure he already knows he has your best regards," she said stiffly. "The feeling is mutual, I'm sure."

He frowned, again feeling awkward and not sure what he should say. Yes, he and her father got along well. He respected Curt, enjoyed the man's company, and was grateful he was in a position to help him. Why did that bother her?

Did she know Curt had offered to sell him the ranch?

He was hesitant to ask, for reasons he couldn't have defined.

"I should go. It's been a long day. I'll bring the boys back from practice tomorrow and take care of Saturday, too."

"Sounds good. I won't be here, but Jax and Dan will be."

She nodded and climbed into her SUV in her fancy leather boots and slim skirt.

He watched her drive away for much longer than he should have, wondering why he felt so awkward around her. Everyone in town seemed to like Ella. Though she had moved back only a year ago, she had somehow managed to fuse herself into the fabric of this small Idaho community.

He liked her, too. That was a big part of the problem. He couldn't be around her without wondering if her skin was as soft as it looked, her hair as silky, her mouth as delicious.

He had to get over this stupid attraction, but he had no idea how.

He was so busy watching after her taillights, he didn't notice the boys had come out until Trevor spoke.

"Hey, Dad. What are you lookin' at?" his son asked.

"Is it a wolf?" Colter vibrated with excitement at the idea. They had driven up to Yellowstone for the weekend a month ago and had seen four of them loping along the Lamar Valley road. Since then, the boys had been fascinated with the idea of wolves, especially after Beck explained the Pine Gulch area was part of the larger far-ranging territory of the various Yellowstone packs.

"Nope. No wolves," he said now. "I'm just enjoying the sight of our pretty ranch."

His sons stood beside him, gazing at the ranch along with him.

This was what should matter to him, passing on a legacy for these boys. He had worked his ass off to bring the Broken Arrow ranch back from the brink since his father died a decade ago. The ranch was thriving now, producing fine cattle and the best quarter-horse stock in the entire region.

He intended to do his best to protect that legacy for his boys and for his younger brother, so he could have something more than bills and barren acreage to give them after he was gone.

He would build on it, too, when he had the chance. Any smart man would take any opportunity to expand his holdings. Beck couldn't let anything stand in the way, especially not a pretty city girl who wore completely impractical boots and made him think things he knew he shouldn't.

Ella's pulse was still racing uncomfortably as she drove the short distance between his ranch and the Baker's Dozen.

Why, oh, why did Beck McKinley have to be so darned gorgeous? She didn't know how it was possible, but he seemed to get better looking every time she saw him.

This crush was becoming ridiculous. She felt like a giddy girl who had never talked to a man before. Completely untrue. She'd been engaged once, for heaven's sake, to a junior partner in her stepfather's law practice.

Okay, she had been engaged for a month. That counted, right?

On paper, Devin had been ideal. Handsome, earnest, ambitious. They enjoyed the same activities, listened to the same music, shared the same friends. She had known him since third grade and dated him all through college. Her mother and stepfather adored him and everyone said they made a perfect couple.

He proposed on her twenty-sixth birthday, with a ring that had been gorgeous and showy. Shortly afterward, they had started planning their wedding.

Well, her mother had started planning her wedding.

Ella's job in the process appeared to consist of leafing through bridal magazines and nodding her head when her mother made suggestion after suggestion about venues and catering companies and dress shops.

Three weeks into her engagement, she found out her father had Parkinson's. Not from Curt, of course. That would have been too straightforward. No, his longtime housekeeper, Alina, wife to his longtime foreman, Manny Guzman, called to let her know he had fallen again. That was a news flash to her, since she didn't know he had fallen before.

After some probing, she learned Curt had been diagnosed a year earlier and had kept it from her. Apparently he had balance issues and had fallen a few times before, requiring help from one of the hands to get back up.

This time, his fall had been more serious, resulting in a broken hip. She had taken leave from her job and immediately caught a flight to Idaho the next day, which hadn't made Devin very happy. After two weeks of him pleading with her to come back, she realized to her chagrin that she didn't want to go back—and worse, that she had barely given the man second thought.

She didn't love him. How could she possibly merge her life with someone she didn't love? It wasn't worth it, only to make her mother happy.

Ella had flown back to Boston, returned his ring and ended the engagement. He hadn't been heartbroken, which only seemed to reinforce her realization that theirs had been a relationship borne out of convenience and familiarity.

They would have been content together. She wanted to think so, anyway, but she wasn't sure they would have been truly happy.

Devin had never once made her insides feel as if a hundred butterflies were doing an Irish step dance. Not like...

She shied away from the thought. Yes, Beck was hot. Yes, she was attracted to him and he left her giddy and breathless.

So what?

She didn't *want* to be attracted to him. It was pathetic, really, especially when it was clear the man thought she was useless out here in ranching country.

Join the crowd, she wanted to tell him. He and her father ought to form a club.

Oh, wait. They already had formed a mutual admiration society that completely excluded her.

She sighed, frustrated all over again at her stubborn father, who couldn't see that she was capable of so much more than he believed.

A blue pickup truck was parked in front of the Baker's Dozen ranch house as Ella pulled up, and she made a face. She recognized the truck as belonging to Chris Soldado, the physical and occupational therapist who came to the house twice a month to work with her dad, both for his ongoing recovery from the broken hip and to help him retain as much use of his limbs as possible as his Parkinson's progressed.

He must be working after-hours. She grimaced at the prospect. His visits always left Curt sore and cranky. More sore and cranky than usual, anyway.

As she let herself in, she found Chris Soldado and her father in the great room. Her father was leaning heavily on his cane while Chris seemed to be putting equipment back into his bag. Chris was a great guy who had been coming a couple times a month for as long as she had been back in Pine Gulch. He was firm but compassionate with Curt and didn't let him get away with much.

"Hi, Chris," she said with a smile.

"Hey there, Ella," he said. He gave her a flirtatious smile in return. "I'm just on my way out. I was telling your dad, he needs to be doing these exercises on his own, every day. That's the best way to retain as much mobility as he can for as long as possible. Make sure of it, okay?"

She tried to nag, but it usually only ended up frustrating both of them. "I'll do that. Thanks."

"This will probably be my last visit for this year. I'll see you in January, Mr. Baker."

Her father made a face but nodded. He looked tired, his features lined with strain.

She let the therapist out, then returned back to her dad and kissed him on the cheek. He needed to shave, something she knew was difficult for him with the trembling of his hands. That was one more area where he didn't want her help.

Maybe she ought to ask Beck to help Curt shave, since he was so good at everything else.

She sighed. "How was your day?"

"I just had physical therapy and that was a high point."

Oh, she missed the kind, loving father of her childhood. Big, hale, hearty. Wonderful.

He was still wonderful, she reminded herself. She just had to work through the occasionally unpleasant bits to get there.

"How about yours?" he asked, which she appreciated. He didn't always think to ask. "You're late getting home, aren't you?"

"Yes. Remember, I told you I would be late for the next few weeks. We had our first practice for the Christmas pageant."

"Oh, right. It slipped my mind during the torture session. How did it go?"

"Good, for the most part. The McKinley twins caused a bit of trouble but nothing I couldn't handle."

"Those boys are rascals," Curt said, but she heard clear admiration in his voice. "Alina left shepherd's pie. She said we just had to bake it but after Chris showed up, I forgot to turn on the oven."

"I can do that. Let me help you to your chair."

"No. I'm fine. If I sit in that recliner, I'll just fall asleep like an old man. I'll come in the kitchen with you."

That was an unexpected gift, as well. She decided to savor the small victories as she led the way to the kitchen. She fussed until he sat on one of the kitchen chairs, then she poured him a glass of water before turning on the oven and pulling out the potato-topped casserole that had always been a favorite of her father.

"So tell me what those twins were up to today," he said. Curt always seemed to get a kick out of Beck's boys and their hijinks.

"Nothing too egregious."

While she made a salad and set the table, she told him stories about the boys. He laughed heartily when she mentioned the bodily noises during "Away in a Manger" and about them trying to hang from the garland, and she was suddenly grateful beyond measure for those twins and their energy, and for providing this lighthearted moment she could share with the father she loved.

Chapter Five

"That was excellent. Really excellent," Ella said, praising the two little cowboys seated at a table in the classroom she shared with the part-time art teacher.

She had arranged for Trevor and Colter to stay after school for a half hour so they could rehearse the cowboy ballad they wanted to sing for their father. She would drive them out to The Christmas Ranch when they were finished.

This had been the most logical rehearsal spot, even if the walls were currently adorned with collage after collage of grinning Santas made out of dry macaroni and cotton-puff beards.

Fortunately, all those Santas checking to see whether they were naughty or nice didn't seem to bother Trevor and Colter McKinley.

"We sound good enough to be on the radio, huh?" Trevor said.

She envied their sheer confidence, even as it made her smile. "Definitely," she answered. "You picked up the words and melody of the chorus perfectly. Why don't we try the whole thing from the beginning? Straighten up in your seat, now. You'll sing your best if your lungs have room to expand and they can't do that when you're all hunched over."

The boys sat up straight and straightened their collars as if they were preparing to take the stage at the Vienna opera house. She smiled, completely charmed by them. If she wasn't careful, these two troublemakers would worm their way right into her heart.

"Okay. Hit it," Colter said.

"Please," his twin added conscientiously.

They had decided that because of time constraints, it would be better if she just accompanied them so they didn't have to learn the words to the song and the unfamiliar guitar chords at the same time. She played the music she had found, the first gentle notes of the Christmas song.

The boys sang the lines in unison, their voices clear and pure and quite lovely. Their voices blended perfectly. She could only imagine how good it would sound if they could learn a little harmony.

They could work on that. For now, she wanted to focus on making sure they knew the words and phrasing of the song.

"That sounded really great," she said, after they went through the song four more times in a row.

"Our dad's going to love it," Trevor declared.

"I'm sure you're right." She glanced at the clock.

"We had better run or we'll be late for practice with the rest of the children. We can run through the song a few more times on the way."

They grabbed their coats and yanked on backpacks while she prepared to close up the classroom.

"We'll meet you by the office," Colter said. Before she could call them back, they headed out of the classroom. She locked the door and was about to follow after when the fifth-grade teacher from across the hall opened her own door.

"Was that really the McKinley twin terrors I heard in here?" Susan Black looked flabbergasted.

"Yes. They asked me to help them prepare a song they could perform as a gift to their father for Christmas."

The older woman shook her head. "How did you get them to sit still long enough to even learn a line? I think I may seriously have to think about retirement before those two hit fifth grade."

"They like to sing. Sometimes it's just a matter of finding the right switch."

"You've got the magic touch, I guess."

She had no idea why the boys were beginning to respond to her, she thought as she walked toward the office, but she wasn't about to jinx things by questioning it too much.

The boys were waiting impatiently for her and raced ahead when she opened the outside door. They found her SUV in the nearly empty parking lot immediately—no surprise, as she'd given them a ride just the day before.

"Thanks again for helping us," Trevor said when

they were safely seat-belted in the back and she was on her way.

"It's my pleasure," she told them.

"Are you still coming tomorrow to ride horses?"

That panic shivered through her and she almost told them to forget about that part of the deal. Two things stopped her. They were proud little cowboys and she sensed they wouldn't appreciate being beholden to her for anything. And second, she knew she couldn't give in to her fear or it would control the rest of her life.

"Are you sure it's okay with your dad?" She couldn't quite keep the trepidation from her voice.

"He won't care and he's gonna be gone, anyway."

"Oh, right. He's looking at a couple of horses."

"Yep. We talked to our uncle Jax and he said he can help us saddle up the easiest horse on the ranch for you."

"That's Creampuff," Colter said. "She's a big softie."

"You'll like her," Trevor assured her. "Even though she likes to wander out when she gets the chance, Dad says he could put a kitten on her back and she'd never knock it off."

"Sounds perfect for me, then," Ella said, trying not to show her nervousness.

"Great. So just wear stuff you can ride in tomorrow. Boots and jeans. You know. Not teacher clothes."

Apparently they didn't approve of her favorite green wool sweater set and dressy dove-gray slacks.

"Got it. I'll see if I can find something a little more appropriate," she said.

"It will be fun. You'll see," Colter said.

She had serious reservations, but tried to swallow them down as they arrived at The Christmas Ranch for rehearsal.

First things first. She had to make it through two more practices before she could have time to worry about her upcoming horseback-riding lesson.

"We were good today, don't you think?"

After rehearsal on Saturday, Ella glanced in the rearview mirror at the two boys sitting in her back seat.

"You really were." She had to hope they didn't hear the note of wonder in her voice. "And yesterday, too. You paid attention, you stayed in your seats, you didn't distract your neighbors. Good job, guys."

"Told you we could be. It wasn't even that hard. We just had to pretend we were dead mice."

"Dead mice who could still sing," Trevor added.

Ella tried to hide her smile. "Whatever you did, it worked perfectly. Let's see if we can do it again next week, through the rest of the rehearsals we have left until the show."

"We will be," Trevor said. "We promised you, and our dad says a man's word is his wand."

It took her a second to fit the pieces together. "I think he probably said bond. That means a commitment."

"Oh, yeah. That was it. A man's word is his bond."

That sounded like something Beckett McKinley would say to his sons.

He was a good father. The boys were high-strung, but their hearts were in the right place. They were working hard to prepare a Christmas gift for their father and that day she had also watched them show great kindness to Taft Bowman's stepdaughter, who had Down syndrome and some developmental delays. She was older than they were by a few years but they still seemed to have appointed themselves her champion.

She should tell Beckett what good young men he was raising. Something told her he didn't hear that very often.

She pushed away thoughts of the man, grateful at least that she wouldn't have to see him today. She was stressed enough about riding the horses. She didn't need to add any additional anxiety into the mix.

As she drove up the snow-packed road to the ranch house, those same horses that had greeted them the first time she brought the boys home raced alongside her SUV, a beautiful but terrifying sight in the afternoon sunlight.

She wouldn't be riding one of those energetic creatures. She would be riding a horse named Creampuff. How scary could something named Creampuff really be?

Terrifying enough that she felt as if her heart was going to pound out of her chest. She let out a breath. Why was she putting herself through this, again? It wouldn't make any difference with Curt. Her father loved her but he couldn't see her as anything but fragile, delicate, someone to be protected at all costs.

She pushed away the thought. This wasn't for her father. She needed to ride again for *herself.* She needed to prove to herself she could do it, that she could overcome her fears and finally tackle this anxiety. The opportunity had presented itself through these twins and she couldn't afford to miss it.

"Where should I park?" she asked as she approached the buildings clustered around the ranch house. "Where do you think we will be having this lesson?"

"Uncle Jax said we could use the riding barn. He said he would have Creampuff all ready for you. But then

Uncle Dan made us promise we'd stop at the house first to grab some lunch and put on our boots."

"That sounds like a good idea. I need to change my clothes, anyway."

Despite the boys' fashion advice, Ella had worn a skirt and sweater to the Saturday rehearsal, as if preparing for a day at school. It seemed silly in retrospect, but she hadn't wanted to appear in jeans. In her experience, she tended to command more respect with her students when she was a little dressed up.

Her riding clothes were packed into a small bag on the passenger seat beside her, but she hadn't given much practical thought to when and where she would actually change into them. She should have had the foresight to do it at The Christmas Ranch before they left.

They directed her where to park and she pulled her SUV into a driveway in back of the house. The boys led the way inside, straight to the kitchen.

They found Daniel McKinley, Beck's uncle, wearing an apron and loading dishes into the dishwasher.

"There you two are. Howdy, Miss Baker."

She smiled at him. As always, she was delighted by his old-fashioned, courteous nature and ready smile.

He was quite a charmer in his day, she had heard—a bachelor cowboy who cut a broad swath through the female population of the county. Now he was over seventy with a bad back and struggled almost as much as her father to get around these days.

"You ready for your riding lesson?" Dan asked, offering her a smile that still held plenty of charm.

Would she ever be? "Yes," she lied. "I can't wait."

"These boys will get you up on a horse, you wait and

see. Best little cowboys I ever did see. They'll have you barrel racing in the rodeo by summer."

That was far beyond what she even wanted to attempt. She could only pray she would be able to stay in the saddle.

"I'm makin' sandwiches, if you want one," he offered. "Nothing grand, just grilled ham and cheese. It's one of the four things I know how to cook."

"What are the other three?" she asked, genuinely curious.

"Coffee, hot dogs and quesadillas. As long as I'm only making them with cheese and salsa. Oh, I can do scrambled eggs, too, if you've got a hankering."

She had to smile, completely enchanted by him. "I'm great with a ham sandwich. Thanks so much for offering."

"It's no trouble. Just as easy to make four sandwiches as it is three, I suspect."

"I appreciate it, anyway. May I help you?"

"You can help me by sitting down and relaxing. Something tells me you don't do enough of that, Miz Baker."

True enough, especially the last month. She would have time to rest after the holidays.

"If it's all right with you, I would like to find somewhere to change into more appropriate clothing for a riding lesson."

"You can use Beck's bedroom. First door on the right."

She instantly wanted to protest. Was there really nowhere else in this big, beautiful log house for her to change, besides Beckett McKinley's bedroom? She didn't want to know where he slept, where he dressed, where he probably walked around in his briefs.

She let out a breath, aware that she would sound completely ridiculous if she raised a single irrational objection to his suggestion.

Nothing left but to accept with grace, she decided. "That sounds good. I'll change my clothes and then come help you with lunch."

He pointed her on her way, his leathery features split into a smile. Unlike her father, Dan McKinley still appeared to have a healthy appetite. He limped around the kitchen but other than that, his skin was firm and pink instead of the sallow tones her father sometimes had.

Curt had probably lost twenty pounds in the months she had been back in Pine Gulch. He was still large-framed, but his clothing all sat loosely on him these days and he wore suspenders to keep up his pants.

It made her sad to see the comparison between the two men, though she reminded herself she couldn't change the course of her father's disease. She could only try to make his world as comfortable and accessible as possible.

She gripped her tote bag and hurried down the hall lined with beautiful western artwork, highlighted by tasteful inset lighting.

As she might have expected, judging by the rest of the house, Beck's bedroom was gorgeous, spacious and comfortable, with a river-rock fireplace in one corner and expansive windows that looked over both his ranch and her father's. It was dominated by a massive log bed, neatly made, with a masculine comforter in tones of dark blue and green.

The room smelled of him, of sagebrush and leather and rainy summer afternoons in the mountains.

She inhaled deeply and felt something visceral and raw spring to life inside her. Oh. She wanted to stand right here and just savor it.

That bed. Her imagination suddenly seemed entirely too vivid. A snowy night and the two of them tangled together under that soft blanket, with all those hard muscles hers alone to explore.

"Snap out of it," she ordered herself, just seconds before she would have pulled his pillow up to her face to inhale.

Good grief. She didn't come here to moon over Beck. She was here to conquer her fears and tackle something that terrified her.

Okay, he terrified her, too. But this was about horseback riding.

With renewed determination, she quickly kicked off her dressy boots and slipped down her skirt, then pulled on her favorite weathered jeans.

Her Christmas sweater with the reindeer and sleigh had been fun for the kids during rehearsal for the program, but would be too bulky and uncomfortable under her coat while she was riding.

She started to pull it over her head but the textured heavy yarn that was part of the design tangled in one of the combs she'd used to pull her hair back. Shoot. If she tugged it too hard, she would rip the sweater and ruin it. She didn't want that. It was one of her favorites, a gift from a friend in Boston.

With her hands above her head and the sweater covering her face, she tried to extricate the design from her hair comb when suddenly she heard the door open.

Panic burst through her and she almost crossed her arms over her chest. At the last minute, she remembered she still had on the plain white T-shirt she wore underneath the sweater.

"Who's there?" she demanded, her face buried in sweater.

"Beck McKinley," a deep voice drawled. "I believe I should be the one asking questions, Miss Baker. It's my bedroom, after all, and to be perfectly honest, I can't begin to guess what you might be doing in it."

She closed her eyes, wishing she could disappear. She should have known. Who else would it be? Wasn't that just the way her luck went? The one person she didn't want to see would, of course, be the one who stumbled in on an embarrassing moment.

She would have far preferred his brother, Jax, who flirted with everyone and could be handled simply by flirting right back.

She ought to just yank down the sweater and rip it, but she couldn't quite bring herself to do that.

"I'm sorry. Your uncle told me I could use your room to change into riding clothes. Didn't he tell you?"

"I haven't talked to Dan since breakfast. I've been holed up in my office on the other side of the house all morning. Riding clothes, Ella?"

She did *not* want to have this conversation with him with her sweater tangled around her head. The only bright spot in this entire miserable predicament was that she was wearing a T-shirt underneath the sweater. She couldn't imagine how mortifying if he had walked in on her in only her bra.

"It's a long story. I can tell you, but would you help me with my sweater first?"

After a pregnant pause, he finally spoke. "Uh, what seems to be the trouble?"

His voice had an odd, strangled note to it. Was he laughing at her? Where she couldn't see him, she couldn't be quite sure. "It's stuck in my hair comb. I don't want to rip the sweater—or yank out my hair, for that matter."

He was silent, then she felt the air stir as he moved closer. The scent of him was stronger now, masculine and outdoorsy, and everything inside her sighed a welcome.

He stood close enough that she could feel the heat radiating from him. She caught her breath, torn between a completely prurient desire for the moment to last at least a little longer and a wild hope that the humiliation of being caught in this position would be over quickly.

"Hold still," he said. Was his voice deeper than usual? She couldn't quite tell. She did know it sent tiny delicious shivers down her spine.

"You've really done a job here," he said after a moment.

"I know. I'm not quite sure how it tangled so badly."

She would have to breathe soon or she was likely to pass out. She forced herself to inhale one breath and then another until she felt a little less light-headed.

"Almost there," he said, his big hands in her hair, then a moment later she felt a tug and the sweater slipped all the way over her head.

"There you go."

"Thank you." She wanted to disappear, to dive under that great big log bed and hide away. Instead, she forced her mouth into a casual smile. "These Christmas sweaters can be dangerous. Who knew?"

She was blushing. She could feel her face heat and wondered if he noticed. This certainly counted among the most embarrassing moments of her life.

"Want to explain again what you're doing in my bedroom, tangled up in your clothes?" he asked.

She frowned at his deliberately risqué interpretation of something that had been innocent. Mostly.

There *had* been that secret moment when she had closed her eyes and imagined being here with him under that soft quilt, but he had no way of knowing that.

She folded up her sweater, wondering if she would ever be able to look the man in the eye again.

"It's a long story. Your sons offered to teach me how to ride horses."

"Trevor and Colter."

She finally gathered the courage to lift her gaze to his. "Do you have any other sons?"

"No. Two are enough, thanks. Why would Trevor and Colter offer to teach you how to ride horses?"

She suddenly didn't know how to answer that. He couldn't know the boys wanted to surprise him with a special song for Christmas, that they were bartering services. Telling him about it would completely ruin the surprise, and she wasn't about to do that to the boys, especially after they were trying so hard to uphold their side of the bargain.

"I guess they felt sorry for me when I told them I couldn't ride. I may have let slip at some point that I'm a little…nervous around horses and I would like to get over it."

He raised an eyebrow. "Let me get this straight. You're nervous around horses, but somehow you thought two seven-year-old boys could help you get over your fear?"

Okay, it sounded ridiculous when he said it like that. What had seemed like a good idea at the time now seemed nothing short of foolish.

"Why not? They're excellent riders and their enthusiasm is…contagious."

"Like chicken pox."

"Something like that." She forced a smile. "They aren't afraid to tell everyone what good riders they are. I figured it couldn't hurt to see if some of that enthusiasm might rub off on me."

It sounded silly in retrospect, but there was nothing she could do about that at this point. The deal had been struck and she didn't want to hurt the boys by pulling out of the arrangement now, when they were so excited to teach her.

Beck continued to watch her with a baffled look on his features. What was he even doing there? She thought he was supposed to be out of town this weekend.

"If you would rather I didn't go riding with them, I understand. I should have asked you first. The boys and I talked about it yesterday after practice. They told me you wouldn't be here but that Dan said it was okay. I guess I assumed perhaps he would talk to you. I don't want to cause trouble, though. If you don't want me here, I can grab my Christmas sweater and go home."

She wouldn't blame the man if he threw her off his ranch. Without telling him about the deal she and the boys struck, she sounded completely irrational.

"No. It's fine. We have a couple of really gentle horses that are good for beginners."

She released the breath she hadn't realized she'd been holding. He didn't *sound* like he thought she was crazy.

"The boys promised me a horse named Creampuff. I like the sound of that name, if she lives up to it."

"That's just the horse I would have suggested. She's about as mellow as it gets."

"Sounds perfect. Thank you."

He tilted his head and studied her. "You can ride our sweet Creampuff on one condition."

"What's that?" she asked, suddenly wary at the look in his eyes.

"You let *me*, not the twins, give you riding lessons."

She instantly remembered standing close to him and the shivery little ache that had spread through her. The more time she spent with Beckett McKinley, the more chance she had of making a complete idiot of herself over him.

"That's completely not necessary," she said quickly. "I'm sure the boys and I will be fine."

"First lesson of horses, you can't be sure of anything. Even the most gentle horse can sometimes be unpredictable. I would hate for something to happen to you." He cleared his throat. "Just like I would hate for something to happen to *anyone* on my ranch, riding one of my horses."

Naturally, he wasn't worrying about her in particular. She told herself that little ache under her breastbone was a hunger pang, nothing more. It certainly wouldn't have been disappointment.

What exactly would riding lessons from Beckett McKinley entail? Did she want to find out?

"The boys were looking forward to teaching me." She tried one last time.

"They can still take the lead and give you some pointers. It will be a good experience for them, actually. I'm sure you've found that teachers often learn more than their students about a subject matter. It's good for them to think about the fundamentals of something that by now seems instinctive to them."

She would have to agree. Teaching someone else how to play a particular instrument always reminded her of the basics.

"They can take the lead but I would feel better if I could be there to keep an eye on things, just in case."

She told herself she didn't want his eyes—or anything else—on her. But what choice did she have? It was his ranch, his sons, his horses.

"I thought you were supposed to be out of town, buying horses."

She didn't want to tell him that she would never have agreed to come here for these lessons if she thought she would run into him. If she had known he would end up finding her half-dressed in his bedroom with a sweater tangled in her hair, she would have locked herself in her own bedroom at the Baker's Dozen.

"Plans changed. We found the horses we needed early on and agreed to a fair price with the owner, so we didn't need to stay for the entire sale. We came back last night."

No doubt that defined most of Beck's life. He made a decision early and then went for it. That was probably fine when it came to horses, but not so good when he made a snap decision about her and couldn't seem to see beyond it.

"You thought I was gone."

"The boys said something about it. I would never

have come to your bedroom to change my clothes if I thought there was any chance you could be here to run into me."

"Were you hoping to avoid me?"

"Don't be silly," she snapped. "Why would I need to avoid you?"

He didn't answer, only raised an eyebrow.

Before she could think of a way to answer, she heard one of the twins from outside. It sounded like Trevor, but their voices were so similar, it was tough to tell them apart when she couldn't see them.

"Miss Ella? Is everything okay? Our sandwiches are all done but Uncle Dan says we have to wait for you so we can eat. He said that's the polite thing to do when you have guests."

He sounded so disgusted, she had to smile. "It is customary, yes."

"How much longer is it gonna take you to get dressed?"

He didn't say it outright, but the implication was clear. *What the Sam Hill is taking you so blasted long?*

"I'm ready now. I'm coming," she called, before turning back to Beck. "I'm sorry you were dragged into this when you probably had other things to do this afternoon. I'll make some excuse to the boys, tell them I changed my mind or something."

"Why would you go and do that, especially after we went to all the trouble to get you extricated from your Christmas sweater?"

The man had a point. Something told her she wouldn't be able to wriggle out of these lessons like she had eventually done with her sweater. She was stuck, so she might as well make the best of it.

Chapter Six

After she left, Beck released his breath, then inhaled deeply. The scent of her still filled his bedroom—peaches and cinnamon, a combination that made his mouth water.

How did Ella Baker manage to twist him into a dozen crazy knots every time he was with her? He felt as trussed up as a calf at a roping competition.

He closed his eyes, reliving how stunned he had been to walk into his own bedroom and discover her standing there, half-dressed, like all his illicit fantasies come true.

Okay, she hadn't really been half-dressed. She had been wearing a plain T-shirt, but he wasn't sure if she was aware it had ridden up with the sweater, revealing about three inches of bare, creamy abdomen.

At the sight of that little strip of skin, his stupid brain

had taken him in all sorts of unruly directions. He had wanted to kiss that patch of skin, to slide off the rest of her clothes, to toss her down on his bed and spend the rest of the day tangled under the quilt with her.

Man, he had it bad.

He opened his eyes as the magnitude of what he had consented to do loomed suddenly as large as the Tetons outside his windows.

Riding lessons. How in the world was he supposed to give the woman riding lessons, when he couldn't stop thinking about all the inappropriate things he would much rather teach her instead?

And what on earth were his boys thinking, to invite her here without talking to him first? He sighed. Those two rascals had the funniest, most convoluted thought processes, especially when they had their minds set on a project. He supposed he should be happy they liked their music teacher enough to want to help her.

Wasn't that what the holidays were all about? Helping others? He didn't see how he could object, really.

She *did* have a phobia about horses. A fairly serious one. He had seen it for himself one day over the summer, when he had been repairing a fence line between the two ranches. Because it had been a lovely July morning, he'd chosen to ride Ace on a trail that connected the two ranches, to the spot that needed repair. He had been minding his own business, enjoying the splendor of the day, when Ella had suddenly jogged into sight on the trail ahead of him, listening to music through earbuds and wearing shorts that showed off her tanned legs.

She hadn't noticed him at first, probably because of the music. When she spotted him and Ace, she had jumped a mile and had scrambled onto a rock beside the trail to let him pass. He had stopped to greet her—the polite thing to do between neighbors—but she hadn't seemed at all in the mood to chat.

He thought it was because she didn't like him. Now he wondered if it had more to do with her aversion to horses.

He wasn't sure if he and the boys could do anything to help that kind of phobia, but he suddenly wanted to try. He would like to be able to give her this. It was a small thing, only a few hours out of his life, but if he could help her get over her fear of horses, he might feel a little less guilty about taking up Curt on his offer to buy the Baker's Dozen.

It only took a few moments for him to realize the task of helping Ella conquer her fear of horses might be slightly harder than he suspected.

"Nothing to be afraid of." He kept his voice calm, slow, just as he would do to a spooked mare. "Creampuff is as easy and gentle as her name. She's not going to hurt you, I promise. It's not in her nature."

"I'm not afraid," she said, which was an outright lie. Her body betrayed her. She trembled, muscles poised as if she was ready to bolt.

"Sure. I believe you," he said, his voice soothing.

Her nervousness temporarily lifted long enough for her to glare at him. "You don't have to patronize me," she said stiffly. "It must be obvious I'm terrified. I don't want to be, but I am."

"You don't have to be afraid, Miss Ella," Colter told her with an earnest look. "Creampuff is so lazy, she only moves every other Sunday. That's what Dad says, anyway."

"Good thing today is Saturday, then," she said, with a slight smile.

"Exactly," Trevor said. "Why don't you start by making friends with her? Dad keeps crab apples in the barn for her, since that's her favorite treat."

That was a good idea to break the ice between her and the horse, one he should have thought of himself. His boys were smart little caballeros.

"Colt, why don't you grab a couple? You remember how to open the box?"

"Yep." Colter headed over to the metal box containing the treat. "We had to put a latch on it after Creampuff here learned how to lift the lid and help herself."

"Did she?" Ella's voice was faint, as if coming from the other side of the barn.

"She would eat those until she's sick, unless we put a few obstacles in her way," Beck answered, still in that calming voice. "Here you are. Give her this, nice and slow."

He handed her a crab apple. "Put it on your palm, not your fingers." He probably shouldn't tell her that if she wasn't careful, Creampuff might munch on her fingers by mistake.

"There. She likes you," he said when the horse lipped the apple from her palm. He also didn't mention that Creampuff would take a crab apple from just about anybody or anything. She had no scruples when it came to her treats.

"How about another?" he asked. Without waiting for an answer, he handed her a second crab apple. She put it on her palm herself and actually smiled a little this time when Creampuff snatched it away before she could even thrust her hand out all the way.

"Now pet her," Trevor suggested. "She likes it when you scratch along her neck. Yep, like that."

"You must think I'm the world's biggest scaredy-cat."

His boys didn't say anything. Though no one could ever call them well-mannered, precisely, sometimes they could be surprisingly polite. This was one of those times. They looked at each other but chose to remain silent rather than agree with her.

"I don't think you're a scaredy-cat," Beck said quietly. "I think something terrible must have happened to you on a horse."

She sent him a swift look, and he could see the truth of his words reflected in the haunted shadows in her gaze. "How did you know? Did my father tell you?"

It didn't exactly take a crack detective to figure it out. She wasn't just nervous, she was petrified.

This hadn't been a good idea. He didn't like seeing her so upset.

"You don't have to do this, you know. There's no law that says you have to ride horses around here."

She was silent, petting the horse. He was happy to see her hands weren't trembling quite as much as they had earlier.

"You might not find it in any Pine Gulch city code," she said after a moment, "but it's one of those unwritten societal laws, understood by everyone who lives here. You have to know your way around horses if you want to truly fit in around here."

He opened his mouth to argue with her, then closed it again. There might be a kernel of truth to what she said, at least in some circles. He had a feeling Curt Baker saw things that way. He was an old-school rancher, through and through. Funny that Curt himself didn't ride, either. Beck had to wonder if that had something to do with whatever had happened to Ella.

"I've always figured most rules were made just so folks could figure out a creative way to break them. Really, Ella. Don't torture yourself. It's not worth it"

She gazed at him, eyes wide as if she didn't expect understanding from him. Her surprise made him squirm. What? He could be as sensitive as the next guy.

She looked at him, then at Creampuff. As he watched, determination flooded those blue eyes.

"I want to do this. I can't let my fear of something that happened when I was eight years old control the rest of my life," she said. "I've given it too much power already."

Eight years old. He tried to picture her, pigtailed and cute and blonde, with that little hint of freckles. What had frightened her so badly?

Whatever it was, he respected the hell out of her for her courage in confronting it.

"Okay, then." His voice came out more gruffly than usual. "Now that you've made friends with Creampuff here, I guess it's time to climb on. When you're ready, I'll give you a hand."

Her hands clenched into fists at her side then unclenched and she nodded. "I'm ready."

Filled with admiration—not to mention this blasted attraction he didn't want—he helped her hold on to the saddle horn and put her boot in the stirrup, then gave her a lift into the saddle.

She held tight to the horn. "I forgot how far off the ground I can feel on the back of a horse."

The twins had mounted by themselves and rode their horses closer to her. "It's great, isn't it?" Trevor said with a grin. "I feel about eight feet tall when I'm on Oreo."

She seemed to be close to hyperventilating. They couldn't have that. He stepped closer and kept his voice low and calming.

"Just hold on to the reins. I've hooked a lead line here and I'm just going to walk you around the training arena a bit, until you feel more comfortable."

"You won't let go?" Her panic was palpable.

He gave her a reassuring smile. "I promise. You got this."

As he led her around the small arena where they held horse auctions and worked to train horses in bad weather, he kept talking in that slow voice about nothing, really. The year he constructed this building, the other barn that was built by his great-grandfather, the house his grandfather had added.

The boys could never have handled this level of fear. He was deeply grateful that his schedule had worked out so he could be here to help her through this.

"You're doing great," he said after about fifteen minutes, when she seemed to have relaxed a little and her features no longer looked so pinched and pale. "You ready to take the reins on your own now?"

"Do I have to?" she asked ruefully. "I was just beginning to breathe again."

He tried to hide his smile. She had grit. He'd give her that. "You don't have to, but you'll never really get a feel for riding a horse until you're the one in command."

She released a heavy sigh. "I suppose you're right. Okay. You can let go."

He twisted the lead line onto the saddle horn and stood by her thigh. "Here are a few basics. Sit up tall, creating a nice, straight line from shoulders to hips. Don't hold the reins taut, just relax them in your hands, and use the least amount of pressure you can to get the horse to do what you want. It's all about pressure and release. The moment she starts doing what you want, going where you want, you let off the pressure."

He went over a few other basic commands but he could see Ella was starting to glaze over.

For all her complacency, Creampuff was a very well-trained horse. She tended to know what her rider wanted before the rider did.

"You got this," he repeated, then stood back to watch.

Ella sat atop the motionless horse for a long moment, then—just as he was about to step in and give Creampuff a verbal command—Ella gave the perfect amount of pressure with her knees into her sides to get her moving.

Though her movements were awkward and stiff, she had obviously been on a horse before. He was a fairly decent teacher but not *that* good that she could instantly pick it up. No, he had a feeling it was more a case of muscle memory. Ella held the reins in the best position and didn't yank them, but instead used slow, steady movements.

She had done this before. Even if it was a long time ago, something inside her remembered.

Colter and Trevor watched from the back of their horses. "You're doing great," Trevor called.

"Keep it up," his brother said. "Way to go, Miss Ella. You'll be riding the rodeo before you know it."

Ella's visible shudder at the suggestion might have

made him smile under other circumstances, if he wasn't so worried about her.

"You *are* doing great," he called. "Now see if you can get her to go a little faster."

"Why on earth would I do that? I don't *want* her to go faster."

He tipped his hat back. "Okay. Take it slow and steady. Nothing wrong with that."

She kept going another twenty minutes, taking the horse around the arena several times, then practicing bringing her a stop again before urging her forward once more. By the time they were done and she rode to a stop in front of him, she looked exhausted but beautifully triumphant.

"You ready to call it a day?"

"Yes. I think so."

He reached up a hand to help her and as she slid off the horse and to the ground, he tried not to notice how wonderful her soft curves felt against him. He was quick to let go when her boots hit the dirt floor.

"How was it?" he asked.

"Not as difficult as I expected, actually." She looked surprised and rather pleased at that discovery. "You were right. Creampuff really is a sweetheart."

"She does live up to her name, doesn't she?" He gave the old horse an appreciative pat as the twins rode up and dismounted.

"You did super good," Colter said.

"Yeah," his brother agreed. "You hardly even bounced around in the saddle."

"I hate to admit it, but there is a certain part of me that would disagree with you right now," Ella said, rubbing the back pocket of her jeans.

The boys giggled while Beck did his best not to shift his gaze to that particular portion of her anatomy.

"Boys, can you take care of the horses? Miss Baker's, too."

The twins had been brushing down their horses since they were old enough to ride. They led the horses away and he turned to Ella, though he kept one eye on the boys, across the arena, as they scrambled to take off saddles and hackamores. They didn't need direct supervision but he still liked to monitor things in case they had trouble.

"That was some good, hard work. A lesson like that deserves a beer. Or at least a soda."

"I wouldn't mind some water," she said.

"I don't doubt it. Overcoming your fear is thirsty business."

In the harsh lights of the indoor arena, her color rose and she looked down.

"Hey. I meant that with upmost respect," he assured her. He led the way into the corner that functioned as the office out here. He reached into the fridge and pulled out a water bottle for her, a beer for him.

"You really did work hard. I could tell it wasn't easy for you."

She sighed and took a healthy swallow from the bottle. A few little droplets clung to her lips from the bottle's mouth and he had to fight the urge to press his own lips there.

"It's so stupid," she said, frustration simmering in her voice. "I don't know why I can't get past it."

"Want to tell me about it?"

She looked at the horses, then back at him with a helpless sort of look. "Not really. But I suppose you have the right to know, especially after all your help this afternoon."

"I don't know about that. But I'd like to hear, if you want to tell me."

She took another swallow and he had the feeling she was biding time as much as slaking her thirst. "You know I didn't grow up on the Baker's Dozen."

Considering he had lived next to Curt his whole life and only saw Ella a few memorable times over the years, until she moved back to Pine Gulch, he was aware of that fact. "I did. I gather your parents were divorced."

"Yes. Eventually. They were separated on and off through most of my early childhood. They would try to make it work for a month or two, usually for my sake, then things would go south and my mom would pack us up and move back to Boston."

"That must have been tough."

"Yes. I adored my father and I always loved coming out to the ranch, even when it was just for a short visit. My favorite times were the summers, when I could be here for weeks at a time. Back in Boston, I dreamed about horses all the time. In the pictures I've seen of my bedroom, there are dozens of pictures on the wall of horses I had either drawn myself or cut out of old ranch magazines I took back with me. I loved to ride. At least that's what they tell me."

That struck him as an odd way to phrase things, but she continued before he could ask what she meant.

"I was three the first time my dad put me on a horse. I don't have a memory of it. Or anything else before I was eight years old."

That seemed awfully late for a first memory.

"Eight? Why eight?"

She looked down at her water bottle with a faraway expression. When she looked back up at him, her expression was bleak.

"That's the year I died."

Chapter Seven

Died? What the hell was that supposed to mean? Shock tangled his tongue, but even if it hadn't, he would have had no idea how to respond.

"I know. That sounds ridiculous and melodramatic," she said, her expression rueful. "But it's the truth. I was dead for about five minutes before they could get my heart started again."

She spoke in a matter-of-fact way, but her hands trembled again, as they had when she first faced the horse arena.

"You were eight? What happened?"

She watched the boys as they competently brushed down the horses. "My mom and I were both here that summer. It was the last time my parents tried to reconcile, I guess, though they didn't tell me that was why we had come back to the ranch. They had been separated on and off most of my life, but neither of them could ever bring themselves to file for divorce. I don't know why but they couldn't seem to take that final step."

"Were you happy about it? About your parents trying to reconcile?"

"I wish I could tell you. Apparently I wanted nothing more than to live here permanently. According to my mom, all I talked about whenever we were in Boston was living here in Pine Gulch and having my own horse and riding whenever I wanted. I think she resented how much I loved the ranch, if you want the truth. She never did."

Yet one more thing he had in common with Curt Baker. The man had never come right out and said it, but Beck had guessed as much.

What was wrong with these Pine Gulch men who insisted on marrying completely inappropriate women who couldn't wait to leave?

"We had only been back about three weeks when I took out a new horse," Ella went on. "I was with my dad and we were just riding above the ranch, nothing too strenuous, but apparently a snake slithered across the trail and spooked the horse and I fell—not just off the horse but about twenty feet down a rocky slope. I ended up with multiple injuries."

His blood ran cold as he pictured it. "You stopped breathing, you said?"

"Yes. My father was right there and he managed to do CPR to eventually restart my heart. I was airlifted to the hospital in Idaho Falls, and then to the regional children's hospital in Salt Lake City."

"How long were you there?"

"Two months. Seven surgeries. I was in a medically

induced coma for weeks while the swelling from the brain injury went down. When I came out of it, there was obvious damage. I didn't remember anything. Not just the accident, but everything that happened before. Total blank slate. I had to relearn how to walk, talk, use a fork. Everything. I still have no memory of what happened the first eight years of my life, only from pictures and what my parents have told me."

He shook his head, trying to imagine how tough that must have been, to lose eight years of her life. He glanced at the boys, who were just finishing up with Creampuff. She was only a little older than they were and had to relearn everything.

No wonder she had been terrified of horses! He wasn't sure he ever would have had the guts to get back on.

"I just have one question."

"What's that?"

His jaw clenched. "Why in *blazes* did you get back on a horse today, after everything you've been through? I would think any sane woman would try to stay as far away as possible from something that's caused so much suffering."

She looked pensive, her fingers curled around the water bottle. "Today wasn't about the horses, Beck. It was about me." She paused. "I keep thinking that if I learn how to ride again, I'll find some piece of me I lost when I was eight."

He couldn't believe Curt had never told him about Ella's accident. Maybe that explained why the man didn't have any horses on the Baker's Dozen. He knew some ranchers thought they were too much trouble and not worth the effort, preferring ATVs and utility vehicles to a good cattle horse. He had always assumed Curt was one of them.

"I guess your parents didn't get back together."

She gave a short laugh. "You could say that. My mother would have been happy if I never came back to Pine Gulch. She blamed my father, said Curt deliberately put me on a horse that wasn't appropriate for an eight-year-old girl with limited experience who wasn't the expert rider she thought she was. She filed for divorce while I was still in the hospital."

How had that impacted Ella? Did she blame herself for her parents' divorce? Did she wonder if they would have been able to finally piece things together, if not for her fall?

He couldn't help seeing her with new compassion and found himself impressed all over again at the courage it must have taken her today to climb up on Creampuff.

"For the first few years after the divorce, she made my dad fly out to Boston for visits, which he hated. They were awkward, tense episodes that weren't comfortable for either of us. When I got older, after the dust from their custody battle settled, I insisted on coming out as often as I could. My dad refused to let me get on a horse. To reduce temptation, he sold them all, even though it was something he always loved. That was a tough pill for me to swallow, but Curt said my mom wouldn't let me come back to the ranch if she found out I had gone riding again. He wasn't wrong, actually."

He couldn't imagine that kind of animosity. Beck's own parents had been happily married until his father's untimely death, even with his mom's rheumatoid arthritis, which limited what she could do around the ranch. His dad had been a loving caretaker as far back as Beck could remember, one of the things he respected most about him.

After his father died, Beck's mother had moved to Florida to be closer to her sister. She was doing well there, though he missed her. She and the boys talked via Skype every Sunday evening.

"I can't believe I didn't know this about you," he finally said.

She made a wry face. "It's not like I go around introducing myself to people by telling them that I spent several weeks in a medically induced coma after falling off a horse."

"But my family lived next door to yours. I should have known. I would have been, what, eleven or twelve? That's old enough to be aware of what's going on in my own community."

On the other hand, Curt Baker had always been a little removed from the greater Pine Gulch society. Beck's parents may well have known and may have mentioned it to him, but since he didn't know Ella personally back then and she was several years younger—and a girl, to boot—he wasn't sure it would have had much impact on him.

"It doesn't matter," she said. "It was a long time ago. Almost twenty years. The doctors all said it was a miracle that I made it through without much lasting damage."

"Nothing?"

"My leg aches in bad weather and I still limp a bit when I'm tired. To be totally honest, I do have the occasional memory lapse. I call it a glitch. Every once in a while, I forget a word that's pretty basic."

"Everybody does that."

"That's what I tell myself. I'm lucky. It could have been much worse."

"It doesn't sound like nothing. It sounds like you've been through hell. Nobody would blame you for never getting on a horse again, Ella. Like I said, it's really not necessary out here. There are plenty of people in Pine Gulch who've never been on a horse yet somehow still manage to live good, productive lives."

She was quiet, her features pensive. "I hate being afraid," she finally said. "Especially of something I once loved."

He had to respect that. "I'm not sure you can force yourself to the other side of a perfectly justifiable fear, simply through willpower."

"Maybe not completely," she acknowledged. "I'm okay with that. Still, I'd like to see if I can regain a little of that passion I once had."

He wanted that for her, too. In that moment, Beck resolved to do whatever he could to help her. "In that case, you'd better come back tomorrow for a second lesson. One hour in a horse arena on the back of a narcoleptic nag like Creampuff isn't enough to inspire passion in anyone."

"I don't know about that. I enjoyed myself far more than I expected."

"Come back tomorrow. Let's see if you can enjoy it even more."

"I could do that." She considered. "It would actually be good timing. Some friends are taking my father to a cowboy poetry event in Idaho Falls and they're supposed to be gone most of the day."

"You're a grown woman, Ella. He can't stop you from riding now, even if he wanted to."

"I know. I usually make him a nice dinner on Sunday afternoons after church. Since he'll be gone, I won't have to do that—or explain why I'm leaving or where I'm going."

"Great. You can just come straight here after church, then. You might as well stay for dinner. We'll probably grill steaks. It's just as easy to toss another one on the coals."

He wasn't sure why he extended the invitation. By her expression, it was clear she was as shocked as he was by it.

"I... Thank you. That would be nice. I'll bring a salad and rolls and some kind of dessert."

"You don't have to do that, but I'm sure the boys would enjoy it."

His side dishes usually consisted of baked potatoes or instant rice.

"Enjoy what?" Trevor asked. They had apparently finished with the horses, who were all fed and watered and turned out to pasture.

"Miss Baker is going to come for another riding lesson tomorrow. I invited her to have dinner with us, too."

"Yay!" Trevor exclaimed.

Colter, he noticed with sudden trepidation, was giving the two of them a speculative look that left Beck more than a little uncomfortable.

What was going through the kid's mind? Beck wasn't sure he wanted to know—any more than he wanted to examine his own thoughts, at least about Ella Baker.

She wasn't sure she should be doing this.

Even as she loaded food into her SUV in preparation

for driving back to the Broken Arrow, Ella was filled with misgivings.

She still had no idea what had prompted Beck to issue this unexpected invitation to dinner and a second riding lesson. Maybe pity. He *had* invited her right after she spilled her entire pathetic story to the man, after all.

More puzzling than his invitation had been how quickly she accepted it, without really thinking things through.

She should have refused. As much as she might have wanted another lesson, another chance to recapture the joy she had once known while riding, she was beginning to think it might not be a good idea to spend more time with Beckett and his boys.

The lesson the day before had eroded her defenses, left her far too open and vulnerable to him. She rarely talked about her accident, even with close friends. It was a part of her, yes, but something that happened so long ago, it hardly seemed relevant to the woman she had become—except as it pertained to her lingering fear of horses.

Why had she confided in Beckett McKinley, of all people?

He had been so patient with her during the lesson and, dare she say, even kind. It was a side of him she wasn't used to seeing. She could admit, she found it wildly appealing.

She wished she could have been able to tell what had been running through his mind when she told him what had happened so long ago. No such luck. The man was still a mystery to her. Every time she thought she had him figured out, he did something to toss all her preconceptions out the window.

This invitation for dinner, for instance. It would have been kind enough to simply invite her over for the lesson. Why add dinner into the mix?

Maybe he just felt sorry for her. The poor, pathetic girl who had nearly died not far from here.

She sighed and climbed into the SUV. She didn't like that idea. But what else could it be?

Though she was tempted to call off the whole thing, she made herself drive through the lightly falling snow to the nearby ranch.

The snowflakes looked lovely as they twirled out of the sky against the pine trees that bordered the road. The perfect holiday scene—except this was her second winter in southern Idaho and she knew the winters here could be anything but idyllic.

Oh, she hoped the weather cooperated for the Christmas program the following week. The children had already worked so hard to learn the songs and would be putting in a full week of intense rehearsals. She hated to think of all their effort being wasted because bad weather kept people away.

That was a hazard of living here, she supposed. You just had to keep your fingers crossed and learn how to take what comes.

Her stomach knotted with nerves as she drove under the Broken Arrow arch, which also had their brand burned into it. She had seen the McKinley men only hours ago at church. Beck had looked big and tough and handsome in his bolo tie and western-cut suit and the boys had looked just as handsome in clean white shirts and similar bolo ties.

They had come in late, hair still wet and Trevor's shirt buttoned wrong, and had waved so enthusiastically at her as they took their seats that Celeste Delaney beside her had whispered a teasing comment about the McKinley twin terrors having a crush on her.

She hadn't responded, even though she wanted to tell Celeste they weren't terrors. They were sweet, good-hearted boys who happened to have a little more energy than most.

She wasn't sure how her feelings for the boys had shifted so abruptly after only a few encounters. A week ago, she would have been one of those rolling her eyes at their antics. Now she saw them through a new filter of affection and even tenderness.

Mostly, they needed a little more direction and restraint in their lives.

She pulled up to the ranch house, her pulse abnormally loud in her ears, aware it wasn't the horse riding that made her nervous this time, but the idea of spending an afternoon with Beck and his adorable sons.

It was too late to back out now, she told herself, as she headed up the porch steps and rang the doorbell. They were planning on her.

Colter answered before the doorbell even stopped echoing through the house.

"Hey, Miss Ella!" he exclaimed, giving her that irresistible gap-toothed grin. "Guess what? Our dog is having puppies, *right now*."

"Is that right?"

"Yeah. She's down in the barn. Dad says we can go down to see her again after you get here."

Beck walked into the foyer in time to hear his son's announcement. He looked gorgeous and relaxed in jeans and a casual collared navy shirt that made his eyes gleam an even deeper blue.

"More excitement than you were probably expecting on a quiet Sunday afternoon."

As if she needed more excitement than the anticipation bubbling through her all morning at the idea of spending the afternoon with him and his boys.

"I would love to see the puppies, if you don't think the mother would mind."

"This is her fifth litter. At this point, I don't think she would care if the high school marching band came through during labor."

She couldn't hide her smile at that image. For a moment, something hot and glittery flashed in Beck's expression as he gazed down at her. Her resident butterfly friends danced harder in her stomach.

He seemed to have lost his cool politeness toward her and she didn't know whether to be relieved or terrified.

She was already ridiculously attracted to him, on a purely physical level. She would be in serious trouble if she actually *liked* him, too.

Something told her it was a little too late for caution now.

After a moment, he cleared his throat. "We can take a look on our way down to the horse barn."

"Sounds good. I have a salad that needs to go in the refrigerator and rolls that will need to continue rising. Mind if I put them in your kitchen first?"

"If it means fresh rolls, you can do anything you want."

Ella was quite certain he didn't mean the words in any suggestible way. That didn't stop her imagination from going a little wild for just a moment, until she reined it back with much more pressure than she would ever have used on Creampuff.

"This way," he said.

She followed him into his updated kitchen, with its stainless appliances and granite countertops.

The day before, when she'd eaten lunch here, she had observed that this was obviously a household of men. The kitchen wasn't messy, exactly, but it was more cluttered than she personally would have found comfortable. The sink had dishes left over from breakfast, and some kind of dried substance, likely from an overflowing pasta pot, covered one of the burners.

Just like the day before, she had a strong impulse to dig in and go to work cleaning things up, but she had to remind herself that wasn't her bailiwick. She was only there for dinner and another riding lesson.

"Sorry about the mess in here." Beck looked a little uncomfortable. "Until a few months ago, we had a nanny-slash-housekeeper, but she was having some health problems so had to take a break. My brother and uncle and I have been trading off household responsibilities until I can find someone new and I'm afraid none of us is very good at it."

The picture touched her, three men working together to take care of these twin boys. She remembered Faith telling her Beck had refused to give his in-laws custody, though the boys had only been toddlers.

Ella was aware of a small, soft warmth fluttering to life in her chest.

"It's a lovely home," she murmured. "I can tell the boys are very happy here."

He offered that rare smile again and for a moment, she felt as if that warmth was swirling between the two of them, urging them inexorably closer.

"I should put this in the refrigerator," she said

quickly, holding out the bowl containing the green salad she had made.

"Let me make a little room." He moved a few things around, leaving her a space amongst a few leftover containers and a half-empty case of beer.

"Now I only need a warm spot for the rolls to rise. Any suggestions?"

"Judy, our old housekeeper, always used the laundry room."

"That works."

He led the way to a large combined mudroom and laundry room. There were two washers and dryers in the space and both were going, sending out humid heat that would be perfect for her wrap-covered rolls.

"Judy always used that shelf up there. It's a little high for you to reach, I can put them up there for you."

"Looks like a perfect spot. Thanks." She handed him the jelly-roll pan of dough balls. Their fingers touched as he took it from her and a shiver rippled over her.

She thought his gaze sharpened but she couldn't be sure. Oh, she hoped he didn't notice her unwilling reaction.

He took the pan but simply held it for a long moment as the tension seemed to thicken between them. He looked as if he had something he wanted to say and even opened his mouth, but the boys burst into the laundry room before he could.

Ella told herself she was relieved.

"Let's go! We want to see the puppies!" Colter said, voice brimming with excitement.

Beck finally looked away to focus on his sons. "We're coming. Grab your coats while you're in here."

The boys complied and Beck finally slid the pan of

rolls onto the high shelf, where the warmth would help them rise more quickly.

"How long until they're ready to bake?"

"I pulled the dough out of the freezer, so it will need to thaw as well as rise. Probably about ninety minutes."

Her dad loved homemade rolls, but it was too much trouble to do very often for only the two of them, so she had started making a big batch every month and freezing the dough.

"That should be about perfect to give us time to see the puppies and ride for a while, if you're still up for it."

"I'm here, aren't I?" she said wryly. "I'm ready."

"Excellent. Let's go."

The twins led the way outside, chattering to each other about Christmas vacation and a school field trip during the upcoming week to The Christmas Ranch, where they both planned to visit Sparkle, the famous reindeer immortalized in books as well as onscreen in an animated movie.

She would have thought their daily rehearsals at the ranch were sufficient holiday cheer, but apparently not.

By default, she and Beckett fell behind the boys a little.

"How's your dad?" Beck said. "I haven't seen him for a few days."

She sighed with remembered frustration. Curt was having a hard time accepting his limitations. That morning, before he left for the cowboy poetry event, she had caught him trying to put up a stepladder to fix a lightbulb that had gone out in their great room. The man had poor balance on solid ground, forget about eight feet up in the air on a wobbly ladder.

"Stubborn as ever," she answered. "I'm beginning to think it must be something in the water up here."

He laughed, the sound rich and deep in the cold December air. "You might be right about that. I've got two boys drinking that same water and they could write the book on stubborn."

He definitely had his hands full with those twins. She had a feeling things weren't going to get easier as they hit their preteen and teenage years.

"Anyway, your dad might be stubborn but he's a good man. After my dad died when I was still too young to know what the hell I was doing here on the ranch, Curt took me under his wing. I learned more from him those first few months than my whole twenty-three years before that."

She hadn't realized his father died when Beck was so young. Sympathy for him helped mute the sting of hearing her father had been willing to help a neighbor learn the ropes of ranching. Too bad he wouldn't do the same thing for his own daughter.

"What happened to your father?"

"One of those freak things. Doctors figured it was a brain aneurysm. He was out on a tractor, perfectly fine one minute, the next he was gone. I'd always planned to take over the Broken Arrow from him, since neither of my brothers was much interested in running the place."

"Jax works here, doesn't he?"

"Yeah, but it took him a while to figure out what he wanted to do. I'm still not convinced his heart's in it, but it's tough to tell with Jax. I always knew I wanted to run the ranch, I just didn't expect to do it so early."

"I'm sorry. That must have been tough on you."

"At first, but good neighbors like Curt stepped in to help me figure things out."

"I'm glad my dad was here for you," she said softly. "And now you're helping him in return."

Beck shrugged, looking embarrassed. "I'm not doing much. I'm glad I can help."

He stopped in front of a different barn than the larger, more modern facility where they had ridden the day before. "Here we are. Guys, remember what I told you. We can watch, if we do it quietly so we don't distract Sal while she's taking care of her puppies."

"We remember," Trevor said solemnly. The boys tiptoed into the barn—which wasn't particularly effective, since they were both wearing cowboy boots.

She followed, not sure what to expect. The barn was warmer than she might have thought, and smelled of straw and old wood and the earthy smells she associated with a ranch.

Beck led the way to a wooden stall about halfway back. She peered over the railing to where a mostly black border collie lay on her side on a blanket that had been spread over the straw.

She looked exhausted, poor thing, as her litter suckled for nourishment.

"They look like little rats," Trevor whispered.

"Beautiful little rats," his brother said loyally, which made Ella smile.

The puppies were small, eyes still closed. They made little whiny noises as they ate.

"Is that all of them, girl?" Beck asked in a low voice. "Looks like she might be done. How many do you count?"

"Seven," Colter said, moving his finger in the air to mark each one. "No, eight."

"Good job, Sal," Beck said softly. The tired mother gave a half-hearted tail wag before returning to care for her litter.

They all watched the little creatures with fascination for a few more moments. It was an unexpectedly intimate moment, standing there by the wooden stall beside Beck and his boys, almost like they were a family unit.

They most definitely weren't, she reminded herself. That sort of thinking could get her into all kinds of trouble.

"We should probably let her rest now," Beck said eventually.

"Will they all be okay out here?" Trevor asked. "It's cold outside."

"But warm in here. Sal and the puppies have everything they need here—warm, soft blankets, with plenty for Sal to eat and drink. My guess is, she'll probably want to sleep for a week after having eight puppies."

"What will you do with them all?" Ella asked.

"I'll probably keep a couple to train, then sell the others. Sal has champion bloodlines and the sire does, too. Those are going to be some excellent cow dogs."

He glanced down at her. "You ready to ride again?"

"I am," she admitted. "Believe it or not, I'm actually looking forward to it."

He gave her a full-on, high-octane smile that turned her insides to rich, gooey honey.

"That is an excellent sign, Miss Baker. Watch and see. We'll make a horsewoman out of you yet."

She didn't share his confidence—but as long as she

no longer had panic attacks when she came within a hundred feet of a horse, she would consider these few days to be worth it.

Chapter Eight

An hour later, she managed to pull Creampuff to a stop squarely in front of the spot at the railing where Beck had stood for the last hour, offering advice and encouragement during the lesson.

"Good girl," she said, patting the horse's withers.

"Wait, was that an actual smile?" he teased. "If I didn't know better, I might think you're enjoying yourself."

"You might be right. I think I've almost stopped shaking. That's a good sign, isn't it?"

"An excellent one." He offered an encouraging smile. "On a day when it's not so cold, you should come out to take a trail ride above the house. It's slow going in the snow, but worth it for the views."

A few days earlier, the very idea would have sent her into a panic attack. Her accident had happened in those very foothills and while she didn't remember it, the specter of what had happened there still loomed large in her subconscious.

The fact that she could even consider such an outing was amazing progress. She shifted in the saddle, satisfaction bubbling through her. She had done it, survived another riding lesson, and had actually begun to enjoy the adventure.

Oh, she had missed this. She really did feel as if she was rediscovering a part of herself that had been buried under the rubble of her accident.

Trevor rode up on his big horse, so loose and comfortable that he seemed to be part of the horse. "Is it time for dinner yet? I'm starving."

"Me, too," his brother said, joining the group.

"I guess that's up to our guest," Beck said. "What do you say, Ella? Want to keep riding or would you like to stop for chow?"

"Let's eat, before you guys start chewing the leather reins."

The boys giggled with delight at her lame joke and warmth soaked through her. There was something so *joyful* about being able to make a child laugh. She had never realized that until going to work in music therapy.

"Chew the reins," Trevor said, shaking his head. "That would taste gross!"

"Yeah, steaks would be much better, all the way around," Beck said. "Why don't you boys take care of the horses and put them up while Miss Baker and I start dinner?"

She slid down without assistance. "I would like to help with the horses, actually. If I intend to start riding again, I need to relearn how to care for them."

His eyes warmed with approval. "Good point. It should only take the four of us a few moments. Boys, let's show Miss Baker how it's done."

Beck couldn't remember the last time he had enjoyed an afternoon so much.

He was growing increasingly intrigued with Ella Baker, forced to completely reevaluate his preconceptions of her as just one more city girl who didn't belong.

She had far more grit than he ever would have believed a few days earlier. Most women who had gone through an ordeal like hers would have stayed as far away as possible from something that represented the trauma they had endured.

Not Ella.

When they had first come into the stables, he had seen how nervous she was. Her small, curvy frame had been trembling slightly as he helped her mount Creampuff, her features pale and set.

It had concerned him a little, especially after she seemed to have enjoyed it the day before. He supposed he should have anticipated her reaction. She had spent many years being afraid of horses, for legitimate reasons. He couldn't expect that to go away overnight, simply because she had an enjoyable experience on an easy mount.

He shouldn't have worried. Within a few moments, she had warmed to it again. After only a few moments, she had visibly relaxed, and by the end of the hour, she had been laughing.

Would she be afraid the next time? For her sake, he hoped she didn't have to fight that battle each time she wanted to ride a horse—though he had to admire the sheer guts she showed by putting herself through it. In his experience, few people demonstrated that kind of raw courage.

He liked her.

Entirely too much.

He frowned at the thought as he hung up the tack on the well-organized pegs. It was hard *not* to like her. She was kind to his sons, she had given up her life back east to come back and care for her father, and she had more courage than most people he'd ever met.

If he wasn't careful, he would do something really stupid, like fall hard for her.

He jerked his mind away from that dangerous possibility. He couldn't. She might be pretty and smart and courageous, but that didn't make her right for him. He would do well to remember she was a city girl. Like her own mother, like Stephanie. Ella was cultured, sophisticated, not the sort of woman who would be comfortable wearing jeans and boots and listening to old Johnny Cash songs.

The thought depressed him more than it should.

They could be friends, though. Nothing wrong with that. A guy couldn't have too many friends, right?

"Everybody ready to go get some food, now that we've all taken care of the horses?" he asked, forcing a note of cheerfulness he didn't feel into his voice.

"Me!" his twins said in unison. Ella smiled and the impact of it was like standing in the middle of a sunbeam.

"We should probably check on the puppies one more time before we head up to the house, if you don't mind," he said.

"Do you seriously think I would mind being able to see those cute puppies again?"

"Good point," he admitted.

The temperature had dropped several degrees by the time they walked outside toward the barn where he had set up Sal for her first few weeks postdelivery. His instincts, honed from years of working the land, warned him they would have snow before morning.

As they trudged through the snow already on the ground from previous storms, he went through his mental weather-preparedness checklist. It wasn't all that lengthy. From his father, he'd learned the important lesson that it was better to ready things well in advance. The Broken Arrow was always set up to deal with bad weather, which made it much easier for this particular ranch owner to sleep at night.

When he wasn't having completely inappropriate dreams about his lovely neighbor, anyway.

In contrast to the gathering storm, the old barn was warm and cozy, a refuge from the Idaho winter.

Sal and her puppies were all sleeping when they peered over the top railing of the stall. Despite Colter's and Trevor's careful effort to tiptoe in on their cowboy boots, Sal must have sensed them. She opened one eye but closed it quickly, busy with the task of keeping eight puppies fed and alive.

Without being asked, Trevor and Colter filled her water and added a bit more food to her bowl. They were such good boys. Yeah, they could be rambunctious at times, but beneath all that energy, they were turning into helpful, compassionate young men.

He couldn't have asked for more.

"She looks exhausted, poor thing," Ella said beside him, her expression soft and sympathetic.

"She's a good mom. She'll be okay after a little rest."

"Until she has eight wriggling puppies climbing all over her."

He grinned. "Shh. Don't say that too loudly or she might decide to hightail it out of here before we get to that point. I don't particularly fancy hand-feeding eight puppies."

"Would she do that?" Ella asked, plainly concerned.

"I'm teasing," he assured her. "Sal knows what to do."

They watched the puppies for a few more moments in silence before he ushered everyone back out into the cold.

"Race you," Trevor said to his brother and the two of them rushed away through the gathering darkness.

"I wish I had even a tiny portion of their energy," Ella said with a sigh.

"Right?"

She shook her head. "How do you keep up with them?"

"Who says I do? There have been more than a few nights when I fall asleep reading to them and only wake up when the book falls to the floor."

She smiled, probably thinking he was kidding. He only wished he were.

"They're good boys. You know that, right?"

He was touched that her thoughts so clearly echoed his own from a few moments earlier. "I do. Once in a while I forget. Like whenever I go to their parent-teacher conferences and hear the litany of classroom complaints. I have to remind myself I wasn't the most patient student, either, yet somehow I still managed to graduate from high school *and* college. My senior year, I was running the ranch, too, and taking night classes."

"It must be challenging on your own."

"Sometimes," he admitted. "There are days I feel like throwing in the parenting towel before we even finish breakfast. It's hard and frustrating and relentless. Each decision I make in the day has to focus on the boys' welfare first. Every other priority is a distant second."

"I can't even imagine." In the fading afternoon light, her features looked soft and so lovely, he had a hard time looking away.

"I'm not really alone, though. Until a few months ago, we had Judy to help us. She did all the heavy lifting when it came to the logistics of caring for the boys when they were smaller."

"You must miss her terribly."

"Definitely. She had been a huge part of our lives since the boys were small. Judy was just about the only mother figure they had. They don't seem to remember their mother much."

"How old were they when she…left?"

He hated thinking about Stephanie and all the mistakes he had made.

"Barely two," he said, his voice pitched low even though the boys had already made it inside.

"She had terrible clinical and postpartum depression as well as anxiety—made harder because, as it turns out, she hated living on a ranch. She missed her family, her friends, the excitement of her life back east."

Their marriage had been an epic mistake from the beginning. He thought they could make a go of things, though now that idea seemed laughable. Still, they had been wildly in love at first. After only a few fiery months, reality had begun to sink in that maybe they couldn't manage to reconcile their differences and then Stephanie found out she was pregnant.

She had cried and cried. He should have clued in to the challenges ahead when he saw her reaction. As for Beck, he had been scared witless one moment, filled with jubilation the next. He had asked her to marry him and it had taken another three months of discussions—and the revelation through her first ultrasound that her pregnancy would provide a double blessing—before she agreed.

Things only went downhill from there, unfortunately. She had struggled fiercely with postpartum depression and hadn't really bonded with the twins. Even before she left to find help, he and the series of nannies he hired until they found Judy had been the ones getting up at night with them, making sure they were fed, providing the cuddles and the love their mother couldn't.

"That must have been tough," Ella said softly.

For both of them. Stephanie had been a mess emotionally and mentally and he had hated knowing he couldn't fix things for her.

"She stuck it out as long as she could, until both of us realized things weren't getting better. She needed help, more help than she could find here. Her parents are both doctors and had connections back east so they wanted her to get help there. It was always supposed to be temporary but the weeks turned into months and then a year. *Soon*, she kept telling me. Just another month and she would be ready to come back."

He sighed as the tough memories flooded back. "Eighteen months after she left, she died from a prescription-drug overdose. Doctors said it was probably accidental."

That *probably* always pissed him off. Even the smallest chance that Stephanie might have deliberately chosen to leave the two cutest kids on the planet just about broke his heart.

Something of his emotions must have shown on his features. Ella made a small sound, her own expression deeply distressed.

"Oh, Beck. I'm so sorry."

"I am, too—for the boys' sake, anyway. They're doing okay, though. They ask about her once in a while, but not so much anymore. They don't remember her. They were only toddlers when she left. They ask after Judy far more often than they do their mother."

"I'm sorry," she said again.

"I don't know why I told you all that," he said. What was it about Ella that compelled him to share details of his life he usually preferred to keep to himself? There was something about her that drew him to her, something more than her pretty eyes and her soft, delicate features.

He liked her. Plain and simple. It had been a long time since he felt these soft, seductive feelings for a woman.

Not that he planned to do a damn thing about it— except spill all his dirty laundry, apparently.

"You're cold. I'm sorry I kept you out here so long."

"I'm not cold," she protested. "Only sad that any woman could deliberately choose to walk away from such amazing boys and—and you."

Was it his imagination or did she blush when she said

that? His interest sharpened. Again, he was aware of the tug and pull of attraction between them.

He wanted desperately to kiss her. He ached with it, the hunger to pull her close and brush his lips across hers, gently at first and then, if she didn't push him away, with a little more intensity.

He caught his breath and inclined his head slightly. Her eyes went wide and she swallowed. He thought she might have even leaned toward him, but at the last moment, before he would have taken that chance, the back door opened.

"Hey, what are you still doing out here?" Trevor asked.

He couldn't very well tell his son he was just about to try to steal a kiss. Trevor didn't give him a chance to answer, anyway, before he went on.

"Hey, can Colter and me watch a Christmas show before dinner?" Trevor asked.

After mentally scrambling for a second, Beck did his best to shift back into father mode. It took great effort, especially when all he wanted to do was grab Ella close and explore that delicious-looking mouth until they were both breathless.

He cleared his throat. "You know the rule. The TV can come on when chores are done."

"They are. I just took the garbage out and Colt finished putting away the dishes in the dishwasher."

He couldn't ask for more than that. "Fine. One show. Fair warning, dinner shouldn't take long. You might have to stop the show in the middle, if the food is ready before the show is over."

"Okay." Trevor beamed, then hurried back inside to tell his brother the good news, leaving Beckett along with Ella and this awkwardness that seemed to have suddenly blossomed between them.

"Ella…"

She didn't quite meet his gaze. "Your boys are hungry. We should probably take care of that."

He was hungry, too, but the choice T-bones he had been marinating all afternoon wouldn't slake this particular appetite.

She was right, though. The boys needed to eat—and he needed to do all he could to regain a little common sense when it came to Ella Baker.

Forty-five minutes later, nerves still shimmied through her from that intense moment on Beck's back step.

Had he really tried to kiss her?

She couldn't be completely sure but was about 95 percent certain. The vibe had certainly been there, crackling through the air between them.

She had done her best to ignore it through dinner, but couldn't seem to stop staring at his mouth at odd, random moments.

She caught herself at it again and jerked her gaze away quickly, setting her napkin beside her plate and leaning back in her chair.

"That was truly delicious," she said, trying for a casual tone. "I'm not exaggerating when I say that was probably the best steak I've ever had. What do you use for a marinade?"

"Nothing too complicated—soy sauce, honey, a little bit of ground black pepper and a splash of olive oil."

"Sometimes the simple things are the best. Thank you again for inviting me to dinner."

"I didn't do anything but grill some steaks and toss a couple of potatoes in the oven to bake. You provided everything else. I should be thanking *you*. Those rolls were little yeasty bites of heaven."

The description pleased her. Why was it so much more fun to cook when people appreciated the effort?

"We're done," Colter announced. "Can we go back and finish our show?"

"Yeah," Trevor chimed in. "The Abominable Snowman guy was just learning how to walk with one foot in front of the other. That's our favorite part."

Ella had to smile, since that had always been her own favorite part of that particular Christmas special.

"Clear your plates first. You can take our guest's, as well, if she's finished."

"I am, thank you."

"Do you want to watch the rest of the show with us?" Trevor asked.

Though the earnestness behind the request touched, Ella glanced at her watch. How had the entire day slipped away?

"Thank you, but it's later than I thought. I should go. I hate to eat and run, but I should probably be home before my father arrives back at the ranch. Sometimes he needs help getting out of his coat and boots."

By the understanding she glimpsed in his gaze, she understood that Beck knew as well as she did that the word *sometimes* was unnecessary. Curt might refuse to admit it, but he *always* needed help. His limitations were growing all the time, something that made her heart hurt whenever she thought about it.

"Let me hurry and wash the salad bowl and the

pan you baked the rolls in, so you can take them home clean."

"Unnecessary. I have other dirty dishes at home I still need to wash. I can easily throw these in with them."

He looked as if he wanted to argue but held his tongue.

"Guys," he said instead to his sons, "can you tell Miss Baker thanks for joining us today?"

"Thanks, Miss Baker," they said in unison, something they did often. She wasn't sure they were even aware of it.

"I'm the one who must thank you for the wonderful day. I'm so grateful to you for sharing your puppies with me and for helping me with my riding lessons again. I owe you. I mean it."

The boys nudged each other, hiding their matching grins that indicated they knew exactly what she meant, that she would in turn help them practice the song for their father before the show the following week.

"You're welcome," Trevor said.

"See you tomorrow. At practice," Colter added, with such a pointed, obvious look, it was a wonder Beckett didn't immediately catch on that something else was going on.

She followed Beck from the dining room to the kitchen. Despite her protests, he ended up washing the pan she had used for the rolls as well as the now-empty salad bowl.

She finally gave up arguing with him about it and picked up a dish towel instead. "While we're at it, we might as well finish cleaning your kitchen. I can spare a few more moments."

This time, he was the one who looked as if he wanted to argue, but after a moment, he shrugged.

She was right, it only took them a few moments. She found the domesticity of the scene dangerously seductive, the two of them working together in the kitchen while the sounds of the Christmas show filtered in from the television that was in a nearby room.

"It really was a great steak," she told him again.

"Thanks. I don't have many specialties in the kitchen, so I'm pretty proud of the few I can claim."

"With reason."

He tossed a spatula in the rinse water and she pulled it out to dry.

"One of the toughest things about us men being on our own now that Judy is gone is figuring out the food thing all the time. She used to leave food in the fridge for us to heat up, but now Jax and Dan and I have to take turns. I think the boys are getting a little tired of burgers and steaks, but that's mostly what I'm good at."

"I hear you. My problem is the opposite. I would like to cook other things, but my dad's a cattleman through and through. Red meat is about all he ever wants, though Manny Guzman's wife prepares meals for us a few times a week and she likes to slip in some chicken dishes here and there."

"You take good care of your father," he said, his voice slightly gruff.

She could feel her cheeks heat at the unexpected praise. "Whether he wants me to or not. He's constantly telling me he doesn't need my help, that I should go back to Boston. That's where my mother lives with her second husband."

"Why don't you?"

She wasn't sure she could articulate all the reasons. "I love my dad. He needs help, no matter what he says, and I'm in a position to offer that help. He doesn't have anyone else. Not really."

She shrugged. "Anyway, I like it here. The people are kind and my job is tremendously rewarding. It hasn't been a sacrifice."

He said nothing, just continued washing the last few dishes, then let the water out of the sink while she wiped down the countertops.

"That should do it," he said when she finished. "Thanks for your help. I've got to say, the kitchen looks better than it has in weeks. None of us enjoys the cleanup portion of the program. That's probably obvious."

"It wasn't bad," she assured him. "You know, even if you don't hire another full-time housekeeper, you could still have someone come in a couple times a week to straighten up for you."

"That would certainly help. Know of anyone looking for a job?"

"Not off the top of my head, but I can ask around." She glanced at the clock on the microwave. "And now I really do have to go. Dad expected he would be home in about a half hour from now. If he makes it home ahead of me, he's going to worry about where I am."

"I'll grab your coat."

He brought it in from the mudroom and helped her into it, which only seemed to heighten her awareness of the heat and that delicious outdoorsy scent that clung to him.

"Thanks again," she said, then reached for her dishes. He beat her to it, picking them up and heading for the door.

"What are you doing?"

"I'll walk you out. Even we Idaho cowboys learn a few manners from our mamas."

"I never said otherwise, did I?"

"No. You didn't," he said gruffly.

Who had? His troubled wife? The thought left her sad.

The storm hadn't started yet. Though it still smelled like impending snow, the clouds had even cleared a little, revealing a few glittery expanses of night sky.

"Oh," she exclaimed, craning her neck. "Look at all those stars. It always takes my breath away."

"Yeah, it's one of the best things about living out here, where we don't have much light pollution."

"A few times when I came here over the summers, my dad would wake me in the middle of the night so we could drive into the mountains to see the meteor shower."

"The Perseids. I do the same thing with the boys. Every August, we take a trail ride up into the hills above the ranch and spread our sleeping bags out under the stars to watch the show."

There was another image that charmed her, the picture of this big, tough cowboy taking his young twin sons camping to show them nature's fireworks show. "That sounds lovely."

"We've got another meteor shower this week. You should check it out."

"Thanks, but I think I'll pass on anything that involves sleeping out under the stars in December."

He smiled as they reached her SUV. She opened the rear door and he slid the pan and bowl inside, then stepped forward to open her door for her.

"Good night," she said. "Thank you again for a lovely afternoon."

"It was my pleasure. The boys loved having you out and...so did I."

His voice was low, intense. Shivers rippled down her spine and she couldn't resist meeting his gaze. All those glittery feelings of earlier seemed to ignite all over again, as if someone had just stirred a hearth full of embers inside her and sent a crackling shower of sparks flaring through her.

They gazed at each other for a long moment and then he uttered a long, heartfelt oath before he lowered his mouth to hers.

Chapter Nine

As his mouth descended and his arms enfolded her against him, Ella caught her breath at the heat and strength of him surrounding her. For a moment, she couldn't think straight and stood frozen in his arms while his mouth brushed over hers once, then twice.

As she blinked in shock, her brain trying to catch up to what was going on, the amazing reality of it seeped in.

She was kissing Beck McKinley—and it was so much better than she ever could have imagined. Still not quite believing this was real, she returned the kiss with all the hunger she had been fighting down for so very long.

She forgot about the boys inside, about the snow spiraling down around them, the cold metal of her SUV seeping through the back of her wool coat.

The only thing she could focus on was Beck—his delicious mouth on hers, the strength of his muscles under her exploring hands, the heat and wonder and sheer thrill of kissing him at last.

She wasn't sure how long he kissed her there in the cold December night—long enough, anyway, that when he pulled away, she felt disoriented, breathless, aware that her entire body pulsed with a low, delicious ache.

"I told myself I wasn't going to do that."

"I... Why?" His words jerked her out of that happy daze.

"Because I was afraid as soon as I kissed you once, I would only want to do it again and again. I was right."

"I wouldn't mind." Some part of her warned her that she probably shouldn't admit that, but the words spilled out before she could stop them.

He gazed down at her, his eyes flashing in the moonlight. He was so gorgeous, rough and masculine. How could any woman resist him?

"I like you, Ella. More than I should."

A thrill shot through her at his words, even though it was tempered by the reluctant way he said them. He liked her, but was obviously not crazy about that fact.

"I like you, too," she admitted. She didn't add that the more time she spent with him, the more she liked him.

Something bright flashed in his gaze and he kissed her again, this time with a fierce intensity that completely took her breath away.

After another moment, he sighed and pulled away, his forehead pressed to hers. "I have to stop, while I still can."

"You don't *have* to."

"It's freezing out here. That snow is going to start in

about ten minutes and the temperature will drop more. I have a feeling it might be pretty traumatic for my boys to find us here after the spring thaw, still locked together."

With clear reluctance, he eased away. "That shouldn't have happened, Ella. You get that, right? I can't...start something with you."

Maybe he should have thought of that little fact before he kissed her until she forgot her own name, she thought tartly. After the heated embrace they had just shared, something had already started between them, like it or not.

Oh, this was going to get awkward quickly. She couldn't just ignore the man. They lived in the same community, were neighbors, for heaven's sake. He was at her father's ranch nearly every day for some reason or other.

How was she supposed to be able to look at him in the grocery store or the library or parent-teacher conferences without remembering this moment—the heat of his mouth on hers, the taste of him, minty and delicious.

"You should probably go. Your father will be home soon, if he isn't already."

"Right." Shaky and off balance, she managed to make her limbs cooperate long enough to climb into her driver's seat.

He stood for a moment, looking as if he wanted to say something else, but ultimately he only gave a little wave, closed the door, then stood back so she could drive away.

Her SUV had a key remote that started with a push button. She fumbled with it for several seconds, aware her hands shook and her thoughts were scattered. After an uncomfortably long moment, she somehow remembered she needed to press the brake at the same time she pushed the button before it could start. Finally she managed to combine all the steps and the engine roared to life.

As she drove away, she forced herself not to check the rearview mirror to see if he was still standing there. Her head spun with a jumble of emotions—shock, regret and, most of all, an aching hunger.

He was right. They shouldn't have done that. How on earth was she supposed to go back to treating him with polite distance, when all she would be able to remember was how magical it had felt to be in his arms?

Beck couldn't force himself to move for several moments, even after the taillights of Ella's SUV disappeared down the drive.

What the hell just happened? He felt as if a hurricane had just blown through his world, tossing everything comfortable and familiar into weird, convoluted positions.

Ella Baker.

What was he *thinking*, to kiss her like that?

He had been contemplating the idea of reentering the dating waters for the last year, had even dipped his toe in a bit and asked out a neighbor, Faith Nichols Dustin. That hadn't turned out so well—for him, anyway. Faith was now married to another rancher and friend, Chase Brannon.

He was happy for them. His heart had never really been involved, but he liked Faith and thought they had many things in common. They had both lost their spouses, were raising their children alone, ran successful ranch operations.

On paper, they would have made a good fit. It wasn't to be, though. Faith and Chase were obviously in love, and Beck was happy they'd been able to find joy together after all these years.

He envied them, really. The truth was, he was lonely, pure and simple. His life wasn't empty. Far from it. He had the boys and the ranch, his brother and his uncle, but he missed having a woman in his life. He missed soft skin and sweet smiles, the seductive scent of a woman's warm neck, the protective feeling of sleeping with someone he wanted to watch over in his arms.

He sighed. In the end, it didn't matter how lonely he was. He couldn't make another mistake like Stephanie. He had the boys to worry about now. If he ever became seriously involved with a woman again, he would have to pick someone he absolutely knew would stick—a woman who loved it here as much as he did, who could not only be *content* with the ranching life, but could also embrace it, hardships and all.

Too bad the one woman he had been drawn to in longer than he could remember was someone so completely inappropriate.

Ella Baker was delicate and lovely, yes. He could look at her all day long and never grow tired of it. She made him want to tuck her inside his coat and protect her from the cold, the wind and anything else that might want to hurt her.

She wasn't for him.

He needed a woman from this world, someone tough and hardy and resilient. Someone who wouldn't mind the wind or weather, the relentlessly long hours a rancher had to put in during calving and haying seasons, the self-reliance that was a vital, necessary part of this life.

He couldn't put his boys through losing someone else they loved, simply because he was drawn to sweet, pretty, delicate types like Ella Baker.

He pressed a hand to his chest, to the sudden ache there. Just a little heartburn, he told himself. It certainly couldn't be something as useless and unwanted as yearning.

His boys were up to something, but damned if Beck could figure out what.

Despite his best and most subtle efforts to probe in the week following that Sunday dinner with Ella, they were being uncharacteristically closemouthed about things.

Still, it was obvious they had secrets. Seemed like they spent half their free time whispering to each other, then going suspiciously quiet whenever he happened to walk in.

He tried to give them a little latitude. It was Christmastime, when everybody seemed to turn into covert operatives, with secrets and hidden stashes of treasure. He had his own secrets right now.

He didn't like that Dan and Jax seemed to be in on the whole thing. More than once, he had seen the boys talking to them, only to shut things off again if Beck walked in.

Knowing something had been stirring at the Broken Arrow all week, he should have been prepared on Friday morning when the boys ganged up and ambushed him at breakfast.

"Dad, can we have Miss Ella over again tomorrow to ride Creampuff?" Trevor asked.

His skin seemed to catch fire just at the mention of her name. The ache in his chest that had been there since their kiss Sunday night seemed to intensify.

He had dreamed about her every single night, but hadn't seen her since then.

"She only rode here two times," Colter reminded him. "That's not enough."

"We promised we would teach her how to ride. If we're gonna do that, it has to be more than two times."

What sort of arrangement had they made with their music teacher? He still couldn't shake the suspicion that there was something fishy about the whole thing from the outset. He thought they were doing a nice thing to invite her out to ride, but he was beginning to wonder if there was something more to it, something he was missing.

What weren't they telling him?

"We thought maybe she could bring us home after practice tomorrow morning and then we can ride in the arena for a while, and then she could go see the new puppies with us," Colter said in what seemed like a deceptively casual tone.

Yes. They were definitely cooking up something.

"And maybe she could stay for dinner again," Trevor suggested blithely. Beck didn't miss the way Colter poked him with his elbow and gave him a shut-up sort of look.

"I don't know about dinner," he said slowly, "but she can certainly come out and ride again, if she wants to. You can invite her at practice. She might be busy, though. It wouldn't surprise me. Everyone seems to be, this time of year."

"We'll ask her," Trevor said. He cast a sidelong look at his brother, who nodded, another of their unspoken twin-talk kind of communications.

"You'll be here tomorrow, won't you?"

"I don't know. Like I said, it's a busy time of year. I'll have to see how my schedule plays out. I have to run into Idaho Falls at some point this weekend to pick up a few things for Sal and the puppies." And for two certain little caballeros for Christmas, but he didn't tell them that.

"I can always run to Idaho Falls for you." Jax looked up from his coffee and his iPad long enough to make the offer.

"Yeah." Colter seized on that. "Maybe Uncle Jax can go to Idaho Falls for you. It would be better if you could be here when Miss Ella comes over."

"Why's that?" he asked with a frown.

The twins exchanged looks that were not at all subtle. He had seen that look before, too many times to count—usually just moments before they did something dangerous or destructive, like jump from the barn loft or try to take out ornaments on the Christmas tree with their little peashooters.

"Because you're, you know, a really good teacher and good with horses and stuff."

Colter's ready response didn't ease Beck's suspicions any.

"Uncle Jax is a good teacher, too, and he's even better than I am with horses." That wasn't always easy for him to admit, but it was true. His younger brother had an uncanny way with them. "Miss Baker will be okay."

Jax had been watching this exchange with unusual interest. Usually his brother kept to himself until at least his second cup of coffee. "Sure," he answered. "For the record, I'm happy to teach Ella Baker anything she would like to know."

Beck knew he had no right to the giant green tide of jealousy that washed over him at the thought of the sweet Ella in his brother's well-practiced hands.

"We're talking about horses, right?"

Jax gave him an innocent look that didn't fool Beck any more than the boys' had. His brother had the same uncanny way with women that he did with animals.

"Sure. That's what I was talking about. What else would be on my mind?"

Beck could only imagine. His brother was a notorious flirt whose favorite pastime, when he wasn't following the rodeo circuit or training his own horses, was hanging out with buckle bunnies who liked to admire his…trophies.

Come to think of it, he wasn't sure he wanted Jax within half a mile of Ella Baker.

"Maybe she can't even come over," Trevor said. "But we can ask her, right?"

He didn't miss the little thread of yearning in his son's voice. It made him wary and sad at the same time. Since Judy retired, they seemed a little more clingy than usual, probably hungry for a woman's softer arms and gentle ways.

"All you can do is ask. Find out if she's available and then we'll figure out the rest."

"Okay. Thanks, Dad."

"Finish your breakfast and load your dishes. You'd better hustle or you're going to miss the bus."

They shoveled in their eggs, then raced to brush teeth, grab homework and don coats and backpacks. Through it all, they continued to whisper, but he sent them on their way without making any progress at figuring out what secrets they were keeping from him.

Ella did her best to put the memory of that kiss behind her. It should have been easy. She was insanely busy as the calendar ticked inexorably toward Christmas.

In addition to the daily practices for the show at The Christmas Ranch, each of the grades at the elementary school was preparing a small performance for their parents—with plenty of music needed—and her middle school choir presented their annual holiday concert.

She also volunteered at the local senior citizen center in Pine Gulch and had agreed to lead carols for their holiday luncheon.

It was chaotic and hectic and…wonderful. She loved being part of the Pine Gulch community. She loved going to the grocery store and being stopped by at least two or three people who wanted to talk. She loved the way everyone waved as she drove past and gave genuine smiles, as if they were happy to see her.

Though she had good neighbors and friends in Boston, she had never known the same sense of community as she did here in Idaho.

Her life had changed drastically since she came to live with her father the previous year.

Occasionally, she missed her job there, her friends, the active social network and many cultural opportunities she found in Boston. She even missed her mother and stepfather and their lovely home in the Back Bay neighborhood.

She wouldn't go back. Her life here was rich and full and rewarding—even when she found her schedule packed with activities.

She hadn't seen Beck all week, but even her busy routine hadn't kept her from spending entirely too much time thinking about him and about that amazing kiss.

She wasn't sleeping well. Each night she fell into bed, completely exhausted, but her stupid brain seemed to want to replay every moment of that kiss, from the first brush of his mouth on hers to the strength of his muscles against her to the cold air swirling around them.

By the time Friday rolled around, she was completely drained. The show at The Christmas Ranch would be the following Tuesday, which meant only three more rehearsals—that afternoon, Saturday morning and Monday after school. With everything else going on, this would be her last chance to practice with Colter and Trevor for their special number.

Now, as they rehearsed one more time in her classroom, her fingers strummed the last chord of the song and she beamed at the boys.

"That time was perfect!" she exclaimed. "I can't believe how well you've picked up the harmony and you've memorized the words and everything. Your dad is going to love this so much. Everyone else will, too."

She wasn't exaggerating or giving false praise. Colter and Trevor actually sounded so good together, she would have loved to record it.

All her instincts told her that if she ever uploaded it to social media, the song would go viral instantly. Their voices blended perfectly and the twins had a natural harmony that brought out all the emotional punch of the song, the angst of a cowboy who has to spend the holiday alone in the cold elements instead of by a warm fire, surrounded by loved ones.

Beyond that, there was something utterly charming about these two redheaded little boys who looked like the troublemakers many thought they were, but when they opened their mouths, they sang like little cowboy angels.

On the night of the performance, she would have to make sure it was recorded. More than one parent had offered to film the entire show. She would have to be sure Beck could obtain a copy, especially since he wouldn't be prepared to record it himself, considering the whole thing would be a total surprise.

"Thanks a lot for helping us," Trevor said.

"You're very welcome. I've enjoyed it. And you boys have been so good during the rehearsals. You've more than repaid me."

"No, we haven't," Colter argued. "We still need to take you horseback riding again. You only went two times and we practiced our song almost every day."

"Our dad said we could invite you to come over again tomorrow after practice, if you have time," his brother said.

"Yeah! You've got to come and see the puppies. They're growing *fast.*"

"Their eyes are open now and they're not always sleeping every minute. They're so cute. You have to see them," Trevor said. "We got to hold one yesterday. Sal didn't like it much but Dad just petted her and talked to her so she didn't get too mad at us."

"I'm glad to hear that," Ella said, charmed despite

herself by the image of Beck giving his boys a chance to hold the puppy.

Only a few weeks ago, she had thought him cold, emotionless. How had she managed to get things so very wrong?

He certainly didn't kiss like he was cold and emotionless. The memory made her ache.

"So do you want to come over after practice tomorrow afternoon?"

With everything on her docket, that was really her only free chunk of time all week to finish her own Christmas preparations, but this appeared to be a matter of honor to the boys. It was clear Trevor and Colter wanted to be sure they repaid her accordingly, after all her work helping them prepare the song.

Beyond that, she felt a little rush of anticipation at the prospect of riding again. She had begun recapturing something she thought had been lost forever and couldn't help being eager to continue on that journey.

"I have a busy day tomorrow, but I think I could make that work. I would love to visit Creampuff again and see Sal and her puppies."

"Yay!" Colter said.

"I'll plan on taking riding clothes again and we can practice after I take you home from rehearsal tomorrow."

"Maybe we can show you how to rope a calf," Colter said.

"I think I'll stick with trying to stay in the saddle," she said with a smile. "Are you sure this is okay with your father?"

Trevor's features fell a little. "He said we could ask you, but he might not be there."

"Yeah. He said he had some stuff to do tomorrow, so our uncle Jax said he could teach you anything you want to know."

"Dad didn't like that very much, though. He was kind of mad at Uncle Jax. He got a big, mean face, but Uncle Jax only laughed."

"Is that right?" she said faintly.

Jax McKinley was a flirt of the highest order. From the moment she moved to town, friends had warned her not to take him too seriously.

"Yeah. Uncle Jax is really good with horses. He even rides broncs in the rodeo and stuff."

"But our dad is even better," Colt assured her. "He's the best cowboy ever."

"And he's nice, too."

"Plus, he can cook good. He makes really good popcorn."

Don't forget that he can kiss like he was born knowing his way around a woman's mouth.

"I'll be grateful to anyone who might be there tomorrow to give me a lesson," she assured them. "Now, we'd better hurry or we'll be late to rehearsal."

As the boys grabbed backpacks and coats and she gathered her own things, she couldn't stop thinking about Beck. Big surprise. What would he think of the boys' special musical number? He would have to possess a heart of lead not to be touched by their effort on his behalf.

They were adorable kids. She would always be grateful she had been able to get to know them a little better these past few weeks.

She had completely changed her perspective about

them, too. Somehow they had worked their charming little way into her heart when she wasn't looking.

The trick after the holidays would be figuring out how to extricate them all.

"I thought you were planning to be in Idaho Falls all day."

Beck fought the urge to rearrange that smirk on Jax's too-handsome face. His brother always seemed to know instinctively which buttons to push. Apparently Beck was more transparent than he thought.

"I took care of everything I had to do in town," he said. "It took less time than I expected. I knew what I wanted and where to get it, so there was no sense dawdling, was there?"

"Words to live by, brother." Jax grinned, obviously taking his words to mean something entirely different from what Beck intended. "Too bad for me, I guess that means you can take over the riding lesson with our pretty little neighbor this afternoon. But I imagine you already knew that."

Beck frowned at his brother's teasing. "I don't know what you're talking about," he lied.

Jax only chuckled. "I guess since you're here, you can do the honors of saddling up all the horses for the lesson. I suddenly find myself with an afternoon free. Maybe I should run into town, do a little Christmas shopping."

"Sounds good." He wouldn't mind if his brother decided to stay away all afternoon.

He checked his watch. Practice was supposed to have ended about fifteen minutes ago, which meant Ella and the boys should be here shortly.

As unwelcome anticipation churned through him, Beckett tried to keep himself busy in the horse barn, readying the horses and the arena for their visitor. He was mostly unsuccessful, with little focus or direction, and was almost relieved when he finally heard a vehicle approach.

He set down the leather tack he had been organizing and walked out to greet them, his heart pounding in his chest.

How had he forgotten how pretty she was? As she climbed out of her vehicle, winter sunlight glinted on her hair and her cheeks were rosy and sweet. She wore jeans, boots and a ranch coat open to reveal another Christmas sweater. Instantly, he remembered that moment in his room the week before, when she had appeared there like something out of a dream he hadn't dared remember.

"Hey, Dad," Trevor said, his features lighting up at the sight of them. "I thought you weren't gonna be here!"

"I took care of my business in Idaho Falls faster than I expected," he answered. They didn't need to know that he had practically bought out the entire toy aisle at the big-box store in his rush to get out of there quickly, before the Saturday rush.

"Great!" Colter said. "This way you can give this Ella her lesson."

The two exchanged delighted grins and an uncomfortable suspicion began to take root.

Something was up, all right, and he had a feeling he was beginning to know what that might be. The little troublemakers had romance on their minds. Somehow they must have got it in their heads that he and their music teacher might make a match of it.

Was Jax in on it? What about Dan? Was that the reason Jax was conveniently taking off and that Dan had made a point of saying he had plans today and couldn't help?

Were they all trying to throw him and Ella together?

His cheeks suddenly felt hot as he wondered if that was the whole reason the boys had come up with the idea for these riding lessons.

This wouldn't do. The idea was impossible. Completely out of the question. He didn't have the first idea how to break it to them.

They were children. They only saw a pretty woman who was kind to them, not all the many reasons why a relationship between Ella and Beck could never work.

He suddenly wished he'd stayed in Idaho Falls, so he could head off this crazy idea before it had any more time to blossom.

Was it too late to drag Jax back to handle the lessons? He still didn't like the idea of his brother here with his flirty smiles and his admiring gaze. Beck would just have to tough it out.

Things would be easier, though, if they didn't stick around here in the intimate confines of the riding arena.

"What do you say we take a quick trail ride up above the house? You can only learn so much while you're riding around in a circle."

"Outside?" Her gaze shifted to the mountains then back to him, her big blue eyes widening.

She had been injured in those mountains, he remembered. He couldn't blame her for being nervous, yet he knew it was a fear she had to overcome if she would ever be able to truly rediscover the joy of riding horses again.

"You'll be okay. We'll keep you safe," he promised. "Do you have warm enough clothing for that?"

"Is anything ever warm enough for the winters around here?"

He had to smile. "Good point. There's no cold like trying to pull a stubborn calf at two in the morning when it's below zero, with a windchill that makes it even colder."

"Brrr."

He looked over her winter gear. "We should have some warmer gloves that will fit you and a snug hat. I would hate to be responsible for you coming down with frostbite."

"You make this whole outing sound so appealing."

Despite her dry tone, he could see the hint of panic in her eyes and in the slight trembling in her hands.

"Don't worry. We won't go far. I've got a fairly well-groomed trail that winds around above the house a little. We can be back in less than an hour. It will be fun, you'll see."

She still didn't look convinced.

"Trust me," he said. "You're never going to love riding a horse again until you let one take you somewhere worth going."

That seemed to resonate with her. She gazed at him, then at the mountains, then finally nodded.

Even if she wasn't for him, the woman had grit. He wanted to tell her so, right there. He wanted to kiss her smack on the lips and tell her she had more gumption than just about anybody he'd ever met.

He couldn't, of course, without giving the boys encouragement that their devious plan was working, so he only smiled and walked back to the barn to bring out the horses.

Chapter Ten

Ella refused to give in to the tendrils of panic coiling through her.

As the boys led out Creampuff and their two horses, saddled and ready to go, she drew in a deep, cleansing breath.

Beck was right. Riding around in an indoor space had been a great introduction for her, but it wasn't much different from a child atop a pony, going around in circles at the county fair. If she truly wanted to get past her fear, she had to take bigger steps, like riding outside, no matter how stressful.

Beck came out leading his own big horse and for a moment, she let herself enjoy the picture of a gorgeous cowboy and his horse in the clear December air.

"Need a boost?" Beck asked as he approached.

She wanted to tell him no, but the placid and friendly

Creampuff suddenly loomed huge and terrifying. "Yes. Thank you," she said.

He helped her into the saddle and gave her thigh a reassuring squeeze that filled her with a complex mix of gratitude and awareness.

"You've got this, El. We'll be with you the whole time."

"Thanks," she mumbled through lips that felt thick and unwieldy.

Beckett mounted his own horse. Ella was again distracted long enough from her worries to wish she didn't have to hold the reins in a death grip so she could pull out her phone and snap his photograph. Her friends back in Boston should have visual proof that she was actually friends with someone who should be featured in men's cologne advertisements.

The Great American Cowboy, at one with his horse and his surroundings.

"Trev, you go in front, then Colt, then Miss Baker," Beck ordered. "I'll bring up the rear. We're just heading up to the springs. You know the way, right, boys? Not too fast, okay? Just an easy walk this time."

"Okay, Dad," Trevor said.

The boys turned their horses and urged them around the ranch house. Creampuff followed the other horses without much direction necessary from Ella as they made their way around the ranch house and toward a narrow trail she could see leading into the foothills.

At first, she was too focused on remaining in the saddle to notice anything else. Gradually, she could feel her muscles begin to relax into the rhythm of the horse. Creampuff really was a gentle animal. She wasn't placid, but she didn't seem at all inclined to any sudden movements or abrupt starts. She responded almost instantly to any commands.

Ella drew in a deep breath scented with pine, snow, leather and horse. It truly was beautiful here. From their vantage point, she could see Beck's ranch, orderly and neat, joining her father's land. Beyond spread the town of Pine Gulch, with the silvery ribbon of the Cold Creek winding through the mountains.

In summer, this would be beautiful, she knew, covered in wildflowers and sagebrush. Now it was a vast, peaceful blanket of snow in every direction.

This was obviously a well-traveled trail and it appeared to have been groomed, as well.

Had he done that for her, so she would be able to take this ride?

Warmth seeped through her at the possibility and she hardly noticed the winter temperature.

Colter turned around in his saddle. "You're doing great," the boy said. "Isn't this fun?"

"Yes," she answered. "It's lovely up here."

Everything seemed more intense—the cold air against her skin, the musical jangle of the tack, the magnificent blue Idaho sky.

After about fifteen or twenty minutes, they reached a clearing where the trail ended at a large round black water tank.

Trevor's horse went straight to the water and the others followed suit.

"This looks like a well-used watering spot."

"Our cattle like to come up here, but if you stuck around long enough, you could also see elk and deer and the occasional mountain lion," Beck said.

"A mountain lion. Oh, my!"

"They're not real scary," Colter assured her. "They leave you alone if you leave them alone."

"We even saw a wolf up here once," Trevor claimed.

"A coyote, anyway," Beck amended.

"I still think it was a wolf, just like the ones we saw in Yellowstone."

"Want to stretch your legs a little before we ride home? We can show you the springs, if you want. There's a little waterfall there that's pretty this time of year, half-frozen."

"Sure."

This time she dismounted on her own and the boys tied the horses' reins to a post there. Beck waded through the snow to blaze a trail about twenty yards past the water tank to a small fenced-off area in the hillside that must be protecting the source of a natural springs from animal contamination. The springs rippled through the snow to a series of small waterfalls that sparkled in the sunlight.

"This is lovely," she murmured. "Do you come up here often?"

"I maintain it year-round. The springs provides most of our water supply on the ranch. We pipe it down from the source but leave some free-flowing. In the winter, this is as far as we can go without cross-country skis or snowshoes. The rest of the year, there's a beautiful backcountry trail that will take you to Cold Creek Canyon. It's really a stunning hike or ride."

"Last year, we rode our horses over to see our friend Thomas."

"That sounds lovely."

What an idyllic place for these boys to grow up. Though they had lost their mother so young, they didn't seem to suffer for love and affection. She didn't envy them precisely—how could she, when they didn't have a mother? Still, she wished she could have grown up on the Baker's Dozen with her parents together, instead of having been constantly yanked in opposite directions.

They seemed so comfortable here, confident and happy and loved.

"You should see the wildflowers that grow up here," Beck said as they headed back to the horses. "There's something about the microclimate, I guess, but in the summer this whole hillside is spectacular, with flowers of every color. Lupine and columbine, evening primrose and firewheel. It's beautiful."

"Oh, I would love to see that." She could picture it vividly.

"You're welcome back, anytime," he said. "June is the best time for flowers."

"I'll keep that in mind."

It always amazed her when she went into the backcountry around Pine Gulch that all this beauty was just a few moments away. It only took a little effort and exploration to find it.

"Can we go back now?" Colter asked. "I'm kind of cold."

"Yeah. Me, too," his brother said, with a furtive look at the two of them. "You don't have to come with us. You two can stay up here as long as you want. We're okay by ourselves."

Before their father could answer, the boys hopped back on their horses and headed down in the direction they'd come up.

She glanced at Beck, who was watching his sons with a look of consternation.

"Those two little rascals." He shook his head with an expression that suggested he was both embarrassed and annoyed.

"What was that all about?"

"It's more than a little embarrassing," he admitted. "I think they're up to something. They've been acting oddly all week."

Oh, dear. She hoped the boys didn't reveal their surprise musical number before the performance in a few days.

"I'm sure it's nothing," she said. "Probably just, you know, typical Christmas secrets."

"That's what I thought at first, but not anymore. Today proved it." He was silent for a moment. "I think they're matchmaking."

She stared. "Matchmaking? Us?"

She felt hot suddenly, then cold. Did the boys know she was developing feelings for their father? Had she let something slip?

"I know, it's crazy. I don't have any definite proof, just a vibe I've picked up a time or two. I'm sorry about that."

Was he sorry because he was embarrassed or sorry that his boys might actually be crazy enough to think Ella and he could ever be a match?

"I... It's fine."

"If this keeps up, I'll talk to them. Make sure they know they're way off base."

"It's fine," she said again, though she felt a sharp pang in her heart at his words. "They are right about one thing, though. It is getting cold up here."

"Yeah. Guess we better head down."

"Thank you for showing me the waterfall, for making me ride up here, when I was afraid to try it. It is beautiful."

"You're welcome. Here. Let me help you mount up again."

She wanted to try herself, but her bad leg was aching from the ride and she wasn't sure she could manage it.

He gave her a boost up. This time, though, because of the stiffness in her leg, she faltered a little and his hands ended up on her rear instead of her waist.

Both of them seemed to freeze for just a moment and then he gave a nudge and she was in the saddle.

He cleared his throat. "I swear, I didn't mean to do that."

"I believe you. Don't worry. I guess it's a good thing the boys weren't here to see, right? They might get the wrong idea."

"True enough."

He looked as if he wanted to say something else but finally mounted his own horse. "You go first. I'll be right behind you. Creampuff knows the way."

She drew in a deep breath and headed down the mountainside.

A wise woman would have jumped back in her car and driven away from Beck McKinley and his cute twins the moment she rode back to the barn. Ella was discovering she wasn't very wise, at least not when it came to the McKinley men.

As soon as they arrived back at the horse barn, the twins came out, two adorable little cowboys. "We can put up Creampuff and Ace for you," Colter offered.

Beck looked surprised, then pleased. "That's very responsible of you, boys."

They beamed at the two of them. "While we do that," Trevor said, "you can take Miss Ella to see the puppies again."

"She has to see how much they've grown," his brother agreed.

"We'll wait until you're done with the horses, then we can all go see the puppies together."

"We've already seen them this morning, when we had to feed them," Colter reminded him. "And you said it's better if Sal doesn't have that many visitors at once. It stresses her. You said so."

"That's right. I did say that." Above their heads, Beck raised his eyebrows at Ella in a told-you-so kind of look.

"Go on, Dad. We promised Miss Baker she could see them."

"I guess I have my orders," he murmured to Ella. "Shall we?"

She didn't see a graceful way out of the situation, so she shrugged and followed him toward the older barn.

"What did I tell you?" Beck said as they headed inside from the cold December afternoon to the warm, cozy building.

"You might be right," she said.

"I'm sorry. I don't know what's come over them."

"You don't need to apologize. I think it's rather sweet. I'm flattered, if you want the truth, that they think I'm good enough for you."

You *obviously don't, but it's nice that your sons do.*

He gazed at her for a moment, before shaking his head. "They're rascals. I'll have a talk with them."

Though she fought the urge to tell him not to do that, at least until after Christmas, she knew he had to set them straight. Nothing would ever happen between her and Beck. He had made that abundantly clear.

They stood just inside the door of the barn. It was warm here and strangely intimate and she had to fight the urge to step forward and kiss away that rather embarrassed expression.

He was gazing at her mouth, she realized, and she saw awareness flickering there in his eyes.

He wanted to kiss her and she ached to let him.

No. That wouldn't do, especially if they wanted to convince the boys there was nothing between them.

She curled her hands into fists instead. "We'd better take a look at the puppies, since that's the reason we came in here."

After an awkward moment, he shrugged. "You're right. Absolutely right."

He turned and headed farther into the barn and she followed him to the stall that housed Sal and her new little brood.

Holding on to her suddenly grim mood was tough in the presence of the eight adorable little black-and-white puppies, who were now beginning to toddle around the stall. They appeared less rodentlike and more like cute puppies, furry and adorable, with paws and ears that seemed too big for their little bodies.

"The boys were right!" she exclaimed. "They've grown so much since I saw them last."

"You can hold one, if you'd like. Sal can be a bit territorial so I'll have to grab one and bring it out to you."

"I'm all right. I'll just watch this time."

"Come back in a few weeks and they'll be climbing all over. She'll be glad to let someone else entertain them for a moment."

"They're really beautiful, Beck."

He gazed down at her with a slight smile and she was aware of the heat of him and the breadth of his shoulders. She felt a long, slow tug in her chest, as if invisible cords were pulling her closer to him.

"Thank you for sharing them with me—and for the rest of today. I'm glad you made me go on that trail, even though it scared me to death."

"I could tell."

She made a face. "Was I that obvious? I thought I was doing so well at concealing my panic attacks"

"There was nothing overt, just a few signs I picked up." He paused. "I hope you realize there's nothing wrong with being afraid, especially after your experience in childhood. Anyone would be. But not everyone would have the courage to try to overcome it."

"I don't think it's *wrong*, necessarily. Only *frustrating*. I don't want to be afraid."

"But you did it anyway. That's the important thing. You've got grit, El. Pure grit."

His words slid around and through her, warming her as clearly as if he'd bundled her in a soft, sweet-smelling quilt just off the clothesline. "I do believe that's the sweetest thing you've ever said to me."

He scratched his cheek, looking sheepish. "It must be the puppies. They bring out my gooey side."

"I like it," she confessed.

As he looked down at her, she again felt that tug in her chest, as if everything inside her wanted to pull her toward him. He must have felt it, too. She watched his expression shift, saw the heat spark to life there. His gaze slid to her mouth then back to meet her gaze and he swallowed hard.

Sunlight slanted in through a high window, making his gorgeous features glow, as if the universe was somehow telling her this was right. She had never been so aware of a man. He could carry her over his shoulders to one of the straw-covered stalls and she wouldn't utter a peep of protest.

The air around them seemed to hiss and snap with a sweet, fine-edged tension, and when he sighed and finally kissed her, it seemed as inevitable as a brilliant summer sunset.

Kissing him felt as familiar and *right* as being on a horse had earlier that afternoon. His mouth fit hers perfectly and he wrapped his arms around her as if he had been waiting for just this moment.

She returned his kiss eagerly, with all the pent-up longing of the previous week, when she had been tormented by heated memories.

Through the thrill and wonder of the kiss, as his mouth explored hers and his hands somehow found their way beneath her sweater to the bare skin of her lower back, she was aware of a tiny, ominous thread weaving through the moment.

It took several more long, delicious kisses before she could manage to identify the source of that little niggling worry, the grim truth she had been trying to ignore.

This was more than simple attraction.

She was falling in love with Beckett McKinley.

The realization seemed to knock the air right out of her lungs and she was suddenly more afraid than she'd been the first time she faced his horses.

He would hurt her. Badly. Oh, he wouldn't mean to—Beck was a good man, a kind one, as she had figured out over the last little while. But he had no real use for her beyond a few kisses. He had made that perfectly clear—as far as Beck was concerned, she didn't belong here. She was no different from his late wife or her own mother.

Like her father, he couldn't see the truth of her, the part that loved afternoon thundershowers over the mountains or the sight of new crops breaking through the ground or a vast hillside covered in wildflowers.

One of the puppies made a little mewling whimper that perfectly echoed how she felt inside. Somehow it gave Ella the strength to slide her mouth away from his.

She caught her breath and tried to make light of the kiss, purely in self-defense. "Good thing your sons didn't come in just now. If they had seen us wrapped together just now, they might have made the mistake of thinking we're both falling in exactly with their plans."

"Good thing," he murmured, looking dazed and aroused and gorgeous.

She had to get out of here, before she did something stupid, like yank him against her again and lose her heart the rest of the way. She drew a deep gulp of air into her lungs and forced a casual smile that she was fairly sure didn't fool him for a moment.

"I should, um, go. I've got a Christmas party tonight with some friends and still have to bake a dozen cookies for the exchange."

He said nothing for a long moment, then sighed. "Should we talk about that?"

She opted to deliberately misunderstand. "The cookies? I'm making my favorite white-chocolate cranberry recipe. There's really nothing to it. The secret is using a high-quality shortening and a little more flour, especially in this altitude."

"I'm sure you know I didn't mean we should talk about the cookies—though those sound delicious. I meant the kiss."

He shoved his hands into the pockets of his coat, as if he was afraid if he didn't, he would reach for her again.

Or maybe his fingers were simply cold.

"There's nothing to say," she said with that fake smile that made her cheek muscles hurt. "The boys can play matchmaker all they like, but we both know it won't go anywhere. I'll just make a point not to visit any cute puppies alone with you again."

While she was at it, she would have to add walking together to her car to that list of no-no's, as well as helping her onto a horse and washing dishes side by side.

Come to think of it, maybe it would be better if they kept a nice, safe, ten-foot perimeter between them at all times.

"I really do have to go," she lied.

"I guess I'll see you next week at the Christmas show."

She nodded and hurried out before she did something else stupid.

Beck followed her out to be sure she made it safely to her vehicle. There were a few icy spots that worried him, but she hurried across the yard to her SUV and climbed inside without faltering or looking back, as if one of his cow dogs was nipping at her heels to drive her on.

He had screwed up. Plain and simple.

For nearly a week, he'd been telling himself all the

reasons he couldn't kiss her again. What did he do the first moment they were really alone together? Yep. He kissed her. He hadn't been able to help himself. She had been so soft and sweet and lovely and all he could think about was tasting her mouth one more time.

The trouble was, he was not only fiercely attracted to her, but he also genuinely liked her.

He meant what he said to her. She had more grit than just about anybody he knew.

If she had the kind of raw courage necessary to ride again after an accident that nearly killed her, why was he so certain she didn't belong out there, that she would turn tail and run at the first sign of trouble?

She wasn't like Stephanie. That was clear enough. Yes, they had both been raised back east in big cities. They both came from wealthy, cultured backgrounds that seemed worlds away from this small Idaho town.

But Stephanie had been…*damaged*. He should have seen that from the start. She had managed to hide it fairly well at first, but when he looked back, he could clearly see all the warning signs he should have discerned much earlier. He hadn't *wanted* to see them. He had been busy growing the ranch, getting ready for the arrival of his sons, coping with a moody, temperamental wife.

If he had been more aware, maybe he could have found help for her earlier and headed off the debilitating depression that came later.

The truth was, he didn't trust himself these days. Things had gone so horribly wrong with Stephanie, and his sons had been the ones to suffer. He couldn't afford to mess up again.

If he didn't have the boys to consider—only himself—he might take the chance to see if these tender young feelings uncurling inside him for Ella Baker could grow into something sturdy and beautiful.

How could he take that risk, though?

If he pursued things between them and she ended up leaving, too, like their mother—and like her own, for that matter—the boys would be shattered.

He couldn't do that to them.

He turned around and headed back to the barn, aware as he walked that Ella had the strength to confront her fears while he was letting his own completely chase him down and wear him out like one of the Yellowstone wolves on a wounded calf.

Chapter Eleven

If he could have avoided it, Beck would have stayed far away from the Baker ranch until he could manage to figure out a way to purge Ella out of his system.

He had a feeling he faced a long battle on that particular front.

Meanwhile, he couldn't avoid the place, especially not while he and Curt were still the copresidents of the local cattle growers association.

They had end-of-year paperwork to finish for the association. It had been on his desk for a week, but he had been putting it off. Finally, the day of the Christmas show the boys had been working so hard on, he knew he couldn't put it off any longer.

It was no coincidence that he tried to time his visit around noon, as he was certain Ella would be busy teaching music at the school and not here to torment him with visions of what could never be.

If that made him a yellow-bellied chicken, he would just have to live with it.

"Thanks for bringing this by," Curt said, gesturing to the folder of papers he needed to sign.

"No problem. I was out anyway," Beck assured him. "I'm heading over to Driggs to pick up the last thing for the boys' Christmas. I commissioned new saddles for each of them, since they're growing so fast and are too big for the ones they've been using."

"Watch those two. They'll be taller than you before you know it."

Since he was six-two and the boys were only seven years old, Beckett was pretty sure he was safe for a few more years on that front, unless they had an explosive growth spur.

"Need anything while I'm out?"

Curt shook his head and Beck couldn't help thinking his friend looked more frail every time he saw him.

"I can't think of anything," he said. "I did most of my shopping online this year, since it's hard for me to get around the crowded stores."

"Got it."

Curt gazed out the window, where a light snow had begun to fall in the last hour. "It's not coming down too much, but you'd still better hurry back from town. We've got a big storm heading this way."

"That's what I heard."

The weather forecast was predicting the storm might break records.

"It's not supposed to hit until tonight, but you never

know. Better safe than sorry. I know you would hate to miss the show tonight at The Christmas Ranch."

"I'll be back in plenty of time. I'm only making one stop to the saddle maker's place."

"Good. Good." Curt reached for the big water bottle on the table beside him but his hands were trembling so badly today that it took him three tries to find the straw.

"How are you doing?" Beck asked. "Really doing?"

It seemed as if they always talked *around* Curt's condition and the challenge it presented, instead of talking *about* it. The older man frowned. For once, he didn't give his stock answer.

"I can't do a damn thing anymore," he said, frustration vying with self-pity in his voice and expression.

"I'm sorry," Beck said, though the words were hardly adequate.

"Parkinson's is the worst. I can barely sign my damn name on those papers. You saw me. If I could climb up on a horse right now, I would borrow one from you. He and I would ride up into the backcountry to die and you'd never see me again."

Man, it was hard to see such an independent, strong man laid low by this debilitating disease.

"That would be a waste of a good horse. Not to mention a good friend," he said quietly.

Curt sipped at his water again, then set it down on the desk in his ranch office. "Have you thought more about buying me out?"

There it was. The other thing he didn't know what to do about.

"Sure I've thought about it. I've run the numbers dozens of times. It's an amazing offer, Curt. I would love the chance to combine our two ranches and build the Baker-McKinley brand into one of the strongest in the world."

"You sound hesitant, though. Is it the asking price? We can negotiate a little."

He could handle the hefty price tag Curt was asking. It would mean leveraging his capital, but he'd had some great years and had money in the bank. What better use for it than taking advantage of the chance to double his usable acreage and water supply, not to mention keeping the Baker's Dozen land out of the hands of developers?

Like everywhere else in the West, this part of Idaho was experiencing a population boom, with people wanting to relocate here for the beautiful views, serenity and slower pace.

As developers built houses and newcomers moved in, they tended to crowd any agricultural operations farther and farther to the outskirts. It was the eternal paradox. People moved to an area because they loved the quiet way of life and what it represented, then immediately set out to change it.

"It's not the price," he said.

"Then what?" Curt persisted. "I'd like to seal this deal as soon as we can."

"What about Ella?" he asked, finally voicing the one concern that seemed to override all the others.

"What about her?"

"How does she feel about you selling the ranch to me?"

Curt flicked off the question with a dismissive gesture. It was obvious from his expression that he didn't consider that an obstacle at all. "She'll be fine with it. It's not like I'm *giving* it to you out of the goodness of my heart, right?"

True enough. He would pay a hefty sum, even slightly above market value.

"Ella stands to inherit my entire estate," Curt went on. "She's all I've got, so the whole kit and caboodle goes to her. Believe me, she's not stupid. She'll be better off having cold hard cash in the bank than being saddled with a cattle ranch she doesn't know the first thing to do with."

The words were barely out of the other man's mouth when Beck heard a gasp from the hallway outside the office.

With a sinking heart, he shifted his gaze and found Ella standing there, holding a tray that looked like it contained a bowl of soup and a sandwich for her father.

The tray wobbled in her hands and he thought for a moment she would drop it, but she righted it at the last moment. She didn't come inside, simply stood there looking devastated.

"Dad," she whispered.

Curt had the grace to look embarrassed. "How long have you been home?"

She ignored the question. "You're selling the ranch? To *Beck*?"

She said his name like it was a vile curse word and he flinched a little. None of this was his idea but he still felt guilty he had even discussed it with Curt.

"I offered it to him. We're still working out terms, but it makes the most sense for everyone."

She aimed a wounded look at Beck, which made him feel sandwiched between father and daughter. "You never said a word to me," she said to him.

He should have mentioned it. Now he wished he had, especially after the first time they kissed.

"Why didn't you tell me?"

Guilt pinched at him, harsh and mean. On its heels, though, was defensiveness. *He* had nothing to feel guilty about, other than not telling her Curt had approached him with an offer to sell. It hadn't been his idea or anything he had deliberately sought out. He had assumed her father had already told her about it.

Anyway, Curt was right. She would inherit the proceeds from the ranch and could live comfortably the rest of her life.

"It makes the most sense for everyone—" he began.

"Not for me! I love this ranch. I'd like to try running it, if my stubborn father would ever let me. I'm trying to learn everything I can. Why do you think I wanted the boys to teach me how to ride?"

"Ride what? I hope you're not talking about horses," Curt interjected, color suffusing his features.

"I am," Ella declared as she finally moved into the room and set down the lunch tray on the desk. "I've been to the Broken Arrow several times to go riding with Trevor and Colter."

"I can't believe you went horseback riding without telling me!"

"Really?" she snapped. "That's what you're taking out of this discussion? Considering you've all but sold my legacy out from under me without bothering to mention it, I don't think you've got much room to be angry about me riding a horse a few times."

"It's not your legacy until I'm gone," her father snapped back. "Until then, I've got every right to do what I want with *my* ranch."

The color that had started to rise on her features

leached away and she seemed to sway. Beck half rose to catch her but earned only a scathing glare for his efforts.

"You certainly would never consider trusting me with it, would you?"

"You have no idea how hard this life is."

"Because you've shielded me from it my entire life!"

"For your own good!"

Now she was trembling, he saw, just as much as she had when facing down her fears and riding a horse.

"I'm twenty-seven years old, Dad. I'm not a broken little girl in a hospital bed. I'm not some fragile flower, either. I'm tough enough to handle running the Baker's Dozen. Why can't you see that?"

Curt's jaw clenched. "You have other talents, honey. You don't need to wear yourself out on this ranch."

"What if I want to? I love it here. You know I do."

"You love it *now*. Who's to say that won't change in a week or month or year from now? You have lived on the Baker's Dozen maybe a total of two years your entire life. I just don't want you to be saddled with more than you can handle."

"That's my decision to make, isn't it?"

"No," he said bluntly. "Beckett can take what I've built over my whole life—and what my father's built and his father—and make it even better. Can you say the same?"

She said nothing, only pressed her lips together. Her eyes looked haunted now, hollow with shadows.

Curt appeared oblivious to her reaction. He shrugged. "I wouldn't sell the ranch to Beck just to hurt you, honey. You know that, right?"

"But it *would* hurt me," she answered. "What hurts

me more is that you will never even give me the chance to try."

She took a deep breath, as if fighting for control, then turned toward the door. "I can't do this right now. Not today. We can talk about it later. Right now, I have to go back to take my afternoon classes then focus on the children's Christmas show. I'll take the things I need for the show tonight. Don't expect me home between school and the performance."

She left without looking again at either of them, leaving behind an awkward, heavy silence.

Curt winced and picked up his water bottle again in hands that seemed to be shaking more than they had earlier. "I didn't want her finding out about our deal like that."

Beck frowned. "We don't have a deal. Not yet."

He was angry suddenly that Curt had dragged him into the middle of things and felt terrible for his part in hurting her. "If Ella wants to try running the ranch, Curt, I don't think I can stand in the way of that."

"She might think she wants it but she has no idea what it takes to keep this place going. She's never had to pull a calf when it's thirty below zero outside, or be up for forty-eight hours straight, trying to bring the hay in on time."

"So she can hire people to help her. You're not doing it on your own, either. Your foreman has stepped up to take on more and more of the load over the last few years. Why can't he do the same for her?"

"It's not the same. I know what I'm doing! I'm still involved in the day-to-day operations. What does Ella know about cattle? She can play four instruments and sings like a dream but she's not a rancher!"

"Not if you don't let her learn, Curt. Why are you trying so hard to protect her?"

"This ranch almost killed her once. I can't let it finish the job."

Curt blurted out the words, then looked as if he wished he could call them back.

Beck sat back, understanding dawning. He had suspected something like that after Ella told him about her accident.

"Your daughter inherited more from you than your eye color, Curtis Baker. She's tougher than you give her credit. You should have seen the grit she used to get back in the saddle, when it was obvious it scared her to death."

"I can't lose her," the man said, his voice low. "She's all I have."

"If you keep treating her like she's incompetent, you might not have much choice," he answered firmly. "You'll lose her anyway."

Ella sat in her SUV at the end of the driveway, trying to control the tears that burned her eyes.

No good deed goes unpunished, right? She thought it would be a nice thing to surprise her dad for lunch by bringing home a sandwich and some of his favorite takeout tomato bisque from the diner in town.

She never expected she would find Beck in her father's office, or walk in on the two of them negotiating away her future.

Her father had no faith in her.

She had suspected as much, but there was something heartbreaking and final about hearing it spoken so bluntly.

She'll be better off having cold hard cash in the bank than being saddled with a cattle ranch she doesn't know the first thing to do with.

Since coming to live here, she had done her best to learn the ropes. When she wasn't teaching music, she had helped with the roundup, she had driven the tractor, she had gone out with Manny to fix fences.

It wasn't enough. It would never be enough. Curtis Baker could never see her as anything more than a weak, frightened girl.

Did she know everything about running a ranch? No. But she was willing to learn. Why wouldn't her father let her try?

She brushed away a tear that fell, despite her best efforts.

She was stuck here. Her father needed her help. She couldn't just abandon him. But how could she face living here day after day with the knowledge that the ranch she loved—the ranch that felt like a huge part of her—would someday belong to someone else?

To Beck?

The pain intensified, bringing along the bitter taste of betrayal. Damn him. Why hadn't he bothered to mention that Curt had approached him about buying the ranch?

That hurt almost as much as her father's disregard for her feelings.

She let out a breath and swiped at another tear. Just as she dropped her hand, a knock on the window of her vehicle made her jump halfway out of her seat.

She turned to find Beck, big and rugged and gorgeous, standing out in the gently falling snow.

She thought about putting her SUV in gear and

spraying him with mud as she peeled out, but that would be childish.

Wouldn't it?

He gestured for her to roll down her window. After a moment, she did but only about three inches. Cold air rushed in, heavy with the impending storm.

"I don't have time to talk to you," she snapped. "I have a class in twenty minutes."

"The school is only a ten-minute drive from here. That means we still have ten minutes."

She set her jaw. Did he think she could just run into her classroom and miraculously be in a mental space to take on thirty-three fourth graders who had been dreaming of sugarplums for weeks?

"What do you want?" she said. Even as she spoke, she was aware she sounded like one of those fourth graders having a verbal altercation with a schoolmate.

"I'm sorry I didn't tell you your father had offered to sell me the ranch. I guess I assumed you and Curt had already talked about it. I thought maybe that was the reason you're sometimes a little…cool to me."

Had she been cool to him? She was remembering a few specific encounters when the temperature had been the exact opposite of cool.

"He never said a word to me. But why would he? As he made it abundantly clear in there, he doesn't need to tell me anything."

Beck sighed. "He should have. Told you, I mean. That's what I just said to him. More than that, I think he should give you a chance to run the Baker's Dozen along with him for a few years, then both of you can decide if you want to sell."

"That's a lovely idea. He would never consider it."

"Have you talked to him about it?"

"Of course! Dozens of times. My father sees what he wants to see. Like I said in there, to him, I'll always be that broken girl in a hospital bed."

"He loves you and worries about you. Speaking as a father, it would be hell to see your child hurt and spend all these years afraid it was your fault."

Curt had sold all his horses after her accident, though he had always loved to ride.

She sighed. "I can't worry about this today," she said. "In a few hours, I'm in charge of a show that involves dozens of children, twenty songs and an audience of three hundred people. I don't have time to stress about my stubborn father right now."

Tomorrow she would. Tomorrow her heart would probably break in jagged little pieces. She would compartmentalize that for now and worry about it after the show. The children had worked too hard for their music director to fall apart because her father had no faith in her.

"I'm sorry," he said again.

"I'm sure you are. Not sorry enough that you would refuse to buy the ranch, though, are you?"

A muscle worked in his jaw but he didn't answer. His silence told her everything she needed to know.

"That's what I thought. I have to go. Goodbye, Beckett."

She put her SUV in gear and pulled out into the driveway, her heart aching with regret and sadness and the tantalizing dream of what might have been.

Chapter Twelve

"Okay, kids. This is it. Our audience is starting to arrive. You've practiced so hard, each one of you. I hope you know how proud of you I am. Each number sounds wonderful and I know you've all put in so much effort to memorize your parts and the words to the music. This show is going to be amazing! Let's make some people happy!"

The children cheered with nervous energy and she smiled reassuringly at them all, though she could feel emotion building in her throat.

This was her second year directing the Christmas show and it might just be her last. If her father sold the ranch to Beckett, she wasn't sure she could stay in Pine Gulch, as much as she loved it here. It would be too difficult to watch.

She snared her thoughts before they could wander

further down that path. Tonight wasn't about sadness and regret, but about the joy and wonder and magic of Christmas. For the children's sake, she needed to focus on the show right now. She would have time to process the pain and disappointment of the day later, when this program was behind her.

"Our guests are arriving now but they will need to eat dinner first. That gives us about thirty minutes before our show. Everyone follow the older girls into the office. We have a special treat in store for you. Celeste Delaney is going to read to you from the newest, still-unpublished Sparkle the Reindeer book!"

An electric buzz crackled through the crowd at that announcement. She knew the children would be excited about the prospect of a new Sparkle book, as everyone adored the charming stories.

When she was certain the children were settled comfortably, Ella returned to the large reception room in the lodge to check on the rapidly filling tables. She greeted a few friends and made small talk as she assessed the crowd.

"We crammed in three more tables, so fifty more people can squeeze in." Hope Santiago came to stand beside her and watch people jostling for space. "I hated to turn people away last year. I hope we've got enough room this year."

It still might be tight, judging by the crowds still coming in.

"How's the weather?" she asked. It wasn't a casual question.

Hope shrugged. "It's snowing a bit but it's not too bad, yet. I still enlisted everybody with four-wheel drive to pick up some of the senior citizens who don't like to drive in the snow. I was hoping we wouldn't have to do that again this year but Mother Nature didn't cooperate. Thanks for signing up Beck, by the way. He's out there now, bringing in his last shuttle group."

So much for trying not to think about the man. She couldn't seem to escape him.

"The show is amazing, El," Hope said, her expression earnest. "You've outdone yourself this year. Every number is perfect. Honestly, I don't know what we would do without you."

She wasn't yet ready to tell her friend The Christmas Ranch might have to do just that next year.

Instead, she forced a smile and prepared to go back and check on the children. To her shock, she came face-to-face with her father, who was just coming in from outside.

What was he doing there? Curtis hadn't said a word to her earlier about attending the show.

An instant later, Beck came in behind him, helping a woman whose name she didn't know navigate the crowd with a walker.

Beck must have given her father a ride. Big surprise. The two of them were no doubt plotting their ranching world domination.

That wasn't really fair, she acknowledged, a little ashamed of herself. Her father and Beck had been friends and neighbors a long time.

Beck looked up from helping the woman and caught sight of her. Something flashed in his gaze, something intense and unreadable.

She let out a breath. Despite her hurt over that scene in her father's office that afternoon, she couldn't help a little shiver of anticipation.

He was going to love the special number his twins had prepared for him out of sheer love. She had no doubt it would touch everyone at the performance—especially Beck.

In a small way, she felt as if the gift was coming from her, as well.

She turned away just as Hope hurried over to her. "We've got a little problem. Somehow two of the angels showed up without their wings. There's no time for someone to fetch them. I know we had extras. Do you remember where we put them?"

"Absolutely. I can picture the box in the storage room perfectly. I'll grab them." She hurried away, forcing herself again to focus on the show and not on her impending heartbreak.

"Oh, Ella. This show has been nothing short of magnificent this year," Celeste whispered backstage as a trio of girls, including her stepdaughter, Olivia, bowed to thunderous applause out on stage. "We could stop there and it would be absolutely perfect. Well done!"

She smiled at her friend. She had to agree. So far the show had gone off without a hitch.

"Is it time for us to go out for 'Silent Night'?" one of the older girls asked.

"In a moment. We have one more special number."

None of the other volunteers or the children in the program had heard Colter and Trevor's song yet, as she and the twins had practiced in secret. Only Hope knew about it, since Ella had to work out the lighting and sound with her and Rafe.

"After we're done, I need you girls to lead the

younger children out, then we'll sing the final number. Boys, are you ready?"

Trevor and Colter both nodded, though their features were pale in the dim light backstage. She had a feeling they would look nervous under any light conditions, as if only now realizing the magnitude of what they had signed up for that long-ago day when they had approached her about singing in the show.

She picked up her guitar from the stand and walked out ahead of the boys, who looked absolutely adorable in matching white shirts with bolo ties and Christmas-patterned vests that Hope had sewn for them. They wore matching cowboy hats and boots and giant belt buckles that were just about as big as their faces.

Oh, she hoped Rafe was videoing this.

Ella sat on a stool as the boys took to the microphone. The crowd quieted, all the restless stirring and rustling fading away.

She had performed enough times to know when she had an audience's attention. With the spotlights on her, it was tough to see Beckett's reaction, but she thought she saw his eyes widen. He would no doubt be completely shocked to see his sons up here onstage, since he had no idea they were performing a duet.

Ella didn't want this number to be about her, but she felt compelled to take the microphone before the boys began.

"It is my great pleasure to introduce to you Colter and Trevor McKinley. They're seven years old. And yes, you guessed it, they're twins."

This earned a ripple of laughter, since that was more than obvious to anyone without cataracts.

Ella waited for the reaction to fade away before

she went on. "A few weeks ago, Trevor and Colter approached me with a rather unusual request. They wanted to perform a special song at this Christmas show as a gift to someone they love very much. They asked me to help them prepare, so it would be perfect. Since then, they have been practicing several times a week with me after school, trying to learn the harmony, the pitch, the dynamics."

She smiled at the boys. "They have worked very hard, which I see as a testament to the value of this gift, which is intended for one person—their father, Beckett."

Though she was a little afraid to look at him, her gaze seemed to unerringly go in his direction. In the brief instant their gazes met, she saw complete shock on his features as people around him smiled and patted him on the back.

"This is his favorite Christmas song, apparently," she went on, "and I have it on good authority he sings it to himself when no one is around."

She didn't look at him now, but she was quite certain he would be embarrassed at that snippet of information. Too bad for him.

"While Trevor and Colter prepared this song especially for their father," she continued, "this is one of those rare and wonderful gifts that benefits more than its recipient. We all are lucky enough to be able to enjoy it. Boys."

She leaned back and softly strummed the opening chords on her guitar. For just a moment, the boys stood frozen in the spotlight, missing their cue by about a half second, but Trevor nudged his brother and a moment later, their sweet young voices blended perfectly as they sang the slow, pensive opening bars.

The crowd seemed hypnotized while the boys sang about spending Christmas Eve in the saddle, about feeling alone and unloved, about finding the true meaning of Christmas while helping the animals.

They had never sung the song so beautifully or with such stirring emotion. When they finished, even Ella—who had heard them sing it dozens upon dozens of times—had to wipe away a tear.

After the last note faded, the crowd erupted into thunderous applause.

"You did great," she murmured over the noise of the crowd. The boys beamed and hugged her, which made more tears slip out.

"Thank you for playing your guitar and teaching us the song," Trevor said solemnly over the noise of the crowd.

Oh, she would miss these sweet boys. She wasn't sure how her heart would bear it.

"You're very welcome," she said. "Now, go find your places for the final song."

The boys rushed to their designated spots as the other children surged onto the stage—angels and shepherds, candy canes and cowboys and ballet dancers in tutus. It was a strange mishmash of costumes, but somehow it all worked perfectly together.

Olivia, who had a pure, magical voice and performed professionally, took the guitar from Ella as they had arranged, and stepped forward to strum a chord. She sang the first line of the song, then the other children joined her to sing "Silent Night" with a soft harmony that rose to fill the St. Nicholas Lodge with sweet, melodious notes.

On the last verse, the senior citizens were encouraged to sing along, which they did with stirring joy.

When the last note died away and the audience again erupted in applause, Hope went to the microphone, wiping away a few of her own tears.

"If you're all not overflowing with Christmas spirit now, I'm afraid there's no hope for you," she declared stoutly, which earned appreciative laughter.

"Wasn't that a spectacular show?" Hope asked.

She had to wait for the audience to quiet before she could speak again. "So many people had a hand in bringing this to you. The fabulous caterer, Jenna McRaven, the high school students who volunteered to serve the meal to you, those who provided the transportation."

She paused and smiled at Ella. "I would especially like to thank the one person without whom none of this would have happened tonight. Our director, organizer, producer and general talent-wrangler, Miss Ella Baker."

The crowd applauded her and she managed a smile. These were her friends and neighbors. They had embraced her, welcomed her in their midst. How would she be able to say goodbye to them?

"Now, I do have a rather grave announcement," Hope went on. Her tone was serious enough that the crowd quieted again and fixed attention on her. "While we were here enjoying this fantastic dinner and truly memorable entertainment, Mother Nature decided to let loose on our little corner of paradise outside with a vengeance. I guess she was mad she wasn't invited to the show so decided to put on her own. As much as I know we all love to visit with each other, I'm afraid that's not a good idea tonight. There will be other chances. We're going to cut things short now and encourage you all to head for home as soon as you can, before conditions get even worse—though if all else fails, we can hitch up the reindeer and sleigh to carry you home. Safe travels to you all, friends. Good night and merry Christmas."

The audience applauded one last time and gave the children a standing ovation, then people began to gather up their coats and bags and stream toward the door.

For the next several moments, Ella tried to hug as many of the children as she could and thank them for their hard work. Through it all, she noticed The Christmas Ranch staff quietly ushering people out.

"I'm sensing urgency here," she said when her path intersected with Hope's through the crowd. "Is it really that bad?"

Hope's eyes were shadowed. "I've never seen a storm come on so quickly," she admitted. "We've already got a foot of new snow and the wind out there is howling like crazy. If the crowd wasn't so noisy in here, you would hear it rattling the windows. I want people to hurry home, but I don't want to incite a panic. It's going to take some time to get everyone out of here."

"I can take more than one group." Somehow, Beckett had appeared at her side without warning and she jumped. She told herself it was only surprise, but she suspected it was more nerves. She was dying to ask how he enjoyed the song, but the urgency of the storm evacuation took precedence.

"Thanks, Beckett. I knew there was a reason I adored you." Hope smiled at him so widely that Ella might have felt a twinge of jealousy if she didn't know Hope adored her husband, Rafe.

"I'll have to factor in taking the boys, too. I'll drop them off in the first batch, then come back for a second trip."

"I can take my father home, so you don't have to do that," Ella said, though she was still so angry with her father, she didn't know if she could be in the same vehicle with him. "If you want, I can also drop the boys off at the Broken Arrow, as it's on our way home. That should free up a couple more spots in your truck for people who need rides home."

He looked torn. "That's true, but I would feel better if you could head straight home, instead of having to detour to our place."

"We'll be fine," she said. She couldn't believe the storm was really that bad. "I have four-wheel drive and new snow tires. I'm not worried."

One of The Christmas Ranch workers came up to ask Hope a question and she walked away to deal with the situation. When they were gone, Beck turned to her, his expression solemn.

"El, I... Thank you for helping the boys with that song. I've never been so touched. It means more than I can ever say."

Warmth seeped through her at the intensity in his voice. "They did all the hard work. I only guided them a little," she said. "Anyway, we made a fair trade. They agreed to give me riding lessons if I would help them learn the song."

Surprise flickered in his eyes. "That's the reason you've been coming out to ride?"

"The opportunity was too good to pass up. I wanted to ride again for a long time. They wanted to learn the song. This seemed the perfect arrangement."

It *had* been perfect, until she made the mistake of falling hard for the boys—and for their father.

"Well, thank you. Every time I hear that song now, I'll remember them…and you."

Before she could answer, Rafe Santiago came over looking harried. "It's crazy out there. Several people have decided to leave their vehicles here and come back for them when the storm passes, so we've got even more to take home. Do you think you could take home Martha Valentine and Ann and Max Watts? They all live on the same street near the park."

"Absolutely." He turned to her. "Are you sure you don't mind taking the boys home? That would help."

"No problem. I'll get them home safely," she promised.

"Thanks."

He gave her one more smile then turned to take care of his responsibilities.

That was just the kind of guy he was. When something needed doing, he would just tip his hat back and go to work.

It was one of the many reasons she loved him.

She couldn't stand here mooning over him when she had her own responsibilities, people who needed her. After one last look at him helping the frail Martha Valentine into her coat with a gentleness that brought tears to her eyes, she turned away to gather up her own charges.

The storm was worse than she had imagined.

The moment they stepped out of the St. Nicholas Lodge, snow blew at them from every direction and the wind nearly toppled them over. Everyone was huddling inside their winter coats as they made their way through the deepening drifts to the parking lot.

"Boys, grab hold of me and my father so you don't blow away." She had to raise her voice to be heard over the whining wind. She wasn't really worried about that, but needed their help more to support her father—something she couldn't tell him.

Fortunately, her vehicle was parked close to the entry and it only took them a few moments.

She opened the driver's side first so she could start the engine to warm up the heater and defrost, then hurried around to help her father inside. Her SUV passenger seat was just a little too high for him and Curt didn't have enough strength to pull himself into it alone.

"Thanks," he muttered when she gave him a boost, clearly embarrassed about needing help.

By the time he was settled and the twins were buckled into the back seat, Ella was frozen through from that icy wind—and she still had to brush the snow from the windows so she could see to drive.

Finally, they were on their way. She took off at a ponderous pace, her shoulders taut and her hands gripping the steering wheel. She could hardly see through the blinding snow that blew across the windshield much faster than her wipers could handle.

Her father looked out the window at the relentless snow while the boys, oblivious to the storm outside or the tension inside, chattered to each other about the show and the approaching holidays.

"We had about ten people tell us our song was the best one," Trevor said proudly.

"You did a great job," she said, tightening her fingers

on the wheel as a particularly strong gust of wind shook the vehicle and sent snow flying into the windshield.

Usually she didn't mind driving in a storm, but this was coming down so fast. Coupled with the wind and blowing snow, it made visibility basically zero.

"Can we listen to the radio?" Colter asked.

"I need to concentrate right now. Can you just hum to yourselves?"

"We can sing our song again," the boys offered.

"I'd like that," Curt said, to her surprise.

While her eyes were glued to the road, she was vaguely aware from her peripheral vision that he had half turned in his seat to face the twins. "I always loved that song. You boys *were* the best thing on the show," he told them.

She couldn't spare a look in the rearview mirror right now. If she did, she was sure the twins would be grinning.

"We'll have to do it without the guitar," Trevor warned.

"That's okay. You can sing without it." Her father turned to her and spoke with a guarded tone. "That won't be too stressful for you while you're driving, will it?"

She shook her head and the boys started singing the song she had heard them practice so many times before. There was something special about this time, in the warm shelter of her vehicle while the storm raged outside.

"That was wonderful," her father said when they finished, his voice gruff. "I'm sure your dad loved it."

"He did," Trevor said. "He came and found us after

and gave us big hugs and said he was so proud of us and had never been so touched."

"He said it was the best gift anybody ever gave him," Colter added. "He said it made him cry and that there's nothing wrong with a guy crying when something makes him too happy to hold it in! Can you believe that?"

She didn't answer as she felt emotion bubble up in her chest.

"It's a good song," her father said gruffly.

"Want us to sing another one? We can do 'Jingle Bells' or 'Rudolph' or 'Away in a Manger.'"

"Sure. We'll have our own private Christmas show," Curt said.

The boys launched into song and she was grateful to her father for distracting them so she could focus on driving.

She could usually make it between The Christmas Ranch and the Broken Arrow in about ten minutes, but she was creeping along at a snail's pace because of the weather conditions.

"Almost there," she finally said after about a half hour. "Your turnoff should be just ahead."

At least she was fairly certain. It was hard to be sure with the poor visibility and the heavy snow making everything look alien and *wrong* somehow.

She turned her signal on, though she couldn't see any lights in either direction, when suddenly her own headlights caught something big and dark on the middle of the road just ahead of them.

It was an animal of some kind. A cow or horse or moose. She couldn't be sure and it really wouldn't matter when two thousand pounds of animal came through the windshield.

Reflexively, she slammed the brakes. She wasn't going fast at all but the road was slick, coated in a thick layer of ice, and the tires couldn't seem to catch. The vehicle fishtailed dangerously and she fought to regain control.

She tried to turn the wheel frantically, with no success. It was a terrible feeling, to be behind the wheel of a vehicle she had absolutely no control over.

"Hang on," she called.

The boys screamed and her father swore as the vehicle went down a small embankment and into a snowbank about ten feet down.

Her heartbeat raced like she had just finished an Olympic sprint and her stomach twirled in an awful imitation of her wheels spinning out of control.

"Is everybody okay?" she asked.

"Yeah," her dad said gruffly. "Gave me a hell of a start."

"We're okay," Trevor said.

She turned around to reassure herself but all she could see in the darkness were their wide eyes.

"Are we stuck?" Colter asked.

She tightened her shaking fingers on the steering wheel. "I don't know. I haven't tried to get us out yet. You're sure you're both all right?"

"Yeah. It was like the Tilt-A-Whirl at the county fair."

Now she remembered why she had always hated that ride.

"Well, that was fun. Let's get everybody home."

Ella put the vehicle in Reverse and accelerated but

the wheels just spun. The snow was too deep here for them to find purchase. She pulled forward a little, then tried to reverse again. She thought she made a little progress but, again, the SUV couldn't pass a certain point.

She went through the same process several times until her father finally stopped her. "You're only making things worse," he said. "Face it. With that incline, this thing doesn't have the horsepower, at least not in Reverse. We're going to need somebody to pull us out."

The boys had fallen silent in the back and she could tell they were beginning to grasp the seriousness of the situation.

It could be hours before someone came by. As the snow piled up, their tracks would quickly be wiped away.

She could still call for help. She could tell Beck how to find them. She reached for her purse and fumbled for her cell phone, scrolling through until she found his number.

She tried to connect but the call didn't go through that time, or the second time she tried.

"What's wrong?" her father asked.

"Why don't I have any service?" she wailed.

"Must be in one of the dead zones around here."

Naturally. It was just her luck to get stuck in one of the few places where she couldn't call for help. "What about yours, Dad?"

"I didn't bring it."

"Why on earth not?"

He didn't answer for a long moment, then shrugged. "What's the point? You know I can't work that damn thing very well."

He could barely hold it in his trembling hands. Hitting the numbers was even harder. She had tried to coach him through speech-to-text methods but he couldn't quite master it.

It wouldn't make much difference. They had the same carrier. If she didn't have service, he likely wouldn't, either.

That gave her very few options.

"In that case, I don't see a choice," she said after a moment of considering them. "I better head to the Broken Arrow for help. Jax and Dan are there. Somebody should be able to pull us out with the one of the ranch tractors."

"You can't wander around in that storm. Just wait here. Beck will be home soon."

"Yes, but all the people he was taking home live south of here, which means he'll likely be coming to the ranch from the other direction. He won't even pass this way."

"When he sees the boys haven't made it home, don't you think he'll come looking for us?"

"Probably." That did make sense and provided some comfort to the worry and grave sense of responsibility she was feeling for the others in her vehicle. "The problem is, he might be shuttling multiple groups of people home. I have no idea how long he'll be at it, and to be honest, I don't feel good about waiting here, Dad. The snow keeps piling up and the temperature is dropping. I need to get you and the twins home where it's safe. The fastest way to do that is to walk to the ranch house. It can't be far. I can be there and back with help in no time."

"I don't like it."

What else was new? She could write a book about the things her father didn't like about her, apparently.

"I'm sorry, but right now I have bigger things to worry about than your opinion of me," she said, more sharply than she intended.

Curt opened his mouth, then closed it again. Good. She didn't have time to argue with him.

"I need you to stay here with the boys and watch over them. I have a full tank of gas. I'll make sure there's no snow obstructing the exhaust, so no worries about carbon monoxide building up inside. You should be fine to keep the engine running and the heater on."

"We can come with you," Colter said.

She had no doubt that the boys would be able to keep up with her. Her father, on the other hand, would not, and she didn't want to leave him here alone.

Torn, she gazed at all three of them. She didn't want to go out into that storm but she didn't dare take her chances of Beck miraculously just stumbling onto them. From the road above, they would be impossible to spot once the snow obscured their tracks, especially with that blowing wind and poor visibility.

This was serious, she realized. This country could be unforgiving and harsh and she would have to draw on all her reserves of strength to help them get through this.

"I need you boys to stay here where it's warm. Do what my dad says, okay? I'll be back shortly."

"Here. Take my coat. It's heavier than yours," Curt said gruffly.

"Mine is plenty warm. You might need yours. I will take the flashlight in the glove box, though."

She reached across him to get it out, grateful she had changed the batteries to fresh ones a few weeks earlier.

"In the back, there's a bag filled with bottled water, some granola bars and a couple of emergency blankets. You're probably not going to need them, but you should know about them, just in case."

"You're prepared," her father said, surprise in his voice.

"I have a father who taught me well about the harshness of Idaho winters."

She wanted to tell him she could learn all sorts of things, if only he were willing to teach her, but this wasn't the time to rehash that argument.

"Sounds like a smart man," he said after a moment.

"About some things, anyway," she said tartly.

Focused on the job at hand, she wrapped her scarf around her face and buttoned up her coat. "I'm going to give you my phone. You don't have cell service here but if I'm not back in a timely manner, you can try climbing up the incline and see if you have better service up there. Give me half an hour to get help first, though. I would rather you didn't leave the vehicle."

After a tense moment, her father finally nodded. "Be careful. I've only got the one daughter, and I'm fairly fond of her."

His words made tears thicken in her throat. Why did he have to be so stubborn?

"I'll be careful. You, too. See you in a little bit." She paused. "I love you, Dad."

She climbed out of the vehicle and whatever he said in response was snatched away by the howling wind that bit through her clothing and stung her face like a thousand knives.

She slipped several times as she tried to make it up the slight hill. Her boots were lined and warm but they weren't meant for heavy-duty hiking, more for walking through the snowy streets of Boston.

By the time she made it back to the road, she was already out of breath and perspiring inside her coat. She stood for a moment to catch her bearings. Everything was disorienting. White upon white upon white.

Fear was heavy on her shoulders. This was serious, she thought again. She had heard horror stories of people being lost in blizzards, their frozen corpses only found months later. Perhaps she would have been better off staying in the car.

But even now, knowing it was just below her, she could hardly see her SUV. Someone with no idea what had happened to them would never find it.

She headed off in the direction of the ranch house, tucking her chin in against the wind, praying she didn't miss his driveway and struggling step by step through the deepening snow.

It was much harder going than she had imagined, but she remained solely focused on doing what she had to, to save her father and the twins.

Shouldn't she have found the ranch road by now?

Panic began to flutter through her. She had to be close, but where was it? She couldn't even see the roadway anymore. She was almost certain she was still on it, but what if she wasn't? What if she had somehow taken a wrong turn and was somehow heading in the wrong direction? She would die out here—and her father and the twins would eventually run out of gas and would freeze to death, too.

What had she done? She should never have trusted her instincts. She should have stayed in the SUV with Curt and the twins. Had she doomed them all?

The panic ratcheted up and she tried frantically to see if she could find a light, a landmark, anything. All she could see was white.

Dear God, she prayed. *Please help me.*

The only answer was the constant whine of the wind churning the snow around her.

She had to keep moving. This had to be the way. There. Was that a light? She peered through the darkness to a spot set back from the road about the correct distance to be the Broken Arrow ranch house.

Was that the log arch over his driveway? She thought so but couldn't quite be sure. Instinct had her moving in that direction, when suddenly a dark shape again loomed out of the darkness.

Ella's instinctive scream tangled in her throat as the dark shape trotted closer. In her flashlight's glow, she suddenly recognized the calm, familiar features of an old friend.

She had never been so very grateful to see another living soul.

"Creampuff! What are you doing out here?" Ella exclaimed. At her voice, the horse ambled closer.

She must have somehow gotten out. She remembered the boys telling her the horse could be an escape artist. Why on earth would she have chosen this particular moment to get out?

Was Creampuff the thing she had almost hit on the road, the shape that had frightened her into hitting the brakes and sliding off the road?

Ella didn't like the consequences, but she was very grateful she hadn't hit the horse.

"You shouldn't be out here," she said to the horse. "It's dangerous."

Creampuff whickered and nudged at her. She seemed happy to see Ella, too.

She suddenly had an idea. It was completely impractical, but if it worked, it might be the answer to her current dilemma.

The storm was so disorienting, she was worried that she would end up miles from her destination. What were the chances that the horse could get her to Beckett's ranch house?

It was worth a try. Better than wandering aimlessly out here on her own. The only trick would be mounting up without a saddle, stirrups or reins—especially when she could barely manage it when she had all those necessary items.

The horse would lead her back to the barn on the Broken Arrow. Somehow she knew it.

If she wanted to save her father and the twins, she had to try.

Chapter Thirteen

"What the hell do you mean, they're not here? They left forty-five minutes before I did!"

Beckett stared at his brother, fear settling like jagged shards of ice in his gut.

"I don't know what to tell you. Nobody is here but Dan and me. We haven't seen a soul. Maybe she took them to her ranch house instead."

Wouldn't she have called him if her plans had changed? He couldn't believe she would simply abscond with his children with no word.

Those ice shards twisted. "Something's wrong."

"You don't know that," Jax said, his tone placating.

"I do. Something's wrong. They should have been here half an hour ago. They're in trouble."

Jax started to look concerned. "Before you run off, why don't you try to call them?"

Good idea. "You call the Baker's Dozen. I'll try their cell phones."

He dialed Curt's first and it went immediately to voice mail. He left a short message, telling the man to call him when he heard the message, then tried Ella's. It rang twice and he thought it would be connected but it shortly went to voice mail, too.

"No answer at the ranch," Jax said. He was beginning to look concerned, as well.

Beck had just spent an hour driving through these terrible conditions. He knew how bad it was out there—just as he knew Ella and her father had left with the boys well before he could load his first group of senior citizens into his vehicle to take them home.

Something was wrong. He knew it in his bones.

He hung up the phone after leaving her a terse message, as well, then faced his brother.

"I'm going to look for them. Call me if they show up."

Jax was smart enough to know when to not argue. He nodded. "What do you need me to do?"

"Stay in touch. For now, that's all."

He rushed out the door, doing his best to ignore the panic. He knew what could happen under these conditions. A few years ago, a rancher up north of them had gotten lost in a blizzard like this and ended up freezing to death just a few feet from his own back door.

The storm hadn't abated a whit in the few minutes he'd been inside. It whistled down through the mountains like a wild banshee. This was going to be one hell of a white Christmas. No doubt about it. He wouldn't be surprised if they ended up with at least two or three feet out of one storm, with much deeper drifts in spots from that wind.

He headed down the long, winding driveway, his heart in his throat and a prayer on his lips.

He had just started down the driveway when his headlights flashed on something dark and massive heading straight for him. If he had been going any faster, he would have inevitably hit it. As it was, he had to tap his brakes, even in four-wheel-drive low, to come to a stop.

It was a horse, he realized as he muscled the truck to a stop and his eyes adjusted to the shifting light conditions.

A horse carrying a rider!

What in the world? Who would be crazy enough to go riding on a night like tonight?

He yanked open his door and stepped out of his truck, boots crunching in calf-high snow, even though Jax had already cleared the driveway once that night.

"Beck! Oh, Beck. I'm so happy to see you!"

"Ella!" he exclaimed.

She jumped off of the horse and slipped to the ground and an instant later, she was in his arms. He didn't know if he had surged forward or if she had rushed to him, but he held her tightly as she trembled violently in the cold.

"What's happened?" he demanded. "Where are the boys?"

Her voice trembled. "I—I slid into a ditch back on the r-road. I don't know how far b-back. I thought it was closer b-but it seemed like f-forever that I w-walked."

"Why were you walking in the first place? Why didn't you call me to come find you?"

"I t-tried. I didn't have cell service. We're off the

road, out of sight. E-even if someone t-tried to find us, they wouldn't be able to. I—I knew I had to f-find help, but I think I must have been lost or missed the road or something. I was panicking but I—I prayed and suddenly Creampuff appeared."

She shivered out a sob that made his arms tighten around her. For just a moment, she rested her cheek against him and he wanted to stay keep her safe and warm in his arms forever.

"It f-felt like some kind of m-miracle."

She was a miracle. She was amazing. If she hadn't faced her fear of horses, she might be wandering out there still. Somehow she had found the strength to climb on a horse without tack or saddle and made her way here, to him.

What would he have done if Creampuff hadn't found her, if she was still wandering around out there, lost in the storm?

He couldn't bear to think about it. If anything had happened to her, it would shatter him. His arms tightened as the feelings he had been fighting for weeks burst to the surface.

He shoved them back down, knowing this wasn't the time or the place to deal with them.

"You're frozen. Let's get you up to the house."

"No! I—I have to show you where to find my dad and the boys. You'll never see my car from the road."

She was so certain of that, he had to accept she was right. "At least hop inside the truck while I put Creampuff in the barn. Jax can take care of her. She deserves extra oats after tonight."

He helped her inside his cab—something he should have done the moment she hopped off that horse, he realized with self-disgust. The heater was blasting and he found the emergency blanket behind the seat and tucked it around her.

"We have to hurry."

"We will. This will only take a moment, I promise."

He closed the door and called his brother as he led the heroic Creampuff toward the barn, thirty yards away.

"Need my help?"

"Maybe. Not yet. Take care of Creampuff for me and give her all the crab apples she wants right now. I'll stay in touch."

He hurried back out to his truck through the storm, trying not to think about how very close they had come to a tragedy he couldn't bear to think about.

Ella had never been so cold, despite the blanket and the blessed warmth pouring full-blast from the heater of Beck's pickup. Occasional shivers still racked her body and Beck continued casting worried looks her way.

"How much farther?" he asked.

She peered out the window at the landscape that seemed familiar but not familiar. Everything was white, blurred by blowing snow.

She recognized that fence line there, and the curve ahead, and knew they had to be close but she could see no sign of her SUV.

"There!" she suddenly exclaimed. "Down there, just ahead. See the glow of my taillights?"

He tapped his brakes and brought the truck to a stop. "Wow. You were right. There are no tracks left on the road and it's well out of view from up here. If you hadn't pointed it out, I would have missed it."

"The engine is still running. I had a full tank of gas so they should have had enough for a few more hours."

He opened his door and frowned when she opened hers, too. "Ella, stay here. You're still half-frozen. I'll get them."

She shook her head. "Dad's going to need help getting up that little slope. It might take both of us."

Her father had grown so frail this past year that she suspected Beck could carry the other man up the slope over his shoulder in a fireman's carry without even having to catch his breath, but after a moment he nodded.

"I'm sorry you'll have to go out in the cold again."

"Only temporarily. I'll be okay."

She opened her door before he could argue further and climbed out, then headed down the slight slope to her snow-covered SUV.

The door opened before she could reach it and her father stuck his head out.

"Ella? Is that you?" he called, peering into the snowy darkness.

"Yes."

"Oh, thank heavens. I've been worried sick," he exclaimed.

With good reason, she acknowledged. She could have died out there—and there was a very good chance her father and the boys might have, too, before help could arrive.

"I brought Beck."

"I knew you could do it."

"How are the boys?" she asked as she reached the vehicle, with Beck right behind her.

"See for yourself," her father said. "They're sound asleep."

Sure enough, the boys were cuddled together under one of her emergency blankets.

Colter was the first one to open his eyes. He blinked at her sleepily, then his gaze caught his father, just behind her.

"Hey, Dad!" Colter smiled. "I think I fell asleep."

"Looks like it. We'll get you to the truck and then home in no time."

"Okay." He yawned, then shook his brother awake. Trevor looked just as happy to see both of them. Neither boy seemed the worse for wear after their ordeal.

"Boys, let's get you back to the truck. It's probably better if I carry you, since your cowboy boots aren't the best for snow. Ella, why don't you stay here where it's warm for a few moments?"

She wanted to offer to take one of the boys and then come back down to help her father, but she wasn't sure she would have the strength to make that trip twice more.

"Me first," Trevor said.

Beck scooped him up onto his back and Ella slid into his warm spot as they headed up the slope. In seconds, the still-blowing snow obscured their shapes from view.

"You guys did okay?" she asked Colter.

He nodded. "You were gone a long time."

"I know. I'm sorry. I had some complications."

"We sang just about every song we knew, then Mr. Baker told us stories about Christmas when he was a kid."

He started reciting a few of the stories, one she remembered her father telling her and another that seemed new. Maybe Curt had told it to her once, but it had been lost along with everything else the summer she was eight.

It seemed like forever but had probably been only two or three minutes when Beck opened the door. "Okay, kid. You're next."

He repeated the process with Colter, leaving her alone with her father.

"You sure you're okay?" Curt said, his voice gruff.

"I got lost. You were right. I probably should have stayed with you until the help arrived."

"That's funny. I was about to say *you* were right. Nobody would have found us until morning, when it would have been too late."

She was spared from having to imagine all the grim possibilities when Beck opened the door.

"Turn off your engine and bring along the key."

"What about my SUV?"

"Jax and I can come down and pull it out after I get you home."

She nodded and did as he said, hoping he would be able to find it again without the gleam of the taillights to light the way.

"I wish I could give you a piggyback ride, too," Beck said to her father.

"I'll be fine. I just need a little support."

In the end, Beck all but carried her father, anyway. She was deeply grateful for his solid strength but also for the gentle way he tried to spare her father's pride as he helped him into the truck's passenger seat. Once he was settled, Ella slipped into the back seat of the crew cab pickup with the boys and Beck headed for the Baker's Dozen, driving with slow care.

Just before he reached their turnoff, she heard her

phone's ringtone distantly. It took her a moment to remember it was in her father's pocket. He fumbled with it but finally managed to pull it out. Before he could hand it over, Curt checked out the display with the caller ID.

"It's Manny. Wonder why he's calling you?"

"Maybe because you usually leave your cell phone at home," she replied, reaching over the seat for her phone.

"Do you know where your padre is?" the foreman asked as soon as she answered. "Is he with you?"

"Yes. We've had a rough evening but should be home soon. Beck is bringing us."

"He can't. Turn around."

"Turn around? Why?"

"You can't get through. One of the big pines along the driveway blew over in the wind and there's no way around it. It's a good thing nobody was driving under it when it fell."

"What's going on?" Beck asked, coming to a slow stop just before the turn.

"The driveway is blocked. We won't be able to get through."

Could this evening get any worse? First she ran off the road, now they were stranded away from home.

"Okay. No problem," Beck answered. "You can just come back to the Broken Arrow with us. I'll feel better about that, anyway."

"Will you be okay for tonight?" Manny asked.

"I suppose," she answered, though she dreaded the prospect. "What about you?" she asked the foreman. "You're stuck on the ranch."

"We're fine. We have plenty of food and so far the electricity is still on. I can take care of everything up here, as long as I know the two of you are safe and have a place to sleep."

"Thanks, Manny. Be safe."

"Same to you."

She hung up. "I guess we're spending the night at the Broken Arrow, if that's okay with you."

"Just fine."

He turned the pickup around slowly and began inching back to his own ranch.

"Dad, what about your prescriptions?" Ella asked, as the thought suddenly occurred to her.

"I took my evening pills before I went to the show, since I wasn't sure what time we'd be back. I'll be fine."

"You're staying at our house?" Trevor asked, excitement in his voice.

"You can have our beds," Colter offered. "Only someone will have to sleep on the top bunk."

"We have plenty of space," Beckett assured them. "We don't have to kick anybody out of bed. We've got a couple spare bedrooms and a comfortable sofa in the family room. You're more than welcome, and in the morning we can head over with chainsaws and clear a path."

"Thank you," she murmured. She really didn't want to spend the night at his house, but unless she wanted to take another merciless trudge through that storm, she didn't see that they had any choice.

"Are you sure you're okay, Dad? Is there anything else I can get you?"

An hour later, she stood in a comfortable guest room with a leather recliner, a wide bed and a flat-screen TV. Her father was already stretched out on the bed with a remote and a glass of water. He wore his own shirt and a pair of pajama bottoms borrowed from Beck's uncle.

She wore another pair, but they were about six sizes too big, baggy and long.

"I don't think so. I haven't been this tired in a long time. I'm probably going to crash the minute the news is over."

If not before. Curt had become good at dozing off while the television still played.

"All right. Good night." She leaned in to kiss his stubbly cheek. As she turned to go, she was surprised when Curt reached his trembling fingers out to touch her arm.

"I didn't say this earlier, but… I was proud of you tonight."

Her father's unexpected words sent a soft warmth seeping through her. "Thank you. I'm happy you enjoyed the program, but it was the children who did all the work."

"I'm not talking about the show, though that was excellent, too. I meant later. When you went to find help. You risked your life for me and those twins of Beckett's. I was never more proud to call you my daughter."

He gave her arm a squeeze and she looked down, wanting to wrap his liver-spotted, trembling fingers in hers and tuck them against her cheek.

"I can do all sorts of things, if you only give me the chance," she said softly.

His hand stiffened and he pulled it away. "You're talking about running the ranch again."

Stupid. She wanted to kick herself. Why bring up a point of contention and ruin what had been a rare, lovely, peaceful moment between them?

"Yes. I am talking about running the ranch. I want to. Why won't you even give me the chance?"

To her chagrin, her voice wobbled on the last word. Exhaustion, she told herself. Still, she couldn't seem to hold back the torrent of emotions. "No matter what I do, you can't see me as anything but the silly girl who fell off a horse."

"You were in a coma for weeks. You nearly died."

"But I didn't! I survived."

"More than that," he said gruffly. "You thrived, especially after your mother took you away from here."

She stared, speechless at his words. "Is that what you think?" she asked, when she could trust her voice. "That I only thrived because Mom took me back to Boston? I grieved every day I was away. I love it here, Dad. I came back, didn't I?"

"To care for a feeble old man. Not because you belong here."

"The ranch is part of me, no matter what you say."

"So is Boston! You have a life there. I can't ask you to give up everything that's important to you. You love music—the opera, the symphony. Not J. D. Wyatt and his Warbling Wranglers. You belong to a different world."

"Yes, I love those things you mentioned. But I also love J.D. and George Jones and Emmylou Harris. The music you and I listened to together. Why can't I have both? Why do I have to choose?"

He appeared struck by this, his brow furrowed as he considered her words. She didn't know what might be different this time, when they had had similar arguments before, but something she said seemed to be trickling through his stubbornness.

"Honey, you don't know anything about running the ranch." She might have been imagining it, but his voice sounded a little less certain.

"You can teach me, Dad. I've been telling you that for months. There's no better time than now. I want to learn from you, while you're still here to teach me. This is my heritage, half of what makes me who I am. I don't understand why you can't see that."

He appeared struck by her words and she decided to quit while she was ahead. Perhaps she had given him something to think about—but why should this time make the difference when all those other times hadn't?

"I don't want to fight with you, Dad. It's been a long day. Can we agree to focus on the holidays and talk about this again after Christmas?"

"That sounds like a good idea." Her father paused. "I love you, you know. No matter what else you think. I love you and I've always been proud of you."

Tears welled up in her throat at this hard, stubborn man she had considered her hero all of her life. "I love you, too, Dad. Get some rest."

Beck slipped into his own room across the hall as he heard her last words and realized she would be coming out at any moment. He didn't want her to leave her father's guest room and find him standing outside the door.

He hadn't meant to eavesdrop, had only been there to check on his guests and see if they needed anything. The slightly raised voices had drawn his attention and he stopped, not wanting to walk in on an argument between Ella and her father.

This is my heritage, half of what makes me who I am. I don't understand why you can't see that.

Her words seemed to howl through his mind like that wind, resonating with truth.

He couldn't buy the ranch out from under her.

Beck leaned against his bedpost as the assurance settled deep in his chest. On paper, purchasing the Baker's Dozen was the smart play. He needed to expand his own operations and grow the Broken Arrow and it made perfect sense to merge the two ranches.

A month ago, he would have jumped at the chance without a second thought, assuming Ella had no interest in ranching and would be happy to take the money and run back to Boston.

He knew better now. He knew her hopes and her dreams and her yearnings. He had seen her face when they went on that ride into the backcountry as she looked at her family's land from the foothills. He had watched her tackle her own fear of horses in order to prove her own mettle. He had seen the courage she showed during a blizzard, her willingness to put her own comfort and safety at risk to help those she loved.

Her heart would break if Curt sold the ranch out from under her.

Beck couldn't do that to her.

He loved her too much.

The truth seemed to blow through him with all the impact of that storm rattling the windows of his room, crashing over him as if he were standing directly under the big pine that had fallen on the Baker's Dozen.

He loved Ella Baker.

He loved her sweetness, her grace, the gentle care she took with his sons. He loved her sense of humor and her grit and the soft, sexy noises she made when he kissed her.

He loved her.

What in heaven's name was he supposed to do about that now?

He assumed the normal course of action in this sort of situation would be to tell the woman in question about his feelings and see if she might share them—or at least see if she didn't reject them outright.

This wasn't a typical situation.

He thought of the precious gift she had helped his boys give him that day, the song that always touched him about a cowboy being alone on Christmas. He didn't want to be alone, like that cowboy. He wanted sweetness and warmth and a woman's smile, just for him.

He wanted Ella.

Did he have the courage to try again? His marriage had left him uncertain about his own instincts, completely aware of all the ways he had screwed up.

He couldn't afford to make a disastrous mistake like that again, but something told him with sweet certainty that allowing himself to love Ella could never be anything but perfect.

She filled his life with joy and wonder, reminded him of everything good and right in his world.

His boys loved her, too. They had thrived under her loving care, in a way he hadn't seen them do with anyone else. Somehow, she had managed to reach them, to sand away a few of their rough edges.

They needed that in their lives. *He* did, too.

Could he find the strength and courage to overlook

all the ugliness of his past to build a brighter future with Ella?

As he stood in his bedroom with the storm raging outside, he wasn't sure he knew the answer to that.

He still hadn't figured it out an hour later as he finally settled the boys for the night and closed the door to their room, confident they were finally asleep.

The combined excitement of their stellar performance at the Christmas show, being trapped in a snowbank during the blizzard and then having their favorite teacher staying in their house seemed to have made sleep elusive, but exhaustion at last had claimed them.

It was late, past midnight, but they could sleep in the next day. He had already received an alert that school would be canceled tomorrow because of the storm, still raging throughout the region. It hadn't surprised him. Nobody would be able to get through on the roads out there until at least noon or later.

He needed to sleep, too. The next day was bound to be a busy one and would start early.

Like his sons, though, he felt too wired to sleep. He had a feeling that if he tried to climb into bed now, he would only toss and turn.

His thoughts were in tumult and he still didn't know what to do about Ella and his feelings for her. Meantime, he decided to grab a drink of water and maybe one of those cookies a neighbor brought over earlier, then head into his ranch office to catch up on paperwork.

He was heading through the great room toward the kitchen when he spotted someone sitting in the darkness, just out of reach of the glow emanating from the

Christmas tree and the dying embers of the fire burning in the hearth.

His gaze sharpened when he realized it was Ella. He had almost missed her.

Had she fallen asleep out here? Her day had been more strenuous than anyone's, between orchestrating that amazing performance earlier, then rescuing her father and the boys.

What was she doing out here? Was she all right?"

Her face was in shadows but he thought he glimpsed the streak of tears on her cheeks, reflecting the colored Christmas lights. As he moved closer, she must have sensed his presence. She looked up then quickly away but not before he was able to confirm his suspicion.

She was crying.

"Oh. You startled me." She swiped her cheeks and kept her face averted, obviously trying to hide them from him. He was torn between wanting to respect her obvious desire for privacy and being unable to bear the thought of her hurting.

Finally he sat beside her on the sofa. "El. What is it? What's wrong?"

"Nothing. I'm fine. It's just…been a long day."

"You need to be in bed. Why are you sitting out here by yourself?" *Crying*, he added silently.

She sighed. "Do you ever have those times when it feels like your mind is spinning so fast you can't keep up with it?"

"All the time. If it's not the ranch I'm worrying about, it's the boys or Jax or Uncle Dan."

Or her father, he wanted to add, but didn't want to upset her more. Most likely, that conversation with Curt was the reason for these tears.

He couldn't bear them, especially when he had the ability to dry them right here, right now.

"Ella, I don't—"

"Beck, I have to—"

They started to speak at the same time, then both faltered. After an awkward little moment, she gestured to him. "It's your house. You first."

He wanted to argue, but couldn't see any point. Better to tell her what was on his mind as quickly as he could.

"You should know, I've decided to tell your father I won't be purchasing the Baker's Dozen."

Her eyes looked huge in the multicolored light from the tree as she stared at him. "You *what*?"

"It was early days in the discussions between us. Whatever you heard today when he and I were talking, nothing has been signed. There's no breach of contract or anything. So I'm officially backing out. I won't buy it."

"But… I don't understand. I thought you needed the watering rights and the pasture land to expand your operations."

"I do. I will, someday, but I'll figure something out when the need is more critical."

"Why?"

He needed to expand the Broken Arrow, but he couldn't do it in good conscience by buying her father's land out from under her.

"You should be running your family's ranch, Ella."

She made a disbelieving sound and though he feared it might be a mistake, he reached for her hand. "You are perfectly capable. You've got exactly all the traits it takes to make a go of things out here. You're tough, spunky and bold. You're willing to learn and you're not afraid to ask for help when you need it. You've shown all those things, again and again. Your father knows it, too—it's just taking him longer than it should to admit it."

Her fingers trembled in his as if she were still cold, and he wanted to wrap her in his arms until her shivering ceased.

"I don't understand," she finally said.

"What's to understand? I'm withdrawing my tentative agreement to purchase the property. It's yours. Curt can show you how to run it, just like he helped me figure things out here after my father died. If he doesn't, *I* will show you the ropes and find other local ranchers to do the same. Wade Dalton. Chase and Faith Brannon. Justin Hartford. You have good neighbors who will want nothing more than to see you succeed."

In the light of the Christmas tree, he saw something bright and joyful flash across her expression—hope and an eagerness to prove herself. For one beautiful instant, she looked exactly what she was, strong and capable of anything.

That's why he was doubly shocked after a moment when she pulled her hand away from his and rose as if to put space between them.

"I don't think I can do that."

"Why not? There's not a single doubt in my mind you'll make a go of it, with or without your father's help."

She gave him one quick look, her lips pressed together and her chin quivering, then she shook her head.

"I…can't. I'm not staying here. I've made up my mind to return to Boston right after Christmas."

Shock tangled his thoughts and his words. Had he misheard her? Not an hour ago, she had pleaded with her father to give her a chance at running the Baker's Dozen and now she was turning tail and taking off? What in Hades had happened?

"Why would you do that? I just told you that I won't be making an offer on the ranch—and I'll make sure nobody else around here does, either. There won't be much I can do about things if Curt decides to sell to an outsider, but I don't think that's what your dad wants, anyway."

As he watched, another tear dripped down her cheek, iridescent in the Christmas tree lights.

"I can't do it," she whispered.

"Are you kidding me? You can do any damn thing you put your mind to. You tamed the twin terrors, didn't you?"

He meant his words as a joke. It seemed to fall flat and she hitched in a breath that sounded more like a sob.

"That's why I…can't stay. Because of the boys and—and you."

Another tear dripped. He couldn't bear this. What had he done to offend her so grievously that she couldn't even stand to stay in the same county with him? He would fix it, whatever it was.

He rose. "I'm sorry. You're going to have to forgive me for being a big, dumb cowboy, but I don't know what the heck you're talking about."

She didn't answer him for several moments, the only sound the relentless wind and the click of branches from the red-twigged dogwoods outside the window.

Finally she swallowed. "I have come to…care deeply for—for Trevor and Colter. I don't see how I could continue to live here, always stuck on the edges of your, er, *their* lives. Just the nice neighbor who once taught them how to sing a song for their dad. I don't want that. I—I want more."

He couldn't catch his breath, suddenly. She was talking about the boys, right? Or did she mean something else? "Ella."

She didn't meet his gaze. "I'm sorry. Forget I said anything. I shouldn't have. It's late and I'm tired and not thinking straight. I'll go to bed now."

She tried to slip past him but he couldn't let her. Not yet. He blocked her path, never more grateful for his size than he was in that moment. "Stop. What are you saying?"

"It doesn't matter."

He tipped up her chin, until she had no choice but to look at him, his strong, amazing Ella. "I think it matters more than anything else in my world right now."

Her mouth wobbled a little again, then tightened with belligerence. "Do you want me to completely humiliate myself? Why not? I've already made a complete fool of myself. Fine. I'll say it. I'm in love with you. Are you happy now?"

She hadn't finished the words before he kissed her fiercely, pouring out all the emotions he had been fighting for weeks. Months, he realized. He had fallen for her when she first came back to Pine Gulch to stay with her father, he just hadn't been able to admit it to himself until now.

He kissed her until they were both breathing hard and the room was beginning to spin and he wasn't sure he would ever be able to bring himself to move from this spot.

"Does that answer your question?" he finally asked against her mouth. Joy continued to pulse through him, bright and shining and as beautiful as any Christmas tree. "*Happy* doesn't begin to cover how I feel to know the woman I love with all my heart shares a little of my feelings."

She stared at him, shock warring with the arousal in her eyes. "You love me? That's impossible."

"Need another demonstration?" He kissed her again, this time with a sweet, aching tenderness he felt from the depths of his soul. He lowered them to the sofa and held her on his lap, teasing and touching and tasting.

"I guess that wasn't really an answer, was it?" he murmured, after another long moment. "Kisses are wonderful, don't get me wrong, but any guy who's attracted to you—which would have to be every sane guy with a pulse—could give you those."

She swallowed, her hands tangled in his hair and her lips swollen from his mouth. "That's right." Her voice sounded thready, low, and made him ache all over again. "You'll have to be more persuasive than that if you expect me to believe you want me and not my father's ranch."

He tightened his arms around her, loving this playful side of her. As he gazed at her eyes reflecting the lights of the Christmas tree, he thought that he had never loved the holidays so very much as he did right now, with his own Christmas miracle in his arms.

"I stand by what I said before. I don't want the Baker's Dozen, and I'll be sure to tell Curt that as soon as I get the chance. We can go wake him up, if you want."

"You really think I would be stupid enough to want to wake my father up right now? I'm a little busy here," she said, pressing her mouth to his jawline in a way that made his breath catch and everything inside him want to slide over her to show her just what her teasing did to him.

He gazed into her eyes, hoping she could see he meant his words. "Curt will come to his senses. I'll make sure of it. As far as I'm concerned, that ranch is yours, to do with as you see fit. If you want to sell all the cattle and start raising alpacas, that's your business."

Beck decided he wouldn't mind spending the rest of his life trying to make that soft, sweet smile appear again.

"I do love alpacas," she murmured. "They're so much cuter than cattle—and think of all the adorable Christmas sweaters I could make out of their wool."

"I can picture it now. And to show you what a great guy I am, I would even let you take those sweaters off in my bedroom, if you wanted."

She laughed. "Wow. That's very generous of you."

This was what he had missed—what he had never really known. This laughter and tenderness, this binding of his heart to hers. It seemed perfect and easy and absolutely right.

He kissed her once more, wishing they could stay here all night wrapped together by the fire and the Christmas tree while the storm raged outside.

"I meant what I said earlier," she said a long time later. "I love you and I love the boys. I wasn't expecting it, but you McKinley men are pretty hard to resist."

"We do our best," he drawled.

His sons would be over the moon to know their not-so-subtle matchmaking had paid off. He hoped that didn't set a dangerous precedent. Maybe he should warn

Jax he had better watch out, or they might turn their attention to him next.

On second thought, Jax was a big boy. He could fend for himself.

He gazed down at her, unable to believe she was really here in his arms. He would never need another Christmas gift as long as he lived. This moment, this night, this woman were beyond his wildest dreams.

He turned serious, compelled to tell her a small portion of what was in his heart. "I love you, Ella. I hope you know that. I wasn't expecting it, either, but nothing has ever felt so right. I love your strength and your courage. I love how sweet you are with my sons. I love that you sacrificed to come back to Pine Gulch and take care of your father, though he's given you nothing but grief in return."

He kissed her again, his heart overflowing with joy and wonder and gratitude. "Most of all, I love that whenever you're near me, I could swear I hear music."

She gave that slow, tender smile he was quickly coming to crave, wrapped her arms around him and let the song carry both of them away.

Epilogue

"I don't know how you did it, but somehow that show was even bigger and better than last year's," Ella's father said as Beck drove away from The Christmas Ranch after her third successful Christmas show in a row.

"You'd better dial it back a bit, babe," her husband said, with that teasing smile she adored. "Everybody's got such high expectations now, you're going to find yourself having to throw a Broadway-quality production in order to meet them."

"I still think last year's show was better," Trevor said from the back seat. "This year Colt and me didn't even get to sing a duet together."

"No, but you played your guitar while all your friends sang 'We Three Kings,'" she answered. "You guys brought down the house, kiddo."

"We were awesome, weren't we?" he said, with that complete lack of humility that always made her smile.

"Hey, Grandpa Curt, what was your favorite part this year?" Colt asked.

Ella knew it always tickled her dad when the boys called him Grandpa Curt, as they had taken to doing since her and Beck's wedding over the summer.

They still usually called her Ella, but had recently asked if she would mind if they called her Mom once in a while. She still teared up every time they did.

As she listened to the twins chatter away to her father, Ella leaned back in the seat and closed her eyes, a wave of fatigue washing over her. The adrenaline rush of finishing a performance was always exhausting, but this seemed to be hitting her harder than usual.

She knew why. After two weeks of achy breasts, mild nausea in the mornings and this unusual fatigue, she'd taken a drugstore test that morning that confirmed her suspicions.

She still hadn't told Beck yet. She was trying to figure out exactly how. Maybe she would wait until Christmas Eve and tell him during their own private celebrations after everyone was in bed and the house was quiet.

Or maybe she would do it tonight. She didn't know how to contain this joy that bubbled through her.

However she told him, she knew Beck would be as happy as she was about adding to their family.

As he drove them toward home, he reached for her hand and brought it to his mouth. He was a big, tough rancher, but every once in a while he did these sweet, spontaneous gestures that completely swept her off her feet.

"You've had quite a day."

She smiled, eyes still closed. "Quite a year, actually."

"It has been amazing, hasn't it?"

Amazing was an understatement. A year ago, she never would have believed her life could be filled with this much joy.

Somehow they were making it work. Shortly after the New Year, her father had finally come to his senses—persuaded in large part by Beck, she knew—and started giving her more and more responsibility at the Baker's Dozen. As of now, she and Curt were comanaging the ranch. She envisioned a day when she and Beck would merge the two operations, as her father intended, but for now the system worked.

She still taught at the elementary school but had surrendered her middle school choir to another teacher.

She even had a small but growing herd of alpacas. The first breeding pair had been Beck's surprise wedding gift to her and she had added three more since then, plus the new offspring of the first pair. She adored them all and had become obsessed with learning all she could about alpaca husbandry.

"Hey, remember last year, when we had that big storm?" Colter said.

"Yeah, and we slid into the ditch and had to wait while you went for help?" Trevor added.

Her journey through the storm had become something of a family legend. Creampuff had earned crab apples for life because of her heroic rescue. Ella still rode her often, as well as the younger, more energetic mare she and Beck had picked out.

"There's the spot, right there," Curt said.

Though it had been a harrowing experience, Ella always smiled when she passed this spot. It had been such a pivotal moment in her life, she would have liked to put a little commemorative plaque on a nearby tree.

A short time later, they pulled up to the ranch house of the Baker's Dozen.

"Can we go see the cria while we're here?" Colter asked.

Cria was the official word for an alpaca baby and her new one was the most adorable thing in the world.

Her father complained the animals were a waste of space, but she couldn't count the number of times she'd caught him sitting by their paddock, just watching them play.

"Sure. Check their water for me while you're there, okay?"

The boys raced off through the cold night to the barn, where the alpaca sheltered in cold weather.

"Let's get you inside," Beck said to her father.

As he helped her father out of the truck, her heart seemed to sigh inside her chest. Every time she saw him offer this kind of patient, gentle care for her father, she fell in love all over again.

Curt's health issues had been the one gray cloud in what had otherwise been a year overflowing with happiness. He was trying a new medicine, though, and so far it seemed to be slowing the progression of his Parkinson's and even reducing some of his trembling.

She knew it was a temporary improvement, but she would take whatever bright spot she could.

The lights were on in the house, which meant Manny and Alina had made it home before them. The ranch foreman and his wife had moved into the big house shortly after Ella's marriage, along with Alina's older brother,

Frank. Between the three of them, they took amazing care of Curt and he seemed to enjoy their company.

At some point, she anticipated that her father would end up moving into the Broken Arrow ranch house with them. He spent much of his time there, anyway, and having him closer would make it easier for her to keep an eye on him. For now, he treasured whatever small portion of independence he still had, and she tried to facilitate that as much as she could.

Now, she saw the Christmas lights were on inside and the Baker's Dozen ranch house was warm and welcoming.

"I'd better go make sure the boys don't try to ruin their good shoes," Beck said after he helped Curt inside.

"I can help you into your room, Dad," she said.

For the next few moments, she was busy easing his swollen feet out of the boots he insisted on wearing and taking off his coat.

"Manny or Frank can help me with the rest," he said.

"All right. I'm glad you came with us, Dad."

"So am I. It really was a great show."

She smiled. "Thanks. I'll be by first thing in the morning to meet with the vet."

Her father tilted his head and gave her a considering look. "You know you're not going to be able to juggle everything when you have that grandbaby of mine, don't you?"

She stared. "How did you know?"

His eyes widened for just a moment, then his expression shifted to a smirk. "You make a poor poker player, honey. That was just a lucky guess—or maybe wishful thinking on my part—but you just confirmed it."

"Don't say anything to Beck," she pleaded. "I haven't told him yet."

"I won't say a word," he promised, then paused. "You picked a good man, Ella."

She smiled. "You don't have to tell me that, Dad. I'll see you in the morning. And don't forget, we have the McRavens' annual party tomorrow night, remember?"

"You ask me, this town has too many damn parties," her father grumbled, though she knew he enjoyed every one of them.

"Good night. Love you."

When she returned to the living room, Beck and the boys had all come back inside and sat in the glow of the Christmas tree they had all decorated here a few Sundays ago. The twins were telling him a story about one of their friends and he nodded solemnly, his gorgeous, masculine features intense as he listened.

As she watched the three of them, her heart couldn't contain all the joy.

Her life was everything she might have wished for and so much more. She had a husband she adored and two stepsons who filled her world with laughter and Legos and tight hugs. She had music and horses, her father, her friends and now this new little life growing inside her.

This was the season of miracles and she would always be grateful for her own—and it had all started with a song.

* * * * *

If you loved this book, be sure to catch up with the Nichols sisters, Hope, Celeste and Faith, in the latest heartwarming holiday stories in
THE COWBOYS OF COLD CREEK
miniseries:

THE HOLIDAY GIFT
(Faith's story)

A COLD CREEK CHRISTMAS STORY
(Celeste's story)

THE CHRISTMAS RANCH
(Hope's story)

Available now wherever Harlequin Special Edition books and ebooks are sold!

THE COWBOY'S
CHRISTMAS MIRACLE

Chapter One

The brats were at it again.

Carson McRaven scowled as he drove under the massive, ornately carved log arch to the Raven's Nest Ranch.

He owned five thousand acres of beautiful eastern Idaho ranch land. A reasonable person might suppose that with that kind of real estate, he had a good chance of escaping Jenna Wheeler and her hell spawn.

Instead, it seemed like every time he turned around, some little towheaded imp was invading his space— sledding down his private driveway, bothering his horses, throwing snowballs at his ranch sign.

A month ago—the last time he had found time to come out to his new ranch from San Francisco—he had caught them trying to jump their swaybacked little paint ponies over his new electric fence. The time before, he had found them building a tree house in one of the trees on *his* property. And in September, he had ended up with a broken window in the gleaming new horse barn and his foreman had found a baseball amid the shattered glass inside.

He couldn't seem to turn around without finding one or more of them wandering around his land. They were three annoying little flies in the ointment of what would otherwise be the perfect bucolic retreat from the hectic corporate jungle of San Francisco.

When he bought the property from Jenna Wheeler, he thought he had been fine with her stipulation that she retain one twenty-acre corner of land for her ranch. He was getting five thousand acres more, bordered by National Forest land. One little nibble out of the vast pie shouldn't bother him. But in the ten months since they closed on the deal, that little nibble sat in his craw like an unshelled walnut.

Every time he drove up Cold Creek Canyon to Raven's Nest and spotted her two-story frame house in the corner of his land, he ground his back teeth and wished to hell he had fought harder to buy the whole property so he could have torn it down to have this entire area to himself.

And to make matters even more aggravating, apparently the Wheeler urchins didn't understand the concept of trespassing. Yes, their mother had paid for the broken window and had made them take the tree house down, plank by plank. After her frustrated reaction when he told her about their steeplechase through his pasture, he would have expected her to put the fear of God into them.

Or at least the fear of their mother.

But here one of them was balancing on the snow-covered split-rail fence that lined his driveway, arms outstretched like he was a miniature performer on a circus high wire, disaster just a heartbeat away while his brothers watched from the sidelines.

Carson slowed the SUV he kept stored at the Jackson Hole airport, an hour away, though he hesitated to hit the brakes just yet.

He ought to just let the kids fall where they may. What was a broken arm or two to him? If the Wheeler hellions wanted to be little daredevils, what business was it of his? He could just turn the other way and keep on driving up to the house. He had things to do, calls to make, fresh Idaho air to breathe.

On the other hand, the boys were using *his* fence as their playground. If one of them took a tumble and was seriously injured, he could just hear their mother accusing him of negligence or even tacit complicity because he didn't try to stop them when he had the chance.

He sighed. He couldn't ignore them and just keep on driving, as much as he might desperately want to. He braked to a stop and rolled down the window to the cold December air. "Hey kid, come down from there before somebody gets hurt."

He was grimly aware he was only a sidestep away from sounding like a grumpy old man yelling at the neighbor's kids to stay the hell off his grass.

The boys apparently hadn't heard the rumble of his engine. They blinked and he could see surprise in all their expressions. The younger two looked apprehensive but the biggest boy jutted out his chin.

"We do it all the time," he boasted. "Kip's the best. Show him."

"Maybe we should go home." The medium-sized one with the wire-rim glasses slanted a nervous look toward Carson. "Remember, Mom told us this morning to come home right from the bus stop to do chores."

"That's a good idea," Carson encouraged. "Go on home, now."

"Don't be such a scaredy-cat," the older one taunted, then turned to the other boy, who was watching their interaction closely, as if trying to predict who the victor would be. "It's okay, Kip. Show him."

Before Carson could figure out a way to climb out of his truck and yank the kid off the fence, the boy took another step forward and then another.

He grinned at Carson. "See? I can go super far without falling!" he exclaimed. "One time I went from the gate all the way to that big pine tree."

The words were barely out of his mouth when his boot hit an icy patch of railing.

His foot slid to the edge though not completely off the log, but his arms wheeled desperately as he tried to keep his balance. It was a losing battle, apparently. His feet went flying off the fence first and the rest of him followed. Even from here, above the sound of his vehicle's engine, Carson could hear the thud of the boy's head bumping the log rail on the way down.

Damn it.

He shut off the vehicle and jumped out, hurrying to where the boy lay still in the snow. The middle boy was already crouched in the snow next to him, but his attention was focused more on his older brother than the injured younger one.

"You're such a dope, Hayden." He glared. "Why'd you make him do it? Mom's gonna kill us both now!"

"I didn't make him! He didn't have to do it just because I told him to. He's got a brain, doesn't he?"

"More of one than you do," the middle boy snapped.

Carson decided it was past time for him to step in and focus attention on the important thing, their dazed brother, who looked as if he'd had the wind and everything else knocked out of his sails.

"Come on, kid. Talk to me."

The boy met his gaze, his green eyes wide and a little unfocused. After a few seconds, he drew in a deep breath and then he started to wail, softly at first and then loud enough to spook up a couple of magpies that had come to see what the commotion was about.

"Come on, Kip. You're okay," the middle kid soothed, patting him on the shoulder, which only seemed to make the kid howl louder.

What Carson knew about bawling kids would fit inside the cap of a ballpoint pen. His instincts were telling him to hop right back into his SUV and leave the boys to fend for themselves. Knowing how rowdy and reckless they were, this couldn't be the first time one of them had taken a tumble.

But he couldn't do it. Not with the kid looking at him out of those drippy eyes and the other two watching him with such contrasting expressions—one hostile and the other obviously expecting him to take charge.

The boy swiped at his tears with the sleeve of his parka and scrambled to sit up in the snow. Carson watched his efforts to make sure he wasn't favoring any stray limbs, but nothing appeared to be damaged beyond repair.

He would let their mother deal with it all, he decided. It would serve her right for letting them run wild. "Come on. I'll give you all a ride back to your house."

The middle boy eyed him warily. "We're not supposed to get in strangers' cars."

"He's not a stranger," the older boy snapped with a return to that belligerence. "He's Mr. McRaven, the dude who stole our ranch."

"I didn't—" Instinctively, Carson started to defend himself, then broke off the words. How ridiculous, that he would feel compelled to offer any explanations at all to a trio of rowdy little hellions.

"You want me to drive your little brother home or would you like to carry him all the way yourselves?" he asked.

The older boys exchanged a glance and then Hayden, the older one, shrugged. "Whatever."

He personally would have preferred the latter option, especially after he scooped up the boy and carried him to the SUV, which resulted in even more tears. Again, he wished fiercely that he had just kept on driving when he'd seen them on his fence. If not for that ill-fated decision to stop, none of this would have happened and right now he would be saddling up one of his horses for a good hard ride into the snowy mountains.

He set the boy in the backseat then turned back to the other boys. "You two coming?"

The middle boy with the glasses nodded and climbed in beside his brother but the older one looked as if he would rather be dragged behind the SUV than accept a ride from him. After a long moment, though, he shrugged and went around to the other door.

The only sound in the SUV as they drove the short distance up the driveway to the Wheeler house was the little one's steady sobs and a few furtive attempts to comfort him.

The two-story cedar farmhouse was charming in its own way, he supposed, with the shake roof and the old-fashioned swing on the wide front porch. But no one could possibly miss that a passel of children lived here. From the basketball hoop above the garage to the Santa Claus and reindeer figures in the yard to the sleds propped against the porch steps, everything shouted *family*.

It was completely alien to him, and all the more terrifying because of it.

For about half a second, he was tempted just to dump the lot of them there at their doorstep but he supposed that sort of callousness wouldn't exactly be considered neighborly around these parts.

Fighting his reluctance, he climbed out of the SUV and opened the rear door, then scooped out the still-crying Kip.

They all moved together up the porch steps but before Carson could knock at the door, Hayden burst through and shouted for his mother.

"Mom, Kip fell down off the fence by the bus stop. It was an accident. Nobody dared him or anything, he just went up by himself and slipped."

Warmth seeped out from the open doorway, along with the mingled aroma of cinnamon and sugar and pine.

The comforting, enticing scents of home.

The Wheeler boys might be wild, fatherless urchins with a distracted mother and more courage than sense. But Carson couldn't help the niggle of envy for what they had, things they no doubt would not even appreciate until much later in their lives.

"You can come inside," the middle boy said shyly. "Mom doesn't like us to leave the door open."

Feeling a bit encroaching for walking into her house, even at the permission of her kid, Carson took a few steps inside, just enough that he could close the door behind him.

He instantly wondered if he had accidentally stepped into one of those annoying Christmas shops in Jackson Hole. Every inch of the foyer seemed to be decorated with greenery or muted red gingham ribbons or ornaments of some sort. A wide staircase led upstairs and the banister was a wild riot of evergreen boughs and twinkling lights. A small trio of fir trees in the corner of the landing were decorated with homespun decorations from nature—pinecones, dried orange slices, even a couple of miniature bird nests.

Through the doorway into the living room, he caught a glimpse of a big evergreen tree, decorated with sloppy paper chains and a hodgepodge of decorations that seemed lopsided, even at a cursory glance.

He barely had time for the few observations to register when the boys' mother bustled into the foyer wearing a red-and-green pin-striped apron and carrying the littlest Wheeler—and the only girl of the bunch.

Jenna stopped dead when she saw him, her ethereal blond hair slipping free of its confines, as usual. "Oh! Mr. McRaven! This is a surprise. Hayden didn't mention you were here."

"I happened to be passing by in time to see the, uh, accident. I couldn't just leave him out there."

"Of course you couldn't," she said. Though her tone

was polite enough, he was quite sure he caught a whiff of skepticism. He tried not to let it rankle.

"Thank you for your kindness in bringing them home. I'm very sorry they troubled you again."

Her tone was cooler than the icicles hanging off her porch. The Widow Wheeler didn't like him very much. She had made that fact abundantly clear over the last ten months since he purchased her property.

Oh, she was polite enough in their sporadic dealings, never overtly rude. But he ran an international technology innovation company, which was a hell of a lot like a good poker game. Keen powers of observation were a vital job skill and he had developed his own to a fine degree. He couldn't miss the tiny shadow of disdain in her green eyes when she talked to him.

"Where would you like me to set your little injured buckaroo here?"

"I'll take him."

She set the little one on the floor and the girl toddled to a wicker basket full of toys in the living room and proceeded to start yanking the contents out, one by one, and tossing them on the floor.

Jenna stepped closer to Carson and reached for the boy in his arms, whose wails had trickled to the occasional sniffle. Carson's leather coat was open and as she took the child from him, her hands brushed against his chest for only an instant.

Even through his cotton shirt, he could feel the warmth of her hands, the small, delicate flutter of them and his stomach muscles tightened.

It was a ridiculous reaction, one that first stunned, then exasperated him. He really needed to expend a little more energy on his social life if he could be attracted to Jenna Wheeler, even on an instinctively physical level.

Sure, she was soft and pretty, with that wispy honey-blond hair and her undeniable curves and those big green eyes all her children had inherited.

But she had that unfortunate baggage shackled around her neck. Four wild kids, the youngest just a toddler.

Apparently, the only thing the injured one of her children needed was his mother. She sat down on a nearby wooden rocking chair. The boy snuggled against her chest and she pressed a kiss on his forehead.

"Hush now, sweetheart. Where does it hurt?"

He sniffled a little and pointed to the back of his head that had conked against the railing. "I hurt my head."

"I'm so sorry." She kissed the spot he showed her, her eyes tender and maternal, and Carson's stomach muscles tightened again, this time with a weird, indefinable *something* he couldn't have explained.

"Better?" she asked.

"A little," the boy answered.

"Jolie and I made your favorite snickerdoodles this afternoon, didn't we, ladybug?" she smiled at the little girl, who beamed back in the middle of pulling the ornaments off the tree. "They're for the party tomorrow but when you feel better, you can go into the kitchen and get one."

Cookies were apparently the magic remedy. Who knew? The boy's sniffles dried up and after only twenty seconds more, he slid off his mother's lap.

"I feel a lot better now," he announced. "Can I have a cookie now?"

"Yes. Grab one each for your brothers."

He flashed his mother a smile and raced from the

room at top speed, leaving Carson alone with the two equally terrifying Wheeler females.

"Thank you again for bringing him home. It's a long walk up the driveway for a kid with an owie."

"I guess I was lucky to be there at the right time," he said.

"He fell off a fence, you said?"

He hesitated, not sure quite how to answer her. She knew his feelings about the boys trespassing on his property and he was suddenly reluctant to dredge all that up. On the other hand, she needed to know what they had been up to.

"The split-rail fence just past where our access roads fork."

"On the Raven's Nest side," she surmised correctly.

"Yeah."

"What was he doing on a fence?" She looked as if she wasn't quite sure she wanted to hear his answer.

"Tightrope walking, apparently."

She let out a long, frustrated sigh. "I have warned them and warned them to stay off your property. I hate that they've put me in this position again."

"What position would that be?"

"Having to apologize to you once more."

Again that sliver of disdain flickered in her eyes and he did his best not to bristle, though he was aware his voice was harder than he would have normally used.

"I certainly don't want to tell you how to be a parent, but you have to do something to get the point across a little more forcefully to them. A working ranch is a dangerous place for three young boys, ma'am."

Her expression turned even more glacial. "I believe

I'm aware of just how dangerous a ranch can be, Mr. McRaven. Probably better than you."

He remembered too late just why she had been forced to sell her ranch to him. Her husband had been killed in a tragic accident on the ranch two years earlier, leaving behind bills and obligations Jenna Wheeler had been unable to take care of without selling the land that had been in her husband's family for generations.

He regretted his tactlessness but his point was still valid. "Then you, more than anybody, should stress those dangers to your boys. There are a hundred ways they could get hurt, as today's accident only reinforced."

"Thank you for your concern," she said with that tight, dismissive voice that seemed so discordant in contrast to her soft feminine features. "I'll be sure to tell them once again to stay away from Raven's Nest."

"Do that."

He shoved on his Stetson, knowing he sounded like a first-class jerk, but he didn't know how else to get the message across to her or her boys except with bluntness. "I know neither of us wants any of your boys to be seriously hurt. But I have to tell you, I refuse to be held responsible if they are, especially when you've been warned again and again about their trespassing habits."

"Warning duly noted, Mr. McRaven."

He sighed in frustration. He successfully negotiated corporate deals all the time, had built McRaven Enterprises into an international force to be reckoned with in only a dozen years. So why couldn't he seem to have any interaction with this woman that didn't end with him feeling he was a cross between Simon Legree and Lord Voldemort?

He needed to have his people make her another offer for this land and the house, he decided. As far as he was concerned, the only way to solve their particular quandary would be for her to sell him this section and move her little family somewhere she could be someone else's problem.

She closed the door behind Carson McRaven, wondering how it was possible for a man to be so very physically attractive—with that dark, wavy hair and eyes of such a deep blue she couldn't help staring every time she saw them—yet have all the personality appeal of a wolverine with a sore snout.

The sale of the ranch had mostly been carried out through third parties. Jenna had known he was some kind of a Bay Area financial wizard and she had met him briefly when he had come to inspect the Wagon Wheel, as it all used to be called. Sure, he had been brisk and businesslike. But she had admired his plans to experiment with more environmentally sound ranching practices and he had seemed decent enough in that short meeting.

Of course, that was before her boys apparently decided to make it their personal mission to be as mischievous as possible—and to do it on Carson McRaven's property.

She couldn't blame him for being frustrated. She was at her wit's end trying to keep them on their side of the property line. But she resented his unspoken implication that her boys were feral banshees allowed to run wild through the mountains.

"Mom, do I still have to do chores?" Kip asked in a plaintive kind of voice. "Hayden says I do."

"I think this once, maybe Hayden can take out the garbage for you, if we ask him nicely."

"My head still hurts."

She pulled him toward her and gave him another kiss, just for good measure. "I don't think it's broken. Bruised a little, maybe, but you've got a pretty tough nut."

"It was scary when I fell."

"You shouldn't have been up on Mr. McRaven's fence, right? I don't want you boys up there again. Next time you might hurt yourself even worse. What if you fell inside the pasture when one of those bulls of his were close by?"

"But I'm really good at it. I like being good at something. Hayden's good at riding the ponies and Drew is good at math and stuff. But I can't do anything."

"You're only six years old, bud. You'll figure out what you're good at soon enough."

"Mom!" Hayden called out. "Can we eat these tart thingies in here?"

"No," she answered as she picked up Jolie and headed back toward the kitchen. "They're for the party tomorrow."

"Everything you make is for some party or a reception or something stupid like that. Why can't we eat any of it?" Hayden complained.

"You can have another snickerdoodle after you feed the horses. I made plenty of those."

"I wanted a tart," her oldest muttered.

Naturally. If she had told him the snickerdoodles were off-limits, that would have been the only thing he wanted. She loved him dearly but this sudden contrariness of his sometimes drove her crazy. Hayden was only ten and she already felt like she was battling all the teen stuff her friends had warned her to expect.

Maybe there was a lesson in that for her, she thought after she had shooed Hayden and Drew out the door to take care of their chores in the barn and returned to preparing for her last holiday party of the season.

Carson McRaven was definitely off-limits to her. Beyond the fact that she disliked him personally, he was a multimillionaire tech investor with a reputation for finding products the world didn't realize it couldn't do without, while she was an overtired widow with a struggling catering business and more obligations than she could begin to handle.

She wasn't genuinely interested in any man. In the first place, when on earth would she have the time for one? Between helping the boys with homework, taking care of Jolie, the upkeep on their remaining twenty acres, taking care of her mother-in-law and starting up a struggling catering business, she had nothing left.

In the second, her heart still ached for Joe and probably always would. After two years alone, she still woke up in the middle of the night sometimes and turned over, trying to snuggle into his warmth, only to find a cold void where he used to be. Just like the one inside her heart.

She pushed away the echo of pain out of long practice as she rolled more cookie-dough balls in the cinnamon sugar mix, then set them on the cookie sheet.

Yes, every time she saw Carson McRaven, her heart seemed to race a bit faster and her stomach trembled. She didn't like her reaction but it was a little easier to comprehend when she told herself it was only because he represented the unattainable.

She almost believed it, too.

Chapter Two

She was impossibly stuck.

Jenna revved the engine one more time and tried to rock her van out of the deep snowbank just outside the turnoff for the Wagon Wheel. Carson McRaven might call it Raven's Nest now but to her this would always be the Wagon Wheel, named after three generations of Wheelers who had worked this corner of eastern Idaho in the western shadow of the Grand Tetons.

She glared at the clock on her dashboard and then at the snow still falling hard outside the van windows. Of all the miserable, rotten, lousy times to be stuck. She had a van full of food and an extremely short window of time in which to prepare it.

She thought she had everything so carefully orchestrated in order to have all the last-minute details ready for the party she was catering that evening. The moment the boys climbed onto the school bus, she had loaded Jolie into her van and driven to Idaho Falls, where the grocery selection was more extensive—and fresher—than anything she could find here in Pine Gulch.

She had budgeted a little over two hours, figuring that would give her time to drive there, shop and then drive home.

Naturally, it started snowing the minute she left Idaho Falls and hadn't let up the entire forty-five-minute drive since then. At least four inches had fallen, laying a slick layer of white over everything.

As frustrating as she found the snow to drive in, it did set the perfect scene for Christmas. The evergreen trees on the mountainside looked as if they had been drizzled with royal icing and Cold Creek matched its name by burbling through patches of ice.

She only wished she had time to enjoy it all. Then again, if she had taken a few extra minutes to slow down and pay attention to her driving instead of her extensive to-do list, she wouldn't be in this predicament. Instead, she had been driving just a hair too fast when she headed over the bridge just before the driveway split, one route going toward Carson McRaven's new, huge log house and the other heading toward home.

Just as she made the turn, her van tires slid and she hadn't been able to pull out of the skid in time before landing in the drift.

She knew better than this. That was the most aggravating thing about the whole situation. She had been driving these Idaho winter roads since she was fourteen years old. She knew the importance of picking a driving speed appropriate for conditions, knew that this section could be slick, knew she had to stay focused on the road—not on the baby-field-green salad she still had to make or the tricky vodka-blush sauce she still hadn't perfected for the penne.

But she had just been in such a big darn hurry to make everything just right for this party. It was her biggest event yet, and the one she hoped would make her the go-to person for catering in this area.

None of which would happen if she didn't manage to extricate herself from this blasted snowdrift.

She shoved the van into Reverse again. If she could just get a little traction, the front-wheel drive on her van might be able to do the job. But try as she might, shifting between Reverse and Drive to try rocking out of the snow, the wheels just spun, kicking up snow and mud and gravel behind her.

Blast it all. She wanted to cry at the delay but she just didn't have the time.

She looked in the rearview mirror to the backseat, where Jolie was babbling quietly to herself in her car seat and playing with her favorite stuffed dog, bouncing him on her lap then twirling him in dizzying circles.

"Well, bug, it looks like we're walking home. We'll go get your daddy's big, bad pickup truck with the four-wheel drive and come back for the food."

No big deal, she assured herself. She only had to walk a quarter mile from here down the driveway to the house. If she hurried, she could make it in ten minutes and be back here in fifteen.

She pulled Jolie out of her car seat. Her daughter beamed at her. "Walk, Mommy?"

"Looks like."

She settled her daughter on her hip, grateful she had

at least had the foresight to wear her boots that morning, even though it hadn't been snowing when she left home.

She had just crossed her slide tracks and started up her long driveway that followed the river when she heard a pickup truck coming down the hill from Raven's Nest.

She only had time to whisper a prayer that it would be Neil or Melina Parker, McRaven's ranch foreman and his wife who served as caretaker when Carson wasn't there, before the pickup pulled up next to her.

Apparently nobody was listening to her prayers today. She sighed as Carson rolled down the passenger-side window.

"You look like you could use a hand."

Her pulse did that stupid little jumpy thing at his deep voice and she could feel her face heat up. She could only hope he didn't notice, probably too busy thinking what an idiot she was for driving into a snowbank like that.

"I was just planning to walk to my house for my pickup. I've got groceries in the back I need to take care of quickly."

"Put your baby back in the van, where it's warm and out of the snow. I should have a tow rope in the pickup truck somewhere. I'll have you out in a second."

She wanted to balk at his commanding tone and tell him to go to Hades but for the first time in her life she understood the old saying about pride being a luxury she simply couldn't afford right now.

She should just be grateful for his help, she reminded herself, even if she found it both humiliating and annoying to be obligated to him once more.

"I'm sorry to trouble you. That's two days in a row now that you've had to come to our rescue."

He made a kind of rueful grimace that plainly told her he wasn't any more thrilled than she was about the situation, while he fished around behind the seat of the pickup and pulled out a thick red braided tow rope. "Here we go."

Before she quite knew how it happened, he was crouched in the snow, attaching the tow to her rear bumper. McRaven probably had more money in loose change than she would see in any lifetime but he didn't seem to have any qualms about dirtying his hands a little. It was an unexpected facet of a man who she was beginning to believe just may be more complicated than she might have guessed. He hitched the other end of the tow around his own pickup's bumper, then came to her window again.

"Okay, now start it up and just steer out when you feel your van pull free of the snowbank. You should be on your way in a minute or two."

She nodded and waited while he climbed back into the truck. Over her shoulder, she watched him engage the four-wheel drive of his truck. He appeared to barely ease forward but just that tiny extra bit of help was enough to accomplish what ten minutes of spinning her tires in the ice and snow hadn't been able to do.

Another life lesson for her, maybe? she wondered ruefully. Accepting a little help in the short-term might be humiliating but could save much heartache and struggle.

She didn't have time to wax philosophical this morning, not when her to-do list felt longer than her driveway and just as slickly treacherous.

"Thank you," she said through her open window when Carson returned to her vehicle to unhook the tow rope.

"No problem. You're going to want to take things slow until that access road gets plowed. I slid about four times coming down the hill from my place."

"I know. I was just in too big of a hurry and wasn't paying attention to how fast I was going. I'll be sure to concentrate better now. Thanks again."

He studied her for a moment, then she saw his blue eyes shift to Jolie in the backseat, who beamed at him and waved.

"Hi, mister," she chirped, which was what she called every adult male of her acquaintance, from her Uncle Paul to the pastor at church to the bagger at the grocery store.

"Hi," he said, his voice a little more gruff than usual, then he stepped back and waved her on.

With her wipers on high, Jenna slowly put the van in gear and inched through the swirling snow that seemed to have increased dramatically in just the few moments since Carson arrived. She was so busy paying attention to the road—and trying to keep from sliding into the icy Cold Creek that paralleled her driveway—that she didn't notice the headlights behind her until she was nearly home.

What was Carson doing? She frowned as his pickup continued to tail her along the winding drive. Maybe something had fallen out of her van when she was stopped and he was returning it. Or maybe he decided she needed more of a lecture on her winter driving skills, or lack thereof.

She wouldn't put it past him. The man seemed to

want to give her plenty of advice on child rearing. Judging by past comments, he apparently put her abilities as a mother somewhere between incompetent and negligible and seemed to think she let her boys run wild and free through the countryside with no supervision.

And now he probably thought she was just as inept at driving. She pulled into her garage and stepped out of her driver's seat to walk back outside, already squaring her shoulders for another confrontation.

"Is something wrong?" she asked coolly when he rolled down his window.

"I just wanted to make sure you made it home safely. I'll send one of my guys over with the tractor to plow the driveway in case you need to get out soon."

She blinked at him as hard, wind-whipped snowflakes stung her cheeks. Her first reaction was astonishment and a quick spurt of gratitude, both that he was concerned at her welfare enough to follow her home and that he would offer to help her plow her road.

One less chore to do, right? she thought. Especially since digging out the driveway wasn't among her favorites.

At the same time, she didn't want him to think she needed to be looked after like some kind of charity case.

"I have a tractor with a front plow," she answered. "I can take care of it. I would have done it earlier but it wasn't snowing when I left for Idaho Falls."

She regretted her words the moment she uttered them. She didn't owe Carson McRaven any explanations."

"I'll send someone," he answered. "Stay warm."

Before she could protest, he hit the button to automatically wind up his window, put his big pickup in gear and drove away.

She watched him go for a moment as the wind howled through the bare tops of the cottonwoods and lodgepole pine along the river. Her neighbor was nothing if not confounding. She couldn't quite peg him into a neat compartment. On the one hand, he was arrogant and supercilious and seemed to think her family's entire focus in life was to annoy him as much as humanly possible.

On the other, he *had* been kind to her boys the day before and he had certainly helped her just now when he really could have looked the other way.

She shivered as the wind cut through her parka and turned back to the garage. She had far more critical things to occupy her mind with right now than obsessing— again—about her new neighbor.

Jolie chattered away as Jenna carried her into the house. Only about one word in three was recognizable and none of them seemed to require a response, but her daughter never seemed to mind carrying on a conversation by herself.

She was a complete joy and far more easygoing than any of the boys had been. She didn't complain when Jenna took her straight from her car seat to her high chair and set some dry cereal and a sippy cup of milk on the tray while she went out to cart the groceries inside from the van.

Just as she was carrying the last armload in, the phone rang. She thought about ignoring it, but with three boys in school, she couldn't take the risk it might be one of their teachers or, heaven forbid, the school principal.

"Phone, Mama. Phone."

"I know, honey. I'll get it."

She quickly set down the bags on the last clear counter space in the kitchen and lunged for the cordless handset before the answering machine could pick up.

"Sorry. Hello," she said breathlessly.

"Hello, my dear."

Jenna smiled at the instantly recognizable voice on the other end of the line. Viviana Cruz was one of her favorite people on earth. She and her second husband had a ranch a little farther up the creek and raised beautiful Murray Gray cattle.

"Viviana! How are you?"

"*Bien, gracias.* And you? How do you do? Busy, busy, I would guess."

"You would be right, as usual, Viv. I'm running a little late, but I promise, all will be ready in time."

"I do not doubt this. Not for *un momentito*. The food will be delicious, I have no worries."

At least one of them was confident, Jenna thought as nerves fluttered in her stomach. This job was important to her, not only professionally but personally. Viviana had taken a big risk hiring her to cater the holiday event she was hosting for the local cattle growers' association, of which she served as president. This was the biggest job Jenna had undertaken since she started her catering business six months earlier. Before this, she had mostly done small parties, but this involved ranchers and business owners from this entire region of southeastern Idaho.

Viv had told her there would be people coming from the Jackson Hole area, as well. She planned to have her business cards out where everyone could see and made a mental note to also stick the magnetic banner on her van that read Cold Creek Cuisine.

"Thanks, Viv. I hope so."

"I was checking to see if you are needing any help."

Unfortunately, the answer to that was an unequivocal *yes* but she couldn't admit defeat yet. She could do this. She had planned everything carefully and much of the food was already prepped. Her sister-in-law and niece were coming over in a couple of hours to help her with last-minute things, so she should be all right.

"I think I'll be okay. Thanks for offering, though."

"You are bringing your children tonight, yes?"

Oh, heavens, what a nightmare *that* would be. "No. Not this time, Viv. My niece, Erin, is coming out to the house to tend to them while Terri helps me serve your guests."

"I so love those little darlings of yours."

She smiled as she put away the groceries, the handset tucked into her shoulder. Viv was one of the most genuine people Jenna knew. She was enormously blessed to have such wonderful neighbors. After the tractor accident that critically injured Joe, all the neighbors along the Cold Creek had rallied around her. Viv's husband, Guillermo, and the Daltons, who owned the biggest spread in the area, had all rushed to help her out.

While she had been numbly running between the ranch and the trauma center in Idaho Falls for those awful weeks Joe was in a coma, they had stepped in to care for her children, to bring in the fall alfalfa crop, to round up the Wagon Wheel cattle from the summer range.

She could never repay any of them.

"They adore you, too," she said now to Viv. "But I think your party will go a little more smoothly without my boys there to get into trouble."

"If you change your mind, you bring them. Christmas is for the children, no?"

Those words continued to echo in her mind as she said goodbye to Viviana a few moments later and hung up, then turned her attention to Jolie who was yawning in her high chair ready for her nap.

Her children certainly hadn't enjoyed the best of Christmases the past two years, but she refused to let them down this year. After tonight, she intended to relax and spend every moment of the holidays enjoying her time with them.

Perfect. It all had to be perfect. Was that such an unreasonable wish?

Her children deserved it. They had suffered so much pain and loss. Their last happy Christmas seemed like forever ago.

Joe had died the day after Christmas two years earlier, and they had known it was coming days earlier. No death of a man in his early thirties could be easy for his family to endure, but her husband's had been particularly tough. He had lingered in a coma for two months after the tractor accident, fighting off complication after complication.

Finally, just when she thought perhaps they had turned a corner and he was starting to improve, when she was certain his eyelids were fluttering in response to a squeeze of her hands or a particular tone of her voice, a virulent infection devastated his system. His battered body just couldn't fight anymore.

The next Christmas would have been hard enough for the boys, so close to the anniversary of their beloved father's death, but they had been forced to spend Christmas with Jenna's brother. Jolie, born five months after her father's death, had picked up a respiratory illness and had been in pediatric intensive care through the holidays, consuming Jenna with worry all over again. Then Pat, Joe's mother, suffered a severe stroke the week before Christmas, so Jenna had been running ragged between both of them.

This year *would* be different. Everyone was relatively healthy, even if Pat did still struggle with rehabilitation in the assisted-living center in Idaho Falls. Jenna's fledgling catering business was taking off and the sale of the Wagon Wheel had covered most of the huge pile of debt Joe had left behind.

She refused to allow anything to mess up this Christmas. Not a blizzard, not a big catering job she felt ill-equipped to handle, not sliding her car into a ditch.

Not even an arrogant neighbor with stunning blue eyes.

"You know you don't have to go to this shindig. I doubt anybody's expectin' you to. This was one of those, what do you call it, courtesy invites."

Carson made a face at his foreman, Neil Parker, as the two of them checked over his three pregnant mares, who were due to deliver in only a few months.

So far all was going well. This particular foal's sire was a champion cutting horse from the world-famous Dalton horse operation just up the road, and Carson had high hopes the foal would follow in his daddy's magnificent footsteps.

"I know that," he answered Neil. "If the local stock growers' association could have figured out a polite way *not* to invite me, I'm pretty sure we wouldn't be having this conversation."

"I doubt it's personal. You just represent change and a different way of lookin' at things, something that worries the old-timers around here. New West versus Old West."

Carson knew that. He knew his purchase of the vast acreage that used to be known as the Wagon Wheel had thrust him onto a hotly debated battleground. All across the West, old-guard ranchers were finding themselves saddled with land that was no longer profitable and practices that had become archaic and unwieldy.

Many of their children weren't interested in ranching and the lifestyle that came with it. At the same time, ranchers fought development and the idea of splitting the land they had poured their blood and sweat into tract subdivisions.

As feed costs went up and real-estate values plummeted, many were caught in a no-win situation.

He knew old-timers resented when new people moved in, especially those who had the capital to enact sweeping, costly changes in ranching practices in an effort to increase yield. It was even worse in his situation since he wasn't a permanent resident of his ranch and only came here a couple of times a month for a few days at a time.

He couldn't avoid the snide comments in town when he came to Pine Gulch. And he knew Neil suffered worse, though his foreman was careful not to share those details with him.

Neil and his wife, Melina, had been with Carson for a decade, first as caretakers of the central California ranch he purchased several years ago and then at the small Montana ranch he still owned.

Carson loved ranching. He loved being out on his horses, loved the wildness and the raw beauty here, loved the risk and the rewards.

It wasn't some big secret why that might be. That year he spent on his grandparents' ranch a few miles away from here had been the happiest, most secure of his life. He wasn't trying to recapture that, only to replicate it somewhere else if he could. And though Raven's Nest was only a small segment of his vast empire, this was where he found the most peace.

He wanted to make it a success and he figured a little proactive public relations couldn't hurt the situation in town. Life would be easier all the way around if Neil didn't have to play politics with obstinate locals.

"I'm not some Hollywood rancher, only looking for a status symbol. We're making something out of Raven's Nest and I need to get that point across. That's the whole reason I'm going to Viviana Cruz's party. You and I have been running Raven's Nest for ten months now and people still won't accept that we're serious about what we're doing here."

He thought of the coolness in Jenna Wheeler's eyes when he had pulled her van out of the snow a few hours earlier and the surprise she had showed when he had done the neighborly thing and told her he would make sure her driveway was shoveled.

He didn't know why her negative opinion of him bugged him so much. Plenty of people hated his guts. It was a normal side effect of both his position and his personality. He hadn't made McRaven Enterprises so successful by being weak and accommodating.

Jenna probably figured she had reason to resent him.

He was radically changing something her husband's family had built over several generations.

He thought of what Hayden Wheeler had said the afternoon before. *He's the dude who stole our ranch.* Had the boy's mother been feeding him that kind of garbage? He didn't like thinking she would be the sort to come off as some kind of martyr. She had listed her ranch for sale and he had paid more than a fair price for it. End of story. It was a business deal, pure and simple.

Hell, he'd even made concessions, like granting her the right-of-way to use the Raven's Nest bridge and access road to the point where her driveway forked off it. Otherwise, she would have had to build a new road and another bridge across the creek, something costly and complicated.

He sighed and pushed the frustration away. What did it matter if she didn't like him? He certainly wasn't trying to win any popularity contests with Jenna.

It *would* be nice, though, if Neil didn't have to fight through the negative perceptions of everybody else in town every time his foreman needed to do business with anyone in the Teton Valley.

"I'm only going to go for a little while tonight," he said to Neil. "I'll shake a few hands, stroke a few egos and be home in time to make sure everything's ready for the guests coming in on Sunday."

"Hate to break it to you, boss, but showing up to one Christmas party with the cattlemen's association probably won't do much to change anyone's mind. Folks around here are set in their ways, afraid of anything that's different."

"What's to be afraid of? We're only trying to find more sustainable ways of doing business."

"You don't have to sell me, boss. I'm on board. I know what you're doing here and I'm all for it. Our overhead is about half of a typical ranch of the same size and the land is already healthier after less than a year. It's working. But what you're doing is fairly radical. You can't argue that. A lot of people think you're crazy to go without hormones, to calve in the summer, to move your cattle to a new grazing spot every couple of days instead of weeks. That kind of thinking isn't going to make you the most popular guy at the cattle growers' association."

"It can't hurt to let people see I don't intend to come out only on the weekends and hide out here at the ranch. I'm not trying to convert anybody, I just want folks to see I'm willing to step out and try to be part of the community."

"A noble effort, I guess."

"You don't mind if I tag along with you and Melina, then?"

"I suppose that would be okay. You want her to find you a date? There's some real nice-lookin' girls around here who'd probably love to hit the town with a guy who has a private jet and one of them penthouses in San Francisco."

Carson narrowed his eyes at his foreman, whose sun-weathered features only grinned back at him. "Thanks, but no," Carson muttered. "I don't need help in the dating department."

"You change your mind, you let me know."

"Don't hold your breath. I'm not interested in a social life, just in a little public relations."

Chapter Three

Two hours later, he reminded himself of the conversation with his foreman as he listened to the Pine Gulch mayor ramble on about every single civic event planned for the coming year, from the Founders' Day parade to the Memorial Day breakfast to the annual tradition of decorating the town park for the holidays.

Public relations, he reminded himself. That was the only reason for his presence. If that meant expiring from boredom, it was a small price to pay.

"This is a nice town, as you'll find when you've been here a little longer," Mayor Wilson assured him. "A nice town full of real nice people. Why, I don't guess there's a more neighborly town in all of Idaho. You could have done a lot worse if you'd settled somewhere else."

"I'm sure that's true," he murmured to the other man, wondering when he could politely leave.

At least the mayor was willing to talk to him. He supposed he ought to be grateful for that. While he wasn't encountering outright hostility from people at the party, he had seen little of that neighborliness Mayor Wilson claimed. Most were polite to him but guarded, which was about what he expected.

The server walked past with more of those divine spinach rolls. He grabbed one as she passed by, hoping she wasn't keeping track of his consumption since he knew he'd had more than his share.

At least the food was good. Better than good, actually. He had come in with fairly low culinary expectations. A stock growers' holiday party in Pine Gulch, Idaho, wasn't exactly high on his list of places to find haute cuisine.

But the menu was imaginative and every dish prepared exactly right. He paid a Cordon Bleu–trained personal chef to fill his refrigerator and freezer here and in San Francisco and he thought the food at this party was every bit as good as anything Jean-Marc prepared.

None of it was fancy but everything he had tried so far exploded with taste, from the mini crab cakes with wild mushrooms to the caramel tart he'd tasted to the spinach rolls he couldn't get enough of.

He could only hope the personal chef he hired from Jackson Hole for the guests who were coming to Raven's Nest in a few days was half as good as this caterer.

The house party was an important one for McRaven Enterprises and he wanted everything to be exactly right, especially since he had a feeling this was his one and only chance to convince Frederick Hertzog and his son, Dierk, to sell their cellular phone manufacturing business to McRaven Enterprises.

Frederick loved all things Western. When Carson learned he and his family were traveling from Germany to Salt Lake City for a ski vacation, he had made arrangements to fly them to Raven's Nest for a few days in an effort to convince the man McRaven Enterprises was the best company to take Hertzog Communications and its vast network of holdings to the next level.

He and Hertzog had had a long discussion the last time they met about some of the range policies Carson was trying to emphasize at Raven's Nest and the man was interested to see those efforts in action.

He expected to have more opportunities to entertain at Raven's Nest. He preferred his solitude while he was here but he had built the house knowing some degree of entertaining was inevitable. It wouldn't hurt to meet the caterer before he left, he decided. He could at least get a business card so he could pass it along to Carrianne, his enormously competent assistant who handled all his event-planning details.

The kitchen was at the rear of the community center. Just before he reached it, another server came through the doors carrying a tray laden with artfully arranged holiday sweets. Cookies and truffles and slices of nut bread.

He focused first on the food, wondering how upset she would be if he messed up her lovely tray by snatching one of those giant sugar cookies. He lifted his gaze to the server to ask and did a quick double take.

"Mrs. Wheeler!"

She wobbled a little and nearly dropped the entire platter. "Mr. McRaven," she exclaimed, in the same voice she might have used if an alien spaceship suddenly landed in the middle of the room. "What are you doing here?"

He raised an eyebrow. "I was invited. Why do you sound so surprised? This is the cattle growers' association holiday party, right? Since I run four hundred head of cattle at Raven's Nest, doesn't that make me eligible?"

She paused for only a moment and then continued to the buffet table, where she set down the tray before answering him. "Yes. Of course. I'm sorry. You certainly have the right to attend whatever party you'd care to. I just...wouldn't have expected you here, that's all. I was surprised to see you. The cattlemen's association is usually old-timers. The local good old boys."

"What about Viviana Cruz? You can't call her a good ole boy and she runs the whole association."

She smiled suddenly, brightly. "Point taken. Viv is definitely her own person. And we all love her for it."

With that smile, Jenna Wheeler suddenly looked as delicious as the food she was so carefully arranging, enough to make his mouth water. Her cheeks were flushed like the barest hint of color on August peaches and her silky blond hair was doing its best to escape the confines of the hair clip holding it away from her face.

He wondered what she would do if he reached out to finish the job, just for the sheer pleasure of watching it swing free, but he quickly squashed the inappropriate reaction. She was an extraordinarily lovely woman, he thought, not particularly thrilled that he couldn't seem to stop noticing that little fact about his neighbor.

"Are you helping the caterer tonight?" he asked.

She shrugged. "I guess you could say that. Is there something wrong with the food?"

"No. Quite the contrary. Everything has been perfect. I'm looking for a business card, in fact."

She blinked at him for a long moment, her big green eyes astonished, then she quickly looked away as if she hadn't heard him, her attention focused on arranging items on the buffet table for better access by the guests.

As the silence dragged on, he realized she wasn't going to respond. "So would you mind getting one for me from the caterer when you have a minute?" he pressed.

Again she gave him that odd look, as if she wasn't quite sure how to handle his request. Finally, she sighed and reached into the pocket of her red-and-green striped apron and pulled out a business card.

A nice touch for the caterer, he thought, to give all his servers business cards to be handed out upon request. He scanned it quickly, then felt his jaw drop.

Cold Creek Cuisine.

Weddings, parties, reunions, or just an unforgettable, intimate dinner for two.

Jenna Wheeler, owner.

"You made all this?" he asked.

She gave him a long, cool look. "Why do you sound so surprised?" she parroted his own words back to him.

He had no good response to that, other than the obvious. "You're a widowed mother of four young children. Quite frankly, I'm astonished you have time to breathe, forget about running a business."

He didn't add that from what he had seen of her children, he would think just keeping them out of mischief would require six or seven strong-willed adults. Armed with cattle prods, for good measure.

"It can be challenging sometimes," she answered.

"But I do most of the cooking when they're in school or sleeping."

Even when he came to Raven's Nest to relax, he could never completely escape work. Carson often had to take conference calls from Europe or Japan at odd hours. He remembered now that he had sometimes seen lights glowing at her house late at night and had wondered about it.

He was struck by another sudden memory. "Is that why you had so many groceries in your van today? I thought maybe you were just stocking up in case of a blizzard."

She laughed out loud and he was quite certain it was the loveliest sound he had heard in a long time. "My boys eat a lot, I'll grant you that. But not quite twenty grocery bags full. Yes, that's why I had so many groceries in my van. It was also the reason for my panic this morning. I had a million things to do before tonight and couldn't really afford the delay of being stupid enough to slide into a snowbank. Thank you again for pulling me out."

"You're welcome. I'm glad I was there. I would have hated missing all this delicious food. Your tandoori beef skewers are particularly wonderful. I don't think I've ever tasted anything like it."

"Thank you." She looked as surprised at the compliment as if he had just reached over and kissed her hard, right here above the maple-pepper-salmon bites.

Not a completely unappealing idea, he had to admit.

None of this made sense to him. Not his sudden fierce attraction to her or the fact that she was here in the first place.

He had paid in the mid seven figures for her ranch, more than its appraised value because he hadn't wanted to quibble and risk missing out on the purchase after he had searched so long for the perfect rangeland for his and Neil's plans for sustainable ranching.

He would think with careful management, she and her children would be well-provided-for the rest of their lives.

But she drove a five-year-old minivan and her house needed painting and she worked after her children were in bed to throw parties for other people.

It was none of his business, he reminded himself. *She* was none of his business.

Except she *did* fix a mean goat-cheese crostini.

"Well, your food is fantastic. Do you mind if I give your card to my assistant who plans my events for me? I expect I'll be doing more entertaining at Raven's Nest in the future. I was hoping to find someone closer than Jackson Hole to handle the catering when I entertain. I never expected her to live just down the hill."

She paused for a long moment and he could clearly see the indecision in her eyes. He sensed she wanted to tell him no but instead she gave a short nod. "I suppose. I should warn you I'm very selective about the jobs I accept. If it doesn't work for my children's schedule, I have no qualms about turning something down. They come first."

"Fair enough."

He would have added more but the woman who had been helping Jenna serve at the party approached them at that moment. She barely looked at Carson but the quick glance she shot at him was icier, even more than Jenna's had been.

"Jenna, the mayor is asking if you have more of your bacon-wrapped shrimp. He's crazy about them, apparently. I told him I would ask."

"I'll have to go check the inventory in the kitchen." She turned toward Carson with an apologetic expression he wasn't completely certain was genuine.

"Will you excuse me? Things are a little hectic."

"Of course," he answered. He watched her go, not at all thrilled to realize the brief interaction with her had been the most enjoyable moments of his evening.

Why wouldn't the man just *leave* already?

Jenna returned to the kitchen after making yet another trip to replenish the buffet table, fighting the urge to bury her face in a pitcher of ice water.

This was becoming ridiculous.

She had made a half-dozen trips out into the holiday-bedecked community center, circulating among the guests with more cheesecake or toffee bites.

Every time, she had vowed to herself she wouldn't pay the slightest bit of attention to Carson McRaven. But the instant she would walk out of the kitchen, her gaze would unerringly find him, no matter where he was standing.

He shouldn't have stood out so glaringly. She had no reason to hone in on him like a heat-seeking missile. It wasn't like he was wearing some fancy tailored Italian-cut suit or anything. He had on perfectly appropriate khaki slacks and a light blue dress shirt under a sport jacket that looked casual but probably cost more than the average fall steer at market.

The man was just too blasted good-looking, with that dark wavy hair and those intense blue eyes. It didn't help that he wore his clothes with a careless elegance that was completely foreign compared to the off-the-rack crowd in Pine Gulch.

She couldn't help noticing him, maybe because he looked like a fierce hawk taking tea with a flock of starlings.

This is the cattle growers' association holiday party, right? Since I run four hundred head of cattle at Raven's Nest, doesn't that make me eligible?

If he was your average rancher, she was Julia Child.

"I can't believe that man had the nerve to show up here."

Jenna swiveled to find her sister-in-law coming through the doors with another empty tray. "What man?" she asked, playing innocent, just as if her thoughts hadn't revolved around him from the moment she had discovered him at the party.

"McRaven!" Terri's glare looked incongruous on her pixie features. "Does the man have to ruin everything? It's not enough that he waltzes away with your ranch and starts building that Taj Mahal on it but now he has to show up all over town like he owns the place."

"He didn't waltz away with anything, Terri. You know that. He paid good money for the ranch. And the house he built is big but it's not obscenely big."

"It's the biggest house in town. I mean, who really needs a twelve thousand square foot mansion out in the middle of freaking nowhere? Do you have any idea what kind of hit he's going to take if he ever tries to sell the place? Who else is going to want to shell out that kind of money in this soft market?"

"Does everything have to come down to real estate with you?"

Terri made a face. "I can't help it. I've got loan-to-values and escrow analyses on the brain."

When her sister-in-law wasn't helping her serve the mad rush of holiday events she had overcommitted to, Terri was studying for her real-estate license.

"McRaven should have taken a good look at the market around here before he jumped in and started building his megahouse," she added.

"I'm guessing he doesn't care about the market. He's got the money and the land. He's free to build whatever kind of house he wants on it."

She had to admit, she hadn't been thrilled that, for ten months, Raven's Nest had seen a constant stream of workers and delivery trucks and construction vehicles, with their dust and noise. The boys had been fascinated by it all but she had mostly found it annoying. And, okay, she had resented that Carson had the endlessly deep pockets to come in and make all the changes she and Joe had only ever been able to dream about in whispered conversations in the dark quiet of their bedroom.

"I still don't think it's right," Terri muttered. "He doesn't belong here. It doesn't help that he comes in looking like he just finished a photo shoot for some sexy men's magazine. No man should be allowed to be that rich and that unbelievably gorgeous. It's just not fair."

"You're a married woman, Terri!" she teased.

"Very happily married," she agreed. "But you have to agree, that man is lethal."

Jenna decided she would be wise to just keep her mouth shut right about now.

"You should see Annalee Kelley putting out the vibe. She's all over him. If Annalee has her way, she'll be the first one in town to see the inside of Raven's Nest. Or at least one of the bedrooms there."

Okay, she didn't want to go there, Jenna decided, and quickly changed the subject.

"How are the crab cakes? They seem to be going fast, don't they?"

Terri looked reluctant to be distracted but finally gave in. "You have, like, three left out there. You've done a fantastic job, as usual, Jen. Everybody's raving about how delicious the food is and at least a half-dozen people begged me for your white-chocolate mousse recipe."

She had been working like crazy to make everything perfect for the party. It was amazing the sense of satisfaction she found.

"Thanks for all your help these last few weeks as everything has been so crazy, Terri. You've saved my bacon."

"You're welcome, hon. I'm just glad this is our last gig for a while. I can't wait for the cruise this week. I'm going to completely put the stupid real-estate test out of my head and just bask by the pool with an umbrella drink in my hand."

Her brother and his family were leaving the day before Christmas for a weeklong cruise on the Mexican Riviera.

"Well, I won't have umbrella drinks but I'll be glad to take a rest, too. It will be nice to have things get back to normal."

"As normal as your life can get when you live just down the hill from the McRaven McMansion. I heard from Melina Parker that he's got guests coming in this weekend. You let me know if there are any naked hot tub parties up there, okay? As much as I despise the man, I might have to come over with Paul's binoculars, just for a little peek."

Oh, as if she needed that visual image in her head. She thrust a platter at her sister-in-law to distract her. "Here. This is the last of the crostini. Try to move them. I don't want to take any home with me."

Terri grinned but obediently headed back out to the party.

The next time Jenna dared venture out of the kitchen, Carson McRaven was nowhere in sight. She told herself that odd, hollow feeling in her stomach was simply relief that he was gone and she could finally concentrate on the job at hand.

It certainly wasn't disappointment.

Chapter Four

"You've got company."

Carson looked up from his computer monitor. His foreman's wife, Melina—who served as housekeeper at Raven's Nest—stood in his doorway, a dust cloth in one hand and an amused smirk on her plump features.

"Can you handle it? This is not really a good time for me to be distracted. I'm videoconferencing with Carrianne right now."

Melina did a little finger wave. "Hi, Carrianne."

His hyperefficient assistant smiled from the computer screen. "Hello, Melina. How are you?"

"Can't complain. Except I woke up this morning with a little sciatica, but that should pass when this miserable cold weather eases a little. Sorry to disturb you two while you're plotting to take over the world or whatever, but I'm supposed to tell you that your visitors are on strict orders to talk to you and no one else."

"Who is it?"

"You'll have to find out yourself, won't you? See you, Carrianne."

Before Carson could protest, she grinned at him and at Carrianne on the computer screen then walked away. He frowned after her. Neither Melina nor Neil were the most docile of employees, which was probably the reason he liked them both so much.

"Is everything all right?" Carrianne asked.

"Damned if I know but I'd better go see. Can you hang tight for a few minutes?"

"Of course."

Even if some emergency kept him away all night and unable to reach her, he knew Carrianne would still be waiting by the computer for him in the morning. She was dependable to a fault—and invaluable for it.

The slightest of headaches thudded in his temples in rhythm with the frustration throbbing through him. He didn't need the distraction right now. He and Carrianne were trying to wrap up several projects before the holidays, a difficult enough task to accomplish via long distance. And even though Christmas was still five days away, the whole business community seemed to have decided to start celebrating early.

His frustration didn't ease when he reached the foyer and found the three Wheeler boys standing inside the doorway, snow dripping from their parkas onto his custom Italian tile floor. The oldest one, Hayden, he remembered, was holding a couple of small parcels.

Cold poured in from the door they had left open to the outside and he caught a glimpse of two ponies tied to the railing of the front porch. Two horses, three boys.

Two must have been forced to double up, a fact he was quite certain didn't please either of them.

"Hi, Mr. McRaven." The medium-sized one with the glasses—Drew, he remembered—seemed to have been elected spokesman for the group.

"Hello, boys. What brings you up this way?"

"Our mom sent us." Apparently, Kip's trauma of a few days earlier had been forgotten. He seemed to consider Carson his best friend, judging by the wattage of the gap-toothed grin he offered that should have looked ridiculous but seemed rather appealing instead.

"This is for you." Hayden barely looked at him as he thrust out the parcels and Carson now saw they were clear holiday-patterned plastic containers filled with some kind of food items.

"We're supposed to tell you to put the spinach rolls in the refrigerator. The cookies you can leave out."

"I hope she gave you snickerdoodles," Kip said with that grin again. "They're my favorite."

"Okay." He had no idea how to respond to this unexpected visit or to their offerings.

"Tell him what we're supposed to say," Drew hissed to his older brother.

Hayden scowled, then spoke in a monotone. "We're supposed to tell you we're sorry for trespassing the other day and thank you for bringing Kip home when he fell off the fence and for pulling out our van yesterday when Mom got stuck in the snow."

"Uh, you're welcome." He had absolutely no experience with neighbors who thought they had to bring him cookies. It was a Mayberry moment he found unexpected and a bit surreal. Still, just the thought of having the chance to enjoy more of Jenna Wheeler's cooking made his mouth water.

"Your house is big," Kip said, looking around the two-story entry that led to the great room. "It's like a castle."

"Grandma Pat says it's a monster city up here." The oldest one stated the insult matter-of-factly. "She says you're only stroking your ego."

It took him a few moments to figure out "monster city" probably meant *monstrosity*. Either way, it annoyed him.

"Does she?" he asked evenly, wondering who the hell Grandma Pat might be.

Drew studied him, those green eyes behind the glasses wary. "Is that something mean? What Grandma Pat said?"

Again, Carson felt out of his depth and wondered the best way to usher his bothersome little visitors out the door. "I guess that depends."

"Grandma Pat says mean stuff like that all the time," he said, apology in his voice.

"She does not, moron. Shut up." Hayden punched his shoulder hard enough to make Drew wobble a little and Carson fought the urge to sit the boy down for a long lecture about not mistreating anybody, particularly smaller brothers.

Drew righted himself and stepped out of reach of his brother. "Mom says not to listen to her when she says something mean because she can't help it. She doesn't always think about what she's saying."

Hayden opened his mouth to defend Grandma Pat but before he could, Kip called out to them from inside the great room. "Hey, where's your Christmas tree?"

How had the kid wandered away so quickly? One minute he'd been there grinning at him, the next he was halfway across the house. Like wayward puppies, his brothers followed him and Carson had no choice but to head after them.

"Don't you have a tree?" Drew asked, his voice shocked.

"I have a little one in the family room off the kitchen." A four-foot grapevine tree his interior designer had left at Thanksgiving, when he visited last.

"Can we see it?" Drew asked.

"Why don't you have a big one in here?" Hayden asked, with that inexplicable truculence in his voice.

"I guess I just haven't gotten around to it."

"Don't you like Christmas?" Kip asked, looking astonished at the very idea.

How did he explain to these innocent-looking boys that the magic of the holidays disappeared mighty damn fast when you lived in the backseat of your druggie mother's Chevy Vega?

"Sure, I like Christmas. I have a tree at my other house in California." One that his housekeeper there insisted on decorating, but he decided he didn't need to give the Wheeler boys that information. "I just haven't had time to put one up here. I've only been here a few days and I've had other things to do."

"We could help you cut one down." Drew's features sparkled with excitement. "We know where the good ones are. We always cut one down right by where the creek comes down and makes the big turn."

"Only this year we couldn't," Hayden muttered. "Mom said it would be stealing since it's on your land now. We had to go with our Uncle Paul to get one from the people selling them at his feed store. We couldn't find a good one, though. They were all scrawny."

The kid's beef was with his mother for selling the land, not with him, Carson reminded himself, even as he bristled.

"You want us to show you where the good trees are?" his brother asked eagerly.

"Drew," Hayden hissed.

"What? Maybe he doesn't know. It would be fun. Just like when we used to go with…with Dad."

The boy's voice wobbled a little on the last word and Carson's insides clenched. He didn't need a bunch of fatherless boys coming into his life, making him feel sorry for them and guilty that he'd had the effrontery to pay their mother a substantial sum to buy their family's ranch.

"We could take you on Peppy," the youngest beamed. "Peppy's the pony me and Drew share."

"Like three people can fit on Pep," Hayden scoffed. "He's so old, he can barely carry the two of you."

"Maybe he could ride his own horse," Drew suggested. "It's not far. So do you want us to help you? We already have our warm clothes on and everything."

"Don't be such a dork. Why would he want our help?"

Hayden's surliness and his brother's contrasting eagerness both tugged at something deep inside him, a tiny flicker of memory of the one Christmas he had been blessed to stay with his grandparents. He had been nine years old, trying to act as tough as Hayden. His grandfather had driven him on a snowmobile to the Forest Service land above their small ranch and the two of them had gone off in search of a Christmas tree.

He had forgotten that moment, had buried the memory deep. But now it all came flooding back—the citrusy tang of the pine trees, the cold wind rushing past, the crunch of the snow underfoot. The sheer thrill of walking past tree after tree until he and his grandfather picked out the perfect one.

He could still remember the joy of hauling it back to his grandparents' home and the thrill as his grandmother had exclaimed over it, proclaiming it to be the most beautiful tree they had ever had.

He and his grandfather had hung the lights later that night and he had helped put the decorations up. He had a sudden distinct memory of sneaking out of bed later that night and going out to the living room, plugging in the lights and lying under the tree, watching the flickering lights change from red to green to purple to gold and wondering if he had ever seen anything so magical.

The next Christmas, he had been back with his mother and had spent the holiday in a dingy apartment in Barstow. The only lights had been headlights on the interstate.

He pushed the memory aside and focused on the three boys watching him with varying expressions on their similar features.

He really did need a Christmas tree. It was a glaring omission, one he couldn't believe he hadn't caught before now when he had been trying to make sure every detail at Raven's Nest was perfect. He had guests coming in the next day who would be sure to wonder why he didn't have one.

He had no good explanation he could offer the Hertzogs, other than his own negligence. He just hadn't thought of it, since Christmas wasn't really even on his radar.

He didn't dislike the holidays, they were mostly just an inconvenience—a time when the whole world seemed to stop working, whether they celebrated Christmas or not.

On the other hand, where the hell was he going to get lights and decorations for a Christmas tree just five days before the holiday?

Carrianne could take care of that, he was quite certain. She would have the whole thing arranged in a few hours, even from California.

"You probably don't even know how to ride a horse, do you?" Hayden scoffed. "That's what Grandma Pat said. She says you probably don't know the back end of a horse from a hole in the ground."

Grandma Pat sounded like a real charmer.

"I do know how to ride a horse, thanks. I've been doing it for a long time now."

"You're just sayin' that."

He sighed at the boy's attitude. He never had been good at ignoring a dare. "Give me ten minutes to wrap some things up in my office, then you're welcome to judge for yourself whether I can ride or not. In the meantime, there's a telephone over there by the fireplace. Why don't you call your mother to ask her permission to go with me?"

The two younger boys couldn't have looked more excited than if he had just offered to let them fly his jet. Hayden, though, looked as if he were sucking on sour apples.

Yeah, kid, I know how you feel, Carson thought as he headed back to his study. He wasn't that thrilled about the whole situation, either. He should never have opened his mouth. He just had to hope Carrianne could arrange things so he wasn't stuck with a perfectly good evergreen he had cut down for nothing.

"You're doing what?"

Certain she couldn't possibly have heard Drew right, Jenna held the cordless phone closer to her ear and slid away from her sewing machine at the kitchen table and moved into the hall, where she could hear better without the whoosh of the dishwasher and the Christmas carols playing on the radio.

"Mr. McRaven doesn't have a Christmas tree," Drew said, in the same aghast tone of voice he might use to say the man kicked baby ducks for fun. "We told him where the good ones are, up above the far pasture, but that we couldn't go there this year to cut one down 'cause you said it was stealin'. But since it's his place now, it's not stealin' so he can get one there if he wants. And we're gonna help him."

Carson was taking her boys out to cut down a Christmas tree for his gigantic new house? Okay, what alternate universe had she tumbled into while she was sewing new pajamas for the boys?

Or maybe she fell asleep over the sewing machine and this was just some weird, twisted dream. He didn't like children and didn't know what to do with them. She didn't need him to voice the sentiment for her to figure it out. She had seen the vague uneasiness in his eyes every time he had been forced to extricate her boys from one scrape or another.

Why would he suddenly decide to take them to find a Christmas tree? It made no sense.

She shouldn't have sent them up to Raven's Nest, she fretted. She had thought the task would be an easy one and would accomplish a couple of purposes—reinforcing to the boys the lesson that it was good manners to express proper gratitude to those who helped them out for one. Getting them out of the house for a while and burning off a little pre-Christmas energy on their ponies was even better.

Now here they were heading off with Carson McRaven to cut down a Christmas tree.

Maybe she should just be grateful instead of worrying about his reasons. The boys had missed not cutting down their own tree this year. The one they found was perfectly adequate but Hayden in particular had been upset at any change in the tradition they had established years ago with their father.

"So can we go with him?"

"I don't think it's a good idea."

"Why not?" Drew, always the thinker, was never content with a simple answer.

How did she explain to her son that she was fairly certain their neighbor considered them on the same level as magpies or whistle pigs—an inescapable annoyance.

"I just don't. If he had truly wanted a Christmas tree, I'm sure he would have found one before now, don't you think?"

"He says he has one in his California house but hasn't had time to get one here since he's only been here a few days. Please, Mom. He needs our help. He said he could use it."

Really? Carson McRaven, cutthroat billionaire businessman said that? He could hire dozens of men to scour the mountainside for the perfect tree. What did he need with three mischievous little boys?

With those killer instincts all her boys had, Drew must have sensed she was wavering. "Please, Mom. Oh please. I promise, we'll be super good."

Jenna sighed. The truth was, she could use a little extra time. Jolie was taking a long nap and she had accomplished more in the last hour than she had done all day.

The pajamas she was working on were supposed to be a surprise on Christmas Eve—the boys' one present she allowed them to open early—and she still needed to finish hemming all three pairs. She enjoyed sewing but didn't have time for it very often. It seemed like every time she took out her machine, she had to relearn how to thread the bobbin and the rhythm of the thing.

What could be the harm in them going with Carson? He had made the offer, for some completely inexplicable reason.

"I suppose it's all right," she finally said. "Behave yourselves and come straight home when you're done."

"Thanks, Mom! Thanks a million! Bye."

Drew hung up before she could give more typical maternal admonishments. She set the cordless phone on the table but she couldn't quite bring herself to return to the sewing machine yet. Her thoughts were still puzzling over why Carson McRaven would do something so incongruous as to invite her boys along on a tree-hunting trip.

Maybe it was the cookies she'd sent along with the boys to thank him for rescuing them the other day.

No, that couldn't be it. Sure, they were good but they weren't quite *that* good.

Drat the man, anyway. He was supposed to be hard and unfeeling and humorless. It was much easier to dislike him when she considered him simply an arrogant rich man who thought his money could buy anything he wanted.

But in the last few days, she could feel something changing. He had rescued her boys, he had pulled her out of the ditch, he had followed her home to make sure she was safe.

She was beginning to think there was more to Carson McRaven than she wanted to believe.

With another heavy sigh, she turned back to her sewing. Christmas was only five days away and she couldn't waste another moment obsessing about the man.

"That's the one, right there." The lenses of Drew's glasses gleamed in the sunlight as he beamed up at Carson from his spot standing proudly by a decent-sized blue spruce.

"That is a nice one," Carson agreed.

"This one's better," Hayden insisted from his spot by a gigantic lodgepole pine. "Yours has a big ugly hole on one side, see?"

"Well, *yours* is way too bushy," Drew retorted. "How do you think you're even gonna fit it into the house? It won't even go through the door!"

An excellent point, Carson wanted to say, but he decided to let them fight it out. He had one picked out already. He had it all figured out. It was just a matter of letting the boys wear themselves out arguing about it for a few more minutes, then he would present his tree as the winner.

In the course of the last half hour with the Wheeler boys, he had begun to finally determine which boy was which and to assess the dynamics between them. In the process, he gained a little more understanding.

Hayden, the oldest, wanted to be boss and was torn between pushing his weight around and trying to pretend he wasn't enjoying their little excursion. Carson knew it was small of him but he had savored the boy's reaction when he had led his favorite horse out of the barn, a high-spirited black named Bodie, and effortlessly mounted him. The boy had taken one look at the sleek, elegant lines of the magnificent horse and at Carson's easy control of him and his eyes had widened to the size of silver dollars.

Make sure you tell your Grandma Pat, Carson wanted to say, but that would have just been petty.

If Hayden had all the tough-guy attitude of the boys, his middle brother was the thinker. He seemed smart as a whip but also inordinately concerned with making sure everyone got along—except when it came to himself and his older brother, anyway.

Kip was eager to please and excited about everything, from the pair of pheasant roosters they scared on the way up the hill to the view of their house from that elevation.

"Here's one," Kip called now from some distance away. "What about this tree?"

"Let's take a look." Carson headed in the direction of the boy's voice and found him standing by the very tree he had already selected. It was a Douglas fir, with those soft, sweet-smelling needles, about sixteen feet tall, he judged, and in the perfect Christmas-tree shape.

"I think it's beautiful," Kip proclaimed.

"I have to agree with Kip on this one, boys. Good eye, kid. It's perfect."

"Thanks, Mr. McRaven!" The youngest Wheeler boy gave him that gap-toothed grin he found so appealing as his older brothers came to stand on either side of Carson.

Drew gave a wistful sigh. "It *is* perfect. Wish I'd seen it first."

"Are you kidding?" Hayden jeered, still determined to be the top dog. "It's too tall. You'll have to cut the top off."

"Not in my great room. The ceiling is eighteen feet high in there. This tree can't be more than sixteen, if that."

"If you say so."

"I do." He hid his amusement at the boy's determined reluctance to admit he might be wrong. "You want to help me do the honors?"

"What honors?"

Carson held up the small chain saw he had brought along and Hayden's green eyes widened with shock and the first flicker of excitement he had allowed himself to reveal. "Cut it down? You want me to help you?"

"If you're up to it."

"Can I help, too?" Kip's voice rose about two octaves in his exhilaration.

Carson hated to squash all that joyful anticipation but it couldn't be helped. He could just picture Jenna Wheeler's soft, lovely features if he returned one of her boys minus a few fingers.

"Not this time," he said, just as if there would ever be another time. "You and Drew need to stand clear. Go on back by the horses."

"Why does Hayden get to help and I don't?" Kip asked.

Carson raised an eyebrow in the same quelling look he gave to employees who pushed him a shade further than was wise. Kip didn't even notice.

"Huh? Why can't I help, too?"

"Because I said so," he answered. As soon as he heard his own words, he remembered all over again why he had always sworn he wouldn't have kids. He had absolutely no desire to become one of those adults who could only speak in clichés.

But he supposed clichés wouldn't be used if they didn't occasionally do the job. Kip gave a little huff of defeat and headed toward the horses, where Drew was already waiting.

"You know how to use a chain saw?" he asked Hayden.

"Don't you?" the boy asked, with just a trace of belligerence in his voice.

"Sure." He walked him through the steps and then started up the chain saw. The boy's eyes were bright with anticipation at the low throb as Carson guided the chain saw to the right spot on the Douglas fir's trunk.

"Now, hold on tight," he ordered. The boy kept his hands on the chain saw, even as it bucked a little on a knot in the tree while they made the cut.

But as the tree toppled away from them, he gave a little shriek and instinctively pressed against Carson's side for just a moment. A weird knot formed in his throat but Carson swallowed it down.

"That was so cool!" Drew exclaimed.

"Yeah! Cool!" Kip echoed.

"Good job, Hayden," Carson told the boy.

"I could have done it by myself without any help," the boy answered, though Carson was quite sure he looked pleased.

"I'm sure you could," he answered.

"How are we going to get it to your house?" Drew asked with a sudden frown.

"I brought along plenty of rope. Bodie's strong enough to pull it down the hill, I think, especially since it's not far. He shouldn't have any problem."

The boys were more of a hindrance than they were a help as he rigged the rope but for once Carson didn't mind their chatter. It wasn't a bad way to spend a December afternoon, he decided. Not a bad way at all.

"If you want, we can help you set it up," Drew said as they finally headed back down the hill toward Raven's Nest.

"And we can decorate it, too," Kip added.

"We're really good at putting up Christmas ornaments," Drew said. "Mom said so."

"Yeah," added Kip. "This year I only broke one thing, a bell that I shook too hard. And it was really old anyway, Mom said."

Carson winced, as a sudden vision danced through his head of broken globes and tinsel strung across every available surface in his house. "Thanks for the offer, but I think it's taken care of. I've got some people who are going to help me with that."

Carrianne had assured him she should be able to have an army of decorators sent over from Jackson Hole as soon as possible. His guests weren't due to arrive until afternoon. By the time the Hertzogs arrived, his house should be brimming with Christmas spirit.

Thanks to the Wheeler brothers. If they hadn't

showed up bearing their unexpected goodies, he would have completely overlooked putting up a tree. He owed them, he supposed. For that, and for the surprisingly enjoyable afternoon.

"We'll stop and let Bodie drop the tree off at my house and then I'll ride you all home."

He told himself quite firmly that he was only being neighborly, making sure they arrived home safely. The offer certainly had nothing to do with any desire on his part to see their mother again.

Chapter Five

Though cleaning out the horse stalls wasn't on her list of top ten enjoyable activities—or top five hundred, come to think of it—it had to be done. Since she'd finished sewing the pajamas and had safely hidden them in her secret spot in a locked closet in the basement furnace room where the boys never ventured, she had decided to tackle another job on her list.

She hummed "Jingle Bells" as she worked, much to Jolie's delight.

"Mommy funny," she pronounced with a giggle.

Jenna smiled. "Thanks, baby."

Even with her singing and Jolie's chatter and her horse Lucy whickering softly for a ride, everything seemed too quiet in the barn. Without the constant hubbub of her boys around, she always felt a little disconcerted, as if something wasn't quite right with her world.

They would be back all too soon, she knew, and then the chaos would start all over again. They would come in hungry and thirsty and arguing about whose turn it was to groom their ponies, Pep and Cola.

"Mommy, out." Jolie pouted from the playpen that wouldn't contain her for much longer. Jenna didn't like using it very often but a barn was a dangerous—not to mention less than sanitary—place for a busy toddler and she couldn't always keep a perfect eye on her.

"Just a minute, honey. Where's your car?"

"Jolie car."

"That's right. It's your car. Let's see it go *vroom vroom*."

Her daughter giggled again and picked up her plastic red car and let herself be distracted. She was such a good baby. Well, not a baby anymore. She was eighteen months old now, putting words together and walking and exploring her world.

She paused with the shovel in her hand, watching the miracle of her daughter as she babbled to her toys. She was a joy. A complete joy. The only tragedy was that her father had never seen his child, had never even known of her existence.

Jenna must have been only a few weeks pregnant at the time of Joe's accident. They had talked about having another child but hadn't yet made a final decision about it. Apparently fate had taken the choice out of their hands. And what a blessing that turned out to be.

Those first few weeks after the accident as he lay unresponsive in a coma, she had been so traumatized she hadn't even realized she was pregnant.

Oh, the signs had been there, just like in her other three pregnancies. She could see that now but at the time she had attributed her exhaustion and the missed periods to the stress of sitting by her husband's bedside day after day, praying for a miracle that never came as his condition continued to deteriorate. The vague nausea she had put down to lousy hospital food and not enough sleep as she rushed between the Wagon Wheel and the hospital day after day.

She found out for certain she was pregnant just a few days after his funeral. New Year's Eve, and it was as if her husband had given her one last precious holiday gift.

Jolie had turned out to be her miracle. Even in the midst of her overwhelming grief—the paralyzing fear now that she was pregnant and on her own with a ranch to run and three little boys—she was forced to be strong for those boys and for the new life she carried.

Her daughter was a gift. All of their children were. Joe had loved them so. She knew he would have adored his little girl, would have spoiled her rotten.

"Mommy sad?" Jolie asked suddenly and Jenna realized she had stopped working and hadn't moved for several moments, just watching the wonder of her child.

"No, baby. I'm not sad." She smiled. "I'm happy. So happy. It's Christmas. The time of hope and love, right?"

"Santa!"

Her brothers had brainwashed her well. "That, too. Let's get this done so we can go inside where it's warm."

She had just laid down fresh straw when Frannie, their old border collie, lumbered to her feet and gave one sharp bark at the same time Lucy whinnied.

That was their not-so-subtle way of making Jenna feel guilty that they were stuck at home while the two ponies got to be out and about with the boys.

"I'm sorry, girls. I promise, I'll take you out one of

these nights, okay? Just the three of us in the moonlight like we used to do."

The horse blew out a breath and Frannie just gave her a sad kind of look. Jolie giggled at her mother and Jenna picked her up and carried her outside to watch for the boys' return.

After the dim light inside the barn, the sunlight gleaming off the snow was blinding for a moment.

Just as she expected, she found her boys approaching the barn on Pep and Cola, Hayden on his own pony and Drew and Kip doubled up.

But to her vast shock, they weren't alone.

Her gaze took in the man on the huge, gorgeous black gelding. He looked like he'd just ridden out of a Clint Eastwood movie—black horse, black Stetson, dark green ranch jacket, all in stark contrast to the snowy landscape.

Her stomach did an odd little twirl and she hefted a squirming Jolie higher in her arms.

"Pretty horsey," the girl crowed with delight. Jenna had a sudden urge to warn her daughter to beware of pretty horses and the dangerous men who rode them.

"Hi, Mom!" Kip and Drew both greeted her with enthusiasm.

"Hi, guys. Hello, Mr. McRaven."

He nodded to her in greeting, his blue eyes gleaming brilliantly in the sunlight for just a moment, and with all her heart, she suddenly wished she hadn't just been mucking out the stalls. She felt at a distinct disadvantage around him, as usual. Just once she would like to encounter the man when she wasn't bedraggled and frustrated and looking like either a scullery maid or a stable urchin.

"How was the Christmas-tree hunt?" she asked.

"Christmas tree!" Jolie clapped her hands.

"We picked a huge one," Kip exclaimed, sliding down from behind Drew, who quickly joined him on the ground.

"We found the perfect tree," Drew added.

"*I* found the perfect tree," Kip bragged.

"Okay, Kip found it. It's perfect. And guess where we found it, Mom? Right in the place we always used to go, above the high pasture. Remember, Mom?"

"I remember," she murmured. As if she could forget eleven years of chopping down Christmas trees.

"It's perfect, isn't it, Mr. McRaven?"

"Pretty close," Carson answered.

"I still think it's too big," Hayden muttered. He climbed down off Cola, the pony his father had given him just a few months before his accident. "You're gonna have to cut off the whole top to get it inside your house, just like I told you."

"We'll have to see. If you're right, you have my permission to say *I told you so* as many times as you want. And next time I'll trust your judgment."

"I'm right. You'll see."

Hayden tugged his pony into the barn, much to Jenna's embarrassment. Her oldest son wasn't usually so rude. She could only hope he had exhibited better manners while he and his brothers had been with Carson.

As he was leaving, Carson gave the other boys a smile and said, "Thanks for your help. I never would have found the tree if not for the three of you."

"It was super fun." Kip grinned.

"Yeah, it was. We can help you find a tree again next year if you want," Drew offered.

Carson looked a bit taken aback by the offer. "Thanks. I appreciate that. Maybe next year I can remember to get a tree earlier than five days before Christmas."

"We can remind you," Drew assured him.

"Great. You do that." His gaze met Jenna's for just an instant but she could swear she felt the sizzle of it right to her toes. Ridiculous. She was holding her squirmy toddler and they were surrounded by horses and boys and one old, tired dog.

Still, when he dismounted and headed toward her, she couldn't help noticing his lean-hipped walk and the way his dark hair curled a little under the hat.

"I didn't know my buying the ranch would interfere with any of your holiday traditions," he said in a low voice that Drew and Kip couldn't hear.

She shrugged. "I knew when I sold the Wagon Wheel that many things would change. Our annual Christmas-tree hunt is the least of the changes."

He frowned. "But it's something your kids enjoy and I don't like being seen as the Grinch who deprived them of that."

"You didn't," she insisted, but he didn't look convinced.

"Look, there are plenty of trees up there, enough to supply us both with Christmas trees for years to come," he said. "You and your family can consider yourself welcome to cut one of your own in the future."

She didn't quite know how to respond to his unexpected generosity. She also couldn't help thinking that even though he seemed uncomfortable making the suggestion, it was rather sweet of him to think of it. And very unlike the hard, implacable businessman she had always considered him to be.

"Thank you. But we found a great one this year, didn't we?" she asked the boys. "My brother Paul owns the feed store in town and he found us a really great one from the shipment he got this year. It's a balsam pine and it smells divine."

Kip and Drew nodded. "You should see how we decorated it," Kip said. "We made strings of popcorn and paper chains and lots of gingerbread-cookie ornaments. They smell super good, too. Only you can't eat them or you'll get sick, Mom says, because they're only decorations. Do you want to see it?"

"I saw it the other day when I brought you home, remember?"

"Oh, yeah." Kip looked disappointed at not being able to come up with another excuse to keep Carson around longer, and Jenna decided she had better step in.

"You boys need to take care of Pep. He's been working hard and is probably ready for a rest and some oats."

Neither of them looked excited at the chore but since they knew it was their responsibility and she wouldn't let them wiggle out of it, they sighed and trudged toward the barn doors, tugging the horse's reins behind them. Frannie hobbled up and followed them inside, leaving Jenna and Jolie alone with Carson.

"Hi, mister." Jolie beamed at him when the boys were gone and Carson gave her a slightly uneasy look.

"Hi," he answered.

"Pretty horsey," Jolie repeated.

"Uh, thanks."

The man looked as if he had no idea how to interact with a little, blond curly-haired cherub. Jenna took pity on his discomfort and distracted Jolie by pulling out her wedding band that she kept on a chain around her neck. The diversion never failed to work and Jolie reached for it with an exclamation of glee.

While her daughter was busy jangling the necklace, swinging it back and forth and holding it up to catch the sunlight gleaming off the snow, she turned back to Carson. "I hope the boys weren't too much trouble."

"They weren't."

She couldn't help the laugh that escaped her, though she regretted it when he gave her an odd sort of look. "You don't have to sound so surprised," she said. "They *can* occasionally act like they're humans and not wild monkeys."

"They were fine. A few spats here and there but nothing too major. Actually, they were a big help finding the tree and it was…fun."

She had the feeling *fun* wasn't something Carson McRaven allowed himself to experience on a regular basis.

"I'm glad," she answered, then paused, remembering his unexpected offer of a few moments earlier. "Tell me they didn't lay some kind of guilt trip on you about our Christmas tree this year and having to find one in town instead of up on the mountain."

"No, not really. Except Hayden," he admitted. "He made a few disparaging comments about your tree being punier than usual."

She sighed. "Hayden would like everything to be the way it was before his father died. He misses him so much. All the boys do, but Joe and Hayden were extraordinarily close, I think because Hayden was the oldest."

"That's understandable."

"I guess you've figured out he's not happy I sold the

ranch. He doesn't understand all the factors that went into the decision." She didn't add that Hayden was also close to his paternal grandmother, who was full of vitriol about Carson McRaven.

Pat's stroke had changed many things. Before it, Joe's mother had been sweet and loving, always willing to lend a hand to anyone in need.

Jenna had to constantly remind herself the brain damage from the stroke was to blame for the changes in Pat's personality now. She had transformed into an angry, bitter woman who sometimes took out her frustration at her physical condition on everyone around her.

"I'm sure it's tough for a kid to see someone else living at the place he always considered home."

"Maybe, but you own the Wagon Wheel now—sorry, Raven's Nest. You have every right to keep every single pine tree on it just as it is. You should feel no guilt or sense of obligation toward me or my family. About Christmas trees or anything else."

"It's all right, Jenna. I really don't mind. You're welcome to take any tree on the ranch next year. Hell, take two or three. We'll plant more."

She studied him for a long moment, trying to gauge his sincerity. He looked as if he meant every word. "Thank you. The boys will be thrilled. And I promise, we won't cut anything without asking permission of you—or of Neil Parker if you're not around. Though to be honest, I'd really like to get through this Christmas before I have to start worrying about next year."

"Fair enough." He returned her smile and she sternly ordered her nerves to stop jumping around just because the man looked devastatingly gorgeous when he wasn't being all tough and serious all the time.

He turned and mounted the horse in one fluid motion. "Tell the boys thanks again for their help this afternoon."

"I'll do that. Goodbye. And if we don't see you again before next week, Merry Christmas."

He studied her a moment and she was quite certain he wanted to say something else but he only touched a finger to the black brim of his hat, wheeled the horse around and cantered down the long drive toward Raven's Nest.

"Bye," Jolie called, somewhat sadly, and Jenna hugged her close, watching after him.

She didn't understand the man. He was hard and austere one moment, until she thought she had him pegged as a rather humorless businessmen only interested in his next deal. But then he showed these flashes of unexpected kindness to her and her family that completely baffled her.

"Mom. Mom!" Kip's dramatically raised voice rang out through the cold air. "Hayden says I'm too big of a baby to ever have my own pony. He says I'll have to share Pep with Drew forever. He's just lying, isn't he? Isn't he?"

She turned her attention to her boys, trying to put thoughts of Carson McRaven out of her head.

He was just her neighbor, a man from a completely different sphere than hers that certainly never involved mucking out stalls and wiping runny noses. Their respective universes would never have collided at all if she hadn't made the fateful decision to sell him the Wagon Wheel.

Three hours later, Raven's Nest rang with the sounds made by the team of designers Carrianne had rounded up, who were decking every hall and jingling every bell.

The tree he and the Wheeler boys had cut down and dragged back had indeed fit perfectly in his great room. The evergreen scent radiated even back to his office and he had to admit the big tree brought a nice, homey touch to the house he was certain the Hertzogs would appreciate.

Though right now as he talked once again via video-conference with Carrianne, he was tempted to call up Frederick Hertzog and cancel the family's entire visit.

"We have a contract," he said. "Sawyer agreed to provide two days' worth of meals while the Hertzogs are here. We have spent the last two weeks nailing down every single detail of the menu with him, down to the frigging after-dinner cheese assortment. Tell the man it's his responsibility to find someone to cover for him if he can't fulfill the terms of our agreement or we'll sue him for breach of contract."

Carrianne's normally serene features were decidedly flustered. "I told him that. You can be certain I was quite clear on our expectations. When vendors agree to do business with McRaven Enterprises, they need to be prepared to honor their commitments. Chef Sawyer assures me that he's tried everyone he knows. But this late in the season, anyone he can recommend in the Jackson Hole area is either taking the holiday off or is already completely booked."

"What are we supposed to do?" He refused to give in to the panic, though he was quite sure that whooshing he heard in his head was the sound of the entire deal heading down the toilet. "They're going to be here by lunchtime and I'm quite sure Frederick Hertzog and his family are expecting a little more than canned soup and tuna sandwiches, which is about all I can prepare."

Carrianne ran a hand through her hair, messing up a few strands, which was definitely a sign that she was upset. "I can check with your personal chef here in the Bay Area and see if he might be available to fly out under these special circumstances or if he can recommend anyone. You will, of course, have to make it worth their while."

"You can be damn sure I'll charge Michael Sawyer for the difference."

"You can hardly fault the man for needing an emergency appendectomy."

"Maybe not. But he should have a contingency plan in case of illness. It's just sound business sense to be prepared for every eventuality."

He thought he had covered all his bases for this visit. But perhaps they should have had a backup chef on standby.

"You know that even if I can find someone here in San Francisco, it's going to take some time to work out all the logistical details for them to travel to Pine Gulch, right? You might be on your own for lunch."

He grimaced, envisioning one nightmare scenario after another. "Just do what you can to get someone here as soon as possible, no matter the cost..."

His voice trailed off as he looked out his office window to the colored Christmas lights flickering in the twilight down the hill.

"Hold it. Wait a minute." He moved the curtain and looked down at Jenna Wheeler's house that seemed like a bright beacon against the wintry night. "Don't call anyone yet, Carrianne. I might be able to fix this mess after all."

"How?"

"Jenna Wheeler."

Carrianne frowned and looked down at something he couldn't see on the screen. "I don't think she's in my Contacts file."

"She wouldn't be. Jenna is my neighbor—the woman who sold me the ranch, remember?"

Carrianne made a sound of shock. "The one with the pestilent children? What does she have to do with any of this?"

Had he really said that about her children? After a few hours in their company, he regretted the harsh words. They weren't pestilent. Energetic and mischievous, maybe, but they were only boys. "Jenna Wheeler might just be able to salvage this situation, if she's willing, anyway. I'll let you know as soon as I talk to her. Just keep your fingers crossed."

Carrianne held up both hands, which were now as tangled as pretzels. "Consider it done," she said promptly.

But as he ended the call and headed for the door, Carson knew it would take more than crossed fingers to convince Jenna Wheeler to help him.

It might just take a Christmas miracle.

Chapter Six

"Can we open another one? Please, Mom? Just one more?"

She shook her head at Hayden, who was gazing at her with pleading eyes. "You know the rule. We only open one book each night until Christmas."

"But we have extras in the basket!" Drew protested. "Christmas Eve is in four more nights and we have six books left in the basket."

She should have known Drew would be the one to notice and point out that fact to his brothers. He would never let a detail like that slip past him.

"I know, honey. But I wrapped extras so we could read two or three books on Christmas Eve. Just in case certain people have a hard time falling asleep."

"Like Kip!" Hayden and Drew both said in unison and she laughed along with them. Her youngest boy was notorious for finding any excuse to stay up late, whether it was Christmas Eve or not.

"I'm not naming any names. But that's the reason for the extra books."

She had started a tradition when Hayden and Drew were barely old enough to sit still long enough for a story, of creating a storybook Advent basket. Each year she wrapped up all their old Christmas picture books in holiday paper and threw in a few new ones to surprise the boys. Every night from December first until Christmas Eve they were allowed to unwrap one book to read for their nightly story.

The tradition helped them countdown to Christmas and also provided Jenna an excuse to reread all their favorite stories. Even Hayden, who was now ten, still seemed to enjoy curling up on the couch by the fire while they read. It was a quiet, peaceful time in the midst of their usual chaotic day and Jenna savored every second.

"We've had our story, now off to bed. We'll open another book tomorrow."

The boys groaned and protested but she persevered and was herding them up the stairs toward their bedrooms when the doorbell suddenly echoed through the house.

"I'll get it!" Kip exclaimed, racing to beat his brothers in the mad dash to the front door.

Who could be knocking on their door this late? It was nearly 9:00 p.m. Maybe one of their Cold Creek Canyon neighbors was out delivering cookie plates or something, she thought as she headed back down the stairs, hoping the doorbell didn't wake Jolie.

"Hi," she heard a deep voice say and her heart accelerated, though she knew that was wholly ridiculous.

"Hi!" Kip exclaimed. "Hey, Mom, look who it is! It's Mr. McRaven! Did you come to see our Christmas tree again?"

"No," he answered. "But now that I've had a good look at it again, I can verify that you were right, it is a nice one."

All three of her boys looked excited at Carson's visit, even Hayden, she saw with some surprise, though he was trying hard to hide it.

She had no idea why he might be there and he apparently had no inclination to immediately explain.

"Come in," Jenna said after an awkward moment. "It's bitter out tonight."

He took off his Stetson as he walked into the house and she fought the ridiculous urge to straighten his wavy hair that had been flattened a bit by the hat.

"It's started to snow again," he said. "There's already another inch or so out there. I guess we don't have to worry about a white Christmas, do we?"

She shook her head, but he still didn't move to enlighten her on his reason for stopping by. Her mind raced with possibilities but she discarded all of them.

"Is something wrong?" she finally asked.

His mouth tightened a little and she saw discomfort in his eyes. "You could say that. I need to ask a favor. A pretty big one."

"Do you need us to help you decorate your tree after all?" Drew asked eagerly.

Carson blinked at the boys in their pajamas. "Uh, no. I had people come do that today. But thanks for the offer."

He seemed so ill at ease, shifting his weight, curling his fingers around the brim of the hat he held, not meeting her gaze for longer than a few seconds at a time. Somehow Jenna sensed this conversation would be easier without the prying presence of three nosy little boys.

"Guys, to bed."

"Oh, Mom," Kip groaned. "We have company. Can't we stay up and talk to Mr. McRaven?"

"Not tonight," she said, her voice firm. "It's late and you've got chores and church in the morning. Come on, up you go."

They all three gave heavy, put-upon sighs but Jenna didn't waver. Apparently they saw she meant business. Though they didn't look thrilled about it, they trudged up the stairs at a turtle's pace.

"Drew, lights out means lights out. No flashlights under the covers so you can read a little more tonight, okay?"

His sigh was even heavier than his brothers' but he nodded and headed into the room he shared with Kip.

When she heard both doors close, she turned back to Carson. "Sorry. They're a little wired this time of year."

"Most kids are, aren't they?"

She nodded, then decided her curiosity couldn't wait another minute. "Sit down. You said you had a favor to ask."

He let out a breath and eased onto the sofa. "Not an easy thing for me, I'll admit."

She smiled, disarmed that he would confess such a thing. She knew exactly how hard it was to ask people for things. Since Joe died, she had tried to remain as self-reliant as possible but it wasn't always easy to do everything on her own.

"I'm in the midst of some...delicate negotiations to purchase a European company," Carson finally said. "I've invited the owner to stay at Raven's Nest for a few days while he's in the States for a ski vacation over the holidays with his family. He's flying up from Salt Lake City in the morning with his family. His wife, his son and daughter-in-law and his two grandchildren."

And this affected her and her family how? Jenna waited, still feeling completely in the dark. "Let me guess. You'd like me to keep the boys away from Raven's Nest while your guests are here."

His eyes widened and she was gratified that he looked completely startled at the suggestion. "No. Nothing like that. "

After another pause, he made a face and plunged forward. "The truth is, I hired a personal chef out of Jackson Hole to take care of the food while my guests are here. Michael Sawyer, with About Thyme Gourmet."

"He's a good choice. Probably the best you can find in the area." She knew the man casually from a few classes she had taken. While personally she found him to be an arrogant jerk, he was a fabulously creative chef.

"Only too bad for me, last night he was hit with acute appendicitis and he's in the hospital for at least two days."

"Oh. I'm sorry. Poor man. What an awful way to spend Christmas." She had firsthand experience how tough it was to be surrounded by hospital walls and beeping monitors and impersonal doctors during the holidays.

Carson blinked. "Right. It is unfortunate for him. But the fact remains that I still have guests arriving in a little over twelve hours and nothing whatsoever to serve them."

Suddenly everything made sense. She rose to her feet in a jerky motion. "No. No way. Absolutely not."

He raised a dark eyebrow. "How do you even know what I was going to ask?"

"What else? You want me to cook for your guests. And my answer is an unequivocal no."

"Why not?"

Could he really be this unbelievably arrogant, so outrageously self-deluded by the sense of his own importance? "It's four days before Christmas Eve, Carson. Did you forget that little detail? You honestly expect me to just drop everything at the last minute—my family, my own holiday plans—just so I can be at your beck and call?"

The heat of her response seemed to take him aback. He blinked at her with complete astonishment. "I'll make it worth your while. Whatever your usual fee would be for two days of work, I'll double it. No, triple it."

She was a professional, she reminded herself. Despite the weird currents between them and her ridiculous attraction to him, he was a potential client offering her a lucrative position. One that might have long-ranging benefits if he was happy with her work and continued to use her for Raven's Nest events.

But before she was a caterer, she was a mother and that had to come first. "I can't leave my children this close to Christmas. I just can't, Carson. We've made plans. I told them the stockmen's party was my last event of the season and I can't break my promise."

"It's just for a few days."

"Which can seem like a lifetime to children. I promised myself I wouldn't let anything ruin their holiday. Not this year."

"Why not? What's so important about this year?"

"You wouldn't ask that question if you had children of your own."

A weird expression flitted across his features but it was gone so quickly she thought she must have imagined it.

"Every year is important when you have children. This is the only time in their lives they'll be ten, eight, six and eighteen months. Next year will be an entirely different dynamic. Time marches on. If I learned anything from Joe's death it's the importance of magnifying every moment I have with my children."

"A lovely philosophy in the abstract. But we're only talking about two days."

"I owe them. Don't you see? We haven't had the best holidays for the past years. Two years ago, their father was dying and we were dealing with the funeral arrangements and everything. Then last year, Jolie, my little girl, was in the hospital with pneumonia. The boys had to spend Christmas with their aunt and uncle while I was at the hospital with her for most of the holidays. I promised them—and myself—this year would be different."

"It's only for a couple of days," he repeated. "You'll still have Christmas Eve and Christmas Day and the whole rest of the holidays."

She had a feeling she could argue with him until her ears turned blue but he wouldn't understand. "No. I'm sorry, but you'll just have to find someone else."

He rose to stand in front of her and she was caught by the plea in his blue eyes. "There is no one else, Jenna.

Not at this late date, not this close to Christmas. Look, I'm desperate. This visit with Frederick Hertzog and his family is important to me."

"And my children are important to me, Mr. Mc-Raven. Far more important than any business deal."

He gazed at her, with her holiday-red sweater and her plain gold hoop earrings and her honey-blond hair piled up on top of her head in a haphazard way that should have looked a mess but somehow managed to look tousled and pretty.

How could she appear so soft and fragile yet be so maddeningly stubborn at the same time?

He considered his options. None of them were very palatable. The idea of serving macaroni and cheese from a box for every meal filled him with cold dread. He supposed he could order in every meal but the restaurant options in Pine Gulch weren't exactly gourmet, either. The coffee shop served decent, honest food but nothing memorable.

There were good restaurants in Jackson Hole or Idaho Falls but both of them were at least forty-five minutes away in opposite directions. A little too far for a quick to-go pickup.

No, Jenna Wheeler was his best alternative. Now if only he could make her realize how limited his choices were.

He narrowed his gaze and tried a little hardball. "You know, I could always decide to lock the gate to the bridge across the creek. It belongs to me now and there was nothing in our sale agreement that obligated me to provide access to you or your family."

She stared at him, sudden fury kindling in her gaze,

and he realized the soft little kitten had sharp claws. "You would really go to such lengths to get your way?"

He sighed, not sure whether he despised himself more for making the suggestion in the first place or because he didn't have the stomach to follow through on it. "Probably not," he admitted. "But I am in dire straits here, Jenna. What about just helping me out with brunch and dinner tomorrow? That would at least give my people time to fly someone else in from the Bay Area for the second day."

She raked a hand through her hair. "I promised the boys we would go sledding after church tomorrow."

"You could still do that, in between meals."

"You have no idea how long it takes to prepare a halfway decent meal of the scope you're talking about, do you?"

"Not really. I'm not much of a cook, I'm afraid. You make it seem effortless, though."

"Effortless. Right." She shook her head but he could sense she was wavering.

"Please, Jenna." He pushed a little harder. "If you do this for me, I promise, I'll never again bring up the idea of you selling the rest of your land to me. I'll never get mad at your boys for wandering where they're not supposed to be. I'll be the perfect neighbor."

"Ha."

Her cynical exclamation was in such contrast to her soft prettiness that he had to laugh.

"I swear it."

She sighed heavily. "How many guests did you say you were expecting?"

"Six total. Frederick and Antonia Hertzog, their son, Dierk, and his wife, Elle, and their children Amalia and

Gregor. They have no food allergies, though Gregor doesn't like anything with onions and Elle insists on low saturated fats."

"What sort of menus have you discussed?"

"I can provide you with everything Sawyer had talked to my assistant about before his unfortunate medical complications. But you don't have to feel obligated to follow his plan. I can be flexible."

This time her laugh was filled with unabashed doubt. "*Can* you? I believe I would like to see proof of that."

Her tart tone made him smile. "I can. Just watch me."

She gave him a long, considering look and he wondered what was going on behind those lovely green eyes.

"So does that mean you'll do it?"

She sighed. "How can I refuse for three times my regular rate and your promise that you won't nag me to sell the Wagon Wheel to you anymore?"

He winced. "You're going to hold me to that, I suppose."

"That's the only reason I would even consider it."

"And people call me a merciless negotiator."

"I'll need your assistant to fax me copies of all the menus tonight and a complete inventory list of the food items Michael Sawyer has already purchased. I may need to make some changes if he was planning dishes I can't fix."

Was that enthusiasm or nerves he could see sparking in her eyes? Whatever it was, she looked bright and vibrant and extraordinarily lovely.

"You can fix anything you'd like," he finally said. "I completely trust your judgment."

Her mouth tightened and the spark went out as if

someone had dumped a foot of snow on her. "No, you don't. You think I'm a terrible mother who can't control her own children."

He stared, genuinely astonished. "When did I ever say that?"

"You didn't have to say the words, Carson. Every time the boys have gotten into trouble on your property and we've had to discuss it, I've seen the reaction in your eyes. You try to hide it but I know you find them frustrating."

Only a few days ago, he would have wholeheartedly agreed with her. But something had changed in the last day or so. He couldn't put his finger on it but he didn't find Jenna Wheeler and her family nearly the abhorrent neighbors he once had.

"They're growing on me," he admitted.

She tilted her head and studied him for a long moment then she smiled. "Good. Because I'm not sure I'll be able to find child care tomorrow morning. If you insist on me cooking for your guests, you just may have to deal with my children coming along to Raven's Nest with me, as well."

For just an instant, panic spurted through him at the idea of three active boys and a toddler racing through his mountaintop haven, knocking over priceless antiques, pressing sticky handprints all over the walls, asking him endless questions he didn't know how to answer.

He squashed it quickly. She was doing him a huge favor and he couldn't quibble about her terms.

Chapter Seven

With a vague sense that she was stuck in some weird dream, Jenna entered the kitchen at Raven's Nest just after 7:00 a.m., four hours before the guests were due to arrive.

She was already cursing whatever ridiculous impulse had convinced her to help Carson.

This was crazy. She had no business being here when she still had presents to wrap, a few last-minute stocking stuffers to find and the guest room to dig out for Pat's annual Christmas Eve visit.

And where was she? Standing in a room that looked as if it were straight out of the pages of some kitchen design magazine.

If she needed yet another reminder of all the differences between the two of them, she only had to look at his kitchen. It was a dream of a room, exactly how she would have laid out her own fantasy kitchen—wide marble countertops, an efficient work space in the middle, double refrigerators, six-burner, professional-grade cooktop, even a wok station. He had everything she could have fantasized about.

Ironic that a man who claimed he didn't cook would have the most gorgeous kitchen she had ever seen. But she supposed she shouldn't be surprised. Carson McRaven struck her as a man of impeccable taste. He wouldn't build a house like Raven's Nest, with its soaring views and careful attention to style and elegance, and stick a subpar kitchen in the middle of it.

Jenna moved to the window, where the only building she could see was her own house, its white paint blending into the snow. The house she loved so much looked humble and rather shabby from this vantage point. Was that what Carson thought when he saw it?

She gripped the sink's edge as sudden panic assailed her. She had no business being here. This was a huge mistake. Someone's idea of a cosmic joke.

What did she know about cooking for people who flew on private jets and had kitchen appliances that probably cost more than her van, even when it had been new?

Breathe, she ordered herself. *You can do this.*

She was on her third round of circle breathing, focusing on her house and the love and laughter she found in it, when she sensed she was no longer alone. She turned and found Carson standing in the doorway watching her. He wore jeans and scuffed boots and a Western shirt and looked as if he would have been more at home herding strays in the high country or slinging longnecks down at The Bandito than standing in this beautiful kitchen with the morning sunlight slanting across his features.

"Morning," he said. "Melina just told me she let you in. Are you ready for this?"

"Wrong question." She did her best to keep the alarm that bubbled through her from filtering into her voice. "I was just thinking I'm not sure I can pull this off."

One corner of his mouth lifted in a devastating smile. "Of course you can. I've tasted your food, remember? Everything you served at the stock growers' party was delicious and I think I finished off what your boys brought over the other day in about half an hour. You're brilliant in the kitchen."

"Brilliant? I wouldn't go that far."

"I wouldn't have asked you to do this if I didn't think you could handle it, Jenna. You should know that."

His words steadied her and she took one more deep breath and pushed the panic away.

"Is everything on schedule, then?"

He nodded. "I'm meeting the Hertzogs' plane in Jackson at ten. I was just about to head out but I wanted to check in with you first. Do you have everything you need?"

She glanced around the gleaming kitchen and almost laughed, though she was afraid if she started, she would end up in hysterics and he would have to cart her away.

What could she possibly need that wasn't contained in this chef's paradise? "I should be fine. According to the inventory Carrianne faxed me last night, I should have enough food to feed several dozen people for a couple of weeks."

"In a couple of weeks, I'll be back in San Francisco

and my company will, knock wood, be the proud owners of Hertzog Communications."

"Unless I screw up and poison everyone today."

He laughed. "Try not to do that, okay? Call me if you can't find something you need and I'll try to pick it up while I'm in town."

"Don't you pay people to fetch and carry for you?" she asked. "I would think Carson McRaven of McRaven Enterprises would be too busy for airport runs and hitting the grocery store."

He hesitated for a moment then nodded. "Yeah, I could send someone to pick them up. But Frederick Hertzog is the sort of man who appreciates the personal touch. A few hours out of my schedule is a small price to pay if it helps convince him McRaven Enterprises will take good care of the company his family built over three generations, first as a telegraph company, then telephones, and now cells."

No wonder the man had created a huge dynasty in such a short time, if he used that sort of sound business sense in all of his dealings.

"I really owe you for this, Jenna."

She gave him a dark look. "Yes. You do. I'm blaming you if my children's Christmas is ruined because their mother had a nervous breakdown."

His laugh was warm and amused and sent chills rippling down her spine. "And where are your children this morning? I thought they would be belly flopping into the swimming pool by now."

"You caught a very lucky break. My sister-in-law called last night after you left and asked if they could come over today and help her make gingerbread houses.

When I told her what I was doing for you, she insisted on taking them to church and then having them spend the afternoon with her. My niece will watch them this evening and then again tomorrow. And you're paying them an outrageous amount for it, by the way."

"Am I? Good for me."

She couldn't contain the laugh that escaped her. It helped ease the tension gripping her shoulders like an eagle's talons—until he smiled back at her and her insides felt as if she had just taken a free fall from the Grand Teton.

She quickly looked away and her gaze rested on one of the small appliances she hadn't noticed before. "Oh, my word. You've got a steam oven! I've been dying to try one of these."

"Well, here's your chance."

He studied her for a long moment and there was a strange light in his eyes at her excitement, something glittery and bright. A thin, tensile current tugged between them and she couldn't seem to look away.

He was the first one to break eye contact. He cleared his throat and eased away from the counter. "I'd better get moving. Give me a call if you find you're in need of anything else."

"I'll do that." To her dismay, her voice sounded raspy and hollow.

After he left, she stood for a moment, wondering what on earth that was all about. This attraction was completely absurd, she reminded herself. She had no business even thinking about Carson McRaven that way.

His kitchen. That was another story entirely. Any

normal, breathing foodie would salivate buckets over this kitchen.

She had the tools, she had the ingredients. Now she just had to do them all justice.

Despite the pep talk she gave herself and the vague comfort she found in knowing Carson had faith in her, nervous tension still seethed and simmered in her stomach all morning as she worked alone in the Raven's Nest kitchen.

As the huge black-rimmed clock over the fireplace ticked inexorably away, that tension grew to full-blown panic. She had pulled out the last batch of cinnamon apple muffins and was stirring the light mushroom sauce for the chicken crepes when she heard a commotion outside the kitchen.

"Sounds like our guests are here," Melina Parker said from the other side of the kitchen, where Jenna had, with desperate gratitude, taken up her offer of help by enlisting her to finish cutting pineapple for the fruit plate.

Nerves jumped inside her but she forced herself to focus on the work at hand. "Thanks again for helping me. I'm afraid I wouldn't even be close if not for you."

"No problem. I can handle slicing and dicing, as long as I don't have to come up with menus or use any creativity," Melina answered. "What else can I do?"

Jenna looked around the kitchen, which was a great deal more disorganized than it had been when she first walked into it three hours ago. "I think the smoked salmon eggs Benedict is ready. And these crepes are just about done. You could take them out to the buffet table, if you don't mind."

"That's why I'm here, darlin'."

Melina headed out of the kitchen with her arms full. When Jenna heard someone come back inside a few moments later, she assumed it was Carson's housekeeper and didn't turn around. She was too busy taking the pineapple-glazed ham out of the oven. "Can you put a few more of the banana-walnut muffins in the basket and take out a couple of the blueberry to even the numbers a little more?"

"Um, sure."

At the unexpected deep voice, she swiveled her head and found Carson standing in the doorway.

"Oh. Sorry. I thought you were Melina."

"I'm not. But I don't mind rearranging your muffins for you."

"You don't have to," she protested. But he had already crossed to the prep sink on the island to wash his hands.

"How's everything going in here?"

Even though he was stepping in to help, she couldn't control her glare. "That reminds me. Go away. I'm not talking to you right now."

He laughed and she found it terribly unfair that even in the midst of the kitchen chaos and her own personal crisis, he could still make her pulse jump.

"The entire house smells fantastic. If everything tastes even a tenth as good as it smells, you have absolutely nothing to worry about."

"Easy for you to say. They're European!"

"What does that have to do with anything?"

"European jet-setters. They probably have their own personal chef trained at Le Cordon Bleu. Do you know where I was trained? Do you?"

"No idea. Where?"

"The greasy-spoon diner in town. Yes, I received

a degree in food sciences but all my practical experiences came from Lou Archeleta, the cook at the diner. I worked there all through high school and he sometimes let me try out new dishes. Oh, this is going to be a disaster."

"Jenna, relax."

He stepped closer and rested a hand on her shoulder. For one crazy moment, she wanted to close her eyes and just soak up the comfort he offered. The strength of the impulse astounded her. It had been so very long since she had anyone to lean on.

At least since Joe's accident. Longer, she supposed. He had been so busy working fourteen-and sixteen-hour days trying to hang on to the ranch that she had learned early in their marriage to be self-sufficient.

Right now the idea of sharing her burdens with someone else for a moment seemed a seductive temptation.

"Everything will be fine." Carson squeezed her shoulder. "I think you'll like the Hertzogs. They're warm and friendly and not at all pretentious. Your food is going to wow them. Trust me."

She wanted to. Oh, she wanted to. Right now it was difficult to remember their relationship was strictly that of neighbors and now client and chef.

Difficult but not impossible, she reminded herself and made a concerted effort to step away from his enticing heat and strength, using the excuse that the cottage potatoes had to be stirred one last time before she transferred them to a serving bowl.

"I guess we're about to find out, aren't we?" she murmured, then arranged a garnish on the potatoes, picked up the serving bowl like a shield and headed into the dining room.

* * *

"What a spectacular view you have here. If I had a home here, I would never want to leave it." Antonia Hertzog smiled at him and Carson wondered why she reminded him so forcefully of his grandmother.

The two women were nothing alike. His grandmother, God bless her, had been short and stout, with broad, sun-baked features and wavy gray hair she kept in a ruthless hairnet. Antonia was slender with ageless features and that innate élan that seemed so effortless in European women.

Still, something about the warmth in her eyes brought his grandmother firmly to mind.

"I fell for the view the first time I saw it," he admitted. He didn't add that very few other places in his life had given him such an instant connection. His grandparents' ranch had felt the same but he supposed his chaotic, nomadic upbringing made it more difficult for him to feel so at home in any particular place.

"I can see why," she answered. "Do you spend much time here?"

"Not as much as I'd like. The house has only been done for a short time. I expect to get away from San Francisco more often in the future."

"A man cannot work all the time," Frederick said, with a meaningful look at his son, Dierk, who was too busy sending a message on one of the company's cutting-edge phones to even notice.

"When may we ride the horses?" Dierk's son, Gregor, asked. Gregor was twelve, two years older than his sister, Amalia, who hadn't said more than a word or two throughout the entire delectable meal.

"That's up to your parents. After brunch would be fine with me."

"May we, Mother?" Amalia asked, her tone as formal as if she were petitioning the queen for a stay of execution.

"You both must have a rest first." Elle Hertzog was as whip-thin as a greyhound and though Jenna's food was divine, she had eaten only a little fruit and half a muffin. "We have already had a rather long morning."

Carson expected protests but both children only nodded solemnly. In his limited experience of children, he couldn't help contrasting the behavior of Amalia and Gregor to the Wheelers. The Hertzog children had impeccable table manners and didn't so much as fidget on their chairs.

He imagined Jenna's boys would have been swinging from the chandelier right about now. They were noisy and busy and troublesome. He wasn't sure why he found their spirited antics so much more appealing.

After their meal, he stayed out of the kitchen as long as he could manage.

The Hertzogs opted to go in their rooms for a short time to unpack and relax before their scheduled afternoon ride, leaving him feeling rather disjointed and at loose ends.

He had a great deal of work he could be doing. Contracts to study, phone calls to make, reports to read.

All of that paled in comparison with the insistent tug he felt toward Jenna Wheeler.

For the life of him, he couldn't understand his powerful attraction to her and he wasn't sure he liked it. Certainly she was a lovely woman, with those stunning green eyes and her soft blond hair and delicate features. He was surrounded by beautiful women all the time, but none of them fascinated him as she did.

He rationalized his trip back to the kitchen by reminding himself that before brunch she had been as nervous as a long-tailed cat at a hoedown, to use one of his grandfather's favorite phrases.

Didn't he owe it to her to set her mind at ease? To reassure her that the food had been devoured by the Hertzogs, who commented several times on how delicious it was?

Only for a moment, he told himself. He could compliment her food, thank her again for helping him, then return to his office in only a few minutes and tackle his workload.

He heard her before he saw her. Her low contralto voice sang a quiet Christmas carol that somehow sounded more lovely in this setting than the opera diva he had been privileged to hear a few weeks earlier in San Francisco.

He stood in the hallway outside the kitchen and let the sweetness of the song wash over him, of babies and mangers and a hope for the future.

When her song ended, he took a couple of breaths then walked into the kitchen, acting as if he had just come from another part of the house. He didn't think she would appreciate knowing he had spied on her for the last five minutes, at least aurally.

At his entrance, she looked up from stirring something in a bowl. "Oh. Hello."

He forced a smile, not at all sure why his chest suddenly ached. "I knew you were good. I didn't realize your food would be the hit of the day so far."

"It was okay, then?" she asked, then winced. "Forget I said that. I swore to myself I wouldn't ask."

"Why not?"

She shrugged and turned back to the mixing bowl. "I'm quite certain you'll tell me if the meals I prepare don't meet your lofty expectations."

"Do I come across as such an ogre, then?"

He meant it as an off-handed comment and didn't really expect a response but she frowned, appearing to give the matter serious consideration. "Not an ogre. Not at all. Just a man who demands perfection. Or as close to it as we mortals can provide."

"In that case, my expectations were far exceeded. Brunch was absolute perfection. Far better, I'm sure, than Michael Sawyer would have provided."

Her smile took his breath away and made that ache return to his chest. "Thank you, Carson. I'm so glad you enjoyed it."

"I wasn't the only one. Frederick and his wife both commented on how delicious the food was."

She smiled again. "I can't tell you what a huge relief that is to hear. Now maybe I can relax a little for dinner."

He suddenly wanted fiercely to kiss away those nerves. The impulse shocked the hell out of him and he moved away a little, using the excuse of going to the refrigerator for a bottle of water.

"Did you have the chance to use the steam oven?" he asked. He knew he ought to leave now but he couldn't quite bring himself to walk out of the warm, fragrant kitchen.

"I did. It was incredible. I steamed the mini Christmas puddings in it. I've never had them turn out so well."

She glowed with excitement as she talked about cooking. He had never known anyone to get so thrilled about Christmas pudding and he had to admit, he found her fascinating. Refreshing.

"I'm glad it worked out."

"I'm going to bake the bread for tonight in it. I can't wait to see how it works. It's supposed to leave the crust hard but the inside perfectly soft."

"You're making the bread?" It was a completely foreign concept to him.

"Of course. You didn't expect me to serve plain old Wonder to your guests, did you? They're European!"

He couldn't help himself, he laughed out loud. For just an instant, her gaze shifted down to his mouth and suddenly the air changed. Those currents started zinging between them again and a blush crept up her cheeks.

He wondered what she was thinking about that turned her skin that lovely rose. And why was she staring at his mouth?

He wanted to kiss her. The impulse took him completely by surprise. He wanted to take Jenna Wheeler in his arms and kiss her right here in this kitchen smelling of cinnamon and spice and everything nice.

He told himself he couldn't do it. She wasn't interested in a kiss—or anything else—and she would probably slap him if he tried.

But maybe not.

He probably could have just backed out of the kitchen and left her to her steam-oven bread baking. But just at that moment, she stirred the contents of the bowl she was holding just a little too hard and the whole thing started to slip out of her hands. He was close enough to lunge after it and for a moment, they both stood together holding the bowl between them.

He could feel the heat of her, the suppressed energy,

and again her gaze flicked to his mouth. He knew he should back away but she was so soft and curvy against him and her mouth was right there and his sudden fierce hunger to taste that soft mouth was more than he could control.

Chapter Eight

She had forgotten what an intense physical experience a kiss could be. Though he touched her with only his mouth, her entire body seemed to sizzle to life, as if all that made her female had been lying dormant since her husband's death.

Every sense seemed heightened, superacute. She could hear the blood pulsing through her veins, the ragged sound of his breathing, could feel his heat seeping into her muscles. He smelled divine, a sensuous mix of laundry soap and a subtle aftershave with notes of bergamot and something woodsy and masculine.

As wonderful as he smelled, he tasted even better, of coffee and cinnamon and something elusive she couldn't identify.

It was an addictive mix, sultry and seductive, and she felt ridiculously like a banana flambé, as if everything inside her was being caramelized and sweetened by his touch.

The most alluring part was that when she was in his arms she didn't feel like a young widow or like somebody's mother. She was only Jenna, a woman who had dreams and hopes and desires of her own.

As he lingered at her mouth, licking at the corner, tasting and teasing, she lost all sense of time and whatever tiny ounce of common sense she might have possessed before he walked into the kitchen.

Oh, it had been far too long. She had forgotten the way a man's touch could make her head spin and her insides flip around with wild joy. She had forgotten the churn of her blood and the yearning heat that stirred up out of nowhere like a dust devil on a July afternoon.

Somehow she was no longer holding the mixing bowl, though she wasn't sure if he had set it on the counter or if she had. Whoever had done it, with her hands free now she couldn't resist wrapping her arms around the strong, tanned column of his neck. She wanted to burrow against him, to absorb his strength inside her.

As the kiss continued, other sensations gradually pushed their way to the forefront of her consciousness. The slow, resolute tick of the big clock above the fireplace, the hard marble countertop pressing into the small of her back, the quiet whoosh of the dishwasher.

What on earth was she doing here? She hadn't touched a man in two years and here she was tangling tongues with Carson McRaven, of all people.

Yes, he was gorgeous and any woman would probably be thrilled to find herself in Jenna's comfortable-soled sneakers right about now.

On a physical level, she couldn't deny she was fiercely attracted to him. But could she have picked a worse male on the planet to grab on to for her jump back into the whole man-woman scene?

Carson was coolly arrogant, used to getting his own way at any cost. Worse than that, he disliked children. Especially *her* children.

She had to stop this somehow. She summoned all her strength and wrenched her mouth from his. With the countertop at her back, she had no way to escape so she slid her hands from around his neck and she used them instead to push at his chest, frantic suddenly for air and breathing space.

He froze for a heartbeat or two and then he stepped back, to her vast relief. They stared at each other and every sound in the kitchen seemed magnified. Her breathing seemed to come in ragged gulps and she had no idea how to react.

What must he think of her? She had responded to him like some sex-starved widow, desperate for a man's touch.

She found it small consolation that he looked thunderstruck, as if his lovely, elegant kitchen were suddenly teeming with bobcats.

She fumbled for words and came up empty. She had no experience in this sort of situation and didn't know the first thing to say to him. He let out a long breath and then raked a hand through his hair.

"Well. That was certainly…unexpected," he finally said.

Heat soaked her cheeks and she wanted to sink through his custom Italian tile floor. "Wasn't it?" she murmured, in as cool a voice as she could muster. She hurried to the sink and washed her hands, then picked up the mixing bowl and resumed stirring the ingredients for the flourless chocolate cake, grateful for any excuse not to have to look at him.

Still, she was intensely aware of him watching her out of those vibrant blue eyes. After a moment, he stepped closer and it was all she could do not to back up a pace.

"I should probably tell you I don't usually do that sort of thing."

She absolutely refused to allow her hands to shake, though it was taking every ounce of her concentration. "Kiss women?" She raised a skeptical eyebrow. "I'll admit, I'm not the most experienced rose in the garden but I find that a little hard to believe, judging by your proficiency at it."

He gave a surprised-sounding laugh but quickly sobered. "I meant I'm not in the habit of accosting employees."

She drew in a sharp breath at the stark reminder of the differences between them and all the reasons she should never have let him touch her. She felt foolish and remarkably naive—quite a feat for a woman who had been married for ten years and had four children.

"You didn't accost me. It was a simple kiss."

"Right."

If she found any solace in this entire situation, it was that Carson appeared as baffled and uneasy as she was by their heated embrace.

"I didn't mean for that to happen."

"Let's just forget it did, all right?"

He looked as if he wanted to argue but before he could form the words, her cell phone chirped out its cheery "Jingle Bells" ring tone. She fumbled in her pocket and for one humiliating moment, she couldn't pull it free, but she was finally able to grasp it and open it to talk.

She had barely said hello before Kip started babbling something about how his aunt had given him a new nutcracker for his collection only Hayden stole it and wouldn't give it back, claiming he was going to throw it in the woodstove.

"Make him stop, Mama! Make him *stop*!"

She sighed. On the one hand, she was grateful for the distraction from Carson. On the other, she truly hated mothering by phone.

"Calm down, honey. He's not going to throw anything into the woodstove. He's just teasing you because you get so upset."

"He's not. He said he was serious."

"Where's your aunt Terri?"

"In the garage talking to Uncle Paul. He's under the truck changing the oil. I got to help hand him a wrench."

"Good job. Let me talk to Hayden, okay?"

While she waited, she caught a glimpse of Carson still leaning against the counter watching her, his expression distant and unreadable.

A moment later, she heard Kip yelling down the hall, "Hayden, Mom wants to talk to you. You better give me back my nutcracker right now or you are in big trouble."

By the time she sorted through the situation and lectured Hayden on not teasing his younger siblings, Carson had left the kitchen.

She hadn't seen him go but she told herself she was relieved. The last thing she needed when she was so stressed about this job was for Carson to stand over her, making her forget her own name, not to mention whether she had added the turmeric to the soup.

She needed to concentrate on the meal she was preparing for dinner, not on the man who kissed her senseless.

Why had he kissed her?

That was the question that echoed through the kitchen the rest of the afternoon and haunted her long after she watched through the kitchen window as Carson and his guests left the ranch on horseback and headed up the trail toward the mountains through a light, powdery snowfall.

She knew why she had responded to him. What sane woman wouldn't? But she wasn't the kind of woman who inspired men like him to passionate embraces. She was a widow with four children, for heaven's sake, not some tight-bodied twenty-three-year-old socialite.

What did it matter? she finally asked herself. It was a fluke that would never be repeated. Somehow she was going to have to focus on the job at hand and not on that stunning, heart-stopping kiss.

She had only a few more meals to cook for him and his guests and then she would retreat to her family and leave Carson McRaven to rattle around alone here in his huge, gorgeous house.

Carson deliberately stayed out of the kitchen the rest of the day, though it was a challenge. With the strength of his fascination for Jenna, he might not have been able to do it if he hadn't spent most of the afternoon out of the house with the Hertzogs—or at least with Frederick and Dierk and the children. Antonia and Elle planned to stay at the house relaxing in the hot tub while Carson and the rest of his guests went riding.

He led them on horses up into the snow-covered mountains above the house, on a trail groomed by one of his men on the ranch's snowcat to make the going a little easier for the horses.

Mother Nature cooperated and provided a gorgeous afternoon, with only a light, feather-soft snowfall that made the entire scene look like something out of a watercolor painting.

He showed them the elk herd that wintered in one of the high pastures and the sixty-foot waterfall that was just beginning to ice over for the season.

Several hours later, they returned to the house tired and hungry just as twilight was settling over the valley and the lights of Jenna's house were beginning to sparkle in the snow.

The Christmas tree he and her boys had cut gleamed a welcome for them in the window and he was suddenly enormously grateful they had nagged him into it. Raven's Nest looked warm and inviting, exactly as he had always dreamed.

"Something certainly smells delicious," Frederick exclaimed as they walked into Raven's Nest after taking care of the horses.

Carson's stomach rumbled at the mingled scents emanating from the kitchen, of meats roasting and yeasty bread and something sweet and chocolaty.

"I am starving," Gregor said.

"We must clean up before we eat," his father said, his voice firm. "We all smell like the horses."

After thanking him for the ride and the tour of the ranch, the four of them headed up the stairs toward their guest quarters. Long after their voices faded, Carson stood in the hallway, fighting his inclination to follow those delectable smells to the even more delectable woman who had created them.

He didn't understand his fascination with her or the inexorable bonds that seemed to tug him toward her, even when he had been away from her for several hours. He only knew he needed to do everything in his power to fight his way free of them.

Despite her astonishingly heated response to his kiss, Jenna Wheeler was not the sort of woman who engaged in casual affairs and he wasn't interested in anything else.

No doubt she had cursed him all afternoon for kissing her. He had made a huge mistake, on many levels. On the most basic, she was an employee, at least temporarily. He had an ironclad rule *never* to fraternize with the many people who worked for him. He didn't like blurring the lines, complicating relationships. And his relationship with Jenna was nothing if not complicated.

More important, she was his neighbor and would be for a long time, especially since he had promised her he wouldn't have his people continue in their efforts to buy her house and land.

He would have dealings with her for years to come. Kissing her again, pursuing this desire that sizzled between them, would only make things awkward for both of them.

He had a sudden wish that things could go back to the way they had been several days ago, when he had found her boys tightrope walking on his fence. Something momentous had changed in that instant and he didn't like it. Not one damn bit.

With a sigh, he forced himself to walk up the stairs to shower and change for dinner. She would only be here a few more hours and then she would be going home for the night to her house and her noisy boys and the chaos of her life.

He only had to make it through dinner.

The task proved tougher than he had hoped. Jenna served the meal herself, dressed simply in black slacks and a white shirt. The clothes were different than the jeans she had worn earlier and he wondered if she had brought the change with her or if she had gone back to her house while he had been out riding.

He was painfully aware of her as she brought out course after course of divine food. A field-green salad with a unique spicy pecan vinaigrette, some kind of mushroom soup he thought he could eat every day for the rest of his life and be perfectly content, and the main course, a choice of either wild rainbow trout in a walnut crust or a savory filet mignon that melted in his mouth.

She didn't meet his gaze once throughout the meal, not even when she served dessert, which was either flourless chocolate cake or a pumpkin-swirled cheesecake.

"Mrs. Wheeler, you have a true gift with food," Antonia Hertzog said as Jenna set an elegantly garnished slice of cheesecake in front of her.

"Thank you," she murmured with a smile. She looked lovely and warm and he couldn't seem to look away from her.

He held his breath as she moved around the table to him and set a serving of the chocolate cake he had requested.

Her breasts barely brushed his shoulder as she set the plate down and he tensed every muscle, his mind unable to focus on anything but the memory of her softness against him when he had kissed her.

"Thank you," he said.

"You're welcome. Does anyone need anything else?"

He could come up with plenty of things but he decided it probably would be wise to keep his mind off of them.

"Do you have any Nutella?" Amalia whispered.

Jenna smiled at the girl, who had barely spoken to Carson though he had spent the entire afternoon with her. "I'm not completely sure, but I think I might have seen some in the kitchen. I'll go look for you."

She returned a moment later and set the jar down near Amalia, who gifted her with a brilliant smile. "Thank you." Her words were so low, Carson could barely hear them.

"No problem. Anytime you need more, it will be on the second shelf in the pantry, near the peanut butter."

"Thank you," the girl said again. Jenna smiled at her again and Carson had a ferocious wish that she would do the same to him sometime.

She turned to leave the room but he finally spoke, compelled in some ridiculous way to keep her a little closer, if only for a moment.

"Everything okay on the home front?" he asked. "No more nutcracker emergencies?"

She finally met his gaze and for just an instant, remembered heat flickered between them but she quickly looked away. "Not this evening. I took a moment to check on them a few hours ago and everyone was settling in for the night."

"Do you live nearby?" Dierk asked, watching Jenna with a male appreciation that made Carson bristle.

"Yes, actually. Just down the hill."

"The house with all the holiday lights?" Elle asked, just a miniscule dash of disdain in her voice.

Jenna either didn't hear it or she chose to ignore it. "That's the one. My family and I are Mr. McRaven's closest neighbors."

"Your home looks so very festive," Antonia said warmly, as if to make up for her daughter-in-law's chilly demeanor. "How many children do you have?"

Jenna smiled "Four."

"Four!" Antonia exclaimed. *"Ach der lieber!"*

"Yes. Three boys and a girl. My oldest is ten and my youngest, the only girl, is eighteen months."

"And their father? What does he do?" Elle asked. This time the supercilious tone was not quite as veiled.

Still, Jenna retained her calm, friendly demeanor. "He was a cattle rancher but he was killed in a ranch accident two years ago."

"Oh, you poor dear." Antonia reached out a hand and covered Jenna with hers. "I am so sorry."

"So am I," Jenna answered. "He was a good man and we all miss him very much."

She turned to leave but Frederick gestured to an extra chair against the wall. "You must have been on your feet all day to prepare such a wonderful feast. Why don't you stay and have dessert with us?"

For an instant Jenna looked taken aback by the offer but then she gave him a regretful smile. "Thank you very much for the kind offer, but I'm afraid I've got a few things to finish up in the kitchen for breakfast in the morning and then I really must return home to check on my children."

"Of course, of course," Frederick said.

She smiled at the group, though she still avoided Carson's gaze. "If anyone needs anything at all, please let me know," she said, then returned to the kitchen, leaving them to their dessert.

"A lovely woman," Frederick said after she was gone.

"Yes. She is." Carson couldn't shake the memory of her delicate features flushed and warm and desirable after their kiss.

"How lucky of you to have a chef living just down the hill, and such a lovely one at that," he said. "Has she worked for you long?"

He briefly thought about explaining the chain of events that had led Jenna to Raven's Nest but decided the truth didn't reflect well on him. Somehow he didn't think Frederick would appreciate the combination of bribery and blackmail it had taken to convince Jenna to cook for his house party. "Mrs. Wheeler doesn't really work for me. She is only here as a favor to me."

Antonia shook her head. "Imagine, four children and no one to help with them. She must be a truly remarkable woman."

Carson was beginning to agree, much to his vexation.

Jenna placed both hands in the small of her back and stretched, trying to work out some of the kinks from standing in a kitchen for fourteen hours.

Her shoulders felt weighted down with exhaustion but it wasn't an unpleasant sensation, more the comfortable tiredness that came from knowing the satisfaction of a job well done. She had worked hard but she found it gratifying that her efforts had been met with such obvious success.

She rotated her shoulders then shrugged off her fatigue to load another dish in the second dishwasher. The plan had been for Melina Parker to help her serve dinner and clean up afterward. But when she showed up earlier in the evening, her features had been tight and nearly gray with pain.

She had pretended everything was all right, apparently forgetting Jenna was raising three mischievous boys and had become quite an expert at worming information out of reticent subjects. After she applied her best interrogation skills on the other woman, Melina finally confessed she had been hit with a terrible migraine.

Though it meant a little extra work for her, Jenna couldn't let her suffer. She had ordered her to rest in a dark room until the headache passed.

It hadn't been too difficult. Really, for all her nerves earlier, the day had gone remarkably well. Her food had been well received and that was the important thing. All of the Hertzogs—with the exception of Elle, who looked as if she typically dined on celery stalks and lemon water—had been effusive in their praise and even Carson had eaten every bite of his filet mignon and a portion of trout, as well.

Not that she was neurotically checking or anything.

She sighed as she loaded another dish into the dishwasher. She had to get out of Raven's Nest before she became completely obsessed with the man.

One and a half more days—four more meals—and then she could return to her own family and Christmas and be able to sleep soundly in the knowledge that with the hefty fee Carson was paying her, she could pay off the small business loan she had taken out to start her catering business.

She had a few doubts about taking such a considerable sum from him but she had convinced herself she deserved it. Throwing together such a meal in only a few hours—especially only a few days before Christmas—was a considerable feat, one that deserved proper compensation.

Besides, he could afford it. The cost of his dishwasher alone would cover her business overhead for six months or more.

She definitely needed to stop thinking about Carson, she reminded herself. She'd made a vow to herself she would put the man out of her head, otherwise she would never get any sleep.

Forcing her mind to think instead about Christmas and all she still needed to do, she reached to return a serving tray onto a top shelf, then winced as the motion stretched the already-tight muscle where her neck met her shoulder. She rubbed at it, trying to work out the knot to no avail.

While she massaged at the ache, she paused to look out the window at the glowing lights of town, just barely visible at the mouth of Cold Creek Canyon.

Carson truly did have a lovely view here, in every direction, really. The soaring western slope of the Tetons was just visible above the smaller mountains around Pine Gulch and from here, Cold Creek glowed silver in the moonlight.

And the house itself was gorgeous, she had to admit, though a bit on the cold side. She would have liked to see a little more life in it. Some children's artwork—and handprints—on the refrigerator, a few toys scattered on the floor, perhaps a school backpack hanging on one of those empty hooks by the door.

The house needed a little life and warmth. Maybe Carson did, too, she thought, then chided herself for letting her thoughts wander back to him.

"You look like you could use a soak in the hot tub."

At the deep voice, she whirled around to find the man who had occupied far too many of her thoughts standing in the doorway, looking ruggedly masculine in the tan slacks and white shirt he had worn to dinner.

To her dismay, despite the lecture she had given herself all evening, her heart started to accelerate and for a moment she could do nothing but stare at him.

Chapter Nine

"I didn't hear you come in."

"You looked as if you were lost in thought. And like a woman who has been on her feet all day."

He took a step into the kitchen and she wondered how it was possible for the massive room to suddenly feel so tight and claustrophobic.

"I was just thinking what a lovely view you have from here. I've been wondering all day why Joe's great-grandfather didn't place his house in exactly this spot. I suppose it was logical in those days to build the homestead close to the creek where they drew their water, but up here makes far more sense from a purely aesthetic point of view."

"I suppose the early Pine Gulch settlers had a few more things on their mind than aesthetics. Survival probably carried a little more weight with them."

"You're probably right."

She knew exactly what it was like to exist purely in survival mode. She had done just that in the terrible months after Joe's death, when she had been fighting so desperately to keep the ranch afloat while she was pregnant and grieving and trying to be strong for her three little boys who had missed their father so much.

But time moved on. She moved on. Day by day, that bleak, wintry world had given way to sunshine. Jolie's birth had been a big part of that. Selling the ranch had helped as well, she acknowledged, despite how much she had agonized about the decision.

"Anyway," Carson said, "you are more than welcome to use the pool or the Jacuzzi anytime. I know you said at dinner you needed to get home to your kids tonight but if you'd like to come early in the morning, please feel free, or even when we leave for the ski resort after breakfast."

She tried to picture herself enjoying a soak in that luxurious indoor hot tub overlooking the valley. It was a lovely image right now with every muscle in her body aching, but she knew she would never be able to bring herself to get quite *that* comfortable in Carson's house.

"Thank you. But right now, all I want is a hot shower and my bed."

For just an instant, something bright and glittery sparked in his eyes and her insides gave a long, slow roll. She drew in a breath and pushed away the reaction, frustrated at her weakness when it came to him.

"Is everything all set for tomorrow?" he asked. "Do you need anything else?"

"I think I'll be fine. According to the menu your assistant sent me, breakfast in the morning was to be macadamia banana pancakes with orange butter. I'm also adding a smoked salmon and asparagus frittata. Is that still acceptable?"

"You're making my mouth water just thinking about it, even though I'm full from the wonderful dinner."

"I thought you all might need more protein before you go skiing. I know it always used to help me to eat a high-protein breakfast before I hit the slopes."

"You ski?"

"I used to snowboard in college, if you can believe that."

He stared at her and she had to laugh. "Should I be insulted that you look so astonished? Do you think I'm too old and settled to be a snowboarder?"

"No. I was just trying to wrap my head around it. You're just full of surprises, aren't you?"

What did he mean by that? She flushed, remembering how she had responded to his unexpected kiss.

"I wasn't a bad boarder, either. It's been a while, though. We used to take the boys to Jackson but I haven't had much time the last few years."

"Why don't you bring the boys and come with us tomorrow?"

Now it was her turn to stare and she forgot about being tired. "Now who's full of surprises? You're inviting my energetic boys to spend the day snowboarding with the international guests whose European business interests you're trying to purchase? Are you completely insane?"

"I'm beginning to think so," he murmured. Or at least she *thought* that's what he said but he spoke too low for her to completely understand.

"Well, thank you for the invitation," she said, "but

I'm going to have to pass, though Hayden would wring my neck if he knew. He's been bothering me since the first snowfall to take him."

"Why don't you, then?"

She shook her head. "Do you have any idea of the logistics that would be involved? I don't think any of their snowsuits still fit, for one thing. They're getting new ones for Christmas but that's still four days away. And beyond that, if my boys and I go off having a grand time at the ski resort with the Hertzogs, how, exactly, do you expect me to prepare your dinner tomorrow night?"

"We could figure something out."

"No. Thank you, but no. That's one of the things on our list for Christmas vacation. You go and have a good time with your guests and I'll stay here and make sure you have something edible at the end of the day."

"If you change your mind, let me know."

She nodded, though, of course, she wouldn't. In her preoccupation with his unexpected invitation, she hadn't paid any mind to what he was doing while they discussed snowboarding but now she realized while she was arguing with him, he had stepped to the sink and started drying and putting away dishes.

"Hey, stop right now," she said suddenly.

He blinked at her. "Stop what?"

"Cleaning up! You don't have to do that. You're paying me a ridiculously obscene amount to take care of those little details."

"I don't mind. I've washed plenty of dishes in my day."

She blinked. "You? The CEO of McRaven Enterprises?"

He gave a rough-sounding laugh. "Fifteen years ago

McRaven Enterprises didn't exist. I was CEO of exactly nothing."

"Fifteen years? You've done amazing things in that short amount of time."

While she had been busy having babies, he had been making his fortune. She supposed that might depress some women but she wouldn't have traded her life for anything, even with all the pain and sorrow on the road of her life's journey.

"I had a few breaks when I was first starting out," he said. "Things have snowballed from there. I've been really extraordinarily lucky."

That wasn't true, she knew. Before she would even consider selling him the ranch, she had researched all she could about him. She knew his reputation for taking faltering or stagnating tech businesses and turning them around.

"You don't have to use false modesty with me, Carson. Everything I've read about you says you're brilliant, that you have almost single-handedly made McRaven Enterprises a force to be reckoned with."

He looked uncomfortable with her praise, almost embarrassed, something she never would have expected. She found it startling and more than a little appealing.

"Not bad for a guy who had to take the GED to get a high-school diploma and barely made it through college taking night classes," he said lightly, with far more self-deprecation than she would have ever imagined.

He reached into the refrigerator for a Perrier and twisted the cap and she had the feeling the action was purely to cover his discomfort from talking about himself.

She didn't remember reading about his early beginnings in any of the articles she had seen about him. Such a humble background made his current success all the more remarkable and clearly reflected that he was a man of focus and determination, something she had already figured out for herself.

She knew she should go home. She had a million things to do, though she also knew from a quick phone call to her niece, Erin, that all the children were sound asleep. Still, she felt strangely content in such quiet conversation with him and she was suddenly reluctant to end it.

"You never married?"

He took a long sip of water. When he lowered the bottle, she saw a change in his expression, as if something dark and sad had slid across it. His mouth compressed into a tight line.

"I was married once. A long time ago."

He spoke reluctantly, as if he didn't share that information with many people, and she almost regretted asking him.

"How long is a long time?" she asked.

"Well, I was barely eighteen. I'm thirty-six now. I guess you can do the math."

She didn't remember reading anything about a marriage or a divorce in any of the articles she had found about him but she supposed if the event had been so long ago, he had probably preferred to keep the information private.

Maybe he wasn't divorced. She pushed the thought away. She would have known when she sold him the ranch if he had a wife hanging around somewhere. The sale documents had been complicated and detailed and surely that information would have come to light.

"They say young marriages have a rougher road. I suppose that must be true."

He sipped at his water again with a faraway look. "It wasn't easy, by any means. Suzanna was only seventeen and we were young and naive and thought we could handle anything."

"Most teenagers do."

That made him smile, though it didn't quite reach his eyes. "Right. Well, both of us were escaping rough home lives and had some sort of idealistic plan to rescue each other, I guess."

He shrugged. "I'm not sure we ever really intended to marry. I don't know that we would have if Suzanna hadn't discovered she was pregnant."

Pregnant? He had a child somewhere?

"That sort of changed everything. We decided we would try to hold things together and try to build a future together, so we scraped together enough for a marriage license and got married at a justice of the peace. I worked construction in the day and washed dishes at night so we could afford an armpit of an apartment in Oakland."

He said he and his wife had both been escaping bad home lives. She wondered what sort of misery he had endured and was grateful again for her own parents who had provided her with nothing but love through her childhood.

"What happened with your marriage?" she asked, though she was almost afraid to hear the answer. Somehow she sensed by his suddenly stark expression that it had a grim ending.

He was quiet for several moments. The only sound in the kitchen was the soft tick of the clock. She thought perhaps he wasn't going to answer and was just about to apologize for her rude prying when he let out a heavy breath. "She died in childbirth, along with our son."

Oh, dear heaven. She never would have expected that answer. Jenna gazed at him as sadness soaked through her. He had lost a wife and a child who never had a chance at life.

She felt as if everything she thought she had known about Carson had just been tossed in a hundred directions.

All this time she had thought him cold, hard, distant. Arrogant, even. He was so reserved with her children—and even with the Hertzog children—but now she wondered if he used that stoic, even stony, demeanor as a mask.

Nothing she said could ease his heartache but she knew firsthand how very much simple condolences could mean to a grieving heart.

"I'm sorry, Carson. So very sorry."

Her low words seemed to echo through the quiet kitchen, reaching deep inside him to a raw wound he thought had healed long ago.

Why the hell was he telling her this? He never talked about Suz and their baby. Never. There wasn't another soul on earth who knew this part of his past, of the guilt and pain that had been his constant companions for so long after her death.

He had been so alone, so angry. Just a stupid, powerless punk, bitter at the world and especially at the substandard hospital's emergency room that had delayed admitting her because they were a poor teenage couple without health insurance, and at the incompetent doctors who hadn't diagnosed her toxemia in time to save either of them.

Mostly he had been consumed with guilt. He had vowed to love and cherish and take care of Suz and their baby and he had screwed up.

He still carried that guilt inside him like an anchor, though he had become so accustomed to it after all these years that it just seemed a part of him now.

He knew it had been his fault she died. If he had done a better job providing for them, it wouldn't have happened. Early in her pregnancy he had taken a construction job with health insurance but had ended up walking out because of the callous way the company treated its workers.

She had wanted to apply for government assistance, as her mother and sisters and everyone else in the inner-city projects where she had grown up had done. But Carson's prickly pride wouldn't allow it. He had promised her he would find another position with insurance before she had the baby, but times had been tough and he had failed. And because of his pride and stupid convictions, his wife and son had died.

He could never forgive himself for that.

He had vowed as he stood over the two side-by-side graves that he would never allow anyone else to depend on him. He couldn't be counted on, nor could he count on anyone else. His childhood had taught him that.

He had worked hard to graduate from college in three years by taking a double load of classes. He had used the small malpractice settlement from the hospital to invest in his first company, a failing Silicon Valley software start-up with a winning product but poor management. He had turned it around in eighteen months then bought another company and another and had been doing it ever since.

Every McRaven company provided extensive health-care programs for its employees, especially prenatal care. It was a primary part of the business model.

None of the success he found would ever ease the guilt over those two lives that had depended on him.

"What was his name?"

He blinked away the past and realized Jenna was watching him closely, her features soft with sympathy.

"Your son," she said when he didn't answer. "What did you name him?"

"Suzanna picked out Henry James. She'd always loved the author—and the name—so that's what I stuck with."

He didn't think about his son as often as he thought of his young wife. He had loved the idea of having a child as much as it had terrified him, but mostly he had been happy because Suzanna had been happy. She glowed with joy and hope at the idea of bringing new life into the world—a minor miracle itself, since her upbringing in deep poverty and despair would have left most women cynical about the future.

Henry James McRaven would have been graduating from high school this year. It was a stunning realization.

"I'm sorry," Jenna said again. She laid a hand on his arm with a comforting kind of gesture that seemed a sweet balm to the aching corner inside him.

"It seems like another lifetime ago. I was a different person."

"But it's one of the things that shaped the man you've become, isn't it?"

"Yes. Without question."

It had been a terrible time in his life, one he wouldn't

wish on anyone, but those years had defined everything that came after.

If Suzanna and Henry had lived, he didn't know what course his life would have taken. He certainly wouldn't have been so driven to prove something to the cold, heartless bitch he called fate.

He studied Jenna, this woman who had somehow managed to reach through his careful barriers and tug out memories and experiences he had always believed he preferred to keep close inside him.

"So what events in your past helped shape the woman you've become?"

She leaned against the marble work island, her head tilted as she appeared to consider his words. "I'm still very much a work in progress."

"Aren't we all?"

A warm intimacy surrounded them in the quiet kitchen. That connection he had been fighting all day seemed to tighten between them.

He should leave right now, before this thing between them grew even stronger. He knew it was the wise course—and he was a man who prided himself on his prudence. But he couldn't seem to make himself move from this spot. He wanted to know about her, he discovered.

"If you had to pick the top three events that shaped you, what would make the list?" he asked impulsively.

She made a face. "No fair asking me to have a coherent thought after I've been on my feet since seven o'clock," she protested. "Anyway, I don't know if I could narrow it down to three."

"Try."

She paused for a moment, her forehead furrowed

in concentration. "Well, I suppose off the top of my head—and purely in chronological order—the first thing would have to be my parents' death in a car accident when I was sixteen. My brother Paul had just turned twenty-one and he became legal guardian to me. I was a sixteen-year-old girl who thought she was invincible and that was the first time I realized the precariousness, the fragility, of life."

"That's one."

Her features grew pensive. "Of course, I would have to include falling in love with Joe the summer before I graduated from college, and then marrying him and moving home to Pine Gulch to stay for good. Hand in hand with that would have to be the births of each of our beautiful children. Those four wise little souls shaped me more than anything else."

She grew quiet, her eyes shadowed. "Then my world and my children's was forever changed two years ago on October 15 when a tractor rolled over on the man I thought I would spend the rest of my life with, crushing our future together. I guess that's three."

A few days ago, he would have thought he had little in common with a woman like Jenna Wheeler. But the pain in her eyes was only too familiar. For a long time after Suzanna's death, he had seen it gazing back at him in the mirror.

"It sucks, doesn't it?" he said.

She was speechless for a moment then she laughed, a low, surprised sound that somehow lifted his spirits.

"It really does. That's the perfect word for it."

He wanted to kiss her again. He had spent all day telling himself why that would be a grievous mistake, but right now none of those reasons seemed very important. She was soft and warm and eminently desirable here in the quiet of his kitchen.

He leaned forward slightly and he could smell her again, that strangely seductive scent of vanilla and cinnamon.

Her gaze met his and in those glittery green depths he saw the same spark of awareness that sizzled through him, the same subtle yearning.

She caught her breath and leaned toward him slightly, her weight canted onto her toes.

His nerves tightened with anticipation and he moved to close the last few inches between them.

At the very last second, just when his mouth would have covered hers, she turned her head and took a jerky step backward.

"Please don't, Carson. Not again." She let out a shaky breath and he saw her hands were trembling.

Frustration burned through him. She had been ready for his kiss, had parted her lips in clear invitation. He knew he hadn't imagined it. "Why not?"

"Because it's completely unfair!" Her voice was heated. "I have no defenses against a man like you."

"What the hell is that supposed to mean?"

She drew her hands to her suddenly rosy cheeks, then dropped them as if the heat there burned her fingers. "I have dated one man seriously in my life and I married him a year later. I'm not the sort of sophisticated socialite who can do the casual affair thing. I'm just not."

"What makes you think that's what I want?"

She gave him an impatient look. "You will break my heart, Carson. I'm sure you won't mean to but you'll do it anyway because that's the kind of man you are."

Her words shouldn't have the power to hurt him but

they sliced him open anyway. "How do you know what kind of man I am?"

Her laugh sounded sharply discordant after the warm intimacy they had just shared. "Look at you. You're like something out of a movie. Gorgeous, rich, successful. I'm the mother of four children, hanging by my fingernails on the ledge of a wild, turbulent world. You will chew me up and spit me out and there will be absolutely nothing I can do about it. When whatever this is is out of your system, I will be left here living just down the hill from Raven's Nest, forced to see your house out my window and remember."

"It doesn't have to be that way."

"You're right. You're absolutely right. We can go back to the place we were before you…before you kissed me this afternoon. I had hoped we were on our way to being, if not friends, at least friendly."

"That's what you want? A friend?"

"Right now I want to go home to my children. I've been away too long. I'll be back first thing in the morning for breakfast."

He wanted to argue with her. To tell her he had never known anything like his attraction to her. But how could he possibly refute what he knew was absolute truth?

"That snow has made everything slick. Be careful."

Her smile was rueful and, he thought, a little sad. "What do you think the last five minutes was all about?"

Before he could answer, she grabbed her scarf and coat off the hook by the back door and headed out into the snow.

A few moments later, he watched her van's headlights cut through the night as she headed down the drive toward her house.

She was right. Somehow they needed to step back a bit. What other option was there? She wasn't interested in anything casual and he would never allow anything else. As soon as Christmas was over, he would be heading back to California, to his deals and his penthouse and the life he had carved out for himself, as empty and cold as that suddenly seemed.

Chapter Ten

"Mom, Hayden won't move so we can see. Make him cut it out!"

Jenna closed her eyes and whispered a quick, fervent prayer for patience. She looked toward the closed kitchen door that led to the rest of the house and then back toward the small couch and love seat where her boys were sitting by the fireplace in their pajamas.

"Come on, guys. Hayden, quit teasing your brothers. You promised. I just need you all to sit quietly and watch Rudolph for a while, okay? And then Aunt Terri will be here to take you back to the house."

"This is a baby show," Hayden grumbled.

"What are you talking about? This is your favorite show!"

"No way. It's totally stupid."

She glared at her oldest. He was such a leader to the

other boys. If they picked up his lead and refused to watch the DVD she had brought, she just might have a mutiny on her hands, which was the absolute last thing she needed when she still had a hundred things to do before breakfast in an hour.

When had her oldest son become too old to enjoy one of the classic Christmas specials? It was a tough age for a boy, she knew. He was ten and struggling to decide if he still wanted to be a boy or a preadolescent. Since his father's death she had watched him as he tried to grow up faster than she thought he should.

She had desperately tried to avoid exactly this scenario—having to bring the children with her to Raven's Nest while she prepared breakfast for Carson and his guests. She thought she had everything arranged and had planned to have her niece, Erin, sleep over so she could spend the morning with the children.

But when she returned to her house the night before, after that awkward encounter with Carson, Erin had apologetically informed her she forgot she had promised to cover a friend's paper route and had to be home to take care of it.

She had hoped to be finished before Jenna had to leave for Raven's Nest but Terri had called her and said the route was taking longer than they planned because of the snow. They expected to be done in the next hour.

She had to keep her fingers crossed and hope the holiday magic of Rudolph and his friends would keep the children preoccupied enough that they wouldn't start ripping apart Carson's house.

If not for Hayden, it just might work. Jolie was still sound asleep in one corner of the couch and the other two boys were at least moderately interested, though she could see the indecision in their eyes. If Hayden called it a baby show, neither Drew nor Kip would be caught dead watching it.

She considered her maternal grab bag of manipulation techniques and decided the fine art of diversion was a proven winner. "If you don't want to watch the show, why don't you come and help me?"

He opened his mouth to protest but then a crafty light entered his green eyes. "Will you pay me as much as you're paying Erin to sit with us? She says she's making a ton."

She smiled. "I guess that depends on how much help you are. While I crack the eggs for the frittata, why don't you come and peel these oranges so we can squeeze them for juice?"

He looked less than thrilled but apparently he decided the possibility of a little coin was more exciting than watching a baby show with his brothers.

It was actually quite enjoyable working beside him while the DVD played quietly in the background. She had discovered these small moments working one-on-one with her children provided an invaluable opportunity for conversation she would normally miss. With four children, she sometimes felt stretched thin when all of them were talking to her at once. She had learned to cherish any opportunity to interact with them individually—even when she was knee-deep in work making a gourmet breakfast for seven people.

For twenty minutes, she and Hayden talked about his favorite subject right now, football, and his favorite team, the Denver Broncos. The time flew past as they talked about passing percentages and wild card play-off slots and player trades. They talked about school and about his friends and his plans for the rest of Christmas vacation.

The time flew past and before she knew it, a quick check of the clock told her it was 7:10 a.m. and Carson's guests were expecting breakfast in twenty minutes.

She just might make it, she thought as she poured the freshly squeezed juice into a crystal pitcher.

The door to the kitchen suddenly opened and her ridiculous heart skipped a beat when Carson appeared in Levi's and an earth-toned sweater. His dark hair was damp and he was freshly shaved and all she could think about for one crazy moment was the stunning heat they had shared the day before.

"Mom, the orange juice is spilling!" Hayden exclaimed.

She looked down and realized she had just wasted a good cup or more of his hard work by letting the pitcher overflow. Juice dripped all over the countertop in a sticky orange mess.

She flushed and reached for the roll of paper towels. "Sorry," she muttered.

"Is the coffee ready?" Carson asked.

"It should be." She couldn't quite bring herself to meet his gaze, though she was painfully aware of him.

"Smells good in here."

She suddenly remembered the scent of him, masculine and sexy, and ordered herself to stop. She would never stop blushing if she couldn't manage to focus on breakfast.

"I was still shooting for seven-thirty for everything to be ready." She forced her voice to be brisk and professional as she finished cleaning up the orange juice and turned her attention to the final thing on her list, the batch of currant muffins she had added to the menu at the last minute. "Does that time still work for you and your guests?"

"Everybody seems to be stirring. Frederick was getting in a swim a minute ago but he looked like he was just ready to get out. We were trying to head to the slopes in Jackson by eight-thirty."

"I love to snowboard," Hayden announced. "My dad used to take me before he died. I'm saving up to buy a new snowboard and I almost have enough."

That was the first she had heard of that particular plan. Last she knew, Hayden was saving to go to a football camp at Idaho State in the summer.

"You've got helpers this morning."

She gave Carson a quick look, trying to gauge his reaction to her children's presence, but he only looked impassive and rather distant. "Yes. I didn't have a choice. If you've got a problem with it, I'm more than willing to let you make your own currant muffins."

He raised an eyebrow. "Did I say I had a problem with it? I was simply making an observation."

She hadn't meant to sound so defensive or confrontational and she worked to moderate her tone.

"My niece is supposed to be tending them for me this morning but something came up and she can't get here for another—" she glanced at the omnipresent clock on the river-rock fireplace "—fifteen minutes. They have promised they'd be on their best behavior until then and so far they've been great. We've been here nearly an hour and you didn't even know they were here, did you?"

"I didn't hear a sound," he assured her as he moved to the coffeemaker and pulled a mug out of the cupboard above it.

He poured a cup but before he could take a sip, Jenna heard a squeaking kind of sound and looked down to see Jolie had awakened while she had been talking to Carson.

Her daughter stood next to her in her red footie pajamas, hanging on to Jenna's pant leg with one hand as she rubbed her bleary eyes.

"Hi, baby."

"Mama. Up."

Jenna was elbow-deep in muffin batter. She looked helplessly down at her daughter. "Oh, honey, I can't pick you up right now. Give me a minute, okay?"

"Mama! Up!" Jolie's voice rose in pitch and intensity and her eyes started to brim with tears. She was such a cuddler when she just woke up and she wasn't happy unless she'd been held for a few moments until she was ready to start the day.

"Do you want me to get her?" Hayden didn't bother to mask the reluctance in his voice.

"No. Want Mama!" Jolie had that stubborn set to her jaw that Jenna recognized only too well, since she shared it with each of her three older brothers. She was just trying to figure out how she could possibly finish the muffins with one hand while holding her daughter in the other when Carson moved toward them.

"Here. Let me try."

She stared in shock as Carson set down his coffee mug and scooped Jolie into his arms. Jenna waited for her daughter's tantrum after finding herself confronted with a stranger. Though her eyes widened and she looked startled, she didn't let out the wail Jenna had expected.

"Um, thanks," she murmured, aware of a weird tightness in her chest as she saw him holding her little girl.

After another moment, Jolie apparently decided she didn't mind her new position.

"Hi," she beamed after a moment, putting out her most adorable vibe.

Now that he had offered to help, Carson looked as if he didn't quite know what to do next with the squirming bundle of toddler. "Hi, yourself."

Jolie patted his cheek. "Nice," she declared.

Jenna knew she should be finishing breakfast but she couldn't seem to look away from their interaction. She saw Carson blink a little at that, then he smiled back at Jolie, a heartbreak of a smile that made her forget everything she was doing.

"Thanks," he answered. "You're pretty nice, too."

Oh, she was a goner.

Jenna could handle a kiss that curled her toes. She could protect herself against shared confidences in the quiet of a kitchen while a soft snowfall drifted down outside.

But she had absolutely no way to shield her heart from a man who could look so completely masculine and sexy—and so adorably flummoxed—holding one of her babies.

Talk about your crazy impulses.

He should have just turned around and walked out of the kitchen the moment this terrifying little creature wandered over to her mother, all big-eyed and soft and sleepy.

He didn't know the first thing about kids, especially girl kids. Jenna's older boys were one thing. They could at least carry on a basic conversation and were somewhat capable of rational thought. At least he assumed as much.

The little girl, though. She was something else entirely.

Her hair was messy, with blond curls sticking in every direction, and she just watched him out of those big, dark-lashed green eyes that were so much like her mother's.

Just what was he supposed to do with her? She babbled something incomprehensible to him. He tried to interpret it so he could answer but she didn't appear to need a response. She just giggled and continued babbling along.

Not sure what to do, he just pretended to follow her gibberish and occasionally made a benign comment as if he understood her.

"Is that right?" he said, which mostly just sent her off into more giggles.

Somewhere in the middle of the nonsensical conversation Carson forgot about feeling foolish. He forgot about his guests and about Jenna watching him out of those wary eyes while she fixed breakfast and about the call to Carrianne he was hoping to find time to squeeze in before they left for the Jackson Hole ski slopes.

All he could focus on was this curly-haired girl with the huge eyes and wide, toothy smile.

He carried her around the kitchen, pointing out different things to her that he had never paid much attention to. The colorful tile backsplash behind the oven, the sprayer on the sink faucet, the ice maker on the refrigerator. She seemed to find everything fascinating as she jabbered at him.

By the time Jenna opened the oven door several moments later and slid in the pan of muffins, little Jolie Wheeler had completely stolen his heart.

"She doesn't usually take to anyone like that, especially men," Jenna said and he wondered if he ought to be insulted by her baffled surprise. "She's just not used to them, I guess, since she really only has interaction with her uncle Paul. I really thought she would be crying by now."

"I guess that just proves not all females run away from me in a panic."

She quickly looked at her boys, who were too busy watching the end of a holiday show to pay them any attention. When she shifted her gaze back to him, she was glaring, her expression clearly conveying that she thought him ill-mannered to mention the day before.

"I didn't run away," she muttered.

"What would you call it?" he asked, while Jolie was occupied suddenly banging a wooden spoon on the countertop.

"Mom, we can't hear the song!" Drew complained and Jenna swiftly slid a silicone cutting board across the countertop to muffle the banging.

"Using a little common sense."

He had promised himself after a sleepless night that he wouldn't push her, that he would try his best to forget his attraction to her. He was a little astonished that he was finding that so difficult to do this morning, especially with all four of her children right there with them.

She looked fresh and lovely this morning, with all her blond hair tightly contained in a French braid. She hardly looked old enough to be the mother of this little one in his arms, forget about three active boys.

"Thanks for your help with her, but you really can give her to one of her brothers. They're all a big help with her."

"She's fine for now, aren't you, bug?"

The girl gave him that wide smile again. "Jolie bug."

He grinned and looked up to find Jenna gazing at his mouth again.

His insides clenched and he suddenly wanted to shove all the children out of the kitchen and take their mother in his arms. He stared at her for a long moment that was only broken by a knock on the back door off the kitchen.

Jenna blinked a few times and he watched her swallow. Then she set down her spoon and hurried to answer the door.

A woman and a teenage girl who looked about fifteen stood in the doorway.

"Sorry we're so late, Aunt Jenna. The papers were delivered to us late and they were huge and took us a long time to roll."

"Lots of last-minute Christmas ads," the woman added as she walked into the room. "So this is the castle kitchen. Swank."

"And the lord of the manor," Jenna muttered, gesturing toward Carson.

He stepped forward to greet them and he saw surprise flicker in the older woman's eyes when she saw the little pajama-clad bundle in his arms.

"Hi." He smiled. "Welcome to Raven's Nest."

"Carson McRaven, this is my sister-in-law, Terri Patterson, and my niece, Erin. Without their help you would be eating dry cereal and peanut butter sandwiches right now."

The woman gave him a guarded look. "Hello," she answered.

Jolie wasn't nearly as restrained. "Auntie!" she exclaimed and clapped her hands in delight.

"Hi, pretty girl." She held out her hands and Jolie lunged into them.

His arms felt curiously bereft without the little girl in them and he wasn't quite sure what to do with them.

Jenna watched Carson shove his hands into the back pockets of his jeans and she tried to decipher his odd expression.

On a different man, she might have thought him hesitant to relinquish the toddler. But that certainly couldn't be true, she decided. The sooner Terri and Erin took the kids out of his hair, the better Carson would probably like it.

"Thanks again for watching the boys today," Jenna said to Erin. "I know you have a million things to do before you leave for the cruise on Christmas Eve."

"I don't have anything else to do. I'm already packed," Erin assured her with a grin. "I have been for two weeks. And with what you're paying me, I'll have even more money to spend in the duty-free stores onboard the ship."

She smiled. Erin was a world-class shopper and often lamented the tragic fact that Pine Gulch didn't have its own mall.

"I should be back at the house in a few hours and then I don't have to be back at Raven's Nest until early afternoon to start the dinner prep."

"No problem," Erin assured her. "Come on, you guys. We can watch the rest of the show at your house."

"This TV is bigger," Kip complained.

"Sorry, you're just going to have to slum it at home," Erin told him with a grin.

As she kissed each of her children goodbye, Jenna was aware of Carson still standing in the kitchen watching out of those blue eyes that seemed to miss nothing.

The next few moments were a flurry of activity— finding coats, grabbing the DVD, ushering everyone out the door.

"Be careful, the steps are a little icy." Jenna offered one last warning, then closed the door behind her family.

Carson was still there, one hip leaning against the kitchen counter. He had picked up his coffee mug again and he sipped at the contents, which must surely be lukewarm by now.

"This really has been a hassle for you to help me, hasn't it?" he said. "I don't know if I fully realized the logistics of it all until right now, watching you herd them all out the door."

"Yes," she said without equivocating. "But you're paying me extraordinarily well to compensate for any inconvenience."

His mouth compressed a little. "That still doesn't make it any easier for you. I suppose you're glad you're only committed to a few more meals. Dinner tonight and then breakfast in the morning and then everything can return to normal."

"Right," she murmured, though she couldn't quite figure out why that prospect should depress her.

Chapter Eleven

She only saw Carson briefly again before he and his guests left for skiing, when she replenished the buffet-style breakfast dishes she had prepared into the dining room.

He didn't look up at her from his spot at the dining table, where he seemed to be engrossed in conversation with the beautifully sophisticated Elle.

She was grateful, she told herself. She didn't need another encounter with him to upset her equilibrium. She was already wasting entirely too much of her time thinking about the man.

They all left shortly after breakfast and the huge rambling house seemed to echo in their absence.

She cleared the breakfast dishes and did as much of the prep work for dinner as she could then stood for a moment in the kitchen.

She had Raven's Nest to herself, and while she knew

she needed to return to her children quickly, she couldn't resist taking a moment to look around, as she had really only seen the kitchen and dining area.

She walked slowly through the great room, with its massive river-rock fireplace soaring two stories high and the Christmas tree Carson had cut with her boys.

Opposite the great room was the indoor pool and Jacuzzi, which had equally impressive two-story windows overlooking the ranch.

Like the kitchen, no detail had been spared in the house, from the carved interior doors to the remote-controlled window shades.

She couldn't deny it was elegant, with graceful lines and comfortable furnishings. She believed they called the decor mountain chic. Sure, a designer might use homespun-looking fabric for the curtains but it no doubt cost a couple hundred dollars a yard.

Even the Christmas tree looked off, somehow. Melina Parker told her Carson had brought in a team of designers to decorate it. Perhaps that was why something about it didn't look quite right. It was beautiful, but perhaps too polished. Or maybe it was the complete dearth of presents underneath it, a sight that sent a weird pang through her heart.

She wandered up the stairs, the railing polished and cool beneath her fingers. At the top of the stairs, she opened a door and realized with some chagrin that this must be the master bedroom.

The room was luxuriously appointed, with its own rock fireplace, a sitting area, a wide wall of windows overlooking her house and the valley and a huge four-poster log bed.

It was lavish and comfortable, she had to admit. But there were no personal mementos in sight. No photographs, no knickknacks, nothing to show the individual personality of the man who lived here.

She found it terribly sad, though perhaps his house in San Francisco was filled with those sorts of accoutrements. Somehow she doubted it. He struck her as a man who had created a self-contained life for himself, one without distractions or unnecessary details.

She trailed a hand over the thick designer comforter on the bed, then jerked herself out of her reverie and ordered herself to stop this fascination with the man and go back to where she belonged.

Christmas was three days away and heaven knows, she still had a million items on her to-do list. She certainly had things she ought to be worried about other than Carson McRaven. The man could buy and sell whatever he wanted and she was fairly certain he would not appreciate her sympathy.

Dinner on his guests' last night was a rousing success, even more spectacular than the night before.

Jenna outdid herself with a choice of roast wild turkey or pork medallions so flavorful he was certain he had never tasted anything so delicious. In addition to creamy mashed potatoes and a fresh green salad with roasted pecans, she provided three kinds of dessert— mocha crème brûlée, cherry brownies with homemade vanilla ice cream and key lime pie.

She had a definite gift, he would give her that much. Most of the time he didn't even think about what he was eating, but Jenna's food was too memorable to ignore.

She could find a job as a personal chef anywhere. If not for the weird currents between them, he would offer her a full-time position at Raven's Nest. As a chef, she was creative and innovative and took risks that still somehow worked.

And amazingly, she presented the entire meal without meeting his gaze one single time.

Melina actually served most of the meal but Jenna came in a few times, once to bring the Nutella out to Amalia and once to answer a question from Antonia about an ingredient in the soup that turned out to be saffron.

Both times, she acted as if Carson didn't exist. So much for the friendship she claimed she wanted with him, though he refused to wallow in the self-pity that seemed, oddly, to hover at the edges of his consciousness.

It had been a strange day all the way around. Though the snow had been light and perfect and the skiing hard and aggressive, he had felt off his stride. He blamed it on the two Wheeler females. He couldn't seem to get Jenna out of his head. The sweet, heady taste of her, those soft, womanly curves, the unexpected heat of her response.

He didn't know when a simple kiss had affected him so profoundly.

But he also blamed some of his distraction on a twenty-five-pound little sprite with curly blonde hair and her mother's green eyes. He didn't like the tug in the vicinity of his heart whenever he thought of little Jolie Wheeler.

"You, my friend, are an excellent host."

Carson jerked his attention back to his guest, sitting across from him in the other plump leather armchair in the Raven's Nest library.

Carson lifted his scotch, forcing himself to focus on his goals at hand. "Thank you. I've very much enjoyed having you and your family at Raven's Nest. I hope you feel welcome to use my home anytime, even when I'm not in residence."

"I wonder if you would be as gracious if I decide not to sell you Hertzog Communications."

Carson raised an eyebrow as he refilled the man's drink. "Am I to take that as some sort of announcement?"

Frederick studied him for a long moment while the fire in the grate crackled between them and then he chuckled. "You are a cool one, McRaven. No, it's not an announcement. The truth is, I made my decision before we even came to Raven's Nest. The company is yours if you still want it. Your offer is generous. I know your record and I've seen how you treat other companies you have acquired. I believe you will treat my employees with great care. They are what matters most to me."

He had won. Carson should be celebrating. This was the heady moment he always savored, the taste of victory on his tongue, more potent than even the finest aged scotch.

Right now he felt rather hollow and had an insane wish that he had someone to share the news with.

"Do you not have anything to say?" Frederick asked.

This wasn't turning out the way he expected. He should be jubilant, not fighting this discordant feeling that everything he thought he wanted had been shaken on its head the last few days.

"Sorry. I'm thrilled. Of course I am. Thank you. Your decision is wonderful news, exactly what I had hoped. You can be sure I will do my best to take good care of all you have worked so hard to build over the years. I'll make a call to the attorneys first thing in the morning and have them start the paperwork."

Frederick made an impatient gesture. "It's Christmas. Do you not think that can wait? Let your people enjoy the holiday. My decision won't change between now and December twenty-sixth."

Carson forced a smile, unused to feeling chided, especially by someone he respected as much as he did Frederick Hertzog.

"You're right," he said after a long moment. "All the details can wait until after the holidays."

Frederick studied him while the fire crackled and hummed. "And how are you spending Christmas after we leave in the morning?"

Carson wasn't quite sure how to answer that question. His plans for a long, solitary ride into the mountains on one of the horses would probably seem rather staid and solitary to a man like Frederick Hertzog, who lived for his family.

"I'm not sure yet," he said, which wasn't exactly a lie.

"Ah. Too many choices?"

"Something like that."

Frederick studied him for another long moment, his eyes entirely too perceptive. "Why don't you have a wife? Children?"

Carson shifted in his chair, deeply uncomfortable with this particular line of questioning. "I guess it just hasn't really been a priority in my life."

"And why not? If you don't mind an interfering old-timer's opinion, a man needs family around him, especially as the years flow past. You might think big, beautiful houses and land and more companies are enough for you. But when you get to be the ripe old age of seventy-five, you learn how little those things matter. Family. That's the important thing. The joy of watching your grandchildren grow, of knowing you have raised a good, honorable son, of having your wife by your side and standing by in amazement as she becomes more beautiful in your eyes with every passing day. That is where you find true joy."

Carson gazed into the flickering fire, wishing he could clap his hands over his ears to shut out the other man's words.

What was happening to him this week? He had come to Raven's Nest five days ago, comfortable in the assurance that his life was rolling along exactly on the track he wanted. His company was successful beyond his wildest dreams, he had found the ideal location for his ranch, he had everything he could imagine.

If he sometimes wondered why he was working so hard, he just figured that was part of living the high life.

But somehow everything was changing. All he thought he had attained seemed empty. Meaningless. For the first time, he was beginning to realize how completely he had shut everyone else out of his life. His friendships for the most part were shallow, his relationships with women always casual.

He had become very adept at relying only on himself. Now he was beginning to wonder if he had made a grave mistake.

It wasn't a pleasant realization or a particularly comfortable one.

She was nearly done.

The Hertzogs had left just a short time ago to meet

their plane at the Jackson Hole Airport. They planned to fly to Aspen for the final leg of their ski journey and she had sent them on their way with breakfast crostini, chicken foie gras sausages and rosemary potatoes.

To her surprise, Antonia Hertzog had given her a hug before she left along with a card with her e-mail address, begging Jenna to keep in touch and to send her recipes for several of the dishes she had served.

Frederick Hertzog had shaken her hand. He had solemnly—but with his eyes twinkling—thanked her for preparing meals "as filling to the soul as to the stomach."

Even Amalia had given her a shy smile and whispered her thanks.

Now all Jenna had left was to wash a few more dishes and finish storing the leftovers that could be heated in clearly marked containers for Carson.

She was glad it was over, she told herself. These two days had seemed endless, though she had loved the work. Having the freedom to create meals with unlimited ingredients had been both challenging and immensely rewarding.

She couldn't do it again, though. Even if Carson offered her a private jet of her own to chef for another of his parties, she would have to decline. Two days at Raven's Nest was more than enough. She couldn't work for him again, not with this insane attraction she couldn't seem to quash.

She would find a way, though. Once she was away from him and back in the flow of her regular life, she wouldn't even have time to think about Carson McRaven or the heat of his kiss or the way he made her insides quiver with sensations she thought she had buried with her husband.

Fifteen minutes later, she dried the last serving tray and returned it to the shelf, then gave one last look around the kitchen to make sure she hadn't forgotten anything.

"I suppose you're glad this is over."

She whirled around to find Carson in the doorway. Her heartbeat instantly kicked up a notch, much to her frustration. So much for the assurances she made to herself that she could put her attraction away.

For some reason, she hadn't expected to see him again before she left. They had no business left between them, since his assistant had expressed payment to her the day before. She had already deposited it in the bank and this morning had transferred payment over to her small business loan, much to her delight.

She hadn't really *wanted* to see him. Yet, here he was in jeans and a casual shirt and those disreputable boots again. She sighed and tried to pretend he didn't affect her in the slightest.

"My children are eager to have their mother back so we can get to some of our holiday traditions," she finally answered.

He stepped into the kitchen and leaned a hip against the work island.

"Like what?"

"Oh, the usual. Nothing very exciting, I suppose. Tonight we're going to drive around and look at Christmas lights around town. Tomorrow is Christmas Eve and we're driving to Idaho Falls to pick up my mother-in-law, who'll be staying a few nights with us. We'll probably go to a matinee or something with her and then dinner, then we'll read stories and play games by the fire until the boys are worn out enough to sleep. Which might be quite late this year, I'm afraid. Hayden tells me he plans to stay up until at least eleven o'clock."

She was rambling, she realized. His blue eyes wore an odd expression. Probably glazed over from boredom, she thought, embarrassed.

"That probably sounds excruciatingly dull to you, doesn't it?"

"You might be surprised," he murmured.

She didn't know how to answer that so she changed the subject. "What about you? What are your plans for Christmas?"

"That seems to be the question on everyone's mind. Actually, I have work today and tomorrow."

"On Christmas Eve?"

"I have several projects in the works right now so I thought I would catch up on the research I need to do for them."

How terribly sad, she thought. Instead of celebrating with family and friends, he planned to hole up in this huge, echoing house by himself and read business reports. She couldn't imagine anything more depressing, though perhaps that was exactly the way he wanted to spend his holidays.

"What about Christmas Day?" she asked, though she wasn't quite sure why she was so insistent on finding out his plans.

"I don't know. Not much. I really don't usually celebrate Christmas, to be honest. I would spend the entire time working but it's hard to do that on your own when everyone else is at home doing their holiday thing. I figured I'd take one of the horses up on the ridgeline trail and then come back and have a drink and a long soak in the hot tub."

She studied him for a long moment, struck at the sudden realization that what she had always taken for coldness, for hardness, actually cloaked a great deal of loneliness. Why had she never realized it before?

"You could come to our place for dinner on Christmas, if you'd like." She spoke quickly, regretting the words almost the moment she uttered them.

He straightened from the work island, his eyes astonished. "I didn't realize you were in the habit of inviting strays to dinner."

If he was a stray, he was a sleek, extraordinarily well-groomed one. She colored a little, feeling foolish all over again at the impulsive invitation. She couldn't rescind it now, though, so she plowed forward.

"One more person at the table certainly won't make much of a difference, especially this year. Usually my brother and his family would be there but they're leaving tomorrow morning on a cruise. It will only be my brood and my mother-in-law."

She made a face as she suddenly remembered one salient point that couldn't be overlooked. "I should warn you, in the interest of full disclosure, that Pat—my late husband's mother—can be...difficult. She had a stroke a year ago and she suffered brain damage from it. I'm afraid, well, it's changed her personality a bit. And not for the better, I'm sorry to say. She was always a strong-willed woman but since her stroke, she's become, um..."

Her voice trailed off and she felt disloyal for even bringing it up.

"Mean?" he asked.

She stared. "How did you know that?"

"Hayden told me a few things she's said about me. Not very complimentary things, I'm afraid."

Jenna winced. She could only imagine what Hayden might have told him. Carson and Raven's Nest were two of Pat's favorite targets for vitriol. She couldn't understand Jenna's reasons for selling the ranch to him and Jenna had never been able to explain to her that her comfortable assisted-living center would never have been in their budget if she hadn't.

"I'm sorry. She's actually a wonderful woman most of the time. She just has her moments."

"But you still have her out to your house for Christmas?"

Jenna sighed at his flabbergasted expression. "She has no other family. Joe was her only son and the Wagon Wheel was her home long before it was mine. What else can I do? My children still love her dearly and she never displays cruelty to them."

"Only to you?"

She flashed him a quick look. The man was too blasted perceptive. "Not much. Anyway, if I haven't completely scared you off, you're welcome to join us for dinner. We'll probably eat around four. My boys enjoy your company and even Jolie seems completely smitten. All afternoon yesterday she wouldn't stop saying mister. Which I'm fairly sure meant you since you're the only new man in her life."

He smiled at that and she gazed at the way it seemed to light up his features.

How did he completely wreck all her grand intentions, just with a simple smile? That crazy hunger surged back through her veins and she could only stare at him.

* * *

He had to kiss her again.

The impulse was so overwhelming, he just about gripped the counter's edge to keep from reaching for her.

She was inviting him to share Christmas dinner with her family. With her boys and her darling little girl and her mother-in-law.

Part of him was totally enraptured by the idea. But it terrified him far more.

What did he know about family Christmases? When he was a kid, December twenty-fifth had simply been another day, another excuse for his mother to drink or shoot up until she passed out and he had to clean her up and put her to bed.

He could remember one happy Christmas from his childhood, the year he had spent with his grandparents.

He had become used to treating the day like any other, just a little more inconvenient since the rest of the world seemed to stop. If he spent the day with Jenna and her family, he was very much afraid he would never be able to go back to those quiet, solitary days he told himself he enjoyed.

"Forget it. I should never have invited you." She turned away and he realized he must have been standing there staring at her for a full minute or more.

"It's silly," she went on. "You don't have to feel obligated. Just pretend I never opened my big, stupid mouth."

The big, stupid mouth he couldn't stop thinking about? The one that haunted his dreams, that he could still taste every time he closed his eyes?

"Jenna—"

"Just forget it," she said. "It was a crazy impulse."

"No, it wasn't. It was very sweet."

Her gaze flashed to his, her eyes wide and surprised and he lost the battle for control. He stepped forward, pulled her against him and kissed her, as he had been dreaming about doing since the first time he had tasted her.

She gasped his name just before his mouth found hers. He might have expected her to pull away, as she had done that first time. Instead, she hitched in a little breath and wrapped her arms around his neck and his tenuous hold on control slipped completely away.

She tasted even better than he remembered from the day before, warm and sultry and sweet at the same time, like juicy sugared peaches.

She responded wildly to his kiss and he pressed against her, relishing her curves and the way her breathing came in aroused little gasps. She opened her mouth for his kiss and her tongue tangled with his.

The heat and taste of her sent blood surging to his groin and he was instantly aroused. He gripped her bottom and pulled her against him and she let out a soft, sexy little sound and twisted her fingers in his hair.

They kissed for a long time, until he couldn't think straight and his body ached for more. "Let's go upstairs," he murmured after several drugging moments. "I've got a huge bed in my room. It's far more comfortable than a marble-topped island."

He knew his words were a colossal mistake the moment he said them. She froze in his arms for only an instant but he didn't want to let her go. Not yet. He couldn't let her pull away this time. He lowered his mouth again and after only a moment, she kissed him back with more of that enticing eagerness that took his breath away.

He wanted more. He had to have her, right now, right here, to hell with comfort or common sense.

He slid his hands under her shirt, to the warm skin at her back and trailed his lips from her mouth to her neck then to the creamy, delicious skin at the vee of her shirt.

She gripped his head to hold him in place for a moment, then he was vaguely aware of her hands falling away just as he dipped a tongue beneath her bra, to the lush swell of one breast.

She pushed at him but he couldn't bring himself to heed her, too lost in his hunger.

"Stop, Carson. Oh, please, stop."

Her whispered words finally pierced his subconscious and he froze, frustration whipping through him.

He stepped away from her but couldn't seem to contain the string of low, bitter curses, a throwback to his rough childhood on the street.

She looked shaken to the core, her eyes wide and almost glassy. Not at his language, he realized. At the wild ferocity of their kiss.

He had let things get completely out of his control, something he never did. She had tried to stop, he remembered with considerable self-disgust, but he hadn't wanted to end the kiss until she actually said the words.

He raked a hand through his hair. "Jenna, I'm..."

"Don't say it. Don't you *dare* say you're sorry." Her breath came in sharp little gusts, her chest heaving up and down as she tried to regain control.

He was. He almost couldn't breathe around the regret—as much for kissing her in the first place as for not being willing to stop.

"I was just going to tell you I won't be coming for Christmas dinner. I need to go back to San Francisco."

Now. Today. To hell with the fact that he'd given his pilot the three days off until the holidays were over. He would take a commercial flight if he had to. He needed to return to a place where his life was sane and normal again, instead of filled with adorable toddler urchins, gabby troublemaking boys or lovely widows with big green eyes and kisses that were rapidly becoming his obsession.

"Now who's running away?" she asked quietly. She lifted her hands to repair some of the damage his fingers had done to her careful hairstyle and he saw she was shaking.

He wanted more than anything to touch her again but he didn't trust himself. "This is insane, Jenna. I'm fiercely attracted to you. More than I've ever been to a woman in my life. I'm not used to…losing control like I just did. I can't let it happen again."

She laughed harshly. "What makes you think I would let you kiss me again?"

He gave her a long look. "Can you do anything to stop it?"

"I just did, didn't I?"

"Eventually. But you didn't want me to stop, did you? Not really."

She just looked at him out of those eyes that suddenly looked bruised and he gave a heavy sigh.

"I don't know what this thing is between us," he said. "But when we kiss, it's like the blowup of a wildfire scorching out of control. It makes absolutely no sense."

"Don't look to me for answers. I don't like it any more than you do."

He needed a clean break from her. That was the only way he could regain any kind of sanity. He needed her and her children out of his life, once and for all—or at least as far out of it as he could manage when they lived just down the hill from Raven's Nest. He didn't like being cruel—the mother-in-law he hadn't even met came to mind—but he couldn't see any other option.

"Look, I'm physically attracted to you, Jenna. I can't deny that. But I never should have kissed you. This was a mistake. I don't want to be attracted to you and I'm sorry I lost control like that. You come with tangles and complications I can't handle. I'm not *interested* in handling them. The whole kid and family thing is not anything I'm looking for and that's what you're all about, isn't it. I'm sorry, but you're just not the kind of woman I want."

She paled a shade or two and he didn't think he had ever despised himself as much as he did right at this moment. "I guess that's clear enough, isn't it?"

"Jenna—"

"No, I appreciate your honesty. I do. And since we're being so up-front and honest with each other, I'll come right out and just say, right back at you. You are absolutely the last man I would be interested in starting anything with. Yes, I find you attractive. But I also believe you're the most manipulative, self-absorbed person I have ever met. You think you have everything you could ever want, but the truth is, your world is cold and empty. I would feel sorry for you except it would be a complete waste of my time and energy, something in short supply in the whole *kid and family thing* I call my life. Goodbye, Mr. McRaven."

She headed for the door and he wanted, more than anything, to apologize, to call her back and tell her he didn't mean any of it. He couldn't, though. Because underneath it all was more than a grain of truth.

He forced himself to say nothing as she grabbed her parka off the hook in the mudroom with a force that nearly ripped it out of the wall, then she stormed out the back door, slamming it hard behind her.

She left an echoing kind of silence between them. The kitchen that had seemed so warm and full of lovely scents when she was there had turned barren, inhospitable.

He stood for a moment, flayed open by her words. *You think you have everything but the truth is, your world is cold and empty. I would feel sorry for you except it would be a complete waste of my time and energy.*

She was exactly right. A week ago, he would have taken great satisfaction in telling her his life was exactly the way he wanted it. Now he didn't know what the hell he wanted.

He needed to get out of there. Now. He pulled out his cell phone to call Carrianne to arrange the details and see how quickly she could find him a way out of the area when he suddenly realized he hadn't seen Jenna's van head down the mountain yet.

He moved to the window overlooking the back driveway and frowned. What was she doing? Her van was still parked there but Jenna was nowhere in sight. He stood for another moment, baffled at the delay, then with growing uneasiness, he opened the door.

His heart clogged his throat and icy panic crackled through him. She hadn't gone to her van because she hadn't made it beyond the back steps. She was lying crumpled at the bottom of the stairs, her eyes closed and her face deathly white to match the snow drifting down to cover her skin.

Chapter Twelve

He shoved open the door, barely aware of the bitter cold that cut through his clothes or the snowflakes that had turned mean and hard.

He rushed down the steps, then scrambled to grab hold of the handrail when his feet started to slip out from underneath him. Why was it so damn icy? He had installed radiant heat under all the sidewalks and steps leading to the house to melt the snow.

Something must have gone haywire with the system. He suddenly remembered her saying that morning to her sister-in-law and children that the steps were a little icy but he hadn't paid much attention to her words.

In her anger at him, Jenna must have rushed out of the house without remembering her own caution or how treacherous it was.

None of that mattered, he thought as he crouched down beside her still form.

"Jenna?" He reached a hand out to cup her cheek, sick fear curdling in his stomach at the cool fragility of her skin. "Jenna? Come on, sweetheart. Answer me."

She made no response at all. He wanted to shake her awake but he was afraid to move her in case she had a spinal injury. He didn't want to cause any more pain than he had already done.

He took his hand away from her cheek and smoothed her hair away from her pale features. He was almost certain it was his imagination when she moved slightly toward him, as if seeking the warmth of his fingers.

"Come on, Jenna. Wake up and we'll get you home."

She moaned a little but didn't open her eyes. He did a quick physical assessment and saw that one arm was tucked underneath her back. Even with his limited experience, he could see something was drastically wrong with the unnatural position of it.

His fault. All of this was his fault. He had goaded her, had done his best to make her as angry as possible with him for his own self-serving reasons, so he could push her away to the safe distance where he kept everyone else in his life.

He should have known the radiant-heat system wasn't working right but he had been so preoccupied the last few days that he hadn't paid any attention to something as critical as her safety.

Hell, she wouldn't have even *been* at Raven's Nest to fall down his steps if he hadn't forced her to go against her better judgment and bribed her into cooking for his house party.

"I'm sorry, Jenna. Just wake up and I'll make it better. Come on." He squeezed her fingers, trying desperately not to remember the last time he had begged a woman he cared about to wake up, eighteen years ago as he watched Suzanna slip into a coma as a result of her eclampsia.

"Damn it, Jenna. Wake up," he ordered, his voice harsher than he intended. "Your kids are waiting for you at home. They need you right now."

That did the trick. She moaned a little more but blinked her eyes open.

Relief coursed through him, hot and fierce. On a purely rational level, he was quite certain it hadn't been more than a minute or so since he opened the back door and found her lying on the steps, but he felt as if he had lived through two or three lifetimes in that miserable span of time.

She moaned a little more and tried to rise to a seated position but he gently pressed a hand to her chest to hold her in place.

"Don't try to move yet, at least until we can figure out what kind of damage you've done."

She blinked up at him like a sleepy kitten. "What... what happened?"

"I didn't see, but I can guess. You must have slipped on the icy steps. Apparently the radiant-heating system isn't working the way it's supposed to. Looks like you must have taken quite a header."

She touched her right hand to the back of her head then moved as if to lift the other arm from beneath her and he saw raw pain spasm across her features.

"Ow! Ow, ow, ow."

Her distressed cry just about broke his heart. "I know. You've hurt your wrist pretty badly. We're going to get some help. What else hurts? I tried to do a quick assessment but I don't really know what I'm looking for."

Her lovely features contorted with pain. "Head. Arm. Ankle."

"I'd say that about covers it. Okay. I left my phone inside. I'm just going to grab it and a blanket for you while I call the ambulance. I'll be back before you know it, okay? Just hold still."

Despite his order, she pushed up with her good arm until she was sitting on the icy step, her hand pressed to the back of her head and the other arm hanging loosely at an awkward angle. "I'm okay. Don't call an ambulance."

"You are very far from okay, Jenna. You've taken a terrible fall."

"Freezing."

He didn't think she had any spinal injuries and he hated the idea of her having to sit out here in the snow while he called for help. Since she had already taken it upon herself to sit up, he supposed there was no harm in taking her in the house.

"Come on. Let's get you where it's warm."

He carefully scooped her into his arms, wondering how she could feel so delicate and be so stubborn at the same time. Her back was cold where she had been lying on the icy steps and he felt sick inside all over again.

He carried her to the sitting area of the kitchen and pulled a knit throw off the corner of the sofa, then turned the gas fireplace on high.

"Don't call an ambulance," she repeated when he crossed the kitchen for his phone. He was relieved to hear she was already sounding more like herself. "I twisted my ankle and bunged up my arm. You don't need to bother the volunteer paramedics with a silly thing like that. They have much more important things to worry about."

Nothing is more important than making sure you're okay, he wanted to say, but he knew he would sound ridiculous.

He could see the determination in her eyes and knew she would not appreciate it if he went against her wishes and called the ambulance anyway.

"Okay," he finally said. "We'll do things your way. I can take you to the hospital in Jackson Hole or the one in Idaho Falls. Your choice."

"Neither. I don't need to go to the hospital."

"Pick one." He could be just as stubborn as Jenna Wheeler and it was high time she realized that.

"Fine," she grumbled. "Jake Dalton at the clinic in town can take care of this. I would appreciate it if you could drive me there."

She looked as if the words just about choked her. Under less stressful circumstances, he might have smiled, but he had a feeling it would be a long time before he found anything amusing, especially since all he could think about was that terrible moment when he had opened the kitchen door and found her lying so still on his steps.

"If you know the number, I'll call and let them know we're on our way."

She gave it to him and he punched it into his phone, thinking he would just call after they were on the road. "Be sure to tell Jake I have to stop at my house first and make sure the kids are still okay."

"We'll call them on the way."

"Carson—"

"Brace yourself." He scooped her up again.

"Honestly," she exclaimed. "This is *not* necessary."

"Says you."

"I can walk if you put me down." Her voice was muffled and he was glad to see color returning to her features. He held her tighter, knowing he shouldn't be enjoying this so much. It seemed slightly warped when she was in such pain that he could find such contentment just having her in his arms.

"It's this or the ambulance. Which would you prefer?"

"Neither," she muttered.

"Too bad," he said as he reached the garage. "I'm not taking any chances, Jenna. You took a hard fall and that wrist looks seriously injured and I can already tell your ankle is going to swell."

"I don't have time for this," she wailed. "Tomorrow is Christmas Eve!"

Guilt pinched at him as he set her in the backseat of the ranch's Suburban. She had wanted to make the holiday idyllic for her children. He remembered her telling him about the last rough two Christmases and how things had to be just right this year.

How was she ever going to do that, battered and sore as she was now?

And how was he ever going to forgive himself for ruining the perfect holiday she had planned out so carefully?

An hour later, Jake Dalton pursed his mouth as he looked at computerized X-rays. "Well, Jen, you've done a real job on yourself."

"I know. I'm such a klutz."

He grinned. "How would I ever pay my bills if not for klutzes like you? I'd be out of a job."

She made a face at him. She knew perfectly well Jake Dalton was probably the most underpaid doctor in Idaho. He opened his clinic at least two days a month for people who didn't have health insurance and he and his wife, Maggie, spent several weeks every summer volunteering in poverty-stricken areas in Central America.

As much as she liked and admired Jake and considered Maggie one of her closest friends, she would rather be just about anywhere else on earth right now than sitting in one of his exam rooms in a hospital gown.

"So do you want the good news or the bad news first?" Jake asked.

"I hate when you say that. Give me the good news first, I guess, so I have something positive to think about while you give me the bad news."

"Well, you've got a mild concussion."

"That's the good news?"

"It could be worse, darlin'. And I'm happy to report that your ankle's not broken, only sprained. You're going to have to stay off it for a day or two but you should be dancing by New Year's Eve."

"I suppose that's something. What about my wrist? Is that the bad news?"

"You could say that. Take a look." He swiveled the computer monitor around so she could see the screen. If the drugs his nurse practitioner wife gave her hadn't already been making her woozy, the X-ray would have done the job. She could clearly see the jagged bones sticking out at an odd angle.

"I guess I'll be in a cast for Christmas. It could be worse, right?"

Jake's face grew solemn. "Jenna, I'm about ninety-nine percent sure you're going to need surgery. That's the bad news I was talking about. This looks beyond something I can take care of here in the office, just because of the break's location. I'm going to get on the phone with the hospital in Idaho Falls and see if they can schedule you in today or tomorrow."

She thought of all her plans, of looking at Christmas lights and reading stories and Christmas dinner with her children's remaining grandparent. "No. No way. Jake, tomorrow's Christmas Eve. I can't ruin this for my kids again."

"I'm afraid you don't have much choice in the matter, at least about the surgery. But nobody said it has to ruin anybody's Christmas. It's most likely an outpatient surgery. You could have it done first thing in the morning and be home by early afternoon."

"Couldn't you just cast it and let me have the surgery after Christmas? Please, Jake." She pleaded with him as a neighbor and as a friend. "I swore to myself I wouldn't let anything ruin Christmas for my boys and for Jolie. You know what it's been like for us. Two years ago Joe was dying and then last year we were dealing with Pat's stroke and Jolie's pneumonia. I can't do the hospital thing again. Everything has to be perfect this year."

"Nothing's perfect, Jenna."

"I know that. I just don't want to see the inside of a hospital this Christmas."

He studied her for a long moment and then he sighed. "You're a hard woman to say no to. Has Maggie been giving you lessons?"

She smiled. "It's a gift we share. What can I say?"

"Look, I can try to set it here. I'm not sure we can

put the bones back into the right position but we can try. It won't be easy."

What in her life was? Jenna thought. "Thanks, Jake. I just need to make it through Christmas and then you can do all the surgeries you want."

"I don't want to do *any* surgeries. My preference would be to have you home safe and sound without mild concussions or sprained ankles or anything."

She nodded, grateful beyond words that Jake had decided to come back to Pine Gulch to practice medicine. He could have taken a job anywhere but he had opted to become a family physician in his own hometown and the entire town owed him a huge debt for it.

"This is going to take a while and we'll have to get you good and loopy. Are your kids okay?"

She hoped so. She had called them on the way here and all seemed to be under control, but with her children, that could change in an instant. "Yes. Erin's with them and Terri said she would run out and help her."

"What about a ride home? Can McRaven stick around and wait for you? You'll be in no shape to drive for a while."

"You can send him home," she said. "Terri or my brother can give me a ride back up the canyon."

"I'll do my best. But I've got to tell you, the man looks pretty settled out there in the waiting room. I don't think he's going anywhere. Let's get you into the procedure room then I'll go talk to McRaven."

Sure enough, Jake returned a few moments later with Maggie and an ominous tray of medical implements— and the news that Carson insisted on staying until her arm was set and casted.

Jenna wanted to protest, but the medication Maggie had given her for the pain was making her far too muddleheaded to think straight.

The next hour passed in a blur. Jake first made sure her entire arm was numb and she was blissfully chatting with Maggie about shoes and shopping and the Daltons' two-year-old, Ada, who was currently spending the afternoon with her grandmother.

Afterward, she vaguely recalled Jake warning her to keep her head averted while he worked the pieces of bone together, then enduring another X-ray to make sure everything was set correctly.

She also had random snatches of memory of Maggie helping Jake cast her arm in a festive red, which she assured them she had to have so she could match her new Christmas dress.

Finally, Jake told her he would drop by her house to check on her the next morning and she was to come back the day after Christmas for another X-ray so they could see if the bones were staying the way he set them.

In the meantime, she was also under strict instructions to stay off her sprained ankle.

"I would give you crutches," Jake said, "but having one arm in a cast makes getting around on them a little difficult. You'll have to use a cane and just be on your honor that you'll keep the weight off that foot."

Jenna nodded, wondering how in the heck she was going to cook Christmas dinner when she couldn't stand up. She would figure something out, she thought. She always did.

Carson jumped up the moment Jake wheeled her into the waiting room and she flushed, embarrassed that he had hung around for her longer than an hour in a room full of crying babies and sniffly children.

"What are you still doing here? My brother or his wife could have given me a ride. Now I've ruined your whole day."

"The day's not over yet," Carson said with a smile and Jenna could swear she heard several of the young mothers in the waiting room give dreamy sighs.

"So you're good to go?" he asked.

She looked to Jake for confirmation. "Just make sure you take the pain pills I gave you on schedule," the physician said sternly. "Don't try to be a hero or I promise, you'll suffer for it later."

She nodded, suddenly weak with exhaustion as Carson took over behind the wheelchair and pushed her out the door toward his black SUV.

She must have dozed off on the six-mile drive up the canyon. She didn't awaken until he pulled up in front of her house and turned off the engine, when the cessation of noise and movement jerked her out of sleep.

The smell of leather and enticing male filled her senses and she blinked her eyes open, to realize that somehow in her sleep she had moved across the seat and was resting her head on his shoulder.

Out of sheer instinct, she jerked her head away, then gasped when pain cut through her like a buzz saw. The acute nature of her wrist and ankle injuries had taken center stage the last hour. Somehow she had forgotten the crack her head had taken and the concussion that had resulted from it.

Still, she made herself pull away from Carson. "Sorry. I didn't mean to fall asleep on you." And she meant that quite literally.

He smiled that devastating smile again. "Don't worry about it. I'm glad my shoulder was here. I thought about just driving so you could rest but I figured you would feel better when you were home."

"I do need to get back to my children. I've been away too long as it is."

He studied her for a long moment and she saw something that looked suspiciously like guilt flicker across his features. "You know you're going to need help, right?" he finally said. "Is there anyone you can call?"

Panic flickered through her whenever she thought about how much her injury complicated her already hectic life, but she ruthlessly shoved it down. "Hayden and Drew can help me."

He raised an eyebrow. "They're just kids. They're not going to know what to do if you start speaking in tongues in the middle of the night from that bump on your head."

"We'll be fine, Carson," she assured him with far more confidence than she felt. "Thank you for giving me a ride to the clinic and for everything."

She suddenly remembered quite clearly the conversation they had been having just before she foolishly stomped out of his house and ended up slipping down the stairs.

You come with tangles and complications I can't handle. I'm not interested in handling them. The whole kid and family thing is not anything I'm looking for and that's what you're all about, isn't it. I'm sorry, but you're just not the kind of woman I want.

How humiliating. She makes a grand, door-slamming exit, intending never to see the man again, and then ends up falling flat on her butt. Now here he was, hours later, forced to babysit her.

Could their relationship become any more awkwardly entangled?

"I really do appreciate the ride," she repeated.

She started to open the car door but he shoved out of his seat and hurried around the vehicle before she could even get it open.

When he jerked the door open, his eyes glittered with annoyance and his mouth was hard and tight.

"You're crazy. That's the only explanation that makes sense. I thought you were just stubborn but I've finally figured out that you're just plain nuts."

She shrugged. She should probably be offended, but she just didn't have the energy right now. "I'm a mother. It's part of the job description."

"Well, crazy or not, I'm not letting you hobble into the house by yourself and I'm not letting you stay here alone. You obviously can't be trusted to take care of yourself, so somebody needs to keep an eye on you, somebody bigger than four feet tall."

"Who did you have in mind?"

His smile was as dangerous as a crouched mountain lion. "I can bunk on your couch."

She stared at him. "Now who's the crazy one? You can't stay here."

"Watch me."

"Carson, tomorrow is Christmas Eve. The last place on earth you want to be is in my crowded house with four jacked-up kids."

Something odd flickered in the depths of his eyes, something she couldn't quite read.

"We'll all have to adapt, won't we? I won't back down on this, Jen. You were hurt at my house, on my watch, and that makes me responsible for you."

"You can set your mind at ease. I fell down the stairs. It was completely an accident. I'm not the sort who will sue you or anything, especially for something that was my own blasted fault."

"I don't care about the legalities."

"I'm sure your McRaven lawyers would love to hear you say that."

"Screw the lawyers. This is deeper than that. I'm responsible for what happened to you. I intend to make sure you're in capable hands."

She shivered a little, remembering just how capable those hands had been earlier. When she caught the direction of her thoughts, she flushed and blamed her reaction on either the lingering exhaustion or the painkillers Jake had given her.

She was too tired to argue with him right now, she decided. She would figure it all out after she had rested and could think straight again.

"Fine. You have no idea what you're walking into but I'm too woozy-headed to talk any sense into you right now. But just remember when you've got kids hanging off you and your head is splitting that I warned you what to expect."

Chapter Thirteen

She did warn him.

Two hours later, Carson stood in Jenna's compact kitchen trying to scrub burned macaroni and cheese off her stove top. Behind him at the kitchen table, Jolie in her high chair was starting to fret and rub her eyes and Kip was gabbing a mile a minute about all the things he wanted Santa to bring him the next night, though for the life of him, Carson couldn't figure out who the kid was talking to.

His brothers certainly weren't paying him any attention. Hayden and Drew were arguing about everything under the sun, from the best place to go fishing in the summer to how to throw a spitball to which of them was better at "Super Mario Galaxy."

He was quite certain his head was going to explode in another sixty seconds.

What the hell was he thinking, imagining even for a moment that he could handle this?

The Wii argument was quickly getting out of hand and he finally had to step in. "Guys. Guys. Come on. Your mom's going to wake up if you keep at each other's throats like this."

Drew instantly backed down. "Sorry, Mr. McRaven," he said.

As he might have expected, Hayden wasn't nearly so cooperative. "Why do we have to listen to you?" he asked in that surly tone Carson had become used to, though he took some small degree of satisfaction that the boy had forgotten to cop his attitude for a large part of the afternoon. Apparently the temporary cease-fire was over.

"You shouldn't even be here," Hayden groused.

Damn straight, he shouldn't. He couldn't have agreed more with the boy. He was completely out of his element here. But he had given Jenna his word and right now he didn't see any other alternative.

At least she wasn't around to see how miserably he was failing her. Jenna had fallen asleep a few hours ago—and he was amazed she had made it as long as she had. When he carried her inside the house, she had insisted he set her on the living room couch in front of their lopsided Christmas tree.

Anyone looking in on the scene might have guessed she had been away from her children for weeks, the way none of them wanted to let her out of their sights. At first he thought they were extraordinarily clingy, until he remembered how frightening the situation must have seemed from their standpoint, children who lost their father just two Christmases ago.

She hadn't seemed to mind having them right there with her. While Carson stood by feeling helpless, she had talked with them for a good half hour even while he could see her energy begin to wane.

Before he could usher the children out of the living room, she was fast asleep, as she had been for the last two hours.

"Look, your mom needs rest," he reminded her boys and the darling little cherub in the high chair with the orange cheese sauce mustache. "I know she'll want to be feeling better tomorrow for Christmas Eve so we all need to give her the chance to take it easy while she can."

"We were supposed to go look at Christmas lights tonight," Kip said with a pout. "My friend Cody says his house has more lights than anyone in Pine Gulch and I want to go see it."

He thought about piling them all into his Suburban and driving into town. It would be a distraction, anyway, and might put Jolie to sleep. On the other hand, the logistics of loading them all in overwhelmed him— quite a humiliating realization for a man who owned dozens of companies and managed to keep track of each one of them.

"Are you still going to be here on Christmas Eve?" Hayden asked crossly.

"I don't know," he answered. *Lord, I hope not.* "I guess that will depend on your mom and how she's doing."

The words were barely out of his mouth when the woman in question appeared in the doorway looking pale and rumpled. Her hair was a little disheveled but she still looked as lovely as ever.

He didn't know when he had ever seen a more welcome sight. Apparently her children shared his sentiment.

"Mommy!" Kip exclaimed and rushed to his mother.

Carson didn't miss her wince as the boy collided with her but she quickly hid it and enveloped him in her arms. A weird ache quivered in his chest as he watched the two of them. She had to be feeling like she'd been run over by a truck right about now, but she still let her little kid maul her.

"I'm sorry." She pushed a stray lock of hair out of her eyes. "I didn't mean to sleep so long. I didn't mean to sleep at all, actually."

"With all the meds they filled you with at the doc's, it's a wonder you lasted as long as you did."

She made a face. "I hate the stuff. I wish I could have convinced Jake that a couple of aspirin would do just fine for me."

"Mommy hurt," Jolie said. She looked adorably empathetic, her little chin quivering as if she was going to cry, too.

Jenna hobbled to her high chair and leaned down to press a soft kiss on the top of her daughter's curls. "Just a little, baby."

"We had macaroni and cheese," Kip announced. "Only it wasn't the good kind like you make with the gooey cheese and the crumbly top."

"Sorry," Carson muttered. "I did my best, but apparently I don't have your skills in the kitchen."

He was the CEO of one of the leading tech innovation companies in the world. He shouldn't feel like a complete loser just because he could only make mac and cheese out of a box.

He would have felt about three inches tall if he hadn't caught Jenna's eyes and seen a glowing light there when she looked at him.

"You did great, Carson. Actually, I'm amazed you're still here and haven't run screaming from the house."

"I was tempted a few times."

Her smile was warm and grateful and he told himself the ache in his gut was just hunger. "I can't thank you enough for sticking around. I'm only sorry I fell asleep and left you on your own. That wasn't in the plan."

"You needed it, just like you need to get off that bad foot. Come and sit down and I can get you a bowl of this orange gunk."

"Mmm. Sounds delicious." She smiled again at him and he was astounded that she could still smile when he knew her pain pills had to be wearing off.

She slid onto the empty chair at the table and he dished up a bowl of the macaroni and cheese and set it in front of her. He found it to be a strange turn of events after the last few days that now he was the one feeding her.

"Thanks. I'm suddenly starving. Even for orange gunk."

His stomach rumbled and he realized he hadn't eaten anything since the breakfast she had served him and the Hertzogs that morning. He dished some onto a plate for himself and slid onto a seat of his own at the table across from her.

It had been years since he'd had the boxed stuff, but to his surprise, it wasn't that bad, especially if a man was hungry enough.

He was further surprised that the boys actually

stopped fighting and sat in relative peace around the table with them while they ate.

"What did you do while I was sleeping?" Jenna asked.

"We went downstairs and played foosball and video games," Drew said. "It was super fun."

"Only because you whipped me six ways to Sunday at 'Wii Sports.'"

Drew giggled and the sound tugged a reluctant smile out of Carson. He had to admit, he had enjoyed that part of the afternoon.

He had been filled with panic when Jenna fell asleep but he discovered the boys were actually quite funny and didn't require much more than a peacekeeper. He found it remarkable that each was such a distinct personality.

And Jolie was a major snuggler. She hadn't wanted to leave his lap, which made swinging a Wii tennis racket a little tough.

"You played all afternoon and then you came up and fixed dinner and everything. I'm really embarrassed I slept so long."

"Don't be. You needed it."

"We tried to be quiet so we didn't wake you up," Drew assured her.

"Some of us did, anyway," Hayden muttered with a dark look to Kip, who Carson had discovered never met a quiet moment he didn't try to fill with chatter.

"I tried," his brother exclaimed. "It's just hard for me."

Carson's gaze met Jenna's and he smiled. As he watched, color crept up her high cheekbones. Why? he wondered, even as that hunger he had been fighting surged up inside him again.

She looked slight and fragile and he still had a hard time believing she was the mother to the four children around the table.

"And we did our chores, Mom, without you even having to nag us," Drew added. "We fed the ponies and Frannie and then we shoveled the snow while Mr. McRaven fixed dinner for us."

"I'm impressed," she told Carson. "What sort of magic obedience school did you send them to while I was sleeping?"

He laughed. "That's my secret." He decided not to tell her he had promised them if they did what he asked, he would get them a copy of a cutting-edge video game one of his companies was creating. It might be bribery, but, hey, a man had to use the tools at his disposal.

Before she could press him, Jolie yawned suddenly, a wide ear-popping stretch of her jaw, and Jenna instantly went into Mommy mode.

"You're exhausted, aren't you, munchkin?" She pushed away the rest of her mac and cheese. "Let's get you to bed. All of you."

The boys grumbled and looked as if they wanted to argue but Carson shook his head with a pointed look to cut them off before they could even start.

"What do I need to do?" he asked Jenna.

She looked confused and a bit befuddled at how quickly her boys fell into line. "The boys can all shower on their own but Jolie needs a bath. Do you think you can help me with that?"

The thought terrified the hell out of him but he had promised to help her. He couldn't just pick and choose the jobs in his personal comfort zone.

"Sure. You'll have to walk me through it, I'm afraid. Bathing little kids isn't exactly in my skill set."

She smiled. "You're in luck, then, because it is in mine. Boys, take turns in the shower and then meet back here in half an hour for our story."

How was it humanly possible for a man to look so utterly, adorably masculine while he tried to figure out how to put a diaper on a little girl?

Jenna sat on the chair Carson had brought in from the kitchen for her and tried to oversee as best she could. It proved tougher than she had anticipated. He really meant it when he said he didn't know what he was doing.

Sitting on the sidelines was frustrating—but a bit amusing, she had to admit.

"No, the tabs go on the back. You slide that section underneath her bottom and then bring those sides around to connect at the front. Yes, that's the way. You did it!"

He looked ridiculously pleased with himself, even as lopsided as the diaper was. She feared Jolie's entire bedding would be soaked before morning. But she had learned early in her marriage that the quickest way to ensure her husband never helped around the house was to criticize the way he did things—or more subversive and destructive, to go behind him and redo things to her satisfaction.

He struggled to put the pink footie pajamas on until she explained her trick of putting the foot without the zipper on first, then the other foot and the arms last. When he zipped her up, Jolie clapped her hands and beamed at him with her wide, toothy grin. Poor Carson looked so bemused, Jenna could tell her daughter had already bewitched him.

She considered it a minor miracle that the boys bathed and put on their pajamas without turning the house into a major battlefield. They did bicker about whose turn it was to open the wrapped storybook for the night.

Tonight's turned out to be one of their favorites, *How the Grinch Stole Christmas*, much to the boys' glee.

"Are you sure you're up to this? Do you want me to read the story?" Carson asked.

"Not a chance. It's my favorite part of the day."

Jenna took a seat on the sofa by the fireplace in the living room with Jolie in her lap while the boys gathered around. Carson took the easy chair by the Christmas tree, much to her surprise.

Jolie fell asleep round about the time the Grinch was dressing Max the dog in his reindeer antlers. Her soft, warm weight was sweet comfort against her. Even though she ached just about everywhere, she wanted the peace of the moment to go on forever.

She glanced over at Carson and found him watching her out of those fathomless blue eyes.

It seemed oddly right to have him there.

Ridiculous, she told herself. He didn't belong here. He was Carson McRaven of McRaven Enterprises. He had a private jet while she had a Dodge minivan with bald tires. He was only doing her a favor by helping her out while she was injured and she would do well not to put any more importance to it than that.

She finished the last page and closed the book.

"We're almost done with the books!" Kip exclaimed. "That means Santa Claus comes tomorrow night!"

Jenna gave an inward wince as she thought of all the presents she still needed to wrap and the stockings that needed to be filled. She nodded. "I know. We have a lot to do tomorrow to get the house ready for him and I'm going to need everybody's help."

"Is *he* still going to be here in the morning?" Hayden asked, with a head jerk toward Carson.

"By *he*, do you mean Mr. McRaven, who has been kind enough to feed you dinner and play foosball and Wii with you?"

"Yeah. Him."

She glanced at Carson but he appeared unoffended by her son's rudeness. "I don't know. We'll have to see what happens tomorrow. Now into bed, guys. Say your prayers and turn off your lights."

They grumbled a bit but after Carson cleared his throat, they quickly subsided. She wondered how on earth was he doing that and could he teach her? as the boys trudged up the stairs to their rooms.

Carson rose. "Let me carry her upstairs for you."

She knew she couldn't argue. "Thanks. I'm not sure I could do it one-handed."

"Not with your cane, anyway."

He scooped Jolie out of her arms a bit awkwardly and she was aware of the heat of his hands as he brushed her chest in the process. "Which one is her bedroom?"

"The pink one. First door on the left."

He nodded and headed for the stairs and she was astonished at the tenderness that welled up inside her as she saw Carson—big and rangy—holding her small, fatherless child with such gentleness.

She didn't think she could hop up the stairs so she opted to scoot after him on her bottom. He stepped out of Jolie's room just as she reached the top of the stairs, wishing for a little dignity.

He frowned at her. "What do you think you're doing?"

"I need to tuck in my boys," she said.

He rolled his eyes but held a hand out to help her to her feet—or foot, anyway. She hobbled into the room Kip and Drew shared and kissed them each in turn then went across the hall to Hayden's football-maniac room, with its huge Broncos posters on the walls and the orange, blue and white theme that was everywhere she looked.

He looked a little disgruntled that Carson was there as well but she was pleased that he still let her kiss him and tuck the blankets around his shoulders. Her oldest was going to be a teenager before she knew it. How much longer would he let his mother kiss him and rub his hair? Forever, she hoped.

"Night, bud. Thanks for your help today. I don't know what I would do without you," she whispered as she kissed him. His cheeks turned a little rosy and she could tell he was pleased.

"I'm not letting you scoot down the stairs again," Carson said after they closed the door to Hayden's room.

She caught her breath as he scooped her into his arms with effortless ease. He carried her down the stairs without even breathing hard.

She was breathing hard enough for both of them, though she did her best to hide her reaction. She didn't want to admit how truly wonderful it felt to be held like this, to be cherished and watched over.

It was only natural. She had been alone for two years, had been forced to rely only on herself for everything her family needed, from mowing the lawn to taking the car to be fixed to repairing a leaky faucet. The chance to lean on someone else for a change shouldn't seduce her so completely, but she felt powerless to control it.

Downstairs, he set her back on the couch and she forced herself to recall his words that morning, a moment that now seemed a lifetime ago.

She wasn't the kind of woman he wanted. He had told her so, straight-out and she couldn't forget it.

"Where's the best place for me to bunk tonight?"

"This is silly, Carson. You don't need to stay here. Hayden and Drew and I should be able to handle things. I don't need a keeper."

His sigh stirred the air between them. "Do we really have to argue about this again? You've got a concussion, a broken wrist and a sprained ankle. How could I possibly feel comfortable leaving you here alone to deal with four kids by yourself, especially with those heavy-duty painkillers on board? Now where's the best place for me to bunk?"

She wanted to argue, but she could clearly see by the stubborn set of his features that he wasn't going anywhere. And as tough as it was to admit, she felt more comfortable having another adult in the house. The painkillers left her loopy and she couldn't go up and down the stairs if, God forbid, the house caught fire or something. Her pride recoiled at needing his help but since the situation was beyond her control right now, she would just have to accept it with as much grace as possible.

"There's a guest room just off the kitchen. It's the room my mother-in-law uses when she visits."

Just another stress she would have to figure out in the morning, she thought with an edge of panic.

"That should be perfect," Carson said.

They lapsed into silence broken only by the crackle of the fire. Outside she could see snowflakes drifting down. It would have been an idyllic scene if not for the undercurrents that ebbed and flowed between them. She couldn't seem to stop thinking about their kiss in his kitchen that morning or the devastating scene that followed it.

"All right," he finally said. "Out with it. I can see your mind is whirling."

She flushed. "Oh, you're psychic now?"

He shrugged. "You have to be a little omniscient when you buy and sell tech companies. But I don't have to be psychic to see those wheels turning. Your face is remarkably expressive, in case you didn't know."

What else could he read on her face? she wondered. Could he see the slow heat she couldn't seem to control around him?

"Joe used to accuse me of having the worst poker face in eastern Idaho."

"You might as well play your hand, Jenna. What's on your mind?"

Of course, she couldn't tell him what she had been thinking so she quickly made something up. "I, um, was just wondering how long before the boys will safely be asleep. Hayden and Kip usually go right to sleep the minute their lights go out, but Drew has a tendency to read under his covers until I catch him at it and make him turn off the flashlight."

"He pick that up from you or his dad?"

She made a face "Me. I used to do the exact same

thing. There are still nights I stay up entirely too late caught up in a good book."

She paused and something about the quiet intimacy of the night made her admit, "It helps to keep the darkness away."

His features softened with sympathy and she instantly regretted her openness. She quickly changed the subject. "Anyway, I still have a few last-minute gifts from Santa to wrap. I need to make sure the boys are all asleep beyond a doubt before I dig them out."

He arched one of those expressive eyebrows. "And how do you expect to wrap presents? With your teeth?"

Her arm ached as if on cue and she gazed down at her cast with no small amount of consternation. "Oh, dear. I hadn't thought that far ahead."

"I can help. I can't guarantee the kind of job I'll do since wrapping presents is another one of those things out of my skill set but I can do my best."

"I can't ask you to do that. You've done enough, Carson. I'll figure something out. Maybe Santa just won't wrap everything this year."

He made an impatient gesture. "Where are your presents and the wrapping paper?"

There was no dissuading the man when he had his mind made up about something and Jenna decided to admit defeat. "We need to make completely sure nobody will be sneaking down the stairs first. Let's give them a few moments and then I'll direct you to my secret stash."

Chapter Fourteen

Carson knew damn well he shouldn't be enjoying this so much.

This wasn't at all how he intended to spend the holidays. He had come to his ranch for two reasons—to host the Hertzogs and to enjoy a little solitude before he returned to the hectic pace of San Francisco.

He certainly never planned to find himself in Jenna Wheeler's comfortable TV room watching *It's a Wonderful Life* on a twenty-inch screen he could barely see and wrapping up action figures.

There were certainly worse ways to pass the time, he had to admit.

"I hope I'm doing this right. I'm not a great gift wrapper."

"They look great." She smiled at him from the couch. "Anyway, the kids don't really care how fancy they look. I doubt they'll even notice. They'll rip all your hard work to pieces in about ten seconds flat."

A weird pang of longing pinched at him. He would like to see Christmas morning at the Wheeler house. The joy and excitement on their faces, the noise and confusion. It would be a completely foreign experience for him but one he suddenly wanted to endure, as crazy as that seemed.

"You know, I can change this," Jenna said, interrupting his thoughts. "You've probably seen this movie a million times."

"Actually, no. I've only seen bits and pieces of it and that was several years ago."

She exaggerated an expression of horror that made him smile. "How can that be? It's completely unnatural."

His smile faded. He thought about making a joke but decided to tell her the truth. "I didn't exactly have the Bedford Falls kind of upbringing."

She gave him a careful look, as if she knew exactly how tough that was for him to admit. "No?"

She was clearly waiting for more. Now that he had opened the door, he wasn't sure he wanted all that information about himself to come slithering out. But the soft compassion in her eyes tugged the words from him.

"My dad ran off before I was born and my mother struggled with depression and drug addiction most of my life. I guess you could say my childhood was on the chaotic side. Foster homes. Shelters. Back and forth with my mom when she would clean up for a while. I spent some time on my grandparents' ranch not far from here, near Ashton. Bill and Nedda Jameson."

Her brow wrinkled with concentration. "Those

names seem so familiar. Wait, I think I knew your grandparents. They used to come into my dad's feed store when I was a kid. I remember your grandfather always had Brach's toffee in his pocket."

He smiled a little at the memory. He had adored his grandparents and would have been happy living at their little ranch forever. But his mother hadn't been on good terms with her parents for years and she became furious when she found out they had applied for permanent custody of him. She came to his school one blustery March afternoon and took him away from Idaho and he had never seen Bill or Nedda again.

He had sneaked a few phone calls to them that first year but Lori always found out and made him sorry enough that he had given up and lost touch with them over the years. The first time he had tried to run away at thirteen, he had called and received a recorded message that the number had been disconnected. He later learned they had died the year before within six months of each other—and that they had never stopped trying to find him.

He pushed the grim memories away. "What about you? I bet you watch this every year, right?"

She shook her head. "Joe never liked it. He said it was so sappy it made his teeth stick together." She smiled a little. "He wasn't as crazy about Christmas as I've always been, though he was a good sport when I went wild decorating the house and baking up a storm for weeks beforehand."

He was astonished suddenly at the jealousy that suddenly pierced him at the thought of the happy years she shared with her husband.

"You must miss him a lot."

She flashed him a quick look and then focused her gaze on the screen. He thought she wasn't going to answer but after a moment she muted the television. "He was a good man and a wonderful father. For the first year, I didn't know how I would go on by myself. But I've learned that everything gets a little easier the more time goes on."

He remembered those first few months after Suzanna and Henry James died, when he was certain every particle of light had been sucked out of his world. Gradually the light found holes to peek through, first tiny pinpricks, then bigger and bigger and he learned that life moved on.

She smiled. "It's Christmas. I certainly don't want to forget Joe—I could never do that—but mostly I want to focus this year on all my many blessings. I have four beautiful children, a roof over our heads that's paid for, good neighbors and friends and a supportive family. I've got a business that's getting off the ground. I'm so richly blessed."

She embraced life, Carson realized. Many women would have used what she had endured as an excuse to be embittered, hardened. But Jenna was like a bright beacon of light to those around her. He had seen it at his house party. The Hertzogs had all responded to her because she glowed with life.

Many in the world would consider him the more richly blessed of the two of them, at least materially. He had enjoyed enormous business success, owned houses in three states, had loyal employees. That was only the start. When was the last time he had taken the time to catalogue all he had or even to spend a moment appreciating it?

He felt small and petty and ungrateful.

He turned back to the gifts, wrapping a pile of books he assumed were for Drew. They lapsed into a not uncomfortable silence, their attention on the movie.

"All done," Carson said sometime later when he finished wrapping the last present in the box, a pretty pink-and-white doll for Jolie. Jenna didn't respond and he looked over and saw her eyes were closed and her breathing even.

She had been through a hell of a day. No wonder she fell asleep just minutes before Clarence the angel earned his wings.

He watched her sleep for a long moment, struck by her fragile loveliness and astounded all over again that it covered such indomitable strength.

She needed to eat more of her own cooking. A few of those divine desserts she made would certainly put a little more meat on those thin bones.

A strange feeling stirred up inside him as he watched her sleep. Something tender and gentle and terrifying. He drew in a sharp breath and did his best to shove it back down in the deep, dark recesses of his heart.

"Jenna? Let's get you up to your bed."

She blinked awake slowly and when her gaze met his, she gifted him with a soft smile so free and unfeigned it took his breath away. To his vast regret, it faded as she returned to full consciousness.

"Sorry to wake you but I figured you would be more comfortable where you can stretch out in your own bed," he said.

"I would. Thanks." She sat and moved as if to stand up but he held out a hand to stop her.

"Don't even think about it. You're going to be in serious trouble if you put your weight on that foot."

She gave him a challenging look. "Will I?"

"Yes. The doc told you to stay off it, remember? I'll carry you up again," he said, though he almost didn't trust himself to touch her with these emotions churning through him.

"I can scoot up the stairs."

"I'll carry you," he repeated. He forced himself to move toward her and scoop her up in his arms. She felt entirely too perfect there, a sweet, warm weight that fit just right, and he wanted to hold her close and not let go.

She didn't meet his gaze while he carried her up the stairs. Both of them were silent and he wondered what she was thinking about that put that color on her cheeks, like the blush of a newly ripe apple.

"I'm the last door on the left," she whispered at the top of the stairs. The narrowness of the hallway forced him to hold her closer and he could feel each breath she took against his chest.

He opened the door she indicated and flipped on the light switch before he gingerly set her down on a wide bed covered in a rich damask.

For some reason, he would have expected her bedroom to be light and feminine. Lavender, maybe, with lace and lots of froufrou pillows. Instead, it was dramatic and bright, with strong solid colors and polished Mission furniture. She had her own small tree here in the window, as all the children did, he had noticed earlier. Her tree was decorated in framed pictures, he guessed of her children.

"Is there anything I can get you before you go to sleep? A nightgown or something?"

Her blush seemed to intensify, though he thought that might just be a reflection of the bold colors.

"I don't think so. I can hop to the bathroom and my dresser is on the way." She paused. "Um, thank you for carrying me and...everything."

"You're welcome." He gazed at her for a long moment, fighting an almost desperate hunger to touch her again. She looked so lovely, her hair tousled from sleep and that skin so rosy and soft that he ached to kiss her.

His gaze met hers and he saw a reflection of his hunger in her green eyes.

Fast on its heels was a growing unease. He could deal with all this much better if he only felt a physical attraction to her. But he was very much afraid it was becoming much, much more.

He shoved his hands in his back pockets to keep from reaching for her. "Good night, then. I'll probably sleep on the couch so I can hear if you need anything."

She opened her mouth as if to argue but shut it again, much to his relief. If he had to stay here another minute, he was going to be on that bed with her, to hell with both her broken wrist and the consequences.

"Good night, Carson. I don't know how I'll ever thank you. You've done nothing but rescue the Wheelers since you've been here."

"That's what neighbors do, right?"

With that lame comment, he backed out of the door while he still could and headed back down the stairs.

Both times he had gone up the stairs, first with Jolie then just now with Jenna, he had been too preoccupied with the Wheeler female in his arms to notice the photo gallery that lined the stairway.

But he couldn't help paying it more attention now as he moved slowly down the stairs. The pictures showed the evolution of a family. There were photographs of all of the children in various stages of development, from infants to toddlers to preschoolers on up. They were beautiful, every one of them.

He was particularly struck by the largest picture on the wall, a posed family portrait taken somewhere outdoors in the midst of what looked like golden-hued fall aspens. He stopped and gazed at it, at the trio of blond, grinning boys who looked a few years younger than they were now, and at the smiling parents behind them. Jenna looked lovely and bright and happy. Beside her stood a man who looked just like he imagined Hayden would look in twenty years or so. His face was tanned and rugged, his blond hair a shade or two darker than Jenna's. He smiled at his family like someone who knew he had everything a man could ever want.

Carson's insides wrenched with sadness for Joe Wheeler, who had been taken from his family and would never see the boys in that picture grow to manhood and who had never even met his beautiful baby girl.

He continued down the stairs, thinking of the love on those shining faces.

He was in a house full of people, but he had never been as keenly aware that he was alone.

The siren smell of coffee and something else delicious dragged her out of sleep the next morning.

Her nose twitched and as she slowly waded back to consciousness, Jenna couldn't figure out why her room was so blissfully quiet. Usually, she was either awakened by her actual alarm clock or by one of her four living, breathing, bed-bouncing alarm wannabes.

What were they up to? Maybe they had decided to let her sleep in a little. Heavenly thought, that. She opened one eye and peeked at her alarm clock, then sat upright, pushing aside the last cobwebs in a burst of panic. Eight-thirty! She never slept until eight-thirty!

She slid off the bed to her feet and then gasped when pain shot through her left leg, at the same time she became aware of a steady, insistent throbbing in her arm.

Oh. Right. Memories flowed back of tumbling down the back stairs at Raven's Nest the previous morning, of looking at those queasiness-inducing X-rays in Jake Dalton's office, of Carson driving her home and fixing mac and cheese for her kids and wrapping her last-minute presents.

He must have put the coffee on. But what about the rest of those smells that had her stomach grumbling? And the kids must be up by now, especially on Christmas Eve morning. How long had he been coping with them on his own?

She wouldn't know until she went downstairs, she thought. She hopped to her bathroom to wash up and change, fiercely wishing she could stand under a hot pulsing shower right now. She spent a frustrating ten minutes trying to pull her hair into a ponytail with only one hand before she gave up and just ended up brushing it out and holding it away from her face with a red bandeau that matched her shirt.

She headed back through her bedroom and opened

the door, only to be confronted with a sign on the wall opposite her room in big, bold, black lettering.

"Do not tackle the stairs," it read, with the second word underlined three times. "I will take you down."

Jenna gazed at the note as she balanced on one foot in her doorway. She supposed she could call down to him, but then she remembered those moments in his strong arms, how she had fought the urge the entire way up the stairs to nestle into that hard chest, to throw her arms around his neck and hold tight.

She felt entirely too delicate, too cherished, in his arms and she didn't want to become accustomed to the sensation, not when he would be returning to California and real life anytime now.

She carefully scooted down the stairs then hopped into the kitchen. The closer she went to the home's center, the more her mouth watered from the smells emanating from it.

She paused in the doorway, astonished at the sight of all her children sitting at the table while Carson stood at the microwave, removing a dish from it.

"Wow. What's all this?"

Carson looked up and his handsome features twisted into a glare. "What are you doing down the stairs? Didn't you read the sign?"

"I did. It just smelled too delicious down here, I had to follow my nose."

"Mom, Santa Claus is coming *tonight*!" Kip gushed, his features glowing like a hundred Christmas trees.

"Santa!" Jolie exclaimed, and banged her spoon on the tray of her high chair.

Her little girl was even dressed, in a holiday sweater and jeans. Warmth soaked her when she realized Carson must have found her clothes, changed her out of her pajamas and her wet diaper, then brought her down here for breakfast.

She gazed at him, looking strong and masculine in this kitchen full of children, and her heart did a long, slow roll in her chest.

Oh, she was in deep, deep trouble with him.

"I know." Jenna smiled at all her children. "Can you believe it's really here?"

They all grinned back at her, even Hayden. For the first time, she had a look at their plates and was astonished at what she saw—muffins and ham and some egg concoction that looked vaguely familiar.

"How did you do all this?" she asked Carson. "I thought you didn't cook."

"I don't. But I'm pretty mean with a microwave. When I was trying to figure out what to fix for breakfast this morning, I remembered all that delicious leftover food at Raven's Nest from the Hertzogs visit, so the kids and I made a quick trip up the hill to raid the refrigerator and freezer."

She had slept through it all? She couldn't quite take it in.

"Did you know Carson has a swimming pool and a hot tub right *inside* his house?" Hayden said.

"I did know that. I saw it when I was cooking for him and his guests."

"He says we can use it anytime we want," Drew said. "Even today. Can we, Mom?"

She had a vivid memory of the day not even a week ago when he had all but ordered her to keep her children off his property. And now he was inviting them to use his pool whenever they wanted? She couldn't quite adjust to the shift.

"That's very kind of Mr. McRaven."

"So can we go?" Kip added his voice to the chorus.

She thought of all the things she had planned for Christmas Eve. Swimming at Raven's Nest wasn't even close to showing up on the list. On the other hand, they seemed almost as excited about the idea as they did about Christmas morning.

"We'll have to see," she said. "We've got to run to Idaho Falls to pick up Grandma today, remember?"

And she had to figure out how to pare down the Christmas feast she had planned to something more manageable for someone with a bum arm and a dicey ankle.

"Have you fed the animals?" she asked.

"Not yet," Hayden said. "We were gonna do that after breakfast."

"And speaking of which, here's yours," Carson said, setting a plate down in front of her with a dramatic flourish that made Drew and Kip giggle.

The boys finished eating just a few moments later and scraped their chairs back. "If we hurry and feed the animals, we'll have more time to swim before we pick up Grandma," Drew said.

Jenna decided not to point out she hadn't yet agreed to the swim idea, though she could already see she would come across as a major grump if she said no for the sole reason that it hadn't been in her plan.

The boys hurried into the mudroom to find their coveralls and boots, leaving her alone with Carson—except for Jolie, who jabbered away in her made-up language.

"Thanks so much for breakfast," she said to Carson.

"That's my line, isn't it? You're the one who fixed it in the first place. I only nuked it."

They lapsed into silence and she was uncomfortable at the realization that her debt to him was growing by the minute.

"Carson, you don't have to stay here today. We can handle things. I'm not disoriented from the concussion anymore. I know this isn't the way you planned to spend your holidays."

"I couldn't have dreamed this scenario up in a million years," he acknowledged. "But it's not bad, either."

She could see no equivocation in his expression and realized he was sincere.

"Well, the other factor is my mother-in-law. You might change your mind about sticking around."

"Ah. The infamous Pat."

She gave a heavy sigh. "She stays here every year, Carson. She has since Joe and I married and moved here. Even after she moved to an apartment in town, she always came back for the holidays. This was her home for thirty years. No matter how wonderful her assisted-living center in Idaho Falls might be, I just can't leave her there by herself during the holidays."

He studied her, then nodded. "Of course you can't. So we'll go get her."

She expected an argument from him about how she didn't need a houseguest when she was injured. His abrupt acceptance left her a bit disoriented. "Just like that? You have no idea what she's like."

"You're her family and she's part of yours. If you want her here, we'll go get her. Are you up for a car ride to Idaho Falls? Even if I have the kids there, I'm not sure I can convince her to come with me if you're not with us."

She smiled suddenly and she would have kissed him if she could have reached him across the table.

"You're a remarkable man, Carson McRaven. You hide that soft heart very well from the rest of the world."

He looked astonished at her words and opened his mouth to argue but the phone rang before he could.

"That's probably Dr. Dalton," Carson said. "He called to check on you earlier. When I said you were still sleeping, he said he would call back to set up a time when he could stop by to see how you were doing."

She had almost forgotten her injuries, the whole reason Carson was there in the first place.

"I guess that's something else we'll have to fit in today," she said as she took the phone from him.

She couldn't help thinking how quickly and naturally they had slipped into a "we." She needed to remind herself all day that Carson's stay was only temporary.

No matter how much she was beginning to worry she wanted it to be otherwise.

"The swim was a brilliant idea," Jenna said four hours later as Carson drove the Raven's Nest's Suburban on the winding ranch road between Pine Gulch and Idaho Falls.

"I have my moments." He smiled at her and Jenna had to fight hard not to let it slip inside her heart. She would see if he still felt like grinning an hour from now after they picked up her mother-in-law.

The calm car ride was such an anomaly that she had to look in the backseat again to make sure the boys hadn't jumped out a few stoplights ago. They weren't sleeping but they all seemed relaxed, content to just look out the window or, in Drew's case, to read a book.

That they weren't bouncing off the interior walls of the Suburban was a minor miracle. Who knew a two-hour swim in Carson's pool would turn them so mellow?

Jolie had fallen asleep in her car seat before they even drove onto Cold Creek Canyon Road and Jenna was feeling comfortable herself, with jazz Christmas carols playing on the stereo and the heater sending out comforting warmth while the wipers beat back a light snowfall.

She fought sleep for a few more miles and jerked herself upright when she found herself dozing off.

"Go to sleep," Carson said. "I'll wake you up when we hit Idaho Falls so you can direct me to your mother-in-law's place."

True to his word, Carson nudged her awake a short time later and she gave him the address. After they pulled up to the elegant facility, they went inside to find Pat waiting on one of the chairs in the lobby of the assisted-living center with her walker and her small suitcase beside her.

"I thought you said two-thirty," she said without preamble. Pat's speech was only slightly slurred, though the left side of her face had been permanently paralyzed from the stroke's aftereffects.

Jenna glanced at the clock above the office desk that said 2:45 p.m. "Sorry we're a little late. Merry Christmas, Mom." She limped forward carefully and kissed Pat's wrinkled cheek.

Pat gazed at her cast and the cane she was using to stabilize herself. "What happened to you?"

"I had a little accident yesterday and slipped on some ice."

"Didn't your boys shovel the walk?" she asked, her tone accusatory.

Jenna was spared from having to tell her where the accident occurred by the boys' impatience to greet their grandmother.

They all hugged her and Pat's stern expression softened at the unfeigned affection from her grandchildren.

Suddenly her gaze landed on Carson, who had carried Jolie inside. "Who are you?" she asked abruptly.

His gaze met Jenna's, a clear question in them. He was asking if he should lie about his identity to make the holiday run more smoothly for her, she realized. She was touched by the thought and even briefly entertained it, then discarded it. Beyond the fact that she couldn't let her children see her trying to carry off a lie, it wouldn't be fair to Carson to make him a party to that kind of deception.

"Mom, this is Carson McRaven. Our neighbor."

Even though half of her face remained stoic and expressionless, the other half clearly showed her outrage. "What is *he* doing here?"

Jenna braced herself, hoping Pat didn't cause a scene in front of the children. "He has been so wonderful to help us since my accident. We would have been lost without him."

"Carson has a pool inside his house, Grandma," Kip said cheerfully. He slipped his hand inside his grandmother's curled-up left one. He was always grateful to have new ears, and besides that, Pat had always adored his chatter. "We went swimming there today and played water basketball and everything. I didn't even have to hold on to the side the whole time. You should have seen me, Grandma."

She looked torn for a moment, as if she wanted to

continue expressing her outrage, but the other boys stepped in to talk to her and she let herself be distracted.

Jenna was quite certain she had never been so grateful for the shortened attention span that was another outcome of the stroke.

She just had to hope they could keep her distracted the rest of the evening from remembering just how much she despised Carson.

Chapter Fifteen

He had never imagined he would ever come so close to decking an old lady—especially a feeble, brain-injured one.

Two hours later, Carson sat at the kitchen table in Jenna's kitchen listening to her mother-in-law's scorching comments to Jenna about everything under the sun. Why were they having soup instead of the roast beef she had been expecting? Why were the rolls store-bought instead of Jenna's famous flaky crescent rolls? Why was the cheesecake leftover pumpkin swirl instead of the raspberry Jenna knew she favored?

He had expected her nastiness to be aimed at him, and Pat hadn't disappointed. He could handle her insults about his having more money than taste and how he was wasting his time with his eco-friendly ranching ideas. But when she started to turn her scathing comments in Jenna's direction, his blood started a long, slow simmer.

He was going to have to say something. Jenna certainly was making no move to defend herself, even after Pat started in on how Kip needed a haircut and Hayden's sweater had a small hole in it and didn't Jenna know how to wash wool, after all these years?

Jenna was unfailingly sweet. She just smiled at her mother-in-law or pretended not to hear the most scathing of her comments.

"You don't really think that hairstyle is attractive, do you?" Pat said out of nowhere. "You look like you just climbed out of bed."

That's it. He couldn't take anymore. He opened his mouth to tell the old bat her daughter-in-law was just about the most gorgeous female he had ever met, but Jenna caught his gaze and shook her head vigorously.

To his shock, she limped to the seat at the table where her mother-in-law sat, leaned down and wrapped her uninjured arm around Pat, hugging her close.

"Mom, I have to tell you how glad I am you could come out to the house with us for Christmas Eve. Remember how awful last Christmas was in the hospital? Isn't it wonderful to be at The Wagon Wheel again, with family around?"

That seemed to stymie Pat. She opened her mouth then closed it again and let her grandchildren's chatter fill the space where her nasty comments had been.

"I think everything's ready. Pat, can you get the children settled in the dining room?"

The older woman nodded and took to the challenge willingly, making Carson wonder if perhaps she lashed out because of her own frustration in her limitations and was only looking for something to do with herself.

Still, he wasn't inclined to quickly forgive her, not

when he had seen the hurt Jenna had tried to hide at the woman's comments.

"I'm so sorry." Jenna turned to him when they were alone in the kitchen. "She seems to be having a particularly bad evening and you're bearing the brunt of it. You don't have to stay and put up with her abuse."

He stopped her by pressing a finger to her mouth. She gazed at him, her green eyes huge, and he quickly dropped his hand but not before taking a guilty pleasure at the warmth and softness of her mouth against his skin.

"She's hitting at you even harder. Why do you put up with her?"

Jenna glanced into the other room to make sure everyone was out of earshot. "She wasn't like this a year ago, I promise you that." She spoke in a low, distressed voice and he had to fight to keep from taking her in his arms. "I wish you could have known her before the stroke. She was sweet and funny. I just keep reminding myself of the woman she used to be."

He had never known anyone like Jenna, who loved so unconditionally and could grit her teeth and smile in the midst of completely unwarranted harsh criticism.

"I promise, she's also not like this all the time. It seems to me the really terrible days are followed by several days when things feel like they're back to normal. I'm keeping my fingers crossed for tomorrow."

She was the eternal optimist. He smiled, unable to help himself from leaning forward and kissing her forehead.

She blinked up at him, clearly as startled by the spontaneous gesture as he had been, but Hayden came into the kitchen and she backed away from him, her cheeks rosy from more than the heat in the kitchen.

To his relief, Pat stayed largely silent as they ate in the dining room, where the boys had set a festive table with a red checkered tablecloth and even Christmas bowls with entwined holly leaves around the edges.

Each of the three kinds of soup were divine and he would never have known it came from her freezer if he hadn't helped her thaw it and stick it in Crock-Pots before they left for Idaho Falls.

After dinner, all of them helped with cleanup then they adjourned to the living room, where her busy, slightly lopsided tree gleamed against the windows.

He stoked up the fire while Pat took the easy chair and Hayden and Drew set up a card table.

The evening passed with astonishing speed as they sang Christmas carols and ate popcorn and played games of cards and Christmas charades.

"All right, that's the last game," Jenna finally said. Jolie had again begun to droop and even Kip had hidden a yawn or two behind his hand.

"There are four presents under the tree in green paper with gold bows. Hayden, can you find them and pass them out?"

"Present!" Jolie summoned enough energy to clap her hands.

"Can we open them?" Kip asked.

"Yes. Only this one, though. The rest have to wait until tomorrow."

Kip and Drew buzzed with anticipation, though Hayden looked bored with the whole thing.

"You're not excited?" Carson asked him in a man-to-man kind of tone.

He shrugged. "It's just pajamas. She makes us some every year. Big deal."

Big deal? Carson looked at the pajamas the other boys were pulling from the paper. They were flannel in complementary plaids and looked just like store-bought pajamas, from what he could tell.

"Your mother made those? As in taking material and thread and cutting out patterns and sewing them?"

"Well, yeah. What did you think I meant?"

He was utterly flabbergasted as he imagined her finding time in her chaotic life to sew four sets of pajamas. His own mother couldn't even be bothered to go to the Salvation Army to buy him a used Matchbox car but Jenna had painstakingly sewn her four children pajamas.

"Go shower and change into them and come down so I can get a picture. Then we can read," she said while he was still reeling from the contrast.

"Do you need me to give Jolie her bath?" he asked.

"I think I'll forgo it and give her one tomorrow. She's so tired she's going to be asleep in a minute as it is."

He nodded and helped change her and dress her in the little red plaid nightgown her grandmother had helped her open.

"I can't believe you made pajamas," he said as he pulled the nightgown over Jolie's curls.

Jenna shrugged. "It's not really hard. Well, the first time was, but I've been making them from the same pattern now for years, except for Jolie's nightgown, of course. I've kind of gotten into a routine."

She was a wonderful mother. He wanted to tell her so but the words seemed to catch in his throat and he turned his attention back to her daughter.

She took several digital photos of them in various poses by the Christmas tree alone and with their grandmother. He insisted on taking his turn behind the camera so she could be included in the picture as well. That offer earned him a grateful smile, then Jenna pulled out their Christmas book Advent basket.

There were still a couple of other wrapped books left but she focused on a small one that had "Christmas Eve" written on it, as well as Hayden's name.

"Why does it have my name on it?" the boy asked. "It's not my turn. I picked one two nights ago, remember?"

"Open it," Jenna answered with a soft smile.

He looked baffled as he ripped the paper away, then he stared for a long moment at the small black book in his hands.

"It's Dad's Bible." His voice was hushed as he traced his fingers over the embossed gold letters. He looked close to tears and Carson felt a lump rise in his own throat.

"We gave him that when he turned twelve years old," Pat spoke from the corner, her voice more gentle than Carson had heard.

Jenna's eyes were moist as well and she pressed her cheek on Jolie's curls. "You're ten now. Almost as old as he was when he got it. I think he would have wanted you to have it now."

Hayden dashed a surreptitious hand against his eyes and straightened his shoulders inside the flannel pajamas his mother had sewn for him.

"Do you want to read the story?" she asked.

"Really? You want me to?"

"Go ahead. Luke Chapter 2."

He turned the pages as if they were made of spun gold and finally found the right section.

"'And it came to pass in those days, that a decree went out from Caesar Augustus…'" he began, his voice solemn.

They all sat spellbound, even Drew and the energetic Kip.

Carson had never heard anything as sweetly powerful as this child's faltering voice reading the story of the first Christmas from his deceased father's Bible. He had to swallow hard several times as emotions seemed to well up inside him.

By the time the boy read the last word, Carson, who had always considered himself a skeptic, was almost ready to believe in miracles.

He hadn't dared look at Jenna while Hayden read. Still, when the boy finished, he shifted his gaze and found her wiping away tears. But she gave a watery smile and pulled Hayden close.

"Perfect. Thank you, Hayden. Your dad would have been so proud of you."

He held the Bible to his chest. "Can I keep it in my room?"

"Yes. I know you'll be careful with it so your brothers can have their turn to read the story from it in the coming years. All right, everyone. It's time for bed."

He might have expected arguments from the boys— it *was* Christmas Eve, after all—but they were subdued as they headed for the stairs.

"I'm off to bed, too," Pat said.

Jenna looked at her with surprise. "Are you sure, Mom?"

"I'm tired," the other woman said, somewhat wasp-ishly. "Been a long day."

"Of course. Do you need help?"

"Just take care of the kids," Pat said.

"All right. Merry Christmas, Mom."

The woman nodded abruptly then shuffled out of the room with her walker.

"I'll take Jolie," he said to Jenna when Pat left. She held the girl out and he scooped her into his arms. She wasn't asleep but she was almost there. Still, she gave him a wide, sleepy smile then rested her cheek against his chest. He pressed a hand on her little back, not at all sure what to do with this wild rush of emotions churning through him.

Jenna hopped up the stairs, putting minimal weight on her ankle. He was loathe to relinquish Jolie so he followed Jenna, the little girl in his arms, as she moved from bedroom to bedroom saying prayers with her boys and giving kisses.

Finally it was Jolie's turn and he carried her to her pretty pink bedroom. He set the girl in her crib and Jenna came forward to settle her in. He started to slip out of the bedroom but Jolie held her arms out.

"Mister, kiss!"

He froze at the door then returned to the crib and leaned down. Jolie threw her tiny arms around his neck and planted a big sloppy kiss on his cheek.

She might as well have carved out his heart and tucked it under her pillow.

"Night night," she said.

"Good night," he answered, his voice gruff.

Jenna smiled at him as if she knew just what he was

going through. She kissed her daughter as well, turned on a low music box by the crib, then turned the light out.

She started to hop down the stairs. Carson looked at her for a half second, heaved a long, frustrated sigh and scooped her up as he had Jolie, trying not to notice all over again how perfectly she fit into his arms.

He made it down the stairs in record time and quickly set her down on the couch in the living room.

"Now what?" he asked, his voice abrupt, mostly because it was taking all his energy and attention to keep his hands off of her.

She smiled, though he thought it looked a little strained. "Now we wait."

"For?"

"For them all to fall asleep, which on Christmas Eve can take forever. But they know Santa can't come until they're down."

She paused and studied him. "Would you like some hot cocoa while we wait?"

He wasn't a big cocoa drinker. On the other hand, having a mug in his hands might help him keep them to himself.

"I'm just going to check on Pat first before I make the cocoa."

"Can I do anything?"

"Just relax."

He nodded and leaned his head against the back of the couch. He had never realized how exhausting the whole family thing could be. He'd been up since before seven when he heard the first stirring from upstairs, and he hadn't slept that great on the narrow sofa to begin with.

He watched the Christmas tree's reflection in the

window while soft instrumental carols emanated from speakers in the corners and wondered what the hell was happening to him.

He must have dozed off for a moment, though not for long. He woke to the smell of chocolate and the vanilla and cinnamon scent of Jenna.

She stood in the doorway watching him, a funny expression on her face.

"Sorry. I didn't mean to wake you," she murmured. "You can go back to sleep."

"No. I'm up." He straightened, wondering how long she had watched him. "How's Pat?"

"Fine. She was nearly asleep when I checked on her. I sometimes forget how exhausting the children can be for someone who's not used to it."

He didn't like thinking he might have the same degree of fortitude as a seventy-year-old stroke victim.

"Sit down. Get off your ankle," he ordered.

She complied with such docile alacrity, he knew she must be hurting. "I left the cocoa in the other room. I was afraid of dumping it all over the carpet if I tried to carry it."

"I'll grab it."

He found the mugs by the stove and had to smile. In typical Jenna style, this wasn't ordinary hot cocoa out of a packet. It was thick and rich and topped with whipped cream and crushed red-and-white peppermint candies.

He shook his head and carried them both to the living room. Jenna had stretched her foot out on the recliner and he set the cocoa on the small table beside her.

"Thanks."

This was nice, he thought. Just the two of them and

the crackling fire and the Christmas tree. It was too nice. He could feel himself start to weave all kinds of scenarios that mostly involved sweeping her off that chair and into his lap.

"Tell me about what Christmases were like when you were a kid," he said.

She looked startled but then began telling him about her childhood, about her parents who had spoiled both her and her brother every Christmas, about big, noisy parties with her extended family.

He listened, sometimes interjecting a skillfully crafted question that would keep her going so she wouldn't ask him about his own Christmas memories.

Some time later, she lapsed into silence. "I'm worse than Kip. I'm sorry. I didn't mean to talk your ear off."

"I didn't mind," he answered, and it was the honest truth. He loved listening to her stories. She could have been reading a cookbook and he probably would have sat here just as spellbound.

She gazed at him and something changed in her eyes, a soft light that stole his breath. Currents zinged between them and he could feel the inexorable tug of desire stretch and pull between them. His blood turned sluggish and he could hear his pulse in his ears.

Jenna jerked her gaze away and focused on the Christmas tree. "I think they're probably asleep by now. It's been an hour."

Had that much time really passed so quickly? He couldn't quite believe it.

"I had better check to make sure they're down," she said, and started limping for the stairs.

Stubborn woman. "I'll do it. Stay here."

He headed back up the stairs and moved from room

to room, looking for any sign of activity. Everyone's eyes were closed, their breathing even. There was always the chance somebody could be faking but he didn't think so. He spent an extra long time in Kip and Drew's room, trying to gauge whether Drew might have quickly hid a book under his blanket when he heard footsteps on the stairs, but he couldn't see anything.

"All snug in their beds," he told Jenna when he returned downstairs.

"Now the fun begins. I'm afraid you're going to have to do most of the work."

She sent him down to the basement several times to bring up all the gifts from her various hiding places, including the gifts he had wrapped the night before.

She sat on the floor by the tree, arranging them all underneath, then filled and hung stockings. The air was filled with the scent of the apple wood fire, with cinnamon from the ornaments, with the sharp, tangy smell of the tree.

"I think that's everything," she said some time later, giving careful scrutiny to the room. "It looks just right, doesn't it?"

"I can't imagine any four children will have a better Christmas," he told her with complete sincerity.

Her smile seemed to light up the dark night. After a moment, it slid away but she continued to look at him.

"I have to tell you something," she said.

He said nothing, waiting for her to continue.

After a long moment, she sighed, fretting with the edge of her festive red cast. "I've been dreading tonight for weeks. Well, this part of it, anyway."

He blinked, astonished. She was all over the whole

Christmas thing. Everywhere he looked, he saw signs that she had been planning this night for a long time.

"You've been dreading it?"

"Don't get me wrong. I can't wait for the morning. But I didn't really want to be alone after the children were in bed for the Santa Claus part. It helped so much to have you here."

Her smile wavered a little but she straightened it again. "And not just because of the heavy lifting, though I was glad for that, too."

He ached inside for all she had lost and for the courage it must take her to reshape her family's traditions without her husband.

"Thank you for letting me be part of it," he answered.

She said nothing for a moment, then before he quite realized what she intended, she stepped forward and kissed him.

Her mouth was soft and tasted of cocoa and peppermint candies, a delicious combination. He recognized the kiss for what it was, quiet gratitude, and he forced himself to remain still as her mouth moved gently against his.

Emotions swirled around them, wrapping them in the quiet peace of the night, and he wanted this slow kiss to go on forever.

Finally she eased away with a tremulous smile, her green eyes catching the lights flickering in the tree, and he was staggered by her loveliness.

"Good night, Carson. Merry Christmas."

"Can you make it up the stairs?" His voice came out gruff.

She nodded and made her way to the bottom of the staircase. She looked at him for a long, drawn-out moment, then gripped the rail and hobbled up the steps.

He sat in the living room for a long time after she disappeared upstairs, watching the fire and the tree lights reflected in the window.

He would have to leave the Wheeler house soon. Too many of the protective walls around his heart were tumbling down. He needed time and distance to shore them back up again.

No matter how high the cost.

"Mom! Is it morning? Can we go down yet?"

Jenna groaned and rolled over. In the glow of the hall light, she saw all four of her children—even Jolie, though she looked half-asleep in Hayden's arms. Jenna was quite certain her brothers had awakened her and dragged her out of bed so they could present a united front.

She looked out the window of her bedroom, where dawn hadn't even started to dress in her pearly gray colors.

"It's barely 6:00 a.m. Are you sure you don't want to sleep a little longer?"

"No!" Kip said loudly. "Santa came. I know he did. Can we go down? Please, Mom?"

She supposed she should be grateful they honored the strict family rule that no one was to go downstairs until they all went down, and that was only after she had a chance to light the fire and turn on the Christmas lights first.

She briefly toyed with trying to get them to go back to sleep, but she realized how futile that would be. "All right. Everybody hop in my bed to stay warm while I go down to make sure everything's ready."

She quickly brushed her teeth, washed her face and pulled her hair back into a ponytail, grateful all over again that she had showered last night after Jake Dalton had given her permission, as long as she covered her cast with plastic.

As she gingerly made her way into the hallway, she smelled coffee brewing. Downstairs, she discovered Carson wasn't on the living room sofa and the blankets and pillows he had used were folded up on the edge.

The fire was merrily crackling away and every light on the tree blazed a welcome.

Had he left? she wondered, and was astonished at how bereft the thought left her. But then she heard a low murmur of voices in the kitchen and her mood instantly lifted.

She followed the sound, grateful her ankle wasn't protesting too strenuously when she put weight on it.

In the doorway, she paused, completely astonished at the sight of Pat and Carson sitting at the kitchen table, coffee mugs between them, looking like old friends.

"Morning," Pat said with her half smile.

Jenna blinked. "Hi."

"Your mother-in-law and I were just talking about some of our newfangled methods at the ranch. I'm going to give her a tour of the accelerated grazing rotation one of these days. In return, she's going to tell me how she and her husband ever got anything to grow on that hundred-acre parcel above the fire road."

Jenna wouldn't have been more startled if the two of them had been in here line dancing to "Grandma Got Run Over by a Reindeer."

"Um, okay," she finally managed to say. "Well, the kids are awake and are dying to come down. I'm afraid they're going to break down my bedroom door any minute now."

Pat chuckled, a rusty sound in the quiet kitchen. "Our Joe was always the same way. He couldn't stand waiting until his dad set up the old movie camera with the six-bulb flash that just about blinded us every Christmas."

Jenna touched her mother-in-law's shoulder and Pat reached a hand up to cover her fingers.

It would be a good day today, she hoped.

They adjourned to the living room, where Jenna gave Carson the video camera duties. With her broken wrist and Pat's trembling, she figured he would get the best images.

"Mom, can we come down *yet*?" Drew called from upstairs. She shared a smile with the other two adults.

"You had better," she answered, "or Santa might decide to come and take all this stuff back to the North Pole with him."

With shrieks of excitement, the boys stampeded down the stairs and the fun began.

Chapter Sixteen

Christmas morning at the Wheeler house was an unforgettable experience.

It was impossible not to be caught up in the children's wonder and glee as they opened their presents and exclaimed over each one, from the Lifesaver book in their stockings to the iPod Hayden apparently had placed at the top of his list.

The children gave Jenna small gifts they had made in school and a new sweater and earrings they confessed their Aunt Terri had helped them pick out. They also had gifts for their grandmother, small knickknacks from the dollar store and framed pictures they had painted to decorate her small set of rooms at the assisted-living center.

To his astonishment, Drew—who had co-opted gift delivery to each recipient—handed Carson a small pile of presents.

"They're from us," Hayden said, when Carson continued to stare at the gifts.

"You didn't have to do that."

"We wanted to," Jenna assured him. "The children and I wanted to thank you for helping us so much these last few days."

They all smiled at him and he swallowed hard and turned to the presents. There were three, each rather clumsily wrapped. Jenna couldn't have done it with her broken wrist so he guessed the boys had pitched in.

The first one he picked up was heavy. He weighed it in his hands and frowned, trying to figure out what it might be. "Is it a rock?" he asked.

Kip giggled. "Open it! Open it!"

He peeled the paper away carefully, aware of an odd need to savor the moment. He opened the plain brown cardboard box and started to laugh. "It *is* a rock!"

"It's a fossil," Drew informed him. "We looked it up after we found it and it's a trilobite. Cool, huh?"

"We thought maybe you could use it as a paperweight, if you want to," Hayden said.

"We found it in the arroyo above the creek bed at the ranch a few summers ago," Jenna added. "There's a really great spot for fossils there."

"We can show you sometime if you want," Drew said.

He forced a smile, immeasurably touched. "That would be great."

"Mister, present!" Jolie pointed to the other two on his lap. The next one was cylindrical and light and he decided not to try to guess.

It was a soup-size can, he saw when he tore the paper, covered in masking-tape pieces and some sort of brown polish that made it look like leather.

"When did you have time to do all this?" he asked Jenna with some astonishment.

"When you went back to Raven's Nest for an hour or so to check in with Neil Parker yesterday when Dr. Dalton was here, remember? We made it then."

He cleared his throat, astounded at the thick emotion welling up inside him for a humble little pencil holder.

The third one was the most unexpected of all. It was the size of a deck of cards and about the same shape. When he tore the paper, he found a slim white box. Inside nestled on a small piece of cotton batting was a bolo tie with a black leather string and a smooth, flat iridescent green stone in the middle.

"It was one of my dad's," Hayden said. "He had a lot. He collected 'em and this one was broken, see, the front fell off. My mom was gonna throw it away but when we were looking for gifts for you yesterday, she remembered it so we fixed it with a polished rock."

"The stone is jasper and it came from the ranch," Jenna told him. "We found it several years ago on the hillside right about where you built your house. I always thought it was so pretty. The boys and I polished it along with some others a few years ago and I've kept it in my jewelry box, hoping I could find something to do with it someday. It fits perfectly on the tie, don't you think?"

He couldn't speak as emotions crowded through him, fast and fierce, so thick he could barely breathe around them.

He looked at Jenna, so lovely and bright, and her children, all watching him out of smiling green eyes that matched the stone on the tie, and his throat seemed to clog up. To his horror, he felt tears burn behind his eyes.

He felt as if all the careful protections he had erected around his heart had just melted to nothing like a snow fort under a blazing summer sun.

In the midst of their chaotic Christmas preparations—and Jenna dealing with a broken wrist and sprained ankle—they had taken time to make him such precious gifts.

He couldn't comprehend it. He gazed at them all and memories crowded through his head. Of Jolie falling asleep in his arms, of Kip telling him knock-knock jokes and laughing so hard at his own punch lines that Carson couldn't understand his words, of Drew swimming like a smart little fish in his pool.

Of Hayden standing a little taller and straightening his shoulders in his plaid pajamas as he read the sweet and joyful Christmas story from the Bible that had been his father's.

He loved them. All of them.

Especially their mother. She had kissed him and laughed with him and shared secrets and he had fallen head over heels with her gentleness and her sweetness and the nurturing care she showed to everyone, even when she was injured and needed it herself.

His gaze met Jenna's. Her smile had slid away and she watched him out of careful, wary eyes. He couldn't bring himself to reassure her, to smile and pretend everything was all right.

It wasn't. He loved her and he wanted her—wanted this—so much it was a physical ache in his chest.

He let out a breath. How the hell had he let this happen in just a few short days? He had spent his entire adult life protecting himself from just this, from coming to care so much, from knowing this heavy, bitter ache in his chest, as if his heart was being flayed open and dragged behind a team of horses.

He couldn't bear it. Suddenly he felt seven years old again, living in a scary flophouse, wondering what terrible thing he had done that year that had been so unforgiveable Santa Claus didn't come yet again, even though he had prayed and prayed and tried his best to be good.

Worse even than that memory was his tenth year, the year after he had spent Christmas with his grandparents and learned how magical the holidays could be.

His mother had taken him away from that, though, and on Christmas she was too high to even remember he was there. He had warmed up the last can of soup in the house for their Christmas dinner and dripped tears into it as he ate it, even though he was ten and too old to cry, remembering the lavish feast his grandmother had made the year before.

He had a terrible fear that next Christmas and every December twenty-fifth for the rest of his life would be like his tenth, only now he would compare them all to this perfect day spent with Jenna's family.

Noisy and chaotic and wonderful.

The year he learned what it meant to be part of a family.

What it meant to love.

The years stretched out ahead of him, barren and cold, and he didn't know what the hell to do about it.

"You don't like them?" Kip's subdued voice pierced his thoughts and Carson realized he must have been staring at the gifts for a long time without saying anything.

He jerked his gaze up to find them all watching him with various expressions on their faces—Jenna looked concerned and the boys' expressions were cautious and a little hurt.

He cleared his throat. He had to say something. He couldn't leave them hanging like this. "I love them. All of them. The pencil holder and paperweight are both going right on my desk at McRaven Enterprises and I'm going to wear the tie the day I return to work. Thank you all so much."

The boys seemed to accept his words and their features relaxed but Jenna continued to watch him out of eyes that had turned a dark green with concern.

He forced a smile, though he was quite certain it didn't make it as far as his eyes. But Kip complained he was starving now that they were done with presents and he wanted to eat. Jenna became distracted as the others joined the chorus and the moment passed.

He had to leave, he realized as she headed into the kitchen. Now, as soon as he could. He couldn't let this family sneak any deeper into his heart. It was already going to hurt like hell trying to go on without them all.

Early in his business career, he had learned there came a time when a man had to cut his losses and walk away while he could.

That time was now.

Something was drastically wrong with Carson. Jenna could see it in his eyes.

She had no idea why the simple gifts she and the children had managed to cobble together for him at the last minute would have merited the bleakness that had entered his expression. He had looked devastated by them and she wished she had never come up with the idea.

She fretted about it as she warmed the oven for the

sweet rolls and the farmer's breakfast casserole she had thawed the night before, grateful all over again that she always kept her freezer well stocked.

She was measuring the ingredients for the maple cream frosting she smeared on her sweet rolls when she glanced up and found Carson standing in the doorway, his Stetson in his hands and his ranch jacket on.

"I have to go," he said, his voice solemn but those blue eyes deep with emotions she couldn't begin to guess at.

She frowned. "Go where?"

"I gave Bill and Melina the day off so I've got to go take care of the Raven's Nest horses."

"Oh, of course. Do you need help? I could send Hayden up with you."

"No," he said, his voice abrupt.

"Okay. Um, I was thinking of moving dinner up to two since we all got up so early. Will you be done by then?"

His gaze met hers and she thought she saw something flicker in his gaze, something almost anguished, but it was gone too quickly for her to be sure. "Probably not."

"We can push it back later. That's no problem."

She was grasping at straws, she realized, desperate to avoid accepting the inevitable, that he was leaving.

"Don't worry about me, Jen." His tone was determinedly casual, though she was almost positive it was an act. "I'll just grab a bite up at the house. You're getting around okay, aren't you? You don't really need me anymore."

Everything inside her cried out an objection to that. She *did* need him. Far more than she dared admit. "My ankle feels much better today." That, at least, was the truth. "Thank you again for helping us through the worst of it."

His hands traced the brim of his hat and he looked as if he wanted to say something but he only nodded.

Something was *definitely* wrong. She could see a distance on his features that hadn't been there that morning. What had put it there? The chaos of the morning, maybe? Or their humble, haphazard gifts?

Really, who gave the CEO of a major technology innovation firm a pencil holder made from a soup can?

Her mind replayed that stunning, tender kiss the night before and the emotions that had swirled around them, between them. Had she imagined the magic of it all?

No. That had been real enough. But Carson had made it perfectly plain that while he might be attracted to her, he didn't want everything that came with her. Wet diapers, runny noses, noisy kids, preteens with truculent attitudes.

He was saying goodbye. She didn't need him to spell it out for her to understand just what this was. He was leaving, returning to his real life, and she could do nothing about it.

"So I guess I'll see you around," he said.

"Okay." She forced a smile that felt too fake, too wide. "Merry Christmas, Carson."

Again that strange something flickered in his eyes but he only nodded. "Same to you."

Without another word, he turned and walked out the door.

Jenna waited for the door to close before she pressed a fist to the hollow ache in her stomach.

He was saying goodbye. Not just for today, she knew. He wouldn't be back. She might bump into him occasionally since he was her nearest neighbor but they would revert to a polite acquaintance again, not the closer friendship they had shared these last few days.

Friendship? That was far too mild a term. She pressed a fist to her stomach again, to the tangled knot of nerves inside her and realized exactly what had happened.

She was in love with him.

With Carson McRaven, CEO of McRaven Enterprises.

How could she have been stupid enough to let this happen?

Falling in love with Joe had seemed so natural. Inevitable, even. They had been good friends in high school but hadn't dated until the summer before her senior year of college. Almost from the first, everything had seemed just right. Everyone said they were perfect for each other and Jenna had thought so, as well.

This torrent of feelings inside her for Carson was different. This wasn't perfect. It scraped at her emotions like jagged stones dragged by a flash flood and she wanted to sit on the floor of her kitchen and weep.

Still, she knew it was love. The only surprise was that she had taken so long to recognize it. She supposed she had been headed there for days, from the moment he showed up on her doorstep looking so completely out of his depth with a crying Kip in his arms.

Oh, what a disaster. Could she see any possible outcome from it other than heartbreak? He wasn't interested in a family and that's all she was, all she cared about.

Her broken wrist ached suddenly but it was nothing compared to the ache in her chest she knew no painkiller from a bottle would ease.

It was Christmas, blast it. Blast *him*. This was a time of peace, of hope. How could she feel so very miserable?

She couldn't let herself wallow in the heartache or all the pain she knew lay ahead. It was Christmas and she had promised her children the best possible holiday.

Somehow she made it through the rest of the day. The children played with their new toys and watched a couple of DVDs and ate Christmas dinner.

The only time she came close to losing it was when Hayden asked her after breakfast when Carson would come back, since he wanted to play a new video game he'd gotten from Santa with him.

When she told the boys he had gone back to Raven's Nest, all of them had been crushed. Jenna had quickly tried to distract them, but it hadn't been easy.

Now, Jolie was asleep and the boys were close to it, exhausted from the day and especially the excitement leading up to it. She tucked them in, hugging them all a little tighter tonight in her gratitude that at least she had this.

"Will Mr. McRaven be back, Mom?" Drew asked, a solemn expression on his features. "I really like him."

Oh, she wished she could take away every disappointment her children had to face in this world. They had all come to care for Carson and would miss him and there was nothing she could do to make it better.

She forced a smile as she brushed a lock of hair away from his forehead. She pressed her lips to the skin the hair had covered. "I'm sure we'll see him again. He lives just up the hill."

"Sometimes. Most of the time he's in California, though."

She let out a breath. "True enough. But he'll be here sometimes and we can see him then."

She kissed Kip and closed their bedroom door, wondering what would be worse—never seeing him again or occasionally catching glimpses of him from afar and knowing she could never have him?

When she returned downstairs, she discovered Pat had gone to bed, as well. They were to take her home the next morning and Jenna purposely had avoided using pain pills all day so they would be out of her system when she had to drive to Idaho Falls.

Aspirin didn't quite cut it against the pain and her wrist throbbed. She told herself that was why she felt so close to tears, but she wasn't really convinced.

Now that the children were asleep and she didn't have the benefit of the distraction they provided, all the loneliness and sorrow she had suppressed all day came rushing back.

As she picked up the last straggling bits of wrapping paper and toy packaging in the living room, her mind replayed the last few days with Carson and a hundred memories washed through her. Sharing hot cocoa with him while the rest of the house slept. His awkward efforts to put Jolie's diaper on. Seeing him in front of the stove scrubbing off dried macaroni and cheese.

That shattering kiss they had shared the night before while the Christmas tree lights twinkled and snowflakes drifted down outside.

How was she going to get through this?

She wiped at her tears. She had to. She had children who counted on her. She couldn't just take time off to wallow in self-pity and loneliness. She gave a heavy sigh and moved to unplug the Christmas tree when she suddenly spied headlights cutting through the dark night.

She frowned, even as her heart quivered in her chest. She peered through the window. It was too dark to tell if it was his black Suburban, but she couldn't imagine anyone else who might be showing up at her house this late.

Of course, she couldn't imagine why Carson might be here, either. But she could always hope.

A moment later, she heard a knock. Her heart pounded as she looked through the peephole.

Carson stood on the other side in his Stetson and ranch coat, his arms loaded with a huge box and an almost wary expression on his ruggedly handsome features.

She jerked the door open. "Carson! What on earth?"

His gaze met hers but she couldn't read his expression. "I didn't have anything for you and your kids. Let me set this down. I've got more in the truck."

She was so gloriously happy to see him, she wanted to limp after him in the snow and throw her arms around him.

On the other hand, she feared seeing him would only make her heart hurt more when he left again.

"How did you manage all this?" she asked when he came inside again. "The stores are closed on Christmas Day. Where did you possibly find one that was open?"

She thought she saw a hint of color climb his cheeks. "San Francisco."

Her jaw dropped. "What?"

He glanced up the stairs. "I guess the kids are in bed."

"Yes. I'm sorry."

"That's okay. They can open their gifts tomorrow. Well, good night. Merry Christmas." He reached for the door handle.

"Wait!" she exclaimed. "You can't just drop all this off and then leave. Aren't you going to explain to me what's going on?"

"Nothing. I just brought you and the kids some presents. I felt bad that I didn't have anything for you today." He paused. "You might as well go ahead and open it."

"Um, okay." She didn't understand any of this. She only knew she was desperately happy to see him and right now she would do anything he asked of her if it would only make him stay a little longer.

She ripped the wrapping paper away, then stared at the box as laughter and tears both fought for control inside her.

"You bought me a steam oven!"

He shrugged, looking embarrassed. "Most women would probably bash me over the head for buying them something to go in the kitchen, but I thought you might see it a little differently."

She couldn't quite believe it. She had wanted one for so long, but it had been way out of her budget! How had he possibly known? Suddenly she remembered when she had first seen his kitchen at Raven's Nest, how she had gushed over everything in it, especially the steam oven. He had noticed such an insignificant moment and tracked one down for her.

"There's more," he said. As she watched, he dumped a bag out on the floor and her heart seemed to turn over as she saw silicone spatulas and chef's cutlery and ball-tipped whisks. There seemed to be every gourmet tool she had ever dreamed about.

She gazed at the pile and then back at him. "Tell me you were joking about San Francisco."

He looked embarrassed again. "I drove to Jackson but everything was closed and to be honest, I didn't know what kind of selection I would find there anyway. On the other hand, I have a business contact who owns a chain of gourmet cooking supply stores in California." He shrugged. "He owed me a favor so he met me at one of his stores and let me in."

"Let me get this straight. You've been to San Francisco and back today."

He seemed inordinately fascinated by the twinkling lights on the garlands going up the stairs. "It's no big deal, Jen. I just wanted to give you something meaningful. And I did promise the boys the video game prototype we were working on. I was able to run by the office and pick that up while I was there and then I found a few other little things I thought they might like."

She could see several huge boxes behind him and had to wonder what his definition of "a few other little things" might entail.

All day she had fought despair, certain that she wouldn't see him again except on a casual basis. Now here he was in her living room bearing gifts for her and her children and she couldn't quite adjust to the rapid shift.

"Why, Carson?"

"I wanted to do something for you and for the kids."

"You didn't need to fly to San Francisco and back in a day to do that."

"I know."

His sigh was heavy and he finally met her gaze and she was astonished at the emotions brimming there. "I told myself I couldn't come back. I didn't plan it. But I was up at Raven's Nest looking down at your house and the smoke was coming out of the chimney and then the boys came outside to play in their new snowsuits and I couldn't take it anymore. I had to leave, so I started driving and before I knew it I was at the airport chartering a flight."

Her heart was pounding so hard she could barely hear herself think. "Why couldn't you come back?"

"Sorry?"

"You said you told yourself you couldn't come back. Why not?"

He gazed at her for a long moment and then he looked away. "I don't belong here with you and your family, Jenna. It was just a brief interlude in both our lives and now it's over."

He was going to leave again. He was even reaching for the doorknob. As she saw things, she had two choices. She could let him go, let him return to his empty life in San Francisco, to that huge empty house on the hillside.

Or she could swallow her pride and offer one more Christmas gift to him, even if he wasn't willing to accept it.

She had no choice. Not really. She stepped forward, until they were only a few feet apart, took a deep breath and plunged forward. "It's not over for me, Carson. I'm not sure it ever will be. I won't forget you or how wonderful it was to have you here these last few days."

His eyes widened and something deep and intense flickered in his gaze. "Jenna—"

"I didn't expect to fall in love with you. I certainly didn't want to. You told me yourself you're not looking for a family. I know that. I accept it. I just…wanted you to know how much you've come to mean to me these last few days. To all of us. The children love you and...so do I."

Before she even murmured the last word, he rushed forward to close the gap between them, grasped her face in his strong, wonderful hands and kissed her so fiercely all the oxygen left her lungs in an instant.

He kissed her with an almost desperate hunger and she reveled in it. She wrapped her good arm around his waist inside his coat, savoring his heat and his strength against her and the joy and peace that soaked through her.

"It killed me to leave you," he whispered against her mouth after several breathtaking moments. "I was completely wrecked, Jenna."

She heard regret and sorrow in his voice and she kissed the corner of his mouth gently. "Why did you, then?"

"Because I'm an idiot. A stupid, terrified idiot afraid to reach for the incredible prize in front of me."

She held him closer, astonished that this could be happening. The night was magical, full of sweet, healing hope.

"I love you, Jenna. That's why I took off. I've loved one other woman in my life and I failed her. I was supposed to be able to take care of her and I couldn't. When she and Henry James died, I thought my life was over. I told myself that if I blocked out anything deep or meaningful, if I focused only on business, I could protect myself from the pain and mess of love. Things were working out just fine, I thought. But then you came along and made me realize how very alone I was."

She held him tighter, astonished and grateful that she had been so very richly blessed in her life to love two such wonderful men.

He kissed the top of her head. "You showed up with your snickerdoodles and your boys and darling little Jolie and knocked down every single one of my defenses."

She smiled against his chest, even as she fought tears of joy. "I get it now. You just love me for my snickerdoodles."

He laughed softly and it was sweetest sound she had ever heard. "And your spinach rolls. And your pumpkin cheesecake. And your crostini. And your hot cocoa with whipped cream and peppermint candy. And your..."

She stopped his recitation with the simple act of throwing off his Stetson and kissing him again.

He settled onto the sofa and pulled her onto his lap. As the tree lights flickered beside them and the fire crackled in the grate, she remembered how she had dreamed of making the ideal Christmas for her family.

She never could have imagined she would find herself here in Carson's arms with this dazzling joy surging through her.

But now, at long last, everything was perfect.

Epilogue

Raven's Nest was in chaos.

Hayden was up in his bedroom upstairs with the door open, playing "Little Drummer Boy" at full volume on the drum set his crazy mother and stepfather bought him for his eleventh birthday a few months earlier.

Amid the "ba-rump-bump-bump-bumps," Drew was chasing Kip around the great room trying to retrieve the book of Christmas mystery stories his little brother had stolen from him. But since Kip was faster than anyone in the house—and knew it—Drew was having a tough time catching him.

Frank—the new border collie puppy the boys had conned Carson into getting that summer—chased after both boys, barking at this fun new game, which Carson supposed was at least a change from the dog yanking all the ornaments off the tree.

Jolie was hanging onto his leg and gabbing a mile a minute about her dolls and the snowman they made earlier and the kitty she wanted for Christmas. And Pat, who had come to spend Christmas Eve with them at Raven's Nest, wanted to know what time they were eating and when she was supposed to take her medicine and how much it cost to heat this mausoleum.

It was Christmas Eve.

And Carson loved it.

He picked up Jolie in his arms and answered Pat. "The radiant-heat system saves a lot of money. I'm going to have to ask Jenna about your prescriptions and what time we're eating. Hang on, I'll be right back."

As he headed toward the door with no small degree of relief, he snagged Kip by the collar of his holiday-patterned sweater as the boy jumped over an ottoman. "Give back your brother's book," he ordered.

Kip giggled but handed the book over willingly with that gap-toothed grin that had only become wider now that he was seven.

"Sorry, Drew."

His brother made a face as he snatched the book out of Kip's hand.

"You guys need to chill out a little, okay?" Carson said, though he knew it was a losing battle. "Santa's going to take one look at this place and think only wild monkeys live here. And last I heard, he doesn't make deliveries to wild monkeys."

"Why not?" Jolie asked with a little frown on her features. "Don't monkeys get presents from Santa?"

"Only if they've been good little monkeys."

"Have I been a good little monkey?" she asked.

He smiled and kissed the top of her blond curls.

"You're always a good little monkey. You're *my* good little monkey."

He was crazy about this little girl, just as he loved her three brothers, drum sets, mischief, barking dogs and all.

"Go tell Hayden to either shut his door or save the recital for after dinner, okay?" he said to Drew as he carried Jolie with him into the kitchen.

Inside, Jenna was standing at the stove stirring something in a pan. By the looks of it, she had about four cooking projects going and his heart bumped at the sight of her, all pink and tousled and warm, just as it always did.

She looked up when they entered and her smile gleamed more brilliantly than the hundreds of lights on the huge Christmas tree in the great room.

He would never get tired of that smile. After six months of marriage, he adored it more than ever.

"Mommy, I'm a good little monkey," Jolie said proudly.

Jenna looked amused. "You are indeed, sweetheart."

"Put me down, please," she directed, in her best princess-of-the-manor voice, and Carson complied. Jolie raced to the sitting area off the kitchen to play with her toys scattered there.

Carson moved behind Jenna and kissed the back of her neck. "Something smells delicious," he said, his voice low.

She leaned against him with that sexy sigh of hers that drove him crazy. "It's my sticky buns."

He breathed in the scent of her, of cinnamon and vanilla and that indefinable—but infinitely sexy—scent that was plain Jenna. "Well, I do love your sticky buns," he murmured. "But I was talking about this spot right here."

He pressed his mouth again to that warm, sweet patch of skin at the back of her neck and she shivered, as she did whenever he touched her.

Their six-month wedding anniversary was in three days and he had a hard time remembering what his life was like before the Wheelers barreled into it.

They had changed everything.

He couldn't help laughing at his own stupidity whenever he thought about how certain he had been a year ago that he had all he could ever want or need. This ranch, his varied business interests, the penthouse in San Francisco.

If he had to, he would gladly trade all of that to hang on to this life he and Jenna were building together.

He had no idea a year ago how much he would love being a stepfather. Helping with homework, fishing trips in the mountains above the ranch, long weekends in San Francisco so he could catch up on work he couldn't finish long distance from Raven's Nest.

His soul filled with a quiet contentment he never realized was missing when he was lying next to Jenna while the wind hurled snow against the windows and the fire in their bedroom fireplace burned down to cinders.

He had been given more precious gifts than he could ever have imagined.

He kissed that spot on her neck again and Jenna sighed softly. "Keep that up and you're going to make me forget all I still have to do."

"That's the idea."

She turned around, her mouth set in a mock frown.

"Well, you'll have no one to blame but yourself if your Christmas Eve dinner is ruined, then."

He couldn't resist kissing away that frown, pretend though it might be. "Even if we had nothing to eat but gunky orange mac and cheese or soup out of a can, Jenna Wheeler McRaven, this would still be the happiest Christmas Eve of my life."

Her eyes softened and she gave him a vivid smile as she returned his kiss.

"Do you know what the best part is?" he asked.

She shook her head, her arms around his waist.

"I have absolutely no doubt that next year will be even better. And the year after that will be better still. And I can't even imagine how great the year after *that* will be."

She rested her head against his chest and he wanted to freeze this moment in his memory—the snow falling outside, the drums still banging away upstairs, the boys' shrieks, the puppy barking, Jolie jabbering to her toys.

The memory album in his head was bulging at the seams.

"I wouldn't be so confident about future Christmases if I were you," she said with a rueful laugh. "We're going to have teenagers by then and I'm afraid all bets are off."

He didn't care. All those years and Christmases stretched out ahead of them, shiny and bright and full of promise like the presents under their tree, and he couldn't wait to unwrap every one.

* * * * *

We hope you enjoyed reading

THE RANCHER'S CHRISTMAS SONG

AND

THE COWBOY'S CHRISTMAS MIRACLE

by

New York Times bestselling author

RAEANNE THAYNE

SPECIAL EXCERPT FROM

HARLEQUIN®

SPECIAL EDITION

*He may have broken her heart twice,
but Declan McGrath has never forgotten Nell Bravo,
and when they end up married in Vegas, he's determined
to make it work. She'll give him until Christmas, but
that's it. Will Declan be able to win her heart before
December 26?*

Read on for a sneak preview of
MARRIED TILL CHRISTMAS,
the final book in New York Times *bestselling author*
Christine Rimmer's beloved miniseries
THE BRAVOS OF JUSTICE CREEK.

"Why me—and why won't you take a hint that I'm just not interested?"

He stared into his single malt, neat, as if the answer to her question waited in the smoky amber depths. "I don't believe you're not interested. You just don't trust me."

"Duh." She poured on the sarcasm and made a big show of tapping a finger against her chin. "Let me think. I wonder why?"

"How many times do I need to say that I messed up? I messed up twice. I'm so damn sorry and I need you to forgive me. You're the best thing that ever happened to me. And…" He shook his head. "Fine. I get it. I smashed your heart to tiny, bloody bits. How many ways can I say I was wrong?"

Okay. He was kind of getting to her. For a second there, she'd almost reached across the table and touched his clenched fist. She so had to watch herself. Gently she suggested, "How about this? I accept your apology. It was years ago and we need to move on."

He slanted her a sideways look, dark brows showing

HSEEXP1117

glints of auburn in the light from above. "Yeah?"

"Yeah."

"So then we can try again?"

Should she have known that would be his next question? Yeah, probably. "I didn't say that."

"I want another chance."

"Well, that's not happening."

"Yes, it is. And when it does, I'm not letting you go. This time it's going to be forever."

She almost grinned. Because that was another thing about Deck. Not only did he have big arms, broad shoulders and a giant brain.

He was cocky. Very, very cocky.

And she was enjoying herself far too much. It really was a whole lot of fun to argue with him. It always had been. And the most fun of all was finally being the one in the position of power.

Back when they'd been together, he was the poor kid and she was a Bravo—one of the Bastard Bravos, as everybody had called her mother's children behind their backs. But a Bravo, nonetheless. Nell always had the right clothes and a certain bold confidence that made her popular. She hadn't been happy at home by any stretch, but guys had wanted to go out with her and girls had kind of envied her.

And all she'd ever wanted was Deck. So, really, he'd had all the power then.

Now, for some reason she didn't really understand, he'd decided he just had to get another chance with her. Now she was the one saying no. Payback was a bitch, all right. Not to mention downright delicious.

Don't miss
MARRIED TILL CHRISTMAS by Christine Rimmer,
available December 2017 wherever
Harlequin® Special Edition books and ebooks are sold.

www.Harlequin.com

HSEEXP1117

An unlikely attraction brings comfort, joy and unforgettable romance this holiday season in this sparkling tale by *New York Times* bestselling author

RaeAnne Thayne

Librarian Julia Winston is ready to ditch the quiet existence she's been living. She's made a list of new things to experience, but falling for Jamie Caine, her sexy military pilot neighbor, isn't one of them. Julia's looking to conquer life, not become the heartbreaker's latest conquest. But when two young brothers wind up in Julia's care for the holidays, she'll take any help she can get—even Jamie's.

Happy to step in, Jamie reveals a side of himself that's much harder to resist. Not only is he fantastic with kids, he provides the strength Julia needs to tackle her list. She knows their temporary family can't last beyond the holidays, but the closer she gets to Jamie, the more she wonders if things could be this merry and bright forever...

Available September 26

Order your copy today!